T0128784

Reconnecting

Ron Stock

authorHOUSE®

AuthorHouse™
1663 Liberty Drive
Bloomington, IN 47403
www.authorhouse.com
Phone: 1-800-839-8640

Published by AuthorHouse 07/20/2012

ISBN: 978-1-4772-4090-8 (sc)
ISBN: 978-1-4772-4091-5 (hc)
ISBN: 978-1-4772-4092-2 (e)

Library of Congress Control Number: 2012912434

Dedicated to my wife Lucille and my Mag 6 buddies
who, in their own wonderful ways, give me great joy and happiness.

Contents

Preface

*A*nyone who has ever attended one of their high school reunions will understand the emotions of anticipation and perhaps even trepidation about facing, possibly for the first time in many years, old friends, sweethearts, and maybe even antagonists—all in one room at once!

Reconnecting with your past at your high school reunion can certainly be intimidating. At the first and only reunion I have attended, fifty years after graduation, my emotions took a roller-coaster ride: There was the exhilaration of meeting up with my best friends again, the exasperation of listening to the braggers tell how successful they had become, and the outright stress of saying hello to my first real high school girlfriend after fifty years, with my wife standing beside me. This book touches on all those feelings.

I was lazy in not attending my tenth and twenty-fifth reunions, using the distance I would have had to travel as my excuse for not showing my face. But when I got the invitation to the fiftieth reunion, something inside me said, "You cannot, *must* not, miss this opportunity to reconnect with your old buddies."

I had not been back to my hometown in the fifty years since my high school graduation, so I was curious to see my friends, go by the house that was my home when I was in high school, and visit the setting of most of my memories, Alfred I. DuPont High School.

At the reunion, and after spending just a few hours with my buddies (in high school, we nicknamed ourselves "The Magnificent Six"), I realized I had made a huge mistake by losing touch with them over the years. After five decades, not much time remains to rekindle our friendships, but after the reunion, I was committed to staying in touch. And more: I wanted to put in writing how much their friendship means to me. This is the reason I wrote *Reconnecting*—to say to these five guys how much I love them.

Reconnecting is intended to memorialize many of the great adventures the Mag 6 shared during our high school years. Considering all our antics, we were lucky not to have been seriously hurt or worse, and not to have been arrested and sent to spend time in the state of Florida's prison system. Nothing we did was malicious toward anyone else—well, almost nothing. Our adventures were just fun happenings the six of us enjoyed during our teenage years. All of the Mag 6 stories recounted here are true.

My girlfriends in *Reconnecting* are strictly fictitious, though some remembrances of those I dated in high school are woven into the fabric of each of the girls in the book. My true-life high school girlfriends were simply a great inspiration for the book's characters. For that, I truly thank them.

I offer a big thanks to my editors, Heidi Mann and Robert Wood. Their collective professionalism meant the smoothing and refinement of the thoughts I laid out on paper (well, on my computer screen). I also thank my graphic designers, Janet Williams and Gregory Mann, for their creative and technical expertise.

I dedicate *Reconnecting* to both the Mag 6 and my wife, Lucille, who sat patiently every night for months while I banged out the story on my laptop. She had not read a word of it till I finished the book and it was "in the can." For her love and support, I dedicate *Reconnecting* to her.

When faced with going to your next high school reunion, take my advice: "GO!" If you do not attend your reunion, you will certainly miss seeing old friends and reconnecting with them, and maybe you will even have let slip by one of the best experiences of your life.

Chapter 1

Sandy Memories
May 2012

*T*he wind is warm through the partially opened window, and even though the car's air-conditioning works perfectly, I'm not tempted to turn it on, as the wind brings me the scent of summer with just that slightest hint of salt and swamp. I am on my way through Jacksonville, Florida, headed to Key West, where almost 25 percent of the population is separated, divorced, or widowed—a perfect place for a guy like me to start over, one more time.

Many of the men in Key West are fleeing a bad divorce or two or even three, and some are trying to distance themselves from their kids who just want the life insurance money when dear old dad finally croaks. As for the kids, they probably don't realize they have to stand in line behind the money-grubbing exes for their share of any insurance payoff.

While in high school and college, I got to visit most cities in Florida, yet somehow I missed Key West. Although it was on my list of must-see places for checking out the "3 B's"—beach, bars, and babes—for some reason, I just never got around to visiting the place. Maybe I was too lazy to drive the added fifty miles from Miami Beach to Key West to see if Key West's beaches were any nicer, the bars any wilder, or the babes any sexier. Miami Beach is hard to beat on all three, so fifty miles more down the road did not happen. Now, well past those carefree days of yore, I'm determined to see what I missed out on just to save a few miles.

Fifty years have flown by, and going to Key West isn't for the "3 B's" anymore, but to take a permanent vacation from the responsibility of caring for my wife Lucinda, who is hopelessly institutionalized in a $10,000-per-month, exclusive Alzheimer's facility. Don't get me or my intentions wrong; I deeply love Lucinda, and I will keep in touch with her doctor and will return home to California on occasion to see her. For forty years she was my closest friend, lover, confidant, and the kind of wife and mother who is usually only found in fairy tales. But now, Alzheimer's disease has built a wall between us to the point that neither I nor our children exist in her version of reality anymore. Each visit has become an exercise in self-torture since she no longer recognizes me, and to see the woman of my dreams, and my realities, look at me like a stranger is more than this old heart can bear.

I hear myself sigh as the miles roll past, and I wipe away a tear with the heel of one hand. Thank God for small favors, at least she is still physically healthy and seems blissful in her own, new world. I realized months ago that the lady I had spent most of my adult life with was gone, the disease having taken her from me just as surely as if the reaper's scythe had descended through cancer or a heart attack, and now I think I've finally gathered the pieces of my broken heart into a neat enough bundle to start a new adventure.

I am looking to take the last breath of happiness before I take my last turn 'round this dusty old rock. I dream of watching Key West's magnificent sunset, hand in hand with "*the one*," and in my dreams I remember. . . .

I remember Stacey, whose smile and charming personality could once light up a room and draw men like moths to a flame, where, if they weren't careful, they would lose themselves in her light. I remember Jackie, whose sultry demeanor could melt the hardest male heart into something akin to warm tapioca pudding. Then there is Ginny, who was as beautiful as a spring day, as sexy as Aphrodite, and brighter than many of my old college professors.

Some fifty years ago, each of the three was once the true love of my life. I am not sure which one will be "*the one*" with me on the beach. Very coincidentally, all three live in Florida, and all three are widows, meaning all three are single, still in the prime of their life, and available to reunite with an old boyfriend—me. After all, I think I've still got what it takes, even after all these years.

I never was much for the whole meet-and-greet thing of dating, hooking up with a new girl every week. And at this point in my life, the thought of going looking for a new girl somewhere out in public is almost as daunting as trying one of those online dating sites. So, rather than look for someone new in my life, I thought I would come back to Florida and contact Stacey, Jackie, and Ginny and find out if any one of them still had any sparks of love for me.

Granted, it's a real stretch to think an old high school sweetheart might still carry a spark, let alone a flame, for me after five decades. So, I'm banking on the theory that girls always carry a small flame in their heart for their first real boyfriend, sort of like the little blue flame of the pilot light in my gas furnace, a tiny little flame but one that never goes out completely.

Like Sleeping Beauty, who awakens from her long slumber at true love's first kiss to find her Prince Charming, I believe maybe one of them—Stacey, Jackie, or Ginny—will find that little pilot light still lit after all these years. Then, with a little time and a little coaxing, maybe I can nurse that tiny blue flame into a roaring inferno and become Prince Charming to one of them once again. It may be a fairy tale to believe a girlfriend from fifty years ago might still carry in her heart a little spark of love that can be awakened like Sleeping Beauty. But can't life sometimes be like a fairy tale?

I *so* hope my fairy tale, my Sleeping Beauty, will come true.

It's not so far to Key West, but I feel the sudden urge for the sand and sea, so I bring the car to a stop in one of the beachfront parking lots along Jacksonville Beach. Tossing shoes and socks into the back seat, I place my feet on pavement that's rapidly growing hot, but I know I'll manage the walk to the sand in spite of the fact that I don't own sandals, and flip-flops always seem to leave a blister between my toes. Tender feet are a family deficiency, I think as I step out of the car; must be something in the DNA.

I dodge the broken beer bottle littering the side of the walkway and, for a brief instant, consider returning for my tennis shoes. But I decide to risk my tender soles on the fifteen-foot walk, for the sheer freedom of not bothering with them. Life, after all, is full of risks to be taken, and only those bold enough will reap the massive rewards of a little cool Florida sand between their toes.

I stop just short of the receding tide and close my eyes. I breathe deeply of the salty air; the sound of the breakers, the warm sun, and the sea breeze take me back in time. The memories come unbidden, cascading through my brain as if in competition with one another to be the first to the surface of my mind or to be the one labeled *fondest*. This beach was once my favorite playground, and returning here today brings me back to the best four years of my youth, to the long summer days and the cool nights spent right here with my car and my friends on this very same sand.

Back in those days, there were no honor meters to try to grab a few dollars from the beachgoer; you simply drove onto the sand and parked where you wanted. The car was the entertainment center of the beach, the latest Elvis song or reruns with "Wolfman Jack" cranking out of the radio from Jacksonville's newest station, WAPE, "The Big Ape," with the Tarzan yells between songs so everyone in earshot knew exactly what radio station was playing. The cooler would be placed in the sand in front of the car, within easy reach, and the ice would be cool and refreshing in the summer sun.

Joining the parade of cars on the beach was *the* social event for those in my age group, and also the best way to go about that most important of activities: meeting girls. One of my friends was so aware of that fact that he named the gathering "The Parade of Poon-Tang."

I open my eyes and return to the present to find that the beach is now just an isolated stretch of sand, sand, and more sand. Not a car can be seen along the strand, motor vehicles long ago banned from the beach by some nutty environmentalist claim that leaky brake fluids and radiator coolants were killing some rare type of sand crab. It's too bad, I think; the types of crabs most often found on the beach in my younger years were the human type and couldn't be killed by simply lying under a leaky '39 Chevy.

Looking down the long stretch of hard-packed sand, I can see the

Jacksonville Beach pier, made of concrete and steel and state-of-the-art. But in my mind, I can still see and smell the creosote-soaked pilings and weathered wood of the old pier, which was lost to a hurricane that ripped along the Florida coast and devastated the city of Jacksonville and its beach. The old wooden structure hadn't stood a chance against the fury of God's winds and the awesome surge of the sea. The pier had been like a summertime friend that I could depend on for fun and adventure, and when it crumbled into the salty depths, it was almost like the death of a childhood companion.

Thoughts of the old pier bring back memories of a night long ago when, at the very end of the rickety wooden structure, a first-time date had jumped from the handrail into the dark, swirling waters below. I can still vividly remember her, in full formal attire from our night at her cotillion dance, silhouetted against the moonlight just before she leapt into the darkness.

Her intentions weren't self-harm; she had simply wanted to prove to me that she was a member of a group of elite Jacksonville Beach swimmers who called themselves "The Jetty Jumpers." The Jetty Jumpers were known throughout the area for their daring in jumping from the jagged rocks of the local jetty into the swirling water, only to swim under the surface for minutes on end against the treacherous currents beating upon the razor-edged stones, before finally making their way safely back to dry ground.

As I watched her swan-dive into the dark waters, her gown flowing like angel wings, I was sure she would be listed as "missing girl" in the next morning's papers and was already trying to figure out how to explain it all to a pair of grieving parents and the Jacksonville police. Well, sure, I thought, we had had a few—maybe *more* than a few—Singapore Slings at Wally's Well, the local watering hole. Maybe it *had* been my idea to wander out to the end of the pier alone with her, but surely it wasn't *my* fault that she had taken the plunge.

I wandered back the length of the pier, down the several flights of steps, and out onto the cool sand, contemplating what my fate might be. No matter how hard I tried, I just couldn't think of a way to explain the events of the previous half-hour to her parents.

I mean, saying "Your daughter took a dare and jumped off the pier;

she wanted to prove what a great swimmer she was, so I dared her" didn't seem like such a good idea when I considered the fact that her father was a former NFL linebacker who would undoubtedly proceed to break me into tiny pieces for standing idly by while his precious little girl jumped from the pier in her $500 formal gown that he had just paid for—especially since the jump had been made on a half-assed dare. On the other hand, telling her father that she had been very drunk at the time and that, before I could stop her, she had leapt from the railing, screaming "YEE HAWW!" on the way down would undoubtedly end up with me being the next person listed as "missing" in the local paper.

I shook my head, wondering why the girl had been shouting "YEE HAWW!" It made no sense at all, but then again, jumping from an ancient wooden pier while wearing a formal ball gown in order to plunge three stories into the dark, swirling water made no sense either. I finally decided that it might be best to let the parents and the cops try to figure out the logic behind the plunge.

As I was about to make the walk to the nearest phone and just take my medicine, my date waddled out of the crashing surf, giggling like mad, her formal dress hanging from her body like a big, white, wet chamois blanket. I can still hear her slightly slurred words: "Hey! Wanna do a duo off the pier? Just me and you?"

I smile in spite of myself at the memory of taking her to my car and peeling off the formal gown; after all, a beautiful, wet, naked, and slightly drunk Jetty Jumper giggling "Yee haw, yee haw" over and over in your front seat is one of those memories that will last a lifetime. We didn't consummate anything that night; she was soaked and coated with sand on every surface and most likely in every orifice. Such activities would not likely have been very comfortable for either of us.

Now, the midday sun turns its full brilliance onto the waves and land, warming the sand under my feet as I turn and head down the beach. My intention is just to walk with my memories as far as I can, yet I am brought up short for a moment to discover a private beach attached to a still more private condo project.

The private beach happened to belong to the Ponte Verde Beach Club, where I had walked many a slightly swaying date down the cool, moonlit sands. I would bring the ladies here, and since I was in good with the doorman and bartender, I would be allowed into the private club where my (usually) under-legal-drinking-age date and I would be served gin and tonics to our hearts' content. Things were much easier back before bars began to get sued and closed down for serving underage patrons. Back in the good old days, the worst that would happen was maybe a citation or a warning, if even that.

Back then, the beaches were great for walking without shoes, plopping down in the cool sand, and just watching the waves gently roll in, a girl under your arm and a little gin and tonic in your belly. At times, the beach itself was better than a movie when it came to entertaining a date. You never quite knew what to expect, and occasionally you would be treated to a show as a gigantic sea turtle hauled herself out of the surf to lay her eggs in the soft sand before lumbering back into the waves.

Let me tell you, if you ever had a date with a few gin and tonics under her belt and you got to watch the momma sea turtle lay her eggs, you could bet your bottom dollar on some action. It seemed that watching that big reptile carrying on the species ignited a passion for some heavy-duty making out. I learned that sea turtles can be valuable in far more pleasant ways than as an ingredient in some exotic soup.

Just south of Ponte Verde Beach was a wonderful little area called "Hill 13," a secluded area of high, snow-colored sand dunes that afforded a grand panoramic view of the ocean. It was the perfect place to take a date. With a big fluffy blanket, something cold to sip on (preferably 3.0 beer), and your girl next to you, the sea and stars would make the rest of the world just melt away as surely as the fresh, salty breeze kept away the sand flies and mosquitoes.

The real attraction of the place was that it was the best location in the area for a teenager to take his date in the hopes that one or both of them would lose their virginity during the evening. Hill 13 had the dubious honor of being the place where a great number of Jacksonville senior high boys experienced their first episode of premature ejaculation as raging hormones, heated passion, and the unexpected sensation of putting on their first condom overcame their . . . umm . . . self-control. I never had that experience myself, of course, but one of my best friends confided his experience of the embarrassing event to me one night after a few (well, more than a few) beers.

I pass the gleaming new concrete and steel pier, wrinkling my nose to try to catch one last whiff of the old creosote-and-salt smell the summer sun would leach out of the wooden structure that extended into the surf in long-ago and better days, and come to what was once Jacksonville Beach's grand, historical boardwalk.

Only a glitzy, restored Ferris wheel remains of what was once a teenage paradise of arcades, corndog stands, fortune teller stalls, souvenir shops, and an enormous bingo parlor. Now all the wonder and color of the place has been stolen by the generic facades of an upscale chocolate shop, a wannabe Starbucks, an overpriced sunglasses and beachwear store, a B-grade family restaurant, and a gallery full of cheesy whale paintings and dolphin sculptures.

Somewhere in the middle of these no-personality, modern monstrosities once stood my all-time-favorite boardwalk stall: Mahoney's SkeeBall Arcade. Honestly, one might wonder why a single skee ball arcade would entrance me more than any of the other attractions of the old boardwalk, but the truth is, the main attraction of Mahoney's SkeeBall was, for me, Coach Mahoney himself.

Each summer would find the owner and operator of Mahoney's SBA dressed in the same faded and frayed Hawaiian shirt, khaki shorts, and flip-flops, sitting out front in a broken-down lawn chair, his khaki-clad ass threatening to drop through to the ground.

Coach Mahoney was one of my high school football coaches who supplemented his meager teacher's salary during the summer with the earnings from the skee ball arcade that had been in his family for decades. He sat out front and always greeted me in his rough, gravelly voice in exactly the same manner: "Hey, Strand, if you wanna play for Notre Dame, stay away from beach bunnies—they make you weak in the knees!" Just like his greeting, my retort was always the same: "Coach, I ain't Catholic, I don't wanna go to college where it snows, and my knees are in great shape. Way great enough for a bunny hop or two!" Coach always laughed at the "bunny hop" line—not sure why.

Coach Mahoney just had that kind of personality, I guess. He was a punchy, happy-go-lucky kind of guy, not married that I knew of, and probably just a few years out of some teachers' college where he had been the starting guard on their forever-losing football team.

He was also my Driver's Ed. teacher, and during lunch we would sneak away in the Driver's Ed. car and cruise down to a clearing by the St. John's River. There, along the river's edge, shoeless and feet in the water, Coach would pull an ice-cold Pabst Blue Ribbon out of his lunch pail and sit back nursing the frosty beer while I tried to skip rocks across the river. That semester I got an "A" in Driver's Education and Coach got another five pounds added to his growing beer belly.

I never knew what happened to Coach Mahoney after I left high school. As I look out at the faux Starbucks, I shake my head a little sadly. Mahoney's SkeeBall Arcade is long gone, having surrendered to what some call progress, and never known by those who now spend their dime to try and win their girlfriend a little fuzzy teddy bear from the racks of prizes at the game booths. The wonderful memories of a certain paunchy, laid-back teacher who helped me grow and develop as a young man will forever remain, along with the recollection of the only "A" I ever earned, by spending a semester throwing rocks in the St. John's River.

With a sigh, I turn and begin my trek back along the now-hot sand. I am a bit eager to get to the rental car and carry on with my (almost) knightly quest to find my Sleeping Beauty. I realize as the sand puffs from beneath my tender soles that I could spend hours recounting memories of those long summers spent with my friends, spread out on the sand with our ratty beach towels, trying to impress each other with the tales of the previous night's impromptu adventure or amorous conquest.

Reaching the parking lot access, I turn back and look out across the gleaming sand at the green and blue, sun-dappled waters, and a last memory comes unbidden to the surface.

It was a long, hot summer day, and felt much like this, when my friends and I rose from lazing in the sun in front of my car to watch as a tourist with Georgia plates on his gleaming, new, chrome and steel pride and joy drove out into the low surf. We watched in silent amazement as the man climbed, smiling, from the '58 Chevy Bel Air and began to wash the road dust off in the briny waters.

9

None of us spoke, though all of us knew that the salt from the water would most likely lead to the fenders rusting off the car within a year or so. We thought we had seen everything, but were forced to rethink ourselves. The smile on the Georgia tourist's face slowly faded into a panicky agony as the quickly rising tide engulfed the car up to its windows. We began to speculate among ourselves that the interior of the car would now most likely rust-rot just as quickly as the exterior, and the floor pans would most likely fall through around the same time the fenders fell off.

The only thing that saved the entire car from a watery grave was the fact that the tourist's agonized cries and angry curses brought a quick response from a tow-truck driver who had already been summoned to pull a teenager's broken-down old heap off the beach.

My friends and I finally lost our composure and gave in to fits of hysterical laughter as the tow truck pulled the once-immaculate '58 Chevy away with salt water streaming from the door and trunk seams. After all, how could anyone be stupid enough to think that the mighty Atlantic was just one big car wash?

I slip the key into the ignition of the rental, and the engine fires. God, I love this place and all the wonderful memories that are held in this one stretch of sand and sea, but as I pull away from the parking spot and turn the car south, I know deep down that I will never return to walk this particular strand again.

Chapter 2

Camelot
1956–1960

*M*y story really begins around fifty years ago in Jacksonville, Florida, a city divided by the St. John's River. The city proper, the naval air station, the airport, and most of the industrial area are on one side of the river, while mostly suburban bedroom communities make up the remainder on the other side. Jacksonville Beach is around fifteen miles from the city center, so there are really three population centers to this northern Florida city: the downtown, the suburbs, and the beach. Located in Jacksonville city are the Prudential Insurance Corporate Headquarters, and the St. Joe Paper Mill, which lends a rotten-eggs aroma to its surroundings when it's running full-tilt.

Jacksonville has long been known by college students all along the east coast as the last stop on the way to spring-vacation sun and fun at Daytona Beach. When heading south from New York, Pennsylvania, and all the other "Yankee" states where wet, dirty snow still litters the ground during spring-break time, Jacksonville is in a prime location as the last best place to stop for a quick gas-up of the parents' car and to load up on potato chips and beer before continuing on south. From Jacksonville, Daytona Beach is just another hundred or so miles down the road, just far enough to be too far to hold in the need to piss out the old beer and replenish the cooler with new beer.

The Jacksonville area is the site of my favorite high school memories, and even now, in moments of quiet solitude, my mind often wanders back to those days between 1956 and 1960 when I attended Alfred I. DuPont

High School. Life was different then—no wars going on, a great deal of prosperity in the wake of World War II, no big government trying to pry into how many times you go to the bathroom and what you do in there each day, never a need to lock doors or windows because neighbors looked out for each other; it was a great and carefree time. Those who grew up in that era will tell you that America was like Camelot, a land of individualism, peace, and security. Too bad it all changed just five years later when, with a twitch of his forefinger, Lee Harvey Oswald put Lyndon B. Johnson in the White House and paved the way for the nation-changing Great Society legislation, which set America on the path to today's screwed-up-ness.

Back in those days there were no computers and no internet, only the old IBM Selectric typewriter. Carbon paper was a business staple. Thermal copy paper was still being used if you needed a second copy of your typewritten letter, which you put in an envelope with an honest-to-God four-cent stamp and dropped into the mail. Sure, the mail was a lot slower, but while you waited the week or more for a response to your letter, you had time to kick back, relax, and enjoy life with the family.

Those were the days when the newest and hottest thing in telecommunications was the Princess Phone, a sleek and sexy little cradle phone that came in designer colors. The graceful lines of the Princess Phone soon replaced the old, bulky, black desk phone as the preferable way to talk by wire. I've never understood why there was a Princess Phone and no Prince Phone; seems to me that sexism in America was perpetuated by Bell Telephone.

There were no hundreds of channels on the old rotary-dial–tuned, remote-control-less, black-and-white TVs of the day. Television amounted to three channels of vanilla, brainless sitcoms like *Life With Father*, *Ozzie and Harriet*, and *My Three Sons*.

Sex on television was depicted only by married couples kissing each other on the cheek. Spouses were never shown in bed together; master bedrooms on TV always had twin beds placed against opposite walls. I could never understand how Fred McMurray had three sons by pecking his wife on the cheek and sleeping in a twin bed. Making the long walk from one twin bed to the other, and then trying to fit two grown adults into a twin bed, having wild, uncontrollable sex for the sake of procreation—well, that image is hard to get out of your mind. Of course, for a teenager, sex in any kind of bed, back seat, broom closet, or in the middle of a hurricane while balanced on a surfboard with sharks circling is probably possible, but ol' Fred McMurray was hardly a teenager.

Doctors made house calls in those days. Yes, doctors made house calls! On the television show *Marcus Welby, MD*, the title character carried his little black bag into homes throughout America. I actually had a doctor come to my house once when I had the flu so bad I couldn't even raise my head to drink Mom's favorite cure for a cold—ginger ale. I hated ginger ale; to me it tasted like carbonated mule piss, with a ginger overtone. I still cannot drink ginger ale today. The doctor, who showed up in grand Marcus Welby style, little black bag and all, gave me a shot in the ass, which only confirmed my opinion of many doctors—they were a pain in the butt. That's an opinion that hasn't changed much for me to this day.

Nowadays, if you are sick, puking, diarrhea, boils, balls falling off, you have to crawl to some impossible-to-find, urgent-care clinic. If the clinic is open, it is usually full of people in worse shape than you, coughing and wheezing, adding only more diseases to your already-diseased state. If you have health insurance so the clinic can bill the insurance company for everything under the sun, they may take care of you. Even if you do have proper and very billable insurance, chances are you still won't see a real live doctor, but a Nurse Practitioner. In order to actually see a living, breathing, honest-to-God doctor, you need an appointment months in advance so that you can sit for hours in his well-appointed, designer-carpeted office with a plasma television selling you the latest drug to keep your stools soft or keep you from dying too soon from veins loaded with cholesterol from eating too many fat-laden, fast-food hamburgers and french fries.

Life was simple, fun, back in those days, and no fears of the bomb— not until 1962 rolled around, with the Cuban Missile Crisis bringing the real possibility of either instant thermonuclear vaporization or hordes of Russian troops suddenly swarming the Florida beaches. With Cuban and Russian missiles parked just ninety miles to the south, everyone was sure that if everything didn't suddenly vanish in a brilliant flash, then we would be out on the beach battling the invading bastards.

Gun sales soared in Florida that year, and Mother and Dad bought the one and only gun they would ever own, a Smith and Wesson .357 Magnum revolver. The blue steel monster was intimidating just lying untouched on a table, but the thought of the mighty roar of the beast as it poured out chunks of lead fit for the destruction of small tanks and large elephants was enough to set my teenaged blood to boiling.

My dad, Glen, was a club champion golfer at the Deerfield Country Club and was definitely more at home managing a slice in high winds than managing some weapon of mass destruction. The thought of my dad tucked in behind some sand dune, decked out in his Bobby Jones knickers and two-tone Foot Joy golf shoes, slinging hot death into an invading Russian horde, was enough to make me nearly bust a gut to keep from laughing. Dad would have been a far more effective defender of the homeland by chipping golf balls at lightning speed with his Ben Hogan 1-iron into the foreheads of the oncoming invaders than pointing that Smith and Wesson hand-cannon and actually trying to hit someone.

Speaking of Dad, this Camelot period in our family life was accentuated by Dad making some serious money in the air-conditioning business. In the post–World War II prosperity, Americans were treating themselves to one of the greatest inventions of the modern age: the home air-conditioning system. Families were tossing out their old window fans and swamp coolers and replacing them with the real thing—honest-to-God, ass-freezing air-conditioning.

Dad did so well financially during that period that he had the cash to build us a new home in a new, upper-class housing development near Alfred I. DuPont High School. That school is no longer so "high"—it has become a middle school, which is still situated on the edge of old Alfred's estate, on land donated by Alfred I. himself. Nice guy; probably needed a tax write-off.

My nickname, "Rollo," was a tag bestowed on me by one of my buddies; not sure which one. There was a cartoon in the daily comic strip in the *Jacksonville Journal* called "Rollo, The Rich Kid." While we were not rich by Alfred I. DuPont's standards, during the Camelot years our family lived very well.

My mother grew up very, very poor. Her dad died when she was eight years old. Her mother worked as a seamstress, which paid very little, and passed away when Mom was just fourteen. Throughout my mother's childhood, Christmas was, if not a literal lump of coal in her stocking, certainly a figurative one. So, having a new home in an affluent neighborhood was a dream come true for her. Even so, she still cut coupons, shopped at JCPenney, and made cold-cut sandwiches for my school lunch. Mom never forgot what it was like to be poor.

In those glory days, Dad purchased a brand new Cadillac El Dorado, solidifying my popularity with my buddies, who stood in line to double-date on Friday and Saturday nights. Hey, let's face it—pulling up in front of your date's house in a new Caddy did a lot to impress not only your date, but also the date's parents, who were watching what kind of car their precious little baby girl got into. Little did Dad or I know that the next four years at DuPont High School would be *my* Camelot, complete with gallant knights and beautiful maidens, the former being my buddies, and the latter being the finest young ladies we could find in the area who were willing to have us.

In 1957, while our new home was being built, Dad and I took a clandestine trip to Miami to pick up a twenty-one-foot Chris Craft cabin-cruiser boat he had purchased on a previous business trip. Somehow, my dad had forgotten to tell Mother the minor detail that he had decided to become a sailor and, so, simply must have a boat.

Good ol' Dad had the idea that if he named the boat after Mom, she would gladly accept the hulking presence of the *Miss Marian* parked in our driveway. I guess Dad thought the honor of having an honest-to-God boat named after her would make Mom swoon and gladly accept the Chris Craft into the family as if it were a puppy or a new baby.

Having had her tubes tied after my sister was born, a new child was the last thing my mother wanted in her life. Even a puppy that would crap all over her new carpet was out of the question. For Mom, the boat was just as bad. Simply put, my mother hated the *Miss Marian*. Mom saw the boat for what it would make of her: a galley cook and maid.

On boating excursions with friends, family, and business associates, with all of us top-side enjoying the sun and fresh air, Dad would open the galley door, lean in, and say to my poor mother relegated to the galley, "Honey, can you hand up a couple of sandwiches, the potato salad, and some cold drinks? Make sure the sodas are cold; reach down in the ice and get some off the bottom of the cooler." My mother, a staunch Christian and not given to cursing, would smile through gritted teeth and reply, "Why, sure, honey; we don't want you and your friends to eat your baloney sandwiches with warm sodas, do we?" Then in a subtle whisper, she would add, "Asshole."

The *Miss Marian*, while the bane of Mom's existence, was another one of my popularity magnets in high school. Memories abound of boating trips with the guys, skiing on the St. John's, beer in the cooler and the radio doing its best to give us the latest tunes. But the most significant feature of the *Miss Marian* was that it could sleep six—or, as I would say, "We can get twelve if the girls don't mind sharing the boat's bed cushions!" We never had twelve for a sleepover on the boat; group sex was years off in the future.

Actually, we never used the boat for any sexual activity, especially at night, as the St. John's River was full of manatee, a big whale-like thing about the size of an aquatic beef cow that could sink a boat if you hit one. Sexual activity in high school, if any, was mostly heavy petting, certainly no intercourse, and usually took place in the front seat of a car, on a darkened road or at the far end of the local drive-in during a Troy Donahue and Sandra Dee melodramatic movie. The *Miss Marian* was a virgin until the day she sank into the Atlantic Ocean, scuttled by a new owner for the insurance money.

Mom didn't shed a tear when she learned the *Miss Marian* was now at the bottom of the ocean in Davey's Jones's Locker.

"Good riddance, and don't ever do that to me again, running off and buying a boat," she told my dad upon learning of the *Miss Marian's* demise.

Little did she know, my dad had only begun to acquire new boats; he subsequently bought a 1939 fifty-foot motor yacht, traded that monster for a thirty-five-foot cabin cruiser once owned by the famous jockey Willie Shoemaker, then traded that one for a Cal twenty-eight-foot sailboat.

Dad never understood the concept that if one of the two best days of your life is when you buy your first boat, the other is when you sell it. A friend told my dad, "Take $1000 and flush it down the toilet. If that doesn't bother you, then you'll enjoy being captain of your own ship." Over the years, Dad flushed a lot of money down the toilet in the form of boats.

My years of Camelot came crashing down in 1962, as the result of my dad losing his cushy job due to the restructuring of his air-conditioning company. The restructuring was orchestrated by some little shit whiz-kid MBA from one of the Ivy League universities. The suddenness of the loss of his job almost killed my dad. He and all the other hundreds of employees who lost their jobs did not see the restructuring coming. Most had not prepared financially for being "out the door" without notice. One or two of the displaced employees even ended their lives due to the embarrassment of being "fired"; in those days, the stigma was more than they could bear, even though the layoffs were company-wide and included hundreds of other employees like them.

All the "toys" our family had were sold to help pay bills and my tuition at Georgia Tech. The Caddy was replaced with a used Ford station wagon, the membership to Deerfield Country Club cancelled, the pool cleaning and landscaping service stopped. I always wondered if the Ivy League MBA jerk realized the impact of his restructuring recommendation on the lower-income folks Mom employed, such as our African American pool-cleaning guy and the Asian yard man, both of whom also got the boot out the door. A life lesson from this experience: "Trickle-down shit happens."

"Rollo, The Rich Kid" became just plain "Rollo." While at Georgia Tech, on a partial track scholarship for the board and books, I also had a little gig as one of the student dorm counselors, which gave me a free dorm room. In addition, I supplemented my income by allowing students to have televisions in their rooms or an occasional girlfriend overnight on the weekend—in exchange for a small cash gratuity.

My parents had borrowed the money for my tuition from one of my dad's brothers, who had made it big-time in the propane gas business. It was just as well that "Rollo, The Rich Kid" ended when it did. I learned the financial lesson that you need a few bucks in the bank or under your mattress to cover your butt when you get fired or outsourced by some Ivy League whiz kid with a brain that only functions in binary code, and some kind of clockwork machinery instead of a heart.

I left Jacksonville in 1964, the year I graduated college. That same year I married Elizabeth, a friend of a friend. I was absolutely and firmly convinced that my new bride and I would live together in blissful harmony and love for the rest of our lives. That assumption proved to be a major mistake. The only saving grace of that union was a son, who means the world to me.

It was during the first year of my ill-fated attempt at marital bliss that my dad, with Mother and my sister in tow, headed for the great state of California. He had accepted a job at General Electric, and overnight, our "East Coast family" became a "West Coast family."

Moving three thousand miles from what we considered home proved life-altering for my whole family. My sister had to give up her senior year at the Florida high school where she had started in the eighth grade. She lost her long-time friends, and then was forced to adjust to kids she didn't know or want to know at Hollywood High. My mother informed me that my sister, when not at school, spent every waking moment locked in her bedroom. That's tough. I wonder if the pencil-necked whiz-kid MBA bastard ever contemplated what impact his restructuring model had on my sister. She would have kicked his ass if she ever caught up with him, and believe me, she could do it!

As for me, after a couple years of our tumultuous marriage, Elizabeth and I separated for more than six months, each realizing that the marriage was not for either of us. But with encouragement from parents on both sides, we moved from where we had been living, out to California to start over. They say you never leave the problems of a marriage behind when you move; you just take them with you. Well, we became living evidence of the truth behind that statement. Three years later, we were in a California divorce court.

Now, fifty years later, I am back at Jacksonville, stopping briefly at Jacksonville Beach to take in some memories of great times. I am on my way to a new life, a new Camelot, to be found in whatever years I have left, and only God knows that number. Whether my Guinevere will be Stacey, Jackie, or Ginny—one of the three girlfriends I loved those many years ago—only time will tell. I do believe my Camelot still has some sand left in its hourglass. Hopefully, the sand will fall to the bottom slowly.

Chapter 3

The Magnificent Six

*E*arly in the morning on what I remember as a shirt-drenching, hot and humid day in September 1959, I was about to set out on my rounds of picking up my best friends to start the first day of our senior year at old Alfred I. DuPont High School. Finishing my usual breakfast of Cheerios and orange juice, I kissed my mother and said to her kiddingly, "Well, this is it—downhill for the next one hundred and eighty days."

She was not amused. Glaring at me, she snorted, "You better make that 'uphill,' buster, if you want to get into a decent college. Your dad has told you a thousand times, 'a student with "C" grades ends up bagging groceries at Winn-Dixie.' Do you want to be a bag-boy the rest of your life?"

"Well, I never saw a starving Winn-Dixie bag-boy with all that free food around him." Backing up, I ducked as a soggy dish towel she had been holding flew by my head. "Look, Rob"—Mom never heard me called Rollo—"you have to buckle down this year with the books. Your dad and I just want the best for you. You know we both love you." My mom came over to me and gave me a big hug and a kiss and pushed me toward the back door to the garage. "Good luck today at school, and tell all the guys I wish them well, too."

With that, I left the house, got into my car, an ambulance-white '39 Ford sedan which seated six adults, four of them squeezed like sardines in the back seat, and headed out to pick up my friends.

Fifty years later, these buddies are still five of the greatest friends I have ever had. In fact, they are the only *real* friends I've ever had. You know, the kind of friends that would have your back no matter what, and wouldn't hesitate to call you an asshole if you were actually being one.

Being the loner of the group, I have seldom had any other male friends as close as these guys. One of the members of our group dubbed us "The Magnificent Six" or "The Mag 6," a take-off on a popular movie of the time called *The Magnificent Seven*. Our Magnificent Six were not magnificent in the sense that Yul Brenner, James Colburn, Horst Buchholz, and the others were. In the movie, the Magnificent Seven were renegade outlaw drifters who saved a small Mexican farming town from being raped and pillaged by a gang of cutthroat banditos.

But our Mag 6 are truly magnificent *friends*, willing to do almost anything for one another, no questions asked. We haven't saved any villages, but we've shared a lot of life and a lot of beer, and no matter the *wheres* or the *whats*, we stick by one another, even after so much time and so many life experiences have passed between us.

"*Lily*"

Lily was the first of the "Mag 6" I picked up. He lived in a modest little one-story just a few blocks from my house. Despite the girlie-sounding nickname, Lily was a guys' guy, low-key, rugged-looking, with an air of innocence about him. He was, and still is, the kind of guy who would do anything for you. He was good at football and track, but despite the prestige this gave him, he wasn't a ladies' man. You didn't have to worry about Lily snaking your date at a party. Usually, he showed up stag, looking to hang out with the Mag 6 or with whoever else showed up stag. I can't remember a single girl he ever had more than two dates with in high school—thus his nickname, "Lily," as in "innocent and pure, like an Easter lily."

Lily didn't smoke, drink beer, or ever take the Lord's name in vain. I thought someday he would become a pastor of a small Baptist church in Mississippi, where his parents were from and where he later played football at a small college. But on second thought, I never knew of Lily going to church on a weekly basis.

Maybe Lily watched church services on television with the emerging "televangelists," like the wild Oral Roberts. On a good Sunday, within the thirty minutes he was on television, Oral could cure half a room of blind and invalid believers. Pushing his palm into their forehead, he would scream in their face, "Heal! Heal! Heal!" Poor souls were probably too scared of old Oral *not* to be healed. I always felt that, once the television cameras were turned off, many of the "healed" TV show participants probably started falling down without their crutches and the "cured" blind walked into doors and walls, their newfound sight suddenly faded to black. Maybe for Lily, the television is where he got his injection of religion. Oral would have been an interesting teacher.

Everyone at DuPont High School liked Lily, to the point that they voted him one of the class officers. I can't remember which—maybe secretary, although that wouldn't make a lot of sense because Lily literally could not write; he just printed. Somehow in his twelve years of school, and probably even in his four additional years of college, Lily never learned the Palmer Penmanship method of writing in longhand; he printed every letter of every word in every sentence he put on paper. With the future age of computer keyboards and text-messaging making handwriting obsolete, Lily was just a little ahead of everyone else—by, say, thirty to forty years.

As popular as he was with the students, we were all surprised that Lily didn't win the Mr. DuPont contest, which many thought to be just a popularity contest. This idiotic fundraising event was the brain-child of someone's mother who headed up the local PTA.

It was later learned that Lily actually *had* won the stupid contest. The results had been announced by the event moderator, who also happened to be the school's quirky, "absent-minded professor" science teacher. The moderator accidentally reversed the envelopes and read the actual winner as the first runner-up and the first runner-up as the winner. Lily was announced as first runner-up, which was perfectly fine with him; he was thrilled with not winning because he didn't want to be forever called Mr. DuPont by his friends. *"Hey, Mr. DuPont, are you doing it with Miss DuPont?"* Or, worse: *"Hey, Mr. DuPont, you and Miss DuPont expecting any little DuPonts?"* Ha! Considering the results of a first-place win, in some contests it's best to come in second.

Of course, the flipside of Mr. DuPont was the Miss DuPont contest.

Ten of our high school's most beautiful, popular, or politically connected girls got selected to participate in what was really not a contest at all. To me, the fix was always in on the winner; the girl most liked by members of the teachers' council, or the girlfriend of the school's biggest ass-kisser, always seemed to win Miss DuPont. I guess some things never change; we can see evidence of this kind of political ass-kissing every election year.

Each year the senior boys tried to get a ringer nominated to be one of the ten girls in the contest. My senior year we hoped Prissy, the class put-out, would get in and we would all vote for her as Miss DuPont. If she had won, it would have been poetic justice for all those girls who were never even selected to be *in* the contest. Each year, our ringer got tossed off the ballot because she did not meet the qualifications due to some unwritten rule the head of the PTA always seemed to manufacture. Prissy was literally "put out" of the contest before she even got on the ballot due to the selection committee stating, "She doesn't have a 'B' or better grade-point average, which is one of the qualifiers for the contest." Funny—that "qualifier" had never been mentioned before.

Word had it that on dates, parking in the woods late at night, Prissy always earned an "A" for her efforts from whatever lucky gent happened to be the owner of the car. For the Miss DuPont contest, I guess her "A" average for parking in the woods didn't count. Too bad; Prissy would have been a great Miss DuPont—much better than the snotty, bratty, spoiled little rich girls who got the title by virtue of Daddy's money, Mommy's influence, and a fake little smile.

That day, when I pulled up in front of his house, Lily was already standing in the driveway with his sister Sarah, who was being taken to school by her dad.

"Hey, Lily," I shouted, "come on and get your butt in the car. First day at school! I want to see which of the hot sophomores has their teats pushed up and out to lure us seniors to ask them on a date!"

Lily's response was instant and sounded a little nervous.

"Rollo, quit talking like that; my sister will hear you and ask my dad what 'teats' are."

Looking across the seat as Lily slid in on the passenger side to ride shotgun, I laughingly responded, "Yeah, and someday your Sarah will be standing out in front of the high school hoping some hot senior is enthralled with *her* teats."

Not amused, Lily reached across the seat and grabbed my shirt just exactly where my right nipple was and pinched it, causing me to scream, "Ouch, asshole, that hurts!"

Lily retorted, "Not as much as you'll hurt if you ever mention my sister like that again."

As we pulled away from Lily's house, my new JCPenney Hawaiian-themed shirt now had a huge wrinkle exactly at my right nipple. I smiled and winked at Lily. "No problem. Sarah has a few more years before she'll be a sophomore, and those little puppies need time to sprout." At that last comment, Lily put another wrinkle in my shirt right next to the first one.

"Spiff"

I don't remember if there was a men's fashion magazine like *GQ* when we were in high school. If such a magazine was around then, Spiff (short for "spiffy"), would have been its poster child. From his Bass Weejuns to his impeccable, double-pleated trousers with a matching weaved belt and a tie-dyed Madras or Lacoste shirt, Spiff was always immaculate in his dress and appearance.

There was never a hair out of place, never a wrinkle in his clothes, never any bad breath or body odor. I always thought Spiff must be the only kid on the planet who slept standing up so he wouldn't even wrinkle his pressed-seam pajamas.

Second on my Mag 6 pickup route, Spiff was always a treat since looking at him was just about the only way the other five of us would ever bother to notice what the men's fashion world was featuring for the season. Every day it was a new outfit, mostly the college preppie look.

While my mother always wanted me to have new clothes for the first day of class, her clothier of choice was JCPenney. Maybe she worked their layaway plan and purchased my clothes by paying for them gradually over time. Eventually, Mom would pick up the layaways, but by then it was usually a season or two later. I swear, my first case of jock-itch came from sweating between my legs as I sat in class all one hot, late-spring day in these wool winter-wear slacks Mom had gotten out of layaway a season late. Regardless, the thought of us all being nicely dressed was important to Mom, even if my clothes did come from JCPenney or Sears. God forbid we should ever shop at the chic men's store in our local shopping center!

I watched in the rearview mirror as Spiff carefully positioned his immaculately garbed butt in the back seat. "Spiff, looks like your mom pulled out all the stops with your clothes for the first day back at school. Is she trying to win you the 'Best Dressed' award?"

"Yeah, Rollo, just because you look like you fell off the turnip truck, don't pick on my clothes. It doesn't cost much more to go first-class. Besides, my girlfriend Halley likes the way I look, as do her friends. What does *Stacey* say about *your* choice of clothes? Oh, oh, excuse me—she dumped you this summer, didn't she? She probably didn't want to be seen with someone who looks like a Polish peasant."

Spiff's grin faded almost immediately as I half-turned in my seat and nearly shouted at him, "You elitist bastard! Stacey is old news. Besides, it was her Protestant-hating mother who caused us to split up. Being a staunch Catholic, she didn't want any Protestant coming within a mile of her daughter. Did you know Stacey is not going to be at DuPont for senior year? Her mom is making her go to some private girls' school. What a tyrant!"

"Wow," responded Spiff, "shipping her to a private school. How is Stacey taking it?"

Pulling away from his house, I looked in the mirror again and said with a tone of sincerity, "Stacey is a beautiful, fun-loving person who has a real hard-ass for a mother. Her dad is an OK guy, not into the Catholic thing, but he doesn't stick up for Stacey with her mom. I feel like Stacey missing her senior year at DuPont is partly my fault. It makes me sick!"

Lily, who had stayed out of the give-and-take with Spiff, now jumped in on the Stacey-not-coming-back-for-her-senior-year bandwagon. "I can't imagine what it would be like to miss my senior year. I don't understand the Catholic-and-Protestant thing. Maybe her mother hates you because you eat cheeseburgers on Friday and not mackerel?" Lily laughed at his own line, and then began making a hand gesture that looked like a fish opening and closing its mouth, and mumbled, "Mackerel snapper, mackerel snapper."

"Knock it off, Lily. At least I *had* a girlfriend this summer, unlike you who spent the summer in your closet. I bet you got to some serious lip-locking, kissing those naked girls in that *Playboy* magazine you have hidden under your bed. Get some paper cuts on those lips?"

Spiff leaned forward and in a sincere tone asked Lily, "What does *Playboy's* Miss September look like? Big balloons? Can I stop by after football practice tonight and take a look?"

"Look, Rollo and Spiff, I don't need a *Playboy* magazine for a date. Besides, I *don't* have one under my bed. My dad would kill me if I ever brought that trash into the house. As for a girlfriend, I just don't want to spend money on some twit who may or may not make out after a couple of dates. I can wait for the right one to come along."

Spiff leaned forward again. "No Miss September? No big balloons? Forget it; I'm not coming by your house tonight."

"*Crazy*"

Every male should have a friend like Crazy. When you get arrested and need someone to bail you out of jail in the middle of the night, no questions asked, Crazy is that kind of guy.

One Sunday morning that summer before senior year, I called Crazy from Jacksonville County Jail at 4:00 a.m., having been arrested along with twenty other friends at a party at the Thunderbird Motel. I almost cried when Crazy answered the phone on the second ring. I pleaded with him to come to the jail and bail me out. I figured I could get home in the morning and tell my folks I had forgotten to let them know I was spending the night at Crazy's house, but timing was a major issue. Crazy simply said, "I'll be there in thirty minutes."

Bing, bang, boom—Crazy was at the jail, money in hand, and I got bailed and home before my parents ever woke up. Crazy saved my life, not only from staying in a jail cell with some guys who looked like they would beat the crap out of me just for the sport of it, but from my dad, who certainly would have beaten the crap out of me for doing something as dumb as getting arrested for partying at a motel.

Like a soldier jumping on a live grenade to save the lives of his buddies, Crazy jumped on my predicament and saved my ass from certain disaster. "Thank you, Crazy," To this day, I'm grateful to him.

You also want Crazy to be with you when you and he, as starting halfbacks on the high school football team, are relegated to the defensive line to play the meanest, baddest-ass team in the conference, our age-old hometown rival, Jackson High. Our football team was good, but not great. We had won only a few games that year before meeting Jackson on the field of combat.

Jackson High School was located in the blue-collar, lower-income area, where most of their players had grown up fighting on the street, as was evidenced by their lack of many of their front teeth, as well as the scars already on a few of their faces. Looking at them during warm-up, I thought we were playing a team just released from the State Reform School.

For this crucial game, our coaches cooked up a plan to put all the big, fast guys on the defensive line, and the big, second-fastest guys as linebackers and defensive ends. The coach didn't care about the defensive backs, as if fully aware that if Jackson High's running backs got that far into our secondary, we wouldn't be able to stop them anyway.

Well, as pissed off as Crazy and I were when we were forced to play defensive guards for that game, to our amazement, the coach's game plan actually worked! Play after play, we stopped their running backs at the line. With our adrenaline flowing, Crazy and I got pumped up and made tackle after tackle on their running backs and quarterback, many in Jackson's own backfield. At the end of the game, the score was DuPont, 12 and Jackson, 6. We had won a football game that even the best bookies in Vegas would never have given us odds of winning.

The reward Crazy and I got for our play was that he was voted Team Captain for the rest of the season, while the local newspaper voted me "Lineman of the Week" from among all the high schools in Duval County. Me, the team's hotshot running back, voted "Lineman of the Week." An honor and a disgrace all rolled into one.

During the game, my leg was broken by an illegal chop block. Thinking the pain was just a cramp, I played the entire game, limping and tackling. Looking down the line as we went into our defensive set, seeing Crazy and he seeing me, and Crazy giving me his big, dumb-ass smile, the terrible pain in my leg magically disappeared. He had that effect on a person—Mr. Pain Killer. You never hurt physically or emotionally when you were with Crazy.

Crazy is also the friend who would spontaneously perform wild, often funny, off-the-wall stunts, such as attempting to break the Guinness record for doing forward flips into the swimming pool in my back yard.

One summer night, several of our group were casually enjoying a swim in my backyard swimming pool. Crazy, on his own without a dare from any of us—well, maybe the beer we were drinking had something to do with it—decided to start doing forward flips off the diving board. After thirty-nine flips, Crazy quit his attempt at breaking the record. Totally exhausted and out of breath, he casually walked to my dad's prize petunia bed and puked his guts out. My kind of guy! Later, we came to find out there was no Guinness record for flips off a diving board, so technically, Crazy holds the world record. And to think, it was set in *my* backyard pool!

Crazy's house was just blocks away from Spiff's; they lived in the same middle-class housing development. Normally, when I would pick up Crazy, he would be standing outside, sort of milling around on the front lawn, pulling up blades of grass, killing time waiting for his ride. This morning, Crazy was not out front. I honked the horn several times, waited for a few minutes. Crazy still didn't appear.

Somewhat irritated, I said loudly as I got out of the car, "I'll go and get Crazy. He probably forgot today was the first day of school. What an idiot."

Crazy's bedroom window was off the walkway leading to the front door, so I squatted down to peek in under the half-drawn blinds. There, sitting on his bed, was Crazy, fully dressed for school, but with a plastic bag full of pennies. He was methodically counting pennies and putting them in what looked to be piles of ten each. What in the world was he doing that for on the morning of the first day of school? I wondered if maybe the nickname we'd given him was more accurate than we knew.

Lightly rapping on the window to get his attention, I yelled, "Crazy, come on! We gotta go! Get your ass out here!"

Looking at me from the bed, he gave me one of his dumb-ass smiles and a thumbs-up, and started toward the front door, scooping up several of the piles of coins.

Back in my car, Lily asked me, "What is he doing? Still in bed stroking his lizard?"

"Gross, gross!" came from Spiff in the back seat. "Our Crazy wouldn't do something like that."

Laughingly, I turned around and said to Spiff, "Oh, come on, if stroking your lizard was a sanctioned event at our high school, you would be a letterman. You would probably have a big lizard on your letter sweater so everyone would know what you do to yourself when your girlfriend won't do it to you."

"Yeah, Rollo, go bite yourself," he retorted.

As I was about to give the needling back to Spiff, Crazy opened the back door of the car and jumped in. I looked at him and asked a simple question: "Crazy, what in the hell were you doing in your room with all those pennies? Robbing your piggy bank?"

Crazy responded, "Chee-vee-vee."

Looking at him in confusion, I asked, "What did you say?"

"Chee-vee-vee," he muttered again.

"What in the hell does 'chee-vee-vee' mean? It doesn't make any sense! Are you feeling OK?" I was a little worried that Crazy might have sort of lost it the morning of our first day of senior year.

Again came: "Chee-vee-vee."

"Chee-vee-vee?" I asked.

"Chee-vee-vee," came my answer.

"No more!" I stated in frustration. I started the car and headed for Star's house.

"Chee-vee-vee" sort of floated forward from the back to the front seat. Then, "Lunch money. Mom forgot to leave me lunch money before she went to work," Crazy sort of whispered. Then, "Chee-vee-vee."

In life, our words—how we speak, how we put together our thoughts in a sentence, even how we string nouns and verbs together to make a sentence—all this defines our personality and, to some degree, our intelligence. Some people have an excellent command of the English language, appearing to be well educated and sophisticated in their manners. Some swear too much, peppering the "F" word into every sentence they utter. They appear less educated and less sophisticated than the well-spoken folks.

Words and phrases also become woven into our culture. Take, for example, "Do you feel lucky, sucker?" or "You can't handle the truth." From many years ago, "Nuts!" or "Play it again, Sam" or "Frankly, my dear, I don't give a damn." "Chee-vee-vee" is an expression that no one understands but Crazy. It certainly defines him as an individualist, maybe one with a right-brain, creative, and carefree outlook on life. For as long as I've known Crazy, no one has ever figured out the meaning of "chee-vee-vee." Only Crazy and God know.

"Star"

Star, nicknamed after the Star of David, is Jewish, but Star also thinks of himself literally as a star, the best at whatever he does: sports, business, girls. In high school, Star wasn't built like some superstar athlete. He was about the size of all of us, just at 6'0, a little on the stocky side at 190, but with some fair speed, which is why he was relegated to playing fullback on our football team. Star wanted to be respected and liked by everyone. He was a very self-conscious person, always comparing whatever to whatever—his clothes to your clothes, his accomplishments on the football field with yours, his girlfriend to yours. He sought equality with everyone he knew and everyone who knew him.

Kiddingly referred to as our "token Jewish member," Star gave our group a certain religious balance: three Baptists, one Methodist (me), one not too sure what his religion was—Oral Roberts on TV maybe—and then Star, our resident Jew. He was sensitive about being Jewish in a mostly Protestant community, although he was not a practicing Jew with the *yarmulke* head cover or synagogue every Saturday. In fact, I never heard of Star *ever* going to synagogue; I'm quite sure he never stepped in one the whole time I knew him.

Other than religion, we were a pretty homogenous group. None of us was African American or of any other ethnic heritage, only Caucasian. When I was in high school, all the schools in Jacksonville were segregated, and it was only years later that it really dawned on me that there were no blacks in our high school. Dumb me thought it had to do with it just *happening* that no blacks lived in our part of town; dumber me, not getting the whole segregation issue, that blacks and whites *didn't live* in the same neighborhoods in Jacksonville in the late 1950s.

As Star got in the car, Lily or Spiff quipped, "Star, looking good for the first day of our senior year! Clothes all pressed, hair brushed, smelling good—what's the cologne . . . Old Spice? . . . Old Jew?" That line produced a round of laughs from everyone.

Star bounced the sarcasm back with "You're just jealous you pigs couldn't afford Canoe, which is what the cologne is. Pam gave it to me this weekend on our date, sort of a sign of her wanting us to go steady."

"Nah, Pam *really* gave you the cologne to cover up the smell of the *gefilte* fish sandwiches your mother packs for your lunch," I fired back at Star.

"You're just pissed Stacey dumped you and all you have for a date for this weekend is your right hand," laughed Star. "Speaking of fish, are you still eating those Long John Silver's Fish Baskets on Friday to kiss Stacey's mother's ass? You really whored yourself out to get in Stacey's pants. Those fish dinners make you smell like the dead mullets we caught at the Coastal Canal a couple of weeks ago."

Crazy piped up from the daze he had seemed to be in—maybe counting all those pennies had crashed his thinking this morning—and said, "We must have caught twenty mullets. Mom is going to put chunks of the fish is some sort of fish stew tonight. Anyone want to come over to my house after football practice for mullet stew?"

Lily started laughing and blurted out, "You know what the sharecroppers in Mississippi call mullets? 'Poor man's lobster.' Crazy is having mullet lobster stew tonight and will be chopping cotton tomorrow!"

Lily was now beside himself with laughter at the thought of Crazy eating mullet stew, me eating Long John Silver's Fish Fun Delight dinners, and Star carrying *gefilte* fish sandwiches to school for lunch. He continued,

"If Jesus had to feed the five thousand with mullet, Fish Fun Delight Dinners, or *gefilte* fish, they all would have left and gone home!"

Star didn't say any more. He avoided confrontation with the group, preferring to go into a silent sulk, but managed one final retort: "You guys are jealous I got the Canoe cologne and you didn't get crap. Score one for the Jew-boy. Ha!"

Not wanting to keep the repartee going with Star, we all let it drop as I pulled my car onto San Jose Boulevard, headed for our final stop. Oz's house was just a couple of blocks from school; he could have easily walked, but didn't want to miss what was going on with the group, and who we were picking on each morning. By the time I got to Oz's house, my car looked like a clown car—five fairly large teenagers packed into the small space, with one more to go. Twelve hundred pounds of testosterone-charged adolescents, nattily dressed and smelling good with the scent of Canoe or Old Jew or Mennen's After Shave—we all had it going for us that first day of our senior year.

"*Oz*"

Oz (short for Ozzie) is the sleeper of our group. Sometimes we called him "Wizard," as in "the Wizard of Oz." Oz, or Wizard, was adept at magically keeping his ass out of trouble when everyone else was getting busted by their parents or the school principal or the Jacksonville police. He was a closet "wild thing"; on the SAT test, Oz scored the highest of our group, but he clearly wanted to be seen as "just one of the guys." He was a combination of all our personalities. Like Spiff, Oz was always fairly impeccable in his dress, and like Star, he was self-conscious about how others saw him. Much like Crazy, Oz was fun-loving and balanced in his approach to life, and like Lily, he was not a skirt-chaser but more laid-back on the girl scene. And like me, he conformed to family pressure to get good enough grades to get into a good college, but deep down within Oz there was that wild streak that ran deep and easily flowed to the surface when he was in the company of someone who also had that "let 'er rip" personality.

During the summer, Oz had made friends with Danny, an off-the-wall, dare-devil troublemaker, whose attitude was "I can do anything to you, and all you can do to me is kill me, which I don't care about 'cause I'm dying anyhow." Unfortunately, that *was* the case; Danny really was dying from a rare and incurable liver disease, which his older brother had already succumbed to just the previous year. Danny had only one year, two max, left in his life when Oz met him and they became friends. The problem for Oz was that Danny was on a destructive path to go out of life with a bang.

One summer night the following year, the summer before we all went off to college, my new girlfriend Ginny and I were all alone in my house, the parents out-of-town and my sister having a sleepover at her friend's place. I was cherishing the opportunity to take advantage of all the features of Mom's dream house: swimming pool, stereo system, air-conditioning, and, of course, my bedroom, with fresh sheets and pillowcase. My plan was: pool, music, then the dream of all horny teenagers—a trip to the bedroom.

The phone rang just as Ginny and I were about to change for a dip in the pool. (No skinny dipping, as friends and family often showed up at the most inopportune times to avail themselves of a quick dip and "Oh, by the way, do you have a dry towel?")

"Rollo, I'm desperate! I'll give you *anything* to come get me *now*! Please, I'm *begging* you!" This, from a frantic Oz, whom I had never heard or seen so shaken.

Concerned, I asked, "Oz, what's the problem? You sound terrible. Are you hurt, been in a wreck? Where are you?"

"Rollo, I'm OK, but there are police cruising the area looking for me. I'm across the river near the 5 Points Theatre, corner drug store across the street from the theatre. Can you come get me?" Oz was begging and sounded fearful.

"Man, I'm with Ginny; can I bring her with me?" I asked, concerned for his well-being.

"Hell, yeah, you can bring Ginny, your dog, anyone; just please come get me, *now*!"

"Oz, I'll be there in thirty minutes. I'm gonna cruise slowly by the drug store and you can jump in."

"Rollo, please hurry!"

Ginny and I jumped in my car and drove across the St. John's River to an area of Jacksonville known as Avondale, a quaint suburban town with a nice movie house, a couple of cute restaurants, and a few service stores, including the drug store where Oz was hiding out from the police.

As we slowly approached, I could see Oz in the shadows of the store entrance. When he spotted my car, he literally ran alongside it, opened the back door, and jumped in, diving to the floor. "Drive, Rollo, drive! Get me out of here!!"

Once across the bridge, back on our side of the river, I turned and said to Oz, "You're safe to come up. Want to tell me why you dragged my ass and Ginny to come rescue you?"

"That asshole Danny and I went to the 5 Points Theater to watch that John Wayne movie that just came out. During the movie, he takes out a bag that I thought had some of his medicine. The jerk had eggs in the bag—*raw* eggs!—and, without saying anything, he started throwing them randomly in the theatre, hitting a few people who started screaming, which caused this idiot to start laughing and throwing a few more eggs, hitting even *more* people and creating a big panic. Then the asshole runs for the exit, leaving me behind to get my ass whipped and arrested. I barely got to the exit before some big guy dripping in yellow egg slop could get to me. If he had caught me, he would have beat the shit out of me and held me for the cops. I didn't know Danny was going to throw eggs!"

Ginny and I were shocked that Oz had gotten caught up in Danny's egg-throwing caper. "You know, Oz, this Danny is crazy. He wants someone to kill him and he doesn't care who he takes with him. Plus, you ruined a great evening Ginny and I had planned." Ginny looked at me, unaware of just *what* I had planned.

"Sorry, Rollo, never again will I go out with Danny—way too crazy for me." And I believed he wouldn't . . . until two weeks later, when he told me that Danny had stopped the car they were in and pulled the same stunt of throwing eggs. This time the egg-throwing was from a bridge overlooking a dance party at a local country club. Dancers in their best formals were covered in the yucky, yellow egg goo. According to Oz, he escaped once more.

Timely for Oz, Danny's disease kicked in and he died within the month. Befitting Danny's contribution to society, Oz stopped by his gravesite a month after his funeral and left a raw, uncooked egg on his headstone.

Now Oz jumped into the back seat with Star, Spiff, and Crazy, trying to squeeze out a little place to sit. As his butt got close to the seat, Crazy pulled his usual routine of sticking something in one of your orifices when you least expected it, be it a slimy, saliva-dripping forefinger in your ear—or even two wet fingers, getting both ears at once—for a "Wet Willy," or a stiffened thumb for a nerve-jarring "ass goose." Well, Oz got his morning wake-up call. "Whoa!" he shouted, as his butt hit one of Crazy's famous "ass gooses."

"Chee-vee-vee," Crazy responded.

"Move, Crazy! Give me some space to sit," barked Oz.

"Chee-vee-vee," Crazy muttered and shifted to give Oz an edge of the back seat for his butt to squeeze into for the five-minute ride to the school parking lot.

"Thanks, Crazy," said Oz, but when Oz turned to talk to Spiff, Crazy put a slimy, saliva-soaked forefinger in Oz's right ear, mumbling to him, "Wet Willy."

"Damn, Crazy!" Oz yelled as he instinctively stuck his own finger in his ear to wipe out the sloppy saliva.

"Chee-vee-vee, "Crazy said, smiling his goofy smile.

Oz started his first day of his senior year with the honor of getting *two* of Crazy's signature moves, both before the car hit the parking lot. What a treat and an honor.

Chapter 4

Alfred I. DuPont High School

*I*spent four of the best years of my life attending DuPont High School and knew the ins and outs of the place better than even the school janitor, but in all that time, I never saw a single picture of Alfred I., even though the school carried his name. I mean, the guy was forever memorialized in the minds of the student body, even in our school song, "To Dear Old DuPont High." As best I can remember, the song was played by the band and mouthed by most of the students at every meeting, pep rally, and assembly: "To dear old DuPont High, we wave our banner proud and true . . ." I can't remember all the words, and far as I know, we never waved a single banner, but hey, it was high school—a lot of things didn't make sense.

Since I never saw a single picture of Alfred I. DuPont, I sometimes wondered what the guy was like. I kind of imagined him as some very rich wacko with bats in his belfry and a closet full of skeletons, but for all I knew, he could've been a communist sympathizer, or a cross-dresser, or even a cross-dressing communist sympathizer. All I knew for sure was that nobody, not even school staff, could tell me very much about the guy, even though our school was named after him.

The one thing I do know, mainly because I witnessed it with my own two eyes, was the fact that old Alfred I. had a huge World War II .50 caliber anti-aircraft gun mounted to the dock next to his luxury motor yacht. This was a fully functional monster of a weapon that was referred to by the gun crews as a "Chicago Atomizer" because it fired a bullet about the size of a large banana at a cyclic rate suitable for killing just about anything in the sea, in the air, or on land.

One summer I took some of my friends on a little outing on the family boat along the St. John's River. We were doing our best to get a good, close look at all the rich folks' waterfront mansions when we spotted Alfred I.'s artillery piece, bolted gray and menacing to the dock. I wondered how Alfred got permission to bolt the thing to his dock, and wondered even more what might possess the man to think he needed such a weapon. I finally gave up trying to figure it out, with the realization that, hey, if you've got enough money, and enough nuttiness, you can get away with almost anything.

Maybe old Alfred I. thought the Russians would cross over from their Cuban staging grounds for a try at invading the U.S. via the St. John's River in Jacksonville, Florida, and that he, in a fit of righteous and patriotic anger, and equipped with his .50 caliber, would save our fair city and the nation from the Red Invasion. Of course, one thought always leads to another, and before long, I had a vivid mental image of Alfred I., awakened early one morning by the roar of Russian landing craft and troop planes. It would have to be early morning, of course, since invasions always have to happen in the early morning, don't they? I could imagine old Alfred dashing out of his mansion and down to the boat dock, slippers flapping and bathrobe trailing cape-like behind him. His cigarette wobbles in its sliver holder, which is clenched between his teeth, as he hauls back on the Chicago Atomizer's charging handle and pours hot lead into those no-good Russian planes, boats, and whatever else, giving them a taste of what happens to people who mess with Alfred I. DuPont.

Later in life, when curiosity got the better of me, I did a little research on Alfred I. DuPont and found out that, even though he was weird enough to have an artillery piece mounted on his boat dock, he was basically a pretty good guy. Well, he did marry his cousin once, but then again, he was married several times, even picking one wife out when she was fourteen years old, then waiting until she was "of age" before adding her to his collection. Alfred had one "oops, shoulda pulled it" moment in his life when he had a child with his office assistant. He also lost an eye during a shooting accident, but subsequently made a ton of money on gunpowder, real estate, and banking. Like I said, he was basically a good guy.

Alfred I.'s estate in Jacksonville is known as "Epping Forest," just like George Washington's mother's Virginia estate. Why, you might ask, was Alfred I. DuPont's estate named after that of a dead president's mother? It seems that George Washington's mother was named Mary Ball Washington. Alfred I.'s third wife, the one he picked out of the crowd when she was fourteen, was named Jessie Ball. Seems that Jessie Ball and Mary Ball Washington were relatives—several generations apart, of course, but still relatives—so Alfred I. named his estate after the estate of his wife's famous relative. No one I ever talked to at Alfred I. DuPont High had any idea the school had a connection to the mother of our first president.

DuPont High School was a nondescript box of a building. Constructed in 1942, it was located in a suburban area and generally only had a few hundred students wandering its halls in search of an education at any given time. Somewhere around 1963, Alfred I. DuPont High School was relegated to the second-class status of DuPont Middle School, having been replaced by Samuel W. Wolfson High School. Gone was the high school that had borne Alfred's name, replaced by a Jewish donor with either more money or more clout than old Alfred had been able to maintain, but then, old Alfred had been dead for a few years and Samuel was still kicking and able to push for his namesake school.

On the first day of senior year, car loaded down with the Mag 6, I pulled into the school parking lot and wheeled into one of the spots reserved for seniors. I had let it be known in the last days of my junior year that this particular parking space was sacrosanct; it was MINE and not to be messed with by any of the other seniors "or else." Never quite figured out what "or else" would be, but I always had the secret hope that just the threat would be sufficient.

I really needed that parking space to be open, since almost every day we would wheel in, tires on that American-made rolling iron screeching on the blacktop, as we were running late and every second counted on the mad dash to our first class. Our late arrival was almost inevitably the result of sitting in Crazy's driveway because he was either counting out change for his lunch or laboring away at his morning constitutional, sitting on the toilet, engrossed in the morning paper's sports page.

The same shout would ring uselessly out across the neighborhood almost every morning when one or the other of us ran short on patience: "Come on, Crazy! Take your dump at school! We're gonna miss roll call in home room!" But it never got Crazy to pinch it off one bit faster; he had his morning routine, and it wasn't to be interrupted by something as minor as getting an education.

We wheeled in that first glorious morning of senior year with actually a few minutes to spare for the first, and probably last, time ever. Still, as soon as the car came to a stop, we were out and moving up the wide concrete walk that led the hundred-and-fifty or so feet from the street to the school. As we walked, we passed groups of other students gathered in their respective cliques: freshmen and sophomores first, then the juniors and seniors closer to the front door.

The junior and senior area of the walk was automatically understood to be "no man's land" by the sophomores and freshmen, and only rarely would a particularly ignorant or thick-headed one cross the unseen line to be heckled and threatened. On this particular morning, however, a sophomore by the name of Jackie had crossed that line and positioned herself outside the door, apparently in search of one of us older, more sophisticated and worldly seniors to date.

As a normal red-blooded American senior high school male, I was a predator on the prowl, and my eyes continually scanned the area to see what juicy young lady I might be able to couple up with during my senior year. Along with the scanning eyes, my brain was constantly weighing both the physical attributes and the possibility of actually getting dates with those young ladies lucky enough to fall under my discerning gaze.

As I looked, the mental notepad filled up with prospects and rejects, each new face or body bringing a response: "No . . . no way . . . huh uh . . . hmmm, maybe . . . NOT even with Crazy's schwantz . . . no . . . no . . . NO!"

The search was looking fruitless, and I was rapidly getting exasperated that there wasn't a single senior or junior girl I wanted to ask out on a date even on a dark night with nobody around, let alone a candidate for a "going steady" relationship. I mean, all the senior and junior girls were great to talk to in class, but visualizing putting my lips to theirs or, even worse, sharing tongue—*bah*! Even the thought was worse than kissing your ugly cousin on the lips at the family Thanksgiving dinner.

I was just starting to shake my head in frustration when my eyes fell on a vision of loveliness. She was standing near the door, dressed to the nines in a tight black skirt that accentuated the smooth swell of her hips. The white blouse would have been a let-down except for the black scarf around her neck which just naturally drew the eye to her pert breasts. *That is good material!* I thought to myself.

I sauntered up to the guys, who had beaten me to our hangout area, and was doing my best to look cool and casual, just in case she glanced my way. "Hey, guys," I asked, even trying to *sound* cool and casual, "wow, who's that girl over there in the black skirt?" I nodded in her direction.

Oz was the one who answered first as, through squinted eyes, he scanned around at the girls. "Don't know. Maybe she's one of those sophomores who blossomed into a full-fledged knock-out over the summer. Man, what a great body."

"Yeah," I replied. "You guys know who she looks like?" When no one offered an answer, I gave it myself: "Kim Novak, she looks like Kim Novak in that movie that was out last year, *Bell, Book, and Candle,* or whatever it was."

Oz turned his squint directly at her and considered for a moment before speaking. "Yeah, you're right, she does kinda have that sultry Kim Novak look about her."

I was staring at "Kim Novak," and even though she was looking in the other direction, it was as if she could sense that I was checking her out. That lovely face slowly turned to me, and she met my eyes with a look that seemed to say that she knew exactly what kind of naughty thoughts were running through my mind. Our eyes met, and her face lit up in a smile that was almost hypnotic in its beauty and intensity. I suddenly realized that she was getting the best of me in our little impromptu staring and smiling contest, and I turned away.

"Oz," I said in a voice a little more thick than usual, "there's something about that girl. Man! It's almost like she can read my mind."

Oz replied wryly, "Well, that would be a short read. The Sunday comics have more depth to them than what you have in that brain of yours."

I returned the quip: "And what did you score on your SATs, 1800?"

Oz replied with a snicker, "Well, Mr. Einstein, about two hundred points higher than *your* SATs."

My retort to the snide remark was forming on my lips when the bell rang for school to start and the hundreds of students milling about out front of the building began to crowd the door like cattle heading into a corral. I just hoped it wasn't the corral outside an academic slaughterhouse.

I half-turned, hoping to see where my Kim Novak had been swept to in the flowing crowd of students, and then my eyes caught her. She was still standing where she had been when I first spotted her, and she was still smiling directly at me. As my eyes met hers, that startling smile went straight to my teenaged bones and a chill ran through me. "Maybe she's a witch," I thought to myself as I headed through the door, "but if she is, she's gotta be the cutest witch ever!"

My senior-year class schedule was categorized as "College Prep." This was a joke among all who knew the school since the only college my high school could prepare you for was one of those "Learn to Drive Semi-Trucks" schools advertised on matchbooks found in low-class diners. Don't get me wrong; my high school teachers were great people, some were fun to know, and others not so much fun at all. But most were either brand new, with the ink still wet on their diplomas from some class IV teachers' college, or were very, very old, some so old that they couldn't stand long enough to teach a full class and spent most of their time sitting while going over material. Actually, those were the *best* teachers because they couldn't easily pop up out of their chairs to scribble on the blackboard, so they taught straight from the textbook. I hated note-taking, and there was never a need to take notes on the textbook "wisdom" of one of these old teachers.

Everybody seems to have had at least one teacher who scared the crap out of them more than anyone else. For me, it was Miss Hamilton, who taught senior English. Miss Hamilton was at least in her sixties and had been teaching since the ark hit the Mountains of Ararat. She was no frills, no bells and whistles, no nonsense in any way, form, or fashion. She was an "I'll only say it once and you'd better get it down on paper, buster" type of teacher with the physical demeanor and appearance of the Wicked Witch of the West from *The Wizard of Oz*. The irony was that the Wicked Witch was played by Margaret Hamilton, a very talented actress who was, I'm sure, in no way related to the terrifying Miss Hamilton, the senior English teacher.

The Wicked Witch of Margaret Hamilton's portrayal and Miss Hamilton shared not only likenesses but also some mannerisms. Just like Dorothy Gale's nemesis, Miss Hamilton would point at you with one gnarled finger and growl, "Come up here, Robert, and let's hear your book report." To this day, the Margaret Hamilton Wicked Witch and Miss Hamilton the English teacher both give me shivers whenever I think of them.

My five Magnificent Six friends, of course, loved nothing better than to see me humiliated in front of the class, especially Miss Hamilton's class, since they knew that the woman scared the crap out of me on the best of days. In their finest fashion, when it was my time to give my oral book report, they would pull out every dirty trick they could think of to try and get me to crack up with nervous laughter and make a fool of myself.

Crazy would shove a couple of #2 pencils up his nose like walrus tusks, cross his eyes, and lean around the student seated in front of him in the hopes of catching my eye without being spotted by Miss Hamilton. Oz would be even more subtle. He would write a big note on letter-sized paper and display it for my attention when Miss Hamilton wasn't looking. The note would usually say "Your fly is down and your wiener is hanging out!" or sometimes just "Wiener!" Oz knew either sign would send me into a fit of uncontrollable laughter.

These tactics were diabolically designed to make me want to throw up from laughing, and were sometimes nearly unbearably hard on my insides. My guts actually hurt after class from the strain of holding the laughter in. But there was one weapon my buddies would pull out of their bag of tricks that was guaranteed to have me rolling on the floor laughing . . . "Freddie the Farter." A great-looking guy who reminded you of a James Dean type, on cue Freddie had the God-given ability to tilt to one side and fart, any place, any time, and as many times as you wanted him to.

Usually Freddie's farts were a non-smelling, high-pitched squeal, close in sound to a dog whistle that some older persons, like Miss Hamilton, would not hear, though all younger persons, like me, could hear it. So when the pencils up the nose or the wiener sign didn't work, Oz would lean over to Freddie, sitting in the next row of desks, and say, "Freddie, we need a fart for Rollo," and Freddie would oblige with a squealer.

The instant after that squeal echoed in my ears, I would be out the door to the boys' bathroom to puke in a sink or toilet of whatever receptacle I could get to first. Later in the day, I would return to Miss Hamilton's class and tell her I woke up in the morning with a cold, and I didn't want to miss her class, but I got sick during my report, and that is why I ran out of her class. Thank God she believed my bullshit. I always wondered if Miss Hamilton really could hear Freddie's farts and was also laughing inside. My bet is that she did, and that the evil old crone just loved watching me suffer.

Each day of school, when my last class was over at 2:30, before football or track practice, I made a beeline to the boys' bathroom for my daily constitutional. The first couple days of senior year, only two or three of my buddies joined me in this routine. After several weeks, the 2:30 bathroom break began to expand in terms of the numbers of guys hanging out before practice. At one point, we had ten to fifteen guys at once trying to use the facilities to either take a whiz or use the toilet. This group became affectionately known as the "2:30 Club."

We would laugh and share the day's best gossip, like news of who was dating whom, snide remarks about our teachers and other students, the typical bantering guys do in a bathroom while taking a dump.

"Rollo, is that you in the next stall?" someone yelled out that first day.

"Yeah, it's me—Rollo." Recognizing Star's voice, I asked, "Star, are you OK? Been sick?'

"No, Rollo, feel great," said Star.

"Been to a doctor lately for a checkup?" I pressed him.

"Nope, I am in great shape. You know that, Rollo. I can take you any day of the week," said Star, his bravado starting to surface.

I shot back, "Well, I just think that whatever you're passing this afternoon certainly can't be normal. I need a gas mask to breathe. Star, you should see a doctor after practice. Maybe that stink is the *gefilte* fish sandwiches your mom is packing in your lunch!"

"Screw yourself, Rollo. Wait a minute, you'd like that too much, right, Rollo?" laughed Star.

Now the other fourteen or fifteen 2:30 Club members joined in the back-and-forth. "Yeah, Rollo and Star, you guys see any new stuff to go after this year?" piped up Spiff.

"Is that you, Spiff?" I could only guess it was, as I sat in a darkened bathroom stall. (The stall lights were always out as the cleaning staff never replaced burned-out light bulbs. Maybe the instructions were too complicated for them to follow. Whatever the reason, most of my senior year at DuPont, my 2:30 constitutional was spent in the dark.)

Spiff replied, "Yeah, it's me, and Oz is out here, too. Not sure where Lily and Crazy are, maybe already in the locker room."

"Probably wanted to miss getting gassed by Star," I shouted out. "Star, flush, flush, flush!"

"No, Rollo, I am going to save it for you for your lunch tomorrow! Certainly better than the baloney sandwiches *you* pass each day," he replied.

Changing the subject, I said so that everyone in the bathroom could hear me, "Anyone know the sophomore who looks like Kim Novak? She is hot."

Some unknown voice answered, "You mean Jackie White? She is a real looker. Not sure if she's going with anyone."

"Who said that?" I inquired.

"It's Nate. My sister's in the same classes as Jackie. She's been over to my house a couple of times. My sister knows her pretty well.'

"Nate, Nate, Nate, I knew it was you!" I continued. "Are you sure it's Jackie White, looks like Kim Novak?"

Nate came back with: "Kim Novak is a stretch, but Jackie *is* different. She has a real mysterious air about her. I can't put my finger on it."

"Yeah," I added, "I saw her looking at me today, and it was as if she could read my mind. I started to walk over and say something to her, but the bell rang and we had to go to class. It was like she *made* the bell ring so I didn't have time to get to her. Strange."

Someone opened the bathroom door and yelled, "Coach wants you guys in the locker room and changing! We have a pep rally today!"

With that, the 2:30 Club meeting came to an end for another day.

Our locker room was built in 1942 and never updated over fifteen years. I'm not sure why the coaches called it a "locker room" as there were no metal lockers for the players. Our clothes were hung on a row of pegs, making it a "died and went to heaven" for petty thieves who would sneak in during practice. Although the locker room was supposed to be locked during practice, the keys were more plentiful than jelly beans in a candy store—everyone had one. Our coaches were too lazy to have the locks changed, so the dummies who left money in their jeans were going home with empty pockets.

Because all your clothes were available to the world to sabotage, routinely your buddies would put hot balm in your Jockey underwear or shaving cream in your Gold Cup socks. If you slipped on your Jockey shorts before checking them and hot balm encased your balls, well, there is no worse pain in the world. Bamboo shoots driven under your fingernails, holes drilled in your teeth, electric shock to your temples would not even compare to hot balm on one's balls. The pain was not only immediate, but long-lasting; sometimes your balls would burn for days.

One of our group—I believe Lily, but no one took credit for it as they were scared shitless—put hot balm in a freshman's jock, causing him to lose three days of school sitting in his mom's bathtub in cold water, crying his eyes out, trying desperately to put out the fire on his little set of balls. His parents sued the school and won some money. "Great Balls of Fire" was our favorite song to sing off-key in the showers. I wonder if the song was the result of someone putting hot balm in Jerry Lee Lewis's Jockey shorts. Coach said he would kick anyone off the team who was caught hot-balming a teammate's balls. After the lawsuit for that freshman, coaches locked up the hot balm.

Rushing into the locker room from my 2:30 Club routine, and already ten minutes late, I quickly changed into my gym shorts. I laughed as the shorts came up and my jock popped out from a heart-shaped hole someone—I immediately suspected Crazy and Lily—had cut in the shorts. I did look funny. Whoever did the seamstress work had found their career niche. I thought to myself, "Shit, *now* what am I going to do?"

Without time to find replacement shorts, I dashed out of the locker room to the auditorium for the pep rally, my jock-covered balls peeking out of my gym shorts through the heart. I thought if I stood in the back of the group, no one would see me. The cheerleaders led all the students in some really stupid cheers: "Stand up, sit down, fight, fight, fight," and "We got spirit, how 'bout you?" Those cheers would not exactly put the fear of God in our opponents—probably just make them laugh their asses off at the ineptness of our team *and* cheerleaders.

Coach got up and made a little speech about how this year's team's win/loss record was going to be a big improvement over last year's three-win season. My guess was that if we won four games, we would be lucky, but at least it would be one more than last year. On our schedule for this year, Coach had booked one more team that should be a snap to beat, St. Augustine Deaf and Dumb Institute.

While I was sitting there contemplating playing a school whose players were all deaf or could not speak, Coach suddenly called my name and said he wanted me to say a few words to the students. Stunned that there would be two hundred people staring at my crotch with a heart cut out of my gym shorts and my jock showing, I grabbed a towel the team trainer was carrying and wrapped it around my waist. I edged forward to where the coach was standing with the microphone. "Here is our starting halfback, number 34, Robert Strand."

With that, our creative cheerleaders gave us their usual "Two bits, four bits, six bits, a dollar, all for DuPont, stand up and holler!" My guess is that not a single one of the twelve cheerleaders had a clue what "two bits" was in money, or if they even knew it was money. I would have been surprised if they could count by two bits to a dollar.

Taking the microphone, I started to say something and got the typical high-pitched squealing feedback that made it impossible to continue. I handed the mike back to Coach, then looked out at the students and gave them the "number one" high sign, and all started to chant, "We're number one, we're number one, we're number one!"

I thought to myself, "Number one till we play Lee High School, our first game; then number zero, as they will kill us." Lee was twice our student size, maybe even three times our size. We were to Lee High School what we hoped St. Augustine Deaf and Dumb would be to us, a rollover game. Oh, well, at least we'd be number one till the end of the week.

Turning to sneak back behind the team, I spotted Jackie White in the front row of students. She was talking to some other girls sitting by her, but the second I looked at her, there with her friends, she turned and looked at me and smiled. "God, she is beautiful," I thought to myself.

Looking back at me, she mouthed the words "Thank you."

"OK, that is spooky," I thought to myself.

Jackie mouthed, "Not really."

I turned back to move to the rear of the stage, thinking to myself, "Shit, she can read my thoughts; she knows everything I am thinking. How does she do that? Whoa!"

Just as I was turning and reflecting on Jackie, Lily suddenly jerked the towel from around my waist. "Yay, Rollo, show everyone the family jewels!"

Now I found myself standing on the auditorium stage in front of the entire student body with my jock peeking through the hole in my shorts. Right away, the jeers started. I thought I heard from somewhere at the back of the auditorium, "Rollo, what you have stuffed in your jock? Tennis balls?" That remark brought down the house. Everyone started to climb on that taunt. "Tennis balls? No, marbles!" "No, not marbles, maybe BBs!"

I swear it was Oz who had yelled first. He was not on the football team, choosing to specialize in spring baseball. That gave him the perfect opportunity to make me look like a fool in front of the student body, which would thrill him to no end.

As I bolted toward the locker room, I glanced back one more time to where Jackie was sitting, but her chair was empty; she was gone. Thank God she did not see that spectacle of me standing onstage with my balls almost exposed to the world. I swore to myself that I would get even with whoever cut up my gym shorts—probably Lily and Crazy. Oz would not be left out of my revenge either, with his yelling his taunt from the rear of the auditorium. Hot balm on their balls would not even begin to match the revenge I would plan for them. Maybe castration would be equal payback.

Football practice was spirited, everyone getting hyped for that week's game with Lee High School. Our coach had brought in a new offense strategy, a double-wing set. Coach thought he had two fast, talented halfbacks that would eat up the offensive yardage against Lee. Lily was one of them, and I was the other.

The double-wing offense involves double hand-offs in the backfield, sort of like running double reverses in the backfield. The only way this type of offense works is if both halfbacks are very, very coordinated, running and handing off the football simultaneously. That was Coach's big mistake with me, as my dexterity was like that of a brick.

During practice, handing off a football to Lily going in the opposite direction was easy; no one was really on us to tackle us. But once we got into a real game, like with Lee High School that Friday night, the double-wing offense looked like a cooked chicken with both its wings pulled off its body and lying in the bottom of the frying pan. The Lee game was a disaster. We found out after the game that Lee had sent one of their coaches who looked young enough to be a high school student to spy on our practice and take our plays back to their team; their coaches devised a great defense against the double-wing. You could count on one hand our total offense yards rushing and passing against Lee High School. Coach dropped the double-wing after the first game of the season. Lee players are probably still laughing at our team.

After practice that first day of school, I took everyone home except Oz, who walked to his nearby house. Going in reverse, Star was the first to be dropped off. "Star, great practice. You doing anything tonight?"

"No, I'm pooped . . . the first day of school, pep rally, practice, I have some homework, my mother wants me at home tonight for a family dinner, spend some time with my sister," Star rattled off.

"Wow, a family group-grope; how sweet," I teased Star, who was often easy to tease, and sensitive to the bone.

He shot back, "At least I don't pig out at the dinner table, shoving food in my mouth to get to a telephone and start calling every girl who gave me the time of day at school today. Wait, for you, no need to eat fast—not a single girl gave you a second look today, pig!'

"Well, Jackie White seems hot for me," I replied, looking in the rearview mirror at Star.

"Jackie White, who the hell is Jackie White? Is she that sophomore you think looks like Kim Novak? God, Rollo, you're robbing the cradle. Get someone in our class, someone like Pam, who I'm taking out," Star said, trying to give me the needle.

"Star, there is not a single senior girl I would ever consider going out with. They all are stuck in their ways, unlike a sophomore girl you can mold and make into a great girlfriend," I replied with some conviction. I wasn't very good at adapting to someone else's taste and style; better for me and them both if they adapted to me.

"Well, hello, Mr. Geppetto the woodcarver, whittling away at his workbench, making Pinocchio. Better watch that nose when you ask Pinocchio if you are the best player on our football team; it will start growing," Star laughed.

Crazy, Lily, and Spiff sat silently engrossed in watching Star and me go back and forth. Maybe the day was wearing on them. As I dropped each off at his house, it was a simple "See you in the morning."

When I walked into my house, my sister and mother were at the dinner table, going over my sister's class schedule. She had just started at DuPont. Dad was traveling the first half of this week, wanting to get home for our Friday night game with Lee High School. (Considering how we got stomped by Lee, Dad should have just stayed out of town, avoiding the embarrassing showing of our team—especially me. Dad was All-Regional Halfback in Illinois when he went to high school. We could have used him on the field against Lee.)

Although DuPont is a small school, I rarely ran into my sister in the hallway or cafeteria. Somehow, the school managed to keep the younger students isolated from the upperclassmen, with different times for lunch and class breaks.

"Hi, Sharon. How was your first day at mighty DuPont? Do you like going to high school?"

"It was great," Sharon replied. "I love my teachers and made some great friends already. I saw you at the pep rally. I told Mom you had a big hole in the front of your shorts. All the girls were so embarrassed. Couldn't you have put on a nice pair of shorts for the pep rally?"

My mother jumped in: "I washed your gym clothes just yesterday and didn't see any holes in your shorts. How did you get a hole in the shorts?"

Not wanting Mom to know Crazy and Lily had cut up a perfectly good pair of shorts, I stretched the truth a little: "I caught them on a nail going out of the locker room to the pep rally and didn't have time to find another pair." I felt my nose getting longer.

"Well, get another pair of shorts out of your dresser drawer and throw that pair away. I don't want you embarrassing our family running around with a big hole in the front of your shorts."

"OK, Mom, I don't want you arrested for housing a pervert," I joked.

"Get the shorts out of your dresser *now*," Mom replied, *not* joking.

"OK, OK! I'm just going to make a quick telephone call before dinner." I quickly slid mention of the phone call into my reply to avoid a debate about the telephone and studying. Pushing phone calls ahead of dinner gave me a good thirty-minute "free zone" when my parents were not tracking my time on the phone.

In my room, I called Nate and asked him if his sister had Jackie's telephone number, which she did. "Thanks, Nate. Tell your sister I said thanks also."

Nate replied, "My sister said Jackie's looking forward to you calling. She thinks you're cute, but a little weird, showing up at the pep rally with a heart-shaped hole in the front of your shorts."

"Great. Wonderful first impression," I said, and hung up.

Quickly, I dialed Jackie's number, expecting it to be picked up by her mother or dad and preparing for the parent screen before they would put their innocent sophomore daughter on the telephone with a degenerate senior boy. But the phone only rang once, and then it was answered: "Hi. What took you so long to call? I've been by the phone for the last thirty minutes," Jackie said immediately upon answering.

Taken aback, I replied, "Jackie? Is this Jackie?'

"Yes, Rob, yes, this is Jackie. Thanks for calling. I didn't mean to be so forward about you not calling sooner. I didn't want to miss your call; my family is going out for dinner, then some more shopping for school clothes. Did Nate's sister give you my telephone number?"

"Yeah, how did you know I would call her for your number? How did you know I would call you tonight and at this time? Do you have a crystal ball?" I asked her kiddingly, trying to break the ice, although with Jackie's forward demeanor, the ice hardly needed any breaking.

She replied in her sultry, smooth voice, "I have a sixth sense about people. I guess I was born with sort of knowing what others are thinking or what they'll do before they do it. My mom has a sixth sense also, more so than me; Dad, too, but he keeps it turned off. It is just something that runs in the family. Does it bother you?"

Stammering, I replied, "N-no . . . I-I . . . I was just thinking it must be neat to know what someone is thinking. Do you know what I am thinking right now?"

"No, I don't try to know what someone I really like is thinking. I want to be surprised. Are you going to surprise me, Robert?" Again, that sultry, smooth-sounding voice. I was getting turned on by this whole notion of Jackie and her sixth sense and her wanting me to surprise her.

In a slightly high-pitched, off-key voice, I asked Jackie, "How about this for a surprise? How about we go out this Saturday night, movie downtown or just eat at Gino's Italian Restaurant?"

"Yeah, let's go to a movie. I like the dark and quiet inside the theatre and the cool air-conditioning. I love cuddling up and watching a good movie; sort of my nature." Jackie let the "cuddling up" part just kind of roll off her tongue.

Now I was getting really turned on with this conversation. Asking Jackie out on a simple date had turned out to be a wonderful, ego-boosting experience. I could not wait to take her to the dark and cool inside of a movie house. This would be really something.

"What about your parents? Don't you need to ask them?" I quizzed Jackie.

Laughing slightly, she replied, "I already asked them, and they're OK with us going out on a date. They trust me."

"How did you . . . ?" I did not finish the question. I knew what Jackie's answer would be: "sixth sense." Instead, I said, "Great! I've got to run for dinner. Maybe I'll see you in school tomorrow."

But the buzz of a dead phone rang in my ear; Jackie had hung up. I guess she knew what I was going to say, so why drag out the conversation any longer? She got what she wanted—a date with me in a dark and cool place to cuddle.

I thought to myself, "Jackie is going to be a very unusual and intriguing person, much different than Stacey. Oh well, something about variety being the spice of life."

"Rob!" Mom called.

"Yeah, Mom, I'm coming," I hollered back, leaving my room and heading for the kitchen, where Mom had prepared her favorite meal for her children, Swanson's macaroni TV Dinner . . . with apple-crisp that tasted like the metal tray it was baked in. Yuck!

Chapter 5

Swats

*T*he "Chief Judge and Executioner," as well as the "Grand High
Inquisitor," at our high school was Mr. Elroy Sitts, the assistant
principal. Sitts was a pretty good-looking guy, tall, maybe 6'2", graying
hair, maybe in his late thirties. He had been a history teacher before
becoming assistant principal, and I figure he was just biding his time till a
position as principal came open at some other high school in the county.
Based on Sitts' behavior, I think the interminable wait was starting to take
a toll on his mental stability and patience. I mean, the guy had absolutely
zero tolerance for any student he suspected of even *thinking* about causing
trouble.

Any time a student was sent to Sitts' office for misbehaving, it was like
a "dead man walking" without hope of pardon or reprieve. Sitts would
listen intently to the student's flimsy excuses for throwing paper wads
in class or back-talking the teacher, then would tell the student that he
considered him or her guilty and that the student must suffer punishment
for the awful transgression.

Sitts was a real "guilty until proven guilty" type of guy. He considered
any student automatically guilty of anything of which they were accused,
much like old Tomás de Torquemada, the master of the Spanish Inquisition,
under whose prosecution over one thousand people were burned at the
stake. Also like Torquemada, Sitts had his own series of levels of *how* guilty
a person was and, thus, how severe the punishment should be. His levels
of guilt ranged from one to four, with throwing paper being a one and
talking back to a teacher being a four.

Threatening a teacher was grounds for immediate suspension, which was sure to be accompanied by punishment from one's parents, but this was never carried out before immediate punishment was rendered by Sitts the Executioner. The one-to-four guilty scale carried with it the corresponding number of swats on the ass with a gnarly old oak paddle—kind of like the ones preferred by fraternity houses of the day for use on new pledges—which Sitts wielded like a headsman's axe.

I had the dubious honor of being selected as "Sergeant at Arms" by Mr. Sitts from among eight of his student office assistants, all of whom were seniors and included Lily, Crazy, and me. Both Lily and Crazy were jealous that I had been selected for the coveted title.

Most of the time, being a student assistant to Mr. Sitts meant running errands around the school grounds or sitting in his office and taking messages while he went to lunch or left the school on business. The Sergeant at Arms also had the duty of keeping Sitts' paddle cleaned, polished, and ready for use. Yep, I was the guy who kept the headsman's axe sharp.

I also had the duty of going to the classrooms and pulling out of class a student who had been reported for misbehaving. I would escort the miscreant to the chopping block and then sit on the sidelines as Sitts carried out his duties as Grand Inquisitor and Chief Judge and Executioner. I could tell by the look on the face of every student I escorted that before the door to Sitts' office closed, sealing them into his dungeon, they already knew they were going to get their ass warmed royally.

My most vivid recollection of Sitts' trademark swatting of a student who had suddenly found himself figuratively clapped in irons and dragged off to the dungeon was the time I was dispatched to a classroom for a freshman named Cooley. I can still remember rapping on the window inset in the door to get the teacher's attention and how, as I spoke the words "Mr. Sitts wants to see a student named Cooley for something he did earlier in the day," the teacher's face went all sorrowful and downcast because she knew what was about to happen to the hapless kid. The expression on her face, and on the face of every student we met in the hallway on our way to Sitts' office, was the sort you see on the faces of the other prisoners in prison movies as they watch the death row inmate taking his final stroll to the noose or gas chamber.

I could tell by Cooley's slightly nonchalant and naïve manner that he had no idea what kind of half-assed trial and speedy execution were in store for him. I took my place and watched Cooley settle into the straight-backed wooden chair across the desk from Mr. Sitts and begin to explain how he hadn't thrown any paper. Cooley said he had only been deflecting a wad which was thrown at him by another student when his motion caught the teacher's eye. I could do no more than watch stoically, even though my thought was, "Awww . . . poor Cooley's about to get his ass swatted for being an innocent bystander."

Mr. Sitts listened quietly, fingers steepled on his desktop, face a mask of seeming sympathy, until Cooley finished his narrative. Then the soft, smooth, southern drawl which purred from Sitts' lips was as soothing as warm milk, but as dangerous, I knew, as a coiled cottonmouth. "Well, *Mr.* Cooley," he said, "your teacher saw you, and *only* you, tossing papers across the classroom. She did not see any other student so engaged. Otherwise, I would have had other students down here also, and not just you. Do you wish to tell the name of this 'other student'?"

Even though he was just a green and ignorant freshman, Cooley knew that the student code of honor required silence in the face of such a question, even asked by the Grand High Inquisitor. Cooley's nervous reply wasn't the least bit believable. "No, Mr. Sitts, I don't know who threw the paper in the first place. I just caught the motion out of the corner of my eye and tried to catch it before it hit me in the face." I had to give the kid credit; he wasn't very bright, but he stuck to his guns, even when staring into the cold blue threat in Mr. Sitts' gaze.

At length, Sitts nodded as if in agreement with some unseen jury and issued his verdict in clipped, but oh-so-smooth, tones: "Guilty as charged, level-one offense, and punishable with one swat," he said with just the very tiniest edge of near-eagerness to his voice.

As I watched, Cooley begged Mr. Sitts to not notify his parents of the transgression and, thus, spare him the secondary ass-burning he would no doubt have received from them; indeed, he would take the swat with no trouble, debate, or conflict at all if Sitts would just agree to not notify his parents.

Sitts, who I secretly thought was just interested in practicing his swing on a one-swat offense, readily agreed to Cooley's terms, and so, the execution of punishment was to proceed immediately. With a nod from Sitts, I took the well-polished instrument of doom from the locked filing cabinet and handed it to him.

A person's immediate impression of Cooley was of a short Pillsbury Doughboy—squat, with fat rolls padding his midsection and, even though he was a Florida resident, a somewhat pasty complexion. He was dressed that day in the classic attire of a nerd of that era: button-down short-sleeved shirt complete with a bunch of pens tucked into a pocket protector, pants a little too short at the hem, and black plastic-framed glasses held together with tape. When Sitts told him to grab his ankles and all Cooley could do was grab his pants at the knees to assume the fateful position, I had a vivid mental image of the Pillsbury icon bending over in Mr. Sitts' office.

Mr. Sitts could have been a professional golfer with his tall frame and long, sweeping arm movements with the paddle. He went from standing stock-still and sort of fondling the paddle to an explosion of forward motion that blurred almost too fast for the eye to follow, and when that forward motion ceased for an instant as the paddle made contact with Cooley's pudgy ass, there was a sound like the blast of a 12-gauge shotgun, and Doughboy looked like one thousand volts of pure electricity had suddenly been poured into him.

The force of the impact lifted Cooley up on his toes, and his glasses went flying to strike the wall about ten feet away, followed a split second later by one of the Bic pens that had been so carefully tucked into his pocket protector. Cooley didn't say a word. The suddenness and instant pain of the violent strike were clearly something he had never experienced before, and he sort of sank slowly to his knees without a word or whimper. Hey, I had to give the kid credit for not crying or squealing like a little girl.

I truly believe Cooley was in a state of shock as I led him out of Sitts' office and back to his classroom. I felt sorry for the kid, and was even a little proud of him for manning up to the horror of the swat. On the way back, I asked him how he was, if he could walk OK without help, or if he needed to see the school nurse. Cooley never uttered an intelligible word during the return march; he just sort of gurgled at every question.

We reentered the classroom, and all the other students fell into a dead silence and sat motionless, as if they had just seen someone return from the dead. Cooley marched stiffly back to his desk, but instead of sitting down on his newly burned ass, he merely stood beside the seat and kind of leaned over toward his open book. His whole demeanor was that of being in a daze. My responsibility completed, I returned to Sitts' office and carefully placed the instrument of doom back in its place in the locked filing cabinet drawer.

Modern educational theory tells us that the threat of getting a few swats by a well-wielded oaken paddle does nothing to alter the behavior of students in the classroom, and many years ago, parental lawsuits put a stop to the practice in school systems. I figure that parents somehow lost touch with reality and began to believe that little Johnny or Sally was perfect, and that any trouble was caused either by other students or by the school system itself. But I can tell you from what I witnessed with Cooley the Doughboy, and the fact that he never again did anything in a classroom that in any way, form, or fashion might land him back in Mr. Sitts' office for another go-'round with that paddle, that *nothing* could have convinced Cooley to ever act out again. If schools today had a Mr. Sitts, Grand High Inquisitor and Chief Judge and Executioner, school attendance would be higher, vandalism lower, and classroom disruptions would be next to zero!

During the first week of my senior year at old Alfred I., I personally almost had a date with destiny at the hands of Sitts the Executioner.

Wow, that was a great week when I look back on it all! As if meeting Jackie and arranging a weekend date weren't memorable enough, the excitement and angst of my close brush with the paddle made it a week I'll never forget. It was made even better by the fact that not only did *I* miss my date with destiny, but so did Oz., Lily, Crazy, Spiff, and Star. What happened? Well, the school principal, Mr. Dennis Berry, a.k.a. "Dingle Berry," caught us all red-handed horsing around when we shouldn't have been.

Back in those heady, and sometimes terrifying, Cuban Missile Crisis days, a lot of school systems had nuclear-attack drills to supposedly prepare for what should happen if the Russians decided to launch a nuclear strike. Some schools taught that students were to "duck and cover," as in duck under their desks and cover their heads. Of course, there was never a question of whether good old American-made classroom furniture would survive a thermonuclear assault.

Alfred I. DuPont High's plan was that all the high school students would walk, or drive their own car with assigned passengers, to the homes of designated parents, then wait thirty to forty-five minutes and return to school after the drill. The idea was that if the missiles and bombs really started to rain from the skies, an assigned bus would go to the assigned homes and pick up the assigned students to be transported to an assigned location in the little town of Hastings, Florida, about a thirty-minute drive away. I always thought this amount of assigning would very quickly fall to *un*assigned bullshit the instant the first real mushroom cloud blossomed over an American city.

But who was, or am, I to judge the infinite wisdom of school administrators who believed such a convoluted plan would lead to better organization and less congestion as parents went along their orderly way down to Hastings to pick up their kids. I reckon the idea was to avoid having panicked parents running around the school, screaming frantically for little Jimmy or Susie to get in the car "RIGHT NOW" so they could haul ass out of Jacksonville.

On the fateful day of my near-first-contact with Sitts' paddle, as soon as the nuke drill began, all members of the Mag 6 piled into my car and away we went to my house, which just happened to be one of the designated pick-up points for the evacuation busses. My mom, being a stay-at-home mom, did her patriotic duty and headed to Hastings, as if she were really going to pick up sis and me from the evacuation master point. This, of course, left the house wide open for us hotshot senior boys to hang out during the drill. (As a freshman, my sister was assigned to go to another designated home in the neighborhood.)

Like any red-blooded American teenagers would do, we made a beeline for the icebox (that's what the refrigerator was still called, even though it had been many moons since actual ice deliveries were made) for something cold to drink and maybe a snack or three. We grabbed Lay's potato chips and Cokes and were all six munching and staring out the kitchen window when, almost as one, six young male voices sounded out two fateful words: "Swimming pool!"

The sound of our joint declaration had barely died away when all six of us were already stripped to our underwear and diving into the cool water. We figured we could go grab a quick swim, dive off the board a few times, trash our wet underwear, dry off, redress, and be back at school by the end of the drill without anyone being the wiser. Well, as it's said, "The best laid plans of mice and men . . ." Uh . . . I can't remember how it's said; just suffice it to say, our plan for a little swim almost got us all in deep shit.

Spiff was taking his turn on the diving board, jumping up and down, aiming for a near orbital height before making his dive. Well, eventually he rose to such a distance that he was plainly visible over the top of the security fence around the house and pool.

The only reason this was a problem is that as Spiff jumped, he sort of turned his head toward the street and locked eyes with Principal Dennis "Dingle Berry" Berry, who just happened, at precisely the most inopportune moment, to be cruising the street, apparently checking to see that students were at their assigned places. Spiff was at the apex of his jump when, in that fraction of a second, he and Dingle Berry locked eyes—an occurrence which surprised them both to the extent that Dingle Berry almost rear-ended a parked car with his late-model Buick, and Spiff toppled sideways as he bounced back down on the board and splashed into the pool in a skin-burning belly-buster.

We all watched Spiff collapse off the board, but, hey, we figured he'd had too much Coke and chips before getting in the water and just caught a leg cramp which made him fall. None of us were the least bit prepared when Spiff's head broke the surface and, spraying water, he yelled, "Principal Berry! He's outside in his car and saw me! I think he's coming in!"

Just as our voices had previously merged over the chance for a school-hours swim, they merged once more in a resounding "Oh, shit!" and the mad scramble to cover our tracks was on.

We were all out of the pool, into the house, and (mostly) dressed within the ninety seconds it took for the doorbell to ring. At the sound of those cheerful little chimes, I was hopping madly down the hall trying to get my last shoe on my wet foot, but for some reason, my big toe was caught on the outside and I wasn't making much headway at getting it in place while hopping at the same time. I bounced past the hall mirror and caught a glimpse of myself—dripping wet hair, soaked shirt, wild eyes—and the only thought in my head was whether Principal Berry would notice that my wet hair wasn't combed.

I whipped open the front door and was still trying to wriggle into my shoe when Principal Berry spoke. "Well, it looks like you have either been in a swimming pool or just got out of the shower, and I hardly believe the latter, as it seems highly unlikely. What have you been doing during this very important nuclear drill, and where are the rest of the boys?"

I couldn't help but grin at my own sheepishness, but I responded as best I could: "Well, Di– . . . umm . . . Mr. Berry, we just thought we could cool off in the pool before going back to class and, umm . . . well . . . you know . . ." Even I thought my answer was a lame try at bullshitting my way out of trouble for getting caught in the act of playing around instead of placing the proper dignity and respect into my actions during what Dingle Berry referred to as a "*very important nuclear drill.*"

Mr. Berry's voice was quiet and calm as he spoke again. "Robert, I want you to get the *boys* together, and you will all meet me in Assistant Principal Sitts' office after the drill has concluded. We will discuss your behavior during my drill and what we should do about said behavior." With that, Principal Dennis Berry turned crisply on his heel and headed back to his car, which was idling in my driveway.

As I watched him walk away, I came to the immediate realization that there would be no "we" meeting in Sitts' office because Dingle Berry wouldn't be there; he preferred for DuPont's own Torquemada to do his dirty work for him. I looked at my watch with the feeling that by four in the afternoon, the rest of the Mag 6 and I would be so sore from having the crap beaten out of us by Sitts' paddle that we might not be able to walk, let alone get into a swimming pool, for months.

I suddenly felt the way I always imagined Jesus must have felt when Pontius Pilate handed him over to the Roman soldiers to the sound of the crowd screaming, "Crucify him, crucify him!" The six of us were fixing to get killed, I was sure.

The drive back to school was quiet, almost serene. I always believed that the prisoners on death row, in the final minutes before taking their last walk down to the lethal-injection room, probably slumped into a quiet, reflective mood and looked back over their lives. I've never heard of jailers having to drag those poor condemned souls kicking and screaming into the room and fighting them tooth and nail to strap them onto the table.

I don't know, maybe the only reason they aren't dragged out shouting "I ain't going!" is because the prison warden secretly slips some drugs into that famous final meal so that when the prisoner's escorts show up outside his door, he's in the mood for a little stroll, regardless of what fate might hold in store. I imagine maybe he meets his jailer with the attitude of "Sure, man, let's stretch our legs a bit and see what's in that little room down the hall. Groovy, dude!"

Sitts wasn't that kind of warden; he would never try to mellow out a prisoner about to be executed, and he certainly wouldn't try to soothe the nerves of a student before putting that oak paddle flush on the seat of their pants. He was a little sadistic, I think.

Surprisingly, Dingle Berry did show up in Sitts' office and spent a half-hour ranting and raving while the six of us looked sheepishly at the cool tile flooring. For at least thirty solid minutes, the man seemed to never even take a breath.

"You boys are so disrespectful of school authority! Your actions of swimming in a backyard pool during the drill make a mockery of just how serious this drill is! We have thousands of enemy troops just miles away, enough bombs and missiles pointed in our direction to obliterate the earth, and this drill was designed to save you and your parents and your friends from death or injury in a possible nuclear attack! You *all* deserve *all* the punishment Mr. Sitts will have for you!"

As Dingle Berry stormed out of Sitts' office, I couldn't decide which would be worse, getting fried to a glow-in-the-dark crisp by a nuclear blast or getting my ass toasted by Alfred I. DuPont's version of Torquemada and his paddle of doom. The images of both danced through my mind and sent shivers up my spine.

Mr. Sitts, who had watched Dingle Berry's rant with his fingers steepled on his desk and a look of cool anticipation in his eyes, looked at all six of us, one at a time, and I swear, the gaze of Lucifer himself couldn't have been icier. Then Sitts' mouth opened and I heard from those thin lips one of the most amazing utterances I have ever heard before or since.

"Gentlemen," Sitts purred like a stalking tiger, "you are a disgrace to this school and your classmates. I would normally issue a level-four punishment, maybe even pushing it to level five for your transgressions of today. But, since most of you are on the football team and have an important game this Friday night against Lee High School, and will be representing Alfred I. DuPont High School in the event, I am afraid I am, for once, forced to reconsider. I feel that giving you each four or five swats may incapacitate you and render you ineffectual on the football field."

Sitts looked deep into each face before continuing. "Therefore, gentlemen, you will have detention for three weeks, beginning today. I will tell Head Coach that you will be late for football practice as you will be in the detention room from three until four every school day for the next three weeks. I have assigned Coach Mahoney as your detention monitor."

I could barely hold my face in the proper near-tearful expression for the scant amount of time it took to exit Sitts' office and get out into the freedom of the hallway. I wanted to sing (but would've scared any small children in the neighborhood). I wanted to dance (but would've looked like a royal weenie). I didn't know which was more divine, escaping the fearful swing of Sitts' paddle or getting good ol' Mr. Pabst Blue Ribbon as our detention room monitor. Since I couldn't sing or dance, I simply clasped my hands together and, with a glance heavenward, whispered, "Thank you, God! Thank you, God! Thank you, God!"

I felt like the death row prisoner, strapped into the electric chair, head shaved and the little steel cap in place, hearing the hum of the transformers waiting to release blue death as the warden stands with his hand on the lever that will turn on the juice when, suddenly, the phone rings. That golden melody of the ringing sound is only surpassed by the words that come next: "Yes, Governor, I understand. You have granted a stay of execution."

But concerning our punishment for the great nuclear-drill swim, it was far better than just a simple stay of execution at the hands of Mr. Sitts and his paddle. In our case, the governor had issued not only a stay, but a full pardon for all prisoners, and we had been remanded into the custody of Coach Mahoney! Thank God, indeed.

Chapter 6

Stacey

*M*y bedroom back in my high school days wasn't exactly what you would consider typical for the era, but it was pretty comfortable. Instead of a single bed, or bunk beds left over from when a younger sibling finally got his own room, I had a pair of twin-sized day beds placed along the walls and meeting at a right angle with a cabinet set into the corner space to hold extra pillows and bed clothes. I remember the Thursday night of the first week of my senior year, when I decided to get in bed a little early just to have some quiet time and think over the past week.

But even as I lay there in the dark, trying to relax and ponder life, my mind kept racing. Whenever I started to grow calm, there would be a new itch to scratch, a new position I needed to roll into, something to interrupt my train of thought. Finally, in the hopes of being comfortable, I grabbed one of the spare pillows from the cabinet, and as I did so, I caught the scent of the freshly washed pillowcase—laundry soap and Florida sunshine. I stretched out, put the pillow over my face, breathed in the aromas of summer, and relaxed into quiet contemplation.

Of course, the first thought in my head was of girls, specifically Jackie, my Kim Novak look-alike who had so bewitched me on the front steps of the school. The fact that she had seemed to know all about our date for the upcoming Saturday, and even that my call was coming well before she picked up, still had me both spooked and intrigued. Her quirky ability to anticipate exactly what was about to happen made her mysterious and alluring, and I was baffled as to how she did it. I lay in the dark with the pillow over my face and pondered whether she would know I was going to kiss her before I even made the first move. It didn't take long to decide that I really didn't care, as long as I got to taste those movie-star lips.

Thoughts of Jackie led quickly to memories of Stacey and the close relationship we had shared over the past year. Stacey had been my very first real girlfriend, and the first girl to whom I had uttered those most monumental words: "I love you."

Telling Stacey I loved her had actually come easily for me. Just beginning to date at age sixteen, I found it easy to fall in love, especially with Stacey! She was vivacious, with a magnetic personality and a Pepsodent smile that could light up a moonless night. Everybody loved being around her, and it didn't take me long at all to join her fan club. Why Stacey picked *me* as her first real boyfriend when she could have chosen *any* boy was a mystery I never dared give much thought to.

We connected one day during my junior year. She was on the swim team, and I was on the football and track teams, so we occasionally ended up attending the same letterman club meetings. (I suppose it would be "letterperson" in today's language of rampant political correctness!) At one of those meetings, fate struck.

I had seen her before, but that day I just felt I *had* to speak to her. I remember opening with the smoothest of pick-up lines: "Hi there, Stacey. I guess you're on the swim team."

She was so nice to me, forgoing the chance to turn my statement of the obvious into an opportunity to dig at me. Instead, she just turned on that big toothy smile that made my heart stop for a second and replied, "Yes, I'm a swimmer. How did you know?"

Being young and dumb, I didn't realize she had just given me a "pass" on my social ineptness and carried on with what I then thought was witty and stunning conversation. "Well, it was probably the little swimmer embroidered on your letter sweater. I don't think non-swimmers get 'em." I grinned and continued, "I heard your name called at roll call for the meeting. Umm . . . that's how I was sure of your name."

"And you're Robert, but your buddies call you Rollo," she said, nodding toward the guys, seated a couple rows ahead of us. "I heard Star call you Rollo. Hmmm . . . Rollo's a really silly name; sounds like you should have a big roll of fat around the middle. You don't look like you have the fat to carry the name *Rollo*."

I could tell she was kidding from her tone and the twinkle in her eye, and I responded with what I thought would be a quip of my own: "Nope, no fat. The name's from a character in the funny pages, 'Rollo, The Rich Kid.' You ever read the funny pages?"

The twinkle never left her eyes and her smile never dimmed as she replied, "No, Rollo, I don't read the funny pages. Seems to me the funny pages are for those with an IQ slightly lower than that of a snake. Are you dumber than a snake?" That last question was punctuated with laughter that sounded like angels singing.

I stared into those beautiful blue eyes and found my heart blinded by her glowing smile and bubbly personality. She had me hooked right then and there, and she knew it. She leaned toward me and whispered in a voice too low for others to hear but loud as a trumpet to my suddenly soaring hormones, "Well, Robert, or Rollo, or whatever you call yourself, why don't you come out to my house this weekend and meet my family? We live out on the river, and we can go for a ride on my parents' boat."

My response was the epitome of poise and manners as I almost fell out of my chair in the middle of the meeting. "Ummm . . . well, uh, OK. Saturday or Sunday?"

Stacey laughed, obviously enjoying my sudden fit of stammering, and shook her head slightly as she replied. "Well, Mr. Quick-on-His-Feet, let's do Saturday, about lunchtime. I'll fix some sandwiches and we'll take the boat out."

The teasing tone never faded as she nodded toward my letterman's jacket. "You run track, I see. What events?"

I fell into her trap without even seeing it coming. "I'm a sprinter, run the 100 and 220. That's how I first lettered."

"Well, Mr. Sprinter, let's hope you're a little faster in asking me out on another date after Saturday." With those words, she apparently considered the matter settled and turned to talk to some other girls, leaving me speechless.

When Stacey turned that smile away, even though I was in a room full of other students, I suddenly felt alone. "Wow, what just happened?" I thought to myself. "Hot girl gets me to her house this weekend to meet the parents and go out for a boat ride, then lets me know I need to ask her out on a second date, all in the space of, like, five minutes." I was astounded, and as the letterman meeting continued, I sat there, completely detached from what was going on around me, and pondered my future with Stacey. Replicating her trademark smile, I also broke into an ear-to-ear grin.

"*Ponderosa*"

The TV western series *Bonanza* made its premier in 1959. Back then, westerns were all the rage, and even today, *Bonanza* can still be caught in reruns. The opening credits of the show began with the Cartwright family, Ben the patriarch, and his sons Adam, Hoss, and Little Joe, riding the range of the "Ponderosa," their mythical one-thousand-square-mile ranch in the Tahoe, Nevada, area.

Each show ended with the closing credits and the iconic image of a late 1800s-style wall map of the Ponderosa catching fire in the middle, then being engulfed in flames. I guess the purpose was to symbolize that there would always be trouble for the Cartwright family, and in each episode there were indeed troubles aplenty. Some bad guy, or group of bad guys, always incurred the wrath of the Cartwright clan and had to be tracked down and taught to regret their actions by show's end.

It didn't take me long to realize that Stacey's home would have been the perfect set for a Florida version of the Ponderosa. It was ideally situated on the bank of the St. John's River and encompassed by hundreds of acres of pine wilderness populated by razor-tusked wild boar, vicious bobcats, rattlesnakes, and zillions of blood-sucking mosquitoes. The main house reminded me of old Ben Cartwright's ranch house—big, rustic, and almost inaccessible to the outside world.

Just getting to the main house was similar to traveling the range and mountains of the Ponderosa; it was a literal pain in the ass. Once you turned off the highway, you had to travel at least a mile down a pothole-filled, gravel road that would jar the tusks out of a full-grown bull walrus. Any attempt to gain speed led to the kind of bodily abuse you normally only got during a teeth-rattling, kidney-beating ride in the bumper cars at the county fair. Not only was the road surface designed to make forward motion very uncomfortable no matter how new your shock absorbers were, but the woods crowded close against the tightly curved road, and with loose gravel under your tires, you had to really take it easy or you would rapidly find yourself and your car a permanent part of one of God's towering conifers.

My bladder was screaming, "Better hurry or I'm going to embarrass you!" when I finally arrived at the main house, and all I could think about was getting out of my car and into a bathroom as hastily as possible without jarring my strained bladder into an humiliating incident. To further complicate my situation, my arrival was heralded by a total of five barking, leaping, paint-scratching Weimaraner dogs that proceeded to jump on and circle my '39 Ford like the old-time images of Indians attacking a wagon train. I could do nothing as I killed the engine but cross my legs to try and mute my bladder. I weighed the options of making a mad dash for the house and becoming a doggie chew toy for the brief remainder of my life or, worse, surviving the ordeal with a few bites taken out of my legs and ass and (maybe) getting to the bathroom on time, or sitting in the car until I reverted to the toilet habits of a toddler.

I was just about to resign myself to bearing the brunt of canine malice when a loud and commanding voice echoed through the pine woods and penetrated my rolled-up windows.

"Down! Down! Down! You in the car, get out and come in. The dogs don't bite. They mostly just bark."

My eyes followed the voice, and there stood Stacey's mother, Diane Purcell. I will never forget my first impression of her: just plain *hot* in a "ranch boss" kind of way in her jeans, riding boots, and men's work shirt, her long hair pulled back in a serviceable ponytail and a cigarette dangling between her slim fingers.

There never was a Mrs. Cartwright on *Bonanza* because old Ben was a widower, but Diane Purcell would have been absolutely perfect for the role. I can imagine that Mrs. Cartwright would have been a tough-talking woman who would take no shit from anyone, especially Ben and the boys. She would eschew gowns and dresses for a button-up flannel shirt, the top button left open to expose the slightest hint of femininity while she rode and roped with the best of the hired hands. Stacey's mom Diane was exactly that type of woman.

I eased my way out of the car. I mean, after all, when someone tells me that the dogs don't bite, they mostly bark, this tells me that there's still a 5 percent margin of error that one or the other of the yapping, jumping hounds might take a chunk out of my butt. I tried not to look too nervous about the dogs and to ignore the fact that they were taking turns hiking their legs on my car as I crossed the dirt yard and extended my hand and a "hello" to Diane Purcell.

She didn't even acknowledge my outstretched hand, instead letting a stream of smoke waft into the air, and skipped the traditional greeting. "Bumpy ride up the road? You look like you need to take a piss. Bathroom's first door on the left just as you go in the house."

Diane Purcell was still looking at me like I was bearing some strange and awful plague into her home as I mounted the steps and let myself in. "Wow," I thought to myself, "what a nice, fuzzy, warm beginning to a relationship with dear old Mom. I wonder if she gives every boy who comes up that hemorrhoid-inflicting road a swift kick in the balls just to get things rolling."

The "friendly" exchange would prove to be the high point of my relationship with Stacey's mom. I figured that if Diane Purcell had in fact been Mrs. Ben Cartwright, in time, Ben and the boys would have shot her ass and buried her in some obscure and unmarked spot on the back forty of the Ponderosa and said she had been kidnapped by Indians or eaten by a bear.

I later learned that the icy greeting I received was just a manifestation of the fact that Diane was overly protective of both her children, but especially Stacey. I came to believe she was going out of her way to try to ensure that Stacey had a better life than she, herself, had.

The family construction business had seen spotty success at best, and even though he had a good heart and the best of intentions, Bob Purcell wasn't the most astute businessman. He was great at working with his hands, but his heart of gold often led him to make loans to his day laborers even when he knew he would never see a dime repaid. Bob Purcell preferred the solitude of fishing the St. John's or hunting on the family property to the bustle of the business world, and rarely pursued his construction business with the aggression needed to make it highly profitable. As a result, the venture just sort of limped along, barely providing enough money to pay the property taxes and keep Bob in shotgun shells.

Diane Purcell wanted more for Stacey than marriage to a man who lacked money and business ambition like old Bob. She wanted a suitor who came with serious family wealth or a free ride to some Ivy League medical school. There was simply no way under heaven that Diane Purcell was going to roll over and approve of her little girl being involved with some horny little, middle-class, typical teenager like me.

To compound the problem of money and ambition, there was also the issue of religion. It was Diane's absolute and mandatory requirement that Stacey's boyfriend be a devout Catholic. This was one rule for which there would be no exception whatsoever under any circumstances.

The instant I pulled up in the yard, Diane Purcell knew I was neither old money nor Ivy League nor Catholic. I don't know—maybe my ambulance-white '39 Ford screamed *"Middle-Class, Future Sears Store Manager, Protestant Schmuck."* I suppose the absence of a rosary or a little crucifix on a chain around my neck was also a dead giveaway. (I later found out that the instant Stacey had mentioned inviting me over that Saturday, her mom had started calling around, inquiring about me and my family. This act, more than any other, confirmed my opinion that Diane Purcell was and would always be a conniving, back-stabbing, sneaky bitch.)

Bob Purcell turned out to be a marginally OK person. He was a simple sort of fellow, though not *dumb* by any means. He was friendly to me, but I never was much of a hunter, so we didn't have a lot in common. I just couldn't stand to see some squirrel or bird get blown to bits with a shotgun. I mean, pitting the destructive force of a 12-gauge over-and-under against a tiny dove or quail just didn't seem either fair or sporting to me. A *real* man's sport would involve the hunter pitting *himself* against the brute power of a pissed-off eight-hundred-pound grizzly bear while armed with only a Swiss army knife. Well, it would definitely be sporting, if suicidal, for the hunter, and would satisfy the bear's appetite quite nicely anyway.

I don't have proof of this, but I suspect that Bob Purcell used his frequent hunting trips to spend as many days as possible away from his wife's bitching and enjoy the peace and solitude of the pine forest. I never went looking, but I imagine that somewhere out in the sun-dappled woods Bob had chopped out a small clearing and made himself a campsite. I picture that campsite complete with a fire pit, logs for sitting and leaning his Browning shotgun against, and a bed of pine needles to stretch out on.

Since pine needles are exactly that—*needles*—and will stick the shit out of you, I imagine Bob had a plastic garbage bag with an old army blanket inside it, stashed away somewhere so he could cover the pine-needle bed when he decided it was time for a nap. I reckon the trash bag probably even contained hunting magazines and a bottle of Kentucky straight bourbon to warm the insides on a cold day.

Just to keep up his charade, every hour or so, I imagine, old Bob would methodically jack a shell into the old Browning and blast away at the clear blue sky, just so Diane would hear the report and figure he was diligently *trying*, at least, to bring home a squirrel, quail, or wild-turkey dinner for the family.

Diane Purcell seemed to be a congenitally bitter woman, and in retrospect, I imagine the fact that Bob came home from the woods empty-handed more often than not just made her conclude that her husband was not only a terrible businessman, but also a lousy shot with a gun. From the way she acted, it was evident that if the house, property, and business were not all held in the name of Bob's family trust, she would have divorced him long ago.

While Bob Purcell found peace and tranquility in his wooded retreat, Diane Purcell sat for hours on end in an old Adirondack lawn chair on the slope leading down to the river, smoking cigarettes one after the other. Occasionally she would go in the house and check on Stacey and her younger brother Peter, but the lawn chair was her throne whenever weather allowed. Never one for housecleaning or cooking, she had a hired housekeeper over twice a week to clean and cook meals to be eaten over several days. If not for the occasional cocktail party at a friend's house and her dutiful excursions to St. Michael's Catholic Church every Sunday, Diane Purcell would have had no social life at all.

As I headed in search of the urgently needed bathroom, Stacey came down from the second floor looking absolutely stunning in her midriff-tied shirt, short shorts, and sparkling white Keds. If not for her appearing at that moment, I might well have borrowed the bathroom, gotten back in my car, bounced back to the highway, and gone home, never to return. Despite my initially stunned reaction to her looks, I hated Diane Purcell the second I met her and experienced her ugly personality. Over the year that Stacey and I dated, nothing ever gave me a reason to change that attitude the least bit.

Stacey looked so beautiful that day, standing at the bottom of the stairs with her all-white outfit a stark contrast to her sun-bronzed skin. Those sea-blue eyes and her hair streaked blonde from swimming in the chlorinated pool, along with that oh-so-white smile, made her look like she should have been on the cover of a magazine instead of standing at the bottom of the stairs in her parents' house near Jacksonville, Florida.

"Hi! Wow, you should be making commercials for Coppertone!" I said when I finally found some words—and I meant it sincerely.

"Gee, thanks. It's just a little something for our boat ride. I have a bathing suit under these clothes so we can swim or ski. Did you bring a swimming suit, or are you just going along to handle the boat ropes and bumpers?" Stacey asked, somewhat jokingly.

"Same as you, bathing suit under these shorts. And yes, I can handle a boat. What kind do you have?" I asked, ready to compare my dad's cabin cruiser to whatever they had here on the Ponderosa.

"1938 Chris Craft, seventeen-foot Deluxe Runabout speedboat, six-cylinder Chrysler Crown engine, mahogany wood, pulls up to four skiers. Think you can handle this boat, Mr. Track Star?"

Thinking of my clunky twenty-one-foot cabin cruiser with twin 35-horsepower Evinrude engines, I said, "I can handle anything you throw my way, Miss Speedo. Let's go! I want to see this monster of a motor boat."

As we headed down to the boat dock, I followed closely behind Stacey so as not to slip and fall on the grass and look like a great big fool in front of her mother, who was sitting in her Adirondack lawn chair with a smoldering cigarette in her hand.

Tied safely to the dock was one of the most beautiful boats I have ever seen: a classic, mahogany speedboat with like-new Naugahyde upholstery in white and sea-foam blue. Built in 1937, this classic Chris Craft Deluxe Runabout must have been passed down through the family, and a bunch of money must have been spent on keeping it pristine. I couldn't believe the family used the sleek, one-of-a-kind speedboat to pull beer-drinking skiers like my friends and me. That would be like a Rolls Royce Silver Cloud motorcar pulling a U-Haul trailer.

I was afraid to even touch the boat or breathe on it, as I did not want to be the person who put a single scratch on that mirror-like finish. I figured Diane would castrate me on the spot for damaging her pride and joy.

Stacey jumped into the captain's chair and fired up the engine. "I was down here earlier to get everything ready for our spin on the river. Sandwiches and drinks are in the cooler. Grab the ropes and bumpers and push us off," Stacey commanded, as any good captain would direct their crew.

"Aye, aye, Captain Bligh, sir," I said, throwing her a salute. "Just don't make me walk the plank if you change your mind about me asking you out on another date!"

The boat cleared the dock, and I jumped into the back seat just as Stacey threw the throttle forward to put the speedboat in gear.

As we pulled away, I glanced toward the house to where Diane was sitting. She was still in the Adirondack lawn chair with what appeared to be a pair of binoculars, watching every move I made with Stacey. It was a good thing the Runabout didn't have a toilet on it because from five hundred yards Diane would have watched me take a whiz. Nothing got by that woman.

Stacey and I skied for an hour or so. First, she pulled me on two skis, and I would occasionally swing outside the wake to show off my athletic ability. Stacey would give me the thumbs-up as I jumped the wake and slid over to one side beyond it. I soon found out she was just humoring me, though; when she got in the water, she took only a slalom ski and began to jump from one side of the wake to the other, clearing the wake by several feet or more. Once she actually did a 360 on the slalom, somehow shooting over the wake, then quickly rotating completely around. I gave her a weak thumbs-up and, shaking my head, laughed at my incompetence by comparison.

Stacey had the athleticism for swimming, skiing, and operating a speedboat, but I was soon to discover she had yet another talent she could perform in the water. She cut the Runabout's engine, leaving the boat to slowly drift with the river's current. We were spread out on the Naugahyde seats, soaking up the sun, when she tilted her head toward me in the rear seating area and said, "Hey, Rollo, where we going on a date?"

At the moment she asked the question, I was entranced, watching some bird circling high above the boat, catching the thermal updraft to just sort of float without flapping its wings. Only half-thinking, I gave the typical answer of a sixteen-year-old male in the presence of a beautiful girl he was trying to impress with his wit and wisdom: "Don't know, haven't really thought about it. Any ideas?"

Apparently having anticipated my dimwit response, Stacey stood up and, looking at me spread out on the back seat, said with a straight face, "Well, how about we go to the Lobster House, have a great dinner, maybe even dance if the band is on that night, then kill the remainder of our second date by getting a room at the Horne Motel on Kings Highway and having sex till I have to be home by 11:00?"

With those momentous words, Stacey dove, laughing, into the water, leaving me in the back seat of the Runabout in a shocked stupor. Did she really mean it—the sex thing? Then, for a brief moment, I pondered, "How much will the Lobster House set me back? I mean, will sex with Stacey at the Horne Motel be worth the cost? What a great name for a motel—Horne, as in *horny*. And what will the *motel* cost? Will the Horne Motel even rent a room to a sixteen-year-old?"

Standing up and looking at Stacey swimming around the boat, I leaned over the edge and said to her, "That's what I heard about you Catholic girls . . . you love sex."

Stacey swam idly up to the side of the boat and extended her hand for me to help her climb back in. I reached down cluelessly and had started to pull her up when she suddenly placed both feet against the hull and hauled backwards, breaking into a gale of laughter as I face-planted into the St. John's. That started it, and we lost all concept of being near-adults. For the next while, we laughed and tried to dunk each other and splashed water in each other's face like a couple of six-year-olds in an inflatable backyard wading pool.

At one point I was shocked when Stacey suddenly stopped laughing and fixed those sea-blue eyes on me intently while treading water. She looked at the boat, and I could almost see the wheels turning in her mind as she calculated its drift and the angle to the shore where her mother sat smoking and watching us with her near-telescope-power binoculars. Then, when she was satisfied that the boat and the current of the river had us completely hidden from her mother's view, she drifted up to me as I treaded water.

Stacey took my face in both her hands and pulled me to her, and without a word, we were suddenly locked in a long kiss. Let me tell you, the mechanics and hydraulics of treading water and kissing a beautiful girl at the same time pose some unique challenges. For one thing, in order for a kiss to be carried out properly, the lips have to be in the perfect position relative to the lips of the other person. When you factor in current, wind speed, and the fact that if lip position is off by as little as one percent you end up lipping the other person's nostrils or chin, it's hard to pull off The Perfect Kiss in a watery environment. But Stacey's kiss could only be described as 100 percent dead-on-center perfect.

While the touch of her lips was chilly due to the cool river water, her breath was warm, and the tips of our tongues exploring each other's mouth were soft. Stacey kept holding my face in her hands to make sure our first kiss would be one I would remember for all eternity. She certainly succeeded. That kiss would forever define Kissing Perfection for me.

Finally, she pulled back from me. All her playfulness had lapsed, and she was suddenly quiet and pensive. Even in the midst of raging teenage hormones, I could sense that she was shaken by her own impulsiveness and not sure quite what to say or where to go from that moment. She just stared a bit bashfully at me while moving her legs slightly to keep afloat.

I felt compelled by the momentous moment to try to say something caring and not stupid, but the best I could come up with was, "That was beautiful, Stacey. I . . . I've never been kissed so tenderly by anyone before. Wow."

At my suave demeanor and flawlessly delivered piece of poetry, Stacey smiled just a bit and said softly, "You're a great kisser. I might have a spot on my kissing team for you."

She shook her head slightly, and the twinkle returned to her eyes. Her smile turned into genuine laughter as she started back toward the Runabout. "Let's get back in the boat before my mother swims out here and drowns you."

In just minutes, we were back in the Chris Craft, and Stacey started the engine and returned us carefully to the dock. Diane was still sitting in the lawn chair with her ever-present cigarette, watching me like a hawk circling a mouse for the entire time it took us to wash down and store the boat and carry the picnic cooler and trash bag up to the house. I sensed it was close to time for me to leave. It was easy to tell that my welcome was worn out as far as Stacey's mom was concerned, and she certainly didn't want me to hang around for chit-chat.

As we stowed the things from our boat ride and I made ready to bump ass back to the highway, I was pretty sure about how the evening would go at the Purcell house. As soon as my car was out of sight, Diane would corner Stacey, demanding to know what we were doing on the boat and in the water, particularly during those long minutes when we were hidden from her watchful eyes. Stacey would be cool and do the proverbial "Oh, Mom!" routine like any good teenage girl, then quickly sidestep the conversation and change the subject to something about her brother or the possibility that Dad would bring home quail for dinner, even though she knew full-well that the only kill he would have made would be a couple of low-hanging pine cones from a nearby tree.

Diane Purcell was still sitting in her lawn chair with her head wreathed in cigarette smoke as I headed for my car. I knew she wouldn't bother to come over to say goodbye, so I said loudly to Stacey, so her mom could hear me, "Thanks for the boat ride and skiing." Then, turning toward Diane, I waved and yelled, "Thanks, Mrs. Purcell, for the sandwiches and for letting us use the boat."

Diane sort of raised her hand to wave, but I swear I saw a middle finger flash my way. "The same to you, Diane," I thought to myself. As I climbed into the Ford, trying to avoid being bowled over by the overenthusiastic pack of Weimaraners in the process, I said softly to Stacey, who was standing alongside my car, "Are we on for a date next Saturday night?"

"Sure, call me and we can decide where we are going. Can we double-date? Mom likes me to go on dates with other couples along. I guess she thinks that makes sure we won't do anything like park and make out . . . or get a room at the Horne Motel." Stacey laughed and slammed the driver's door.

"I can get Star and Pam to go with us next Saturday. Movie at the Florida Theatre? Not sure what's showing but after the movie, we can cruise through the Texas Drive-In restaurant to see who's there with a date. Then we can go to the Horne," I said with a grin.

I laughed, put the car in first gear, and slowly pulled away from the house, careful not to run over one of Diane Purcell's prized Weimaraner dogs, who had now decided to try to chew holes in my tires even as the car was in motion. Oh, I had to fight myself hard to override the temptation to just whip the wheel around and take out one or two of the stupid animals.

As I rounded the first bend and bounced my ass out of sight of the house, I spotted a lone person walking up the road. As I got closer, I could see it was Bob Purcell headed home, shotgun cradled under his arm. Not wanting to stop to engage in a conversation, I eased past him, gave him a little hand-wave, and kept driving. Bob did not even look at me or return the wave. He seemed focused on the tops of his hunting boots as he trudged up the road. Looking in my rearview mirror, I shook my head as I thought I saw Bob weave a little as he walked. A thought shot through my mind: "Maybe a little too much Kentucky straight. Boy, he's going to catch shit from Diane, but hell, I bet that's a regular thing anyway."

Stacey and I dated for almost exactly one year. Dates in the late 1950s were mostly movies and then something to drink at the Texas Drive-In or inside at the Huddle House restaurant. Sometimes we would park on an isolated street or at the community park overlooking the river and "make out," which amounted to little more than a lot of heavy-duty kissing.

Remember, this was before the sexual revolution, when condoms or "chancing it" were the only readily available methods of contraception. That meant no intercourse in high school, as no girl was going to stay in the mood while her boyfriend unwrapped a year-old condom that had been in hiding in his wallet and then tried to roll it onto his penis in the dark, with one hand, while the other hand was under the girl's Maidenform bra for what was referred to as "bare tit."

When you were limited to engaging in amorous activities in the front seat of the family car, seldom, if ever, did things progress beyond the making-out stage. The genital-touching stage was usually one step away from asking the girl to marry you. Most couples were virgins on their wedding night. Times have changed, and I certainly don't think all these changes are for the better.

Our dating came to a crashing conclusion the night Diane caught Stacey on the phone after midnight, talking with me. When I heard the phone go suddenly dead, I pictured Diane with the telephone wires in her hand, having jerked them from the wall in anger. The next day, Stacey called, crying, and said her mother forbade us to date any longer. Stacey was completely beside herself. Like Romeo to Juliet, I said I would find a way for us to see each other. With much bravado, I firmly committed, "Screw your mom; she isn't going to break us up!"

For several months, we tried the clandestine-dating routine; one Mag 6 buddy or the other would pick Stacey up so Diane would think he was Stacey's date for the evening. We had what I thought was the perfect plan: At the bend in the drive, just before the Purcell house came into view, I would get out of the car and stand on the dirt road, waiting on the two of them to come back to pick me up.

To be honest, standing there by myself in the pitch darkness, I was scared shitless every single time that something would charge out of the woods and attack me, carrying away my limp, dead body to feed to the rest of the pack for their Saturday night dinner.

Once Stacey and whichever of the Mag 6 had "help Rollo" duty had picked me up, we would go and get my buddy's date. After the movie or whatever, we would reverse the process, dropping off his date, and then leaving me standing, scared shitless again, in the dark on that godforsaken dirtbag road. My buddy would escort my Stacey to her front door, where she, at the end of every "date with a Mag 6 member," would say, "Good night. I had a great time!" just loud enough to delight her mother, who was undoubtedly hiding behind the blinds or peeking between the drapes, clueless that the much-hated Protestant boy had in fact been the one making out in the back seat with her daughter that night.

At some point in the last month of our relationship, we both knew the fragility of the secret routine. Stacey was scared one of Diane's friends would see us at a movie or restaurant and tip her off about what was going on behind her back. If Diane knew Stacey was cheating on her, Stacey would be grounded for the rest of her teenage years. To make sure we would not see each other in school, Diane made Stacey change high schools; she would attend Kennedy Catholic High School for her senior year.

It wasn't long after finding out about the upcoming change of schools that the flame on our love candle slowly flickered and then went out. Besides, I had a sneaking suspicion that a hotshot former DuPont student was putting the moves on Stacey and that, seeing no future with Rollo, she had started taking a date or two with him behind my back.

On what turned out to be our last date, which consisted of meeting at a party at Oz's house, I confronted Stacey with my suspicions that she was dating someone else. She replied in a very straightforward, sincere manner, "Robert, you were my first love. I will always love you and the times we had together, you putting up with my mother, standing in the dark waiting to be with me, all of it. I love you, but we can't go on like this now. Maybe after high school, who knows. Please, don't ever forget me."

With that, she reached into her large purse and pulled out a crumpled brown paper bag, which she handed to me. In the bag I found my class ring and framed class photo, engraved, "To the One I Love, Robert." I knew that Stacey and I were now just a wonderful memory. As I stood staring into the paper bag at the framed photo with the inscription, I thought to myself, "Good thing I didn't put Stacey's name on it. Now I can give it to someone else."

The closing credits of *Bonanza* had the wall map of the Ponderosa catching fire and then exploding into flames before burning to a sooty crisp. That pretty much described my first teenage love affair—hot, fiery, then suddenly nothing but smoldering ashes.

As I lay in my bed that Thursday of the first week of senior year, my memories of Stacey faded from my mind. The sleep sandman was doing his thing, and I was starting to drift off. Before my mind totally shut down for the night, I thought of Jackie White and wondered, "Will she be my next true love? Will we kiss on the first date? Will it be The Perfect Kiss?"

As I pondered these questions, from down the hall came a harsh command: "Robert, turn out you light and go to bed! You have school tomorrow!"

"Yes, Ma," I replied and flipped off the desk lamp by my bed. I couldn't wait to see what tomorrow would bring.

Chapter 7

Black Friday

On September 24, 1869, America had one of its lowest days ever, financially speaking. That day will live on in infamy as "Black Friday" because so many rich Americans suddenly became dirt-poor after losing their ass in the gold market. It was their own fault, actually; they were trying to corner the gold market and make themselves all the richer, but when the federal government put the brakes on the plan by flooding the market with gold from the Federal Reserve, it knocked the bottom out of the inflated gold prices and kicked the greedy jerks right in the proverbial wallet.

Since that day when so many fat cats suddenly became suicidal, half-starved alley cats, there have been many other "Black Fridays," especially in the stock and commodities markets, and any number of people have experienced financial ruin since that day so long ago. So now, anytime a person has a really shitty Friday and decides to name that day their own "Black Friday," they are in the good company of all those nineteenth-century rich folks who got their financial butts kicked.

Almost ninety years to the day later, in September 1959, my very own personal Black Friday struck and kicked me square between my legs. Like all the Fridays in September, this particular one was a school day, but the day started going to hell before I had even made it to my first class.

The trouble started first thing when I was standing in the hallway waiting for the opening bell and Jackie approached me with tears in her lovely eyes. I, of course, didn't see the tears right away. As a typical teenage boy, I was far too busy staring at that short, pleated skirt and at how such a simple thing as having the top two buttons open on her high-collar blouse could add such sensuality to her appearance.

But I soon couldn't help but catch on because she was shaking and her voice was little more than a hoarse whisper: "I can't go out with you on Saturday night . . . I'm so sorry." She was almost crying out loud as she continued, "My mom and dad are making me go to a family *conclave* at our fishing camp outside Hastings. Please, please, don't be mad at me!"

"Shit," I said to myself, though I was careful not to speak out loud and upset her even more, "there goes my chance for making out with Jackie this weekend."

Since I had enough instinctual knowledge of females to at least not make a fool of myself on this one occasion, I reached down and took hold of her hand. I pulled it to my chest and, looking into her teary eyes, said as sincerely as I could, "No problem, Jackie. Waiting another week to go on a date will only make our hearts grow fonder for each other." Yeah, it was a corny line, but I really meant it, and she ate it up.

"Oh, Rob, you are so wonderful. I'll dream of our date the whole time I'm at the camp with all those people I don't even know. Any chance you'd like to come see me at the camp on Saturday? We could sneak away and go to a movie in Hastings."

"Jackie, I'd love to be with you anywhere, here or in Hastings, but I've promised my dad I'll do some work around the house on Saturday. We'll just have to wait another week."

What I told her was basically the truth, as my dad always had a list of Saturday chores for me to do. Early each Saturday morning, without fail, Dad taped it to our sliding glass door in plain sight of anyone heading out to the back yard and the swimming pool.

Usually, the chores amounted to cutting the grass and cleaning the pool, though sometimes Dad would throw in some major project, like painting the fence or cleaning his *Miss Marian*. Yet, as much as I longed to spend time with Jackie, slaving away at a list of chores would be more fun than spending all day at a camp with a bunch of adults I didn't know. Besides, there would be very little chance of sneaking away and being alone together under so many watchful adult eyes. As I had told her, we'd just have to wait another week to see where our newfound relationship would take us.

"Rob, can I see you at lunch? I have a little surprise for you, something to remind you of me this weekend when we are apart."

Eyeing Jackie, I couldn't help but think, "When someone looks like Kim Novak, what in the hell can she give me to remind me even more how hot she is?'

"Sure, see you in a few hours."

With that, the bell rang for my first class of the day, which was Basic Spanish. It was taught by Ms. Alvarez, and she was a pro because even though she had been born in the United States, she had gotten her undergraduate degree from some university in Mexico City. She had lived there with her grandparents to learn the culture and language while preparing to fulfill her dream of returning to the United States to teach high school students the Spanish language and customs of Mexico.

Now many years later, Ms. Alvarez was a very lovely, but very old, lady, who looked to be ninety years old, maybe from too much Mexican sun as a student. She was hard of hearing and had poor eyesight, but was a tenured teacher counting the days to retirement, either in Jacksonville or back in dear old Mexico.

The blackness of this personal Black Friday continued in her class with an exercise in which each student had to stand by their desk and read a verb, conjugate it, and then give its definition from a list in the Spanish text book. Looking at the verbs, my mind went absolutely *blank*. I started to mumble the Spanish words, but I sounded like an alien who had just landed in a spaceship from the planet Uranus: "*Habb larr, yo habb low, too habb ace, el habb lah . . . .*"

Apparently not wanting the class to suffer my slaughtering of her beautiful Spanish language any longer, Ms Alvarez turned her dark, almond-shaped eyes toward me and said, "Rob, *gracias*, you can sit down, and now Susan Sutton will do our next word."

I was never asked again to stand and read in her Spanish class. Too bad Ms. Alvarez didn't teach "Uranus-ese"; I might have gotten an "A" in her class.

During lunch, I met up with Jackie, and from the moment I laid eyes on her, I could tell that her mood had improved 100 percent since our tearful encounter in the hallway just a couple hours before. I noted the difference in how she was standing and in how her whole demeanor had lost that downcast pall. I was so self-satisfied with the way my little "hand to heart" maneuver had worked that if anyone had been paying attention, they would have noticed a little added cockiness to my swagger.

I was also hoping that delaying our first date for a week would pump up Jackie's hormones. I hoped that, in her mind, suffering through her parents' conclave, then the following five days at school, and all the related heart pangs would somehow make our first date all the sweeter.

Jackie was standing in the serving line for the usual macaroni and cheese surprise, one of the cafeteria's signature dishes. The surprise was what you might find attached to the noodles; it might be a strand of long black hair from one of the servers lying placidly in the sticky cheese sauce, or a sliver of tooth-shocking aluminum foil from the container the mac–and-cheese had been packaged in, and if you were really lucky, you might get a fat black housefly still kicking from playing touch-and-go with the sticky cheese goop.

I was the epitome of suave, debonair, cool as I sidled up to her and spoke those words of magic: "Hi, Jackie."

"Oh, hi, Rob," she replied in a warm, soft tone. "I want to tell you how much your thoughtfulness this morning means to me. You could've been a real jerk about us not going out this weekend."

The instant she turned to me, I was lost, trapped in those sultry, smoky, deep-set gray eyes, and the best comeback I could muster was, "I can wait an extra week for the perfect date." I was surprised at my own ability to bullshit when the words just rolled off my tongue, and Jackie loved it.

She moved closer to me and then reached up as if to whisper something in my ear. I cocked my head slightly to hear her, curious as to what she wanted to tell me secretly. But instead of whispering right away, she put one very soft hand on the side of my face, paused to let the warmth of her touch sink in, then whispered in that lovely voice, "I'll make it worth the wait. I promise, it will be something very special for you." With that, she reached up with her other hand to hold the back of my head and kissed my cheek.

I was really turned on by her promise of "something very special for you." I'd be lying if I didn't admit that the Black Friday pain was turning swiftly to a heightened and very pleasant sensation. If Jackie had continued to whisper in my ear for just a few seconds longer, her warm breath stroking my ear lobe and neck, I believe my own mood shift would have been so obvious I would have really embarrassed myself there in the cafeteria.

A seventeen-year-old male's libido switches on with the slightest provocation, especially when stroked by a hot girl's warm breath in one's ear, accompanied by a kiss on the cheek. On a scale of one to ten on the erection meter, anything that stimulates the ears causes it to register an immediate five, and be on the fast track to a ten in a potentially embarrassing fashion.

I told Jackie I wouldn't be able to talk with her till the next Monday. Tonight I had the opening football game, and I'd already told her about my chores around the house for Saturday. Having declined her invitation to the camp, I didn't spell out that I'd likely also spend some time running with the Mag 6, maybe enjoying a last-of-the-season jaunt to the beach. But I did explain that Sundays were the mother-mandated family day of church and other activities, usually hanging around the house or a trip on the St. John's in the *Miss Marian* with a few of the family friends.

Jackie was OK with waiting and whispered again into my ear, this time declaring: "I will count the minutes till Monday."

She reached into the stylish little purse she was carrying, pulled her hand back out, and then took one of my hands, turned it over, and pressed into my palm something that felt like a round coin and chain. I looked at it and saw it was a pendant of some sort with an illustration of a couple of dragons. I figured it must be symbolic of our team mascot, the DuPont Dragons. For a minute, I stood staring at the pendant and turning it over and over. Finally I said, "Wow, Jackie, where did you get this pendant with a DuPont Dragon on it? It's really cool."

Not directly answering my question, she replied, "The dragons represent strength and protection. Wear the pendant for good luck. It'll keep you from getting hurt in the game tonight. I can't have you damaged for our date!" And with that, Jackie planted another soft kiss on my cheek. The erection meter hit 7.0, causing me a bit of discomfort as I tried to fit the dragon pendant and chain in my pocket without either injuring myself or making the state of my sudden arousal evident.

After eating a light dinner and getting good wishes for the game from my family, I drove over to DuPont to put on my football uniform, forgoing the shoulder pads for the bus trip to the stadium. Putting my valuables in a safe place, I took the change from my pants and saw the pendant and chain. Thinking about Jackie's claim that it would bring me strength and protection, I coyly put it over my head, tucking the pendant inside my t-shirt, under my uniform jersey. Chuckling to myself, I thought, "Funny, I don't feel any stronger."

Little did I know that the mystical protective forces of the dragons on the pendant were already shielding me from harm. Only once during the entire season did I ever get a scratch on me, and that was when I had taken off the pendant for a shower the night before the Jackson High game and had forgotten to put it back on. That was the game when the tibia in my left leg got broken. That night, after limping home with my leg taped, planning to head for the doctor the next day, I found the pendant and chain on my dresser. I put the dragon pendant back on and never took it off the rest of the year. I wasn't going to chance getting hurt again.

The Black Friday bad-luck streak continued into the big Lee High football game, ending as a big fat flop for DuPont High. Yep, we got our asses stomped with a 50–0 final score. This came as no surprise to anyone in the know, especially since Lee High was so much larger than DuPont and had five times the winning tradition at football.

The only real surprise was that, when the Friday edition of the *Jacksonville Journal* hit the newsstands, it featured a full front page in the sports section devoted to a preview of the game with a quarter of the page taken up by a photo of me and Lee High's top defensive lineman. It was also a surprise that Rex Edmonson, the *Journal's* sportswriter, had gone way out on a limb and predicted that the game would be a toss-up. The 50–0 end score forever tarnished Rex's reputation as a reliable predictor of high school sports teams. He never covered any of our games again but, instead, gave them to whatever high school journalism intern happened to be handy at the *Journal* on the given day.

My own game performance was a huge disappointment to my team, myself, and, most of all, my dad, who had visions of me being a highly-recruited big-college running back. Lee picked apart our double-wing offense like pulling feathers from a slaughtered chicken. It was as if Lee had our playbook—which, in fact, they did. So the whole game was a matter of *pluck . . . pluck . . . pluck.*

Lily and Crazy, both halfbacks, and Star, our fullback, did all they could, but we were outmanned, out-sized, out-planned, and out of luck. They blocked and ran with true spirit, but at the end of the game, you could count their net running yardage on both hands and feet, even with a missing toe or two.

Spiff, our starting left offensive tackle, got bent backwards on almost every offensive play by Lee's All-Conference defensive tackle, who later starred at the University of Florida. Spiff was outweighed by his opponent by more than fifty pounds, which was OK for Spiff, as he didn't want the extra weight to ruin his 32-inch-waist, slim-and-trim look. But on the field that night, the bigger guy almost ruined Spiff's face for him. Good old Oz was in the stands watching the slaughter, about which he later commented that Custer had better odds at the Little Bighorn than we had against Lee High.

The stadium lights severely compromised my ability to see the football when it was thrown my way. On a couple of plays, the football actually bounced off my helmet because I didn't even see it coming. I guess "spastic" would be a fair description of how I looked on the field, trying to catch the football as it careened off my head. In fairness to my spastic ball-catching performance, DuPont High School didn't have a lighted field, so we had never practiced under stadium lights. Boy, was that a mistake! The Lee game started at 7:00 p.m. in the Gator Bowl under blazing stadium lights, and I was so blinded by the glare that even a seeing-eye dog couldn't have helped me catch that ball.

I was sitting at the kitchen table after the game, trying to drown my sorrows in a cold root beer and wishing it were a Budweiser, when my dad put his hand on my shoulder. "Not a great night, but the season is just one game old. You'll do better with your running game next week against a team more matched to DuPont." I knew he was referring to our upcoming game against the St. Augustine Deaf and Dumb High School. I shook my head bitterly as I realized that even I would have qualified for a school for the disabled, under the "blind" category. Dad had said nothing about my football-catching abilities; maybe he recognized my spastic eye-hand coordination as a skill that could improve in the coming weeks.

As it turned out, it was all academic, as the coaches moved me to defense the following Monday and I never ran the ball again for DuPont—and never again humiliated myself in front of hundreds of DuPont spectators, cheerleaders, and fellow players with my signature spastic ball-catching routine.

That night, my dad told me that a boyhood friend's son, Chet Ostrowski, was currently playing defensive end for the Washington Redskins football team and that the Redskins were in town to play the next night, Saturday, in an exhibition game against the Chicago Bears. The Redskins were staying at the Thunderbird Motel, and Dad had called Chet and set it up for me and any of my friends to go over on Saturday afternoon and meet some of the players. Dad wouldn't be with me on Saturday—it was his golf day, and even the Washington Redskins couldn't get Dad to give that up. He squeezed my shoulder in consolation before wandering off to get his clubs ready for his usual Saturday golf outing.

On Saturday, I picked up the Mag 6, all of whom were anxious to go meet some of the Redskins players. We all piled into my car and drove over to the Thunderbird Motel—the same motel I got arrested in a few months later, along with other underage teenagers, for partying in one of their rooms. We all beat the charge of underage drinking and some minor room damage when it was proven that one of the underage party hosts bought the party's liquor at the motel bar. The Thunderbird management wisely decided not to press charges, not wanting the judge to find out they had been serving alcohol to minors.

Using the motel's front-desk guest phone, I asked for Chet Ostrowski, who, amazingly, picked up on the second ring and invited us to his room. Like a parade of baby ducks following their mother, we made our way through the halls, passing some mammoth individuals who could only be professional football players. Chet was most pleasant, talked about his dad and how his dad knew my dad from playing football at the University of Missouri. Chet was a defensive end, about 6'1", 230 pounds, and looked like a movie star. I bet the ladies went crazy for this guy.

While talking to Chet, we couldn't help but notice his roommate, Bubba, a huge defensive tackle, 6'6" and maybe 285 pounds. While that's not big even by high school standards nowadays, these guys filled up the room with their bulk. What caught our attention most about ol' Bubba was that he was lying half-naked in bed, flipping his penis back and forth like it was a noodle on a fork. I couldn't understand what he was doing, maybe keeping time in his mind with the tune he was humming. Chet looked at him and shook his head with just a hint of disgust on his face and asked, "Would you boys like to meet some of the other players? I don't think Eddie LeBaron, our quarterback, is around, but Sam Barker, our All-Pro kicker, is somewhere outside. I heard him yelling at someone before your came to the room."

Chet led us back out into the hall, and we headed toward the outdoor swimming pool, as he figured some of the Washington players might be soaking up some Florida sun. Turned out he was right. At the pool we met Dick James, a 5'9" second-team halfback we immediately took a liking to. He was personable, friendly, not at all pretentious, even though he was a pro football player. While all of us were much taller than Dick, he was very muscular, with what appeared to be a gymnast's body.

While we were talking to Dick James beside the Thunderbird Motel swimming pool, we suddenly heard loud screams coming from the parking lot. Looking in the direction of the screams, we beheld, of all things, a golf cart rapidly inbound toward the pool. Perched on the cart and driving it like a bat out of hell was All-Pro Sam Baker, as well as two of the motel's housekeepers, both of whom were African Americans, both in their late thirties, and both screaming like banshees.

Somehow, Sam Baker had commandeered the motel's housekeeping cart, along with the maids. He was maneuvering it around the shrubbery, lounge chairs, and other motel guests, and was headed directly for the swimming pool. I don't know if Sam was drunk, but he was laughing uncontrollably and had a glazed look in his eyes, determined to get to the pool with the cart and its cargo. The maids were screaming hysterically, "Gets me off this thing! Gets me off this thing!"

The golf cart, Sam Baker, and the two housekeepers hit the swimming pool, and the cart sank to the bottom in an instant, leaving Sam sort of floating around in the pool spouting water like a whale. The two maids yelled for help, as it was apparent neither could swim, and without a minute's hesitation, a number of the Redskins players jumped into the pool to save them from going under. Sam Baker continued his imitation of a breached white whale in what looked like a sort of self-satisfied oblivion.

Our group hung out around the pool for a couple of hours till the team left for the Gator Bowl and the exhibition game with the Chicago Bears. I met Eddie LeBaron that night at the game, and was lucky enough to get to work as ball boy for the Redskins because Dick James had recommended me to the training staff at the pool earlier in the day.

Unlike today's huge quarterbacks, Eddie LeBaron was 5'9" and 168. He had been drafted by the Redskins in the tenth round, 123rd overall. He wasn't highly rated, but at his size, who would ever expect that he would eventually be a four-time Pro Bowler? After a distinguished record with the Redskins, he went on to a respectable law career. Unfortunately for Eddie LeBaron, that Saturday night at the Gator Bowl, the Chicago Bears' "Papa Bear" spanked little Eddie's butt, and his teammates' butts, all night long.

Later on Sunday, after family and church time, the Mag 6 and I picked up Dick James and a couple of other players whose names escape me now and took them skiing on the river in my dad's boat. Dick bought beer for the trip, which he gladly shared with us. He was just as agile on skis as I imagined he'd be in a gymnastics routine, never falling, bouncing from one side of the wake to the other with ease. The other players weren't as athletic as Dick, and for most, it was their first time on water skis.

What they lacked in skiing ability, they made up for in their beer-drinking skills, and almost to a man, the whole group was pretty blasted by the time we got back to the dock. They were probably trying to forget the 55–12 ass-whipping they had gotten the previous night. They were drinking in good company, as we were also trying not to remember our strikingly similar margin of loss from Friday night.

I came away from my ball-boy duties and my Black Friday weekend with a team-autographed game football given to me by one of the Redskins' secondary coaches and some of the best and worst memories of my entire life. I kept that football for years until, somehow during my college days, it disappeared. I think my mother gave it to a neighbor's young son, thinking it nothing more than a beat-up relic from my high school football days.

Oh, well, so much for collecting cherished mementoes; they usually end up in the trash or a weekend garage sale, or given to some kid who trades your treasure for a tempting box of Milk Duds or Jujubes. I bet my mother didn't even ask for any candy—let alone money—when she handed away my Redskins souvenir.

Chapter 8

Spellbound

Early the next morning, Monday, the raging of my beer-flooded bladder woke me from a fitful sleep. One glance at the glowing hands of my alarm clock told me that it was 4:46 a.m. For a moment, I lay there in the quiet darkness, not wanting to leave the warmth of the sheets, but soon enough I realized that there was no way to ignore a half gallon of beer trapped in my cup-sized bladder. I got up and stumbled out into the hallway toward the bathroom.

Most of the night I had tossed and turned, replaying in my head what it had been like to watch Ben Scotti and the rest of the Washington Redskins throw empty beer cans at whichever one of their teammates was riding the skis at the time. It was amazing how much these grown men acted as badly as, or worse than, teenagers. "Well," I thought to myself as I fumbled for the bathroom light, "after getting their asses handed to them by the Chicago Bears, who could blame them for wanting to blow off a little steam."

I bellied up to the commode, braced one hand against the wall, and as I began to relieve my aching bladder, I shook my head at the thought that it was just my luck that the only real sleep I had all night had been interrupted by the urgent need to piss. Then I remembered the dream that had been haunting me as I lay sleeping.

No sooner had my mind registered a slight memory of the dream than it instantly sprang into sharp focus. In the dream, I had been standing in a grassy meadow in the dewy predawn. In the middle of the field was Jackie, a vision of esoteric loveliness, clad in a long flowing gown of the purest white, her platinum blonde hair falling like a cascade of sunshine. The only adornment to her dress was a simple, yet oddly shaped, pendant hanging from a cord of black leather around her neck.

In her hand was a candle of ebony-colored wax, whose flame flickered and danced in the misty air. Just as the first rays of dawn passed the horizon and set that platinum hair alight like the halo of an angel, she began to sing and dance. Her voice was lilting and sweet; it was as if all nature was holding its breath just to hear the words. As she began to spin and twirl, her dainty bare feet sent drops of dew flying like drops of molten gold. The words of her song were foreign, Celtic perhaps, though I knew Jackie had no knowledge of any Celtic languages. (It wasn't as if Florida high schools included Celtic as part of the curriculum.)

I shook my head as I finished and flushed; how could Jackie know a Celtic song? Must have been too much beer and pepperoni pizza still wandering around my brain. Less than three minutes later, I had washed my hands and was back in bed and immediately asleep. My eyelids had no more closed and my breathing settled down than I fell back into the same dream as before. Jackie twirled around the clearing. Though the candle flickered, somehow it never went out, and she seemed to offer the fire to the four directions as she held it out and spun.

She leapt lightly back to the center of the clearing, white gown flowing like a snowdrift, and raised her hands to the sky. Just as our eyes met, the dawn light was suddenly blotted out by an enormous shadow. I turned my eyes skyward and was met by one of the most terrible sights I had ever seen in reality or nightmare.

There, wheeling through the sky with grace and power that would be the envy of any eagle, was an enormous red-scaled dragon. Its ragged wings like those of a gigantic bat swept around the great beast, catching the thermals to bear it aloft as it dove and spiraled through the air. Talons like bars of iron tipped the clawed feet at the end of the monster's two muscular legs, and the sinuous tail spun and writhed as the monster opened its spike-toothed maw and sent great gouts of fire into the misty morning.

The nightmare creature spiraled directly above my smiling Jackie. Then, suddenly it spread its wings like blackened sails and dropped from the sky like an enormous falcon swooping in for the kill . . . and it was diving directly for Jackie! Its huge jaws were agape as if to devour her.

I started to scream, to warn her of the approaching doom, but my words were swallowed up in the gusts of wind produced by the huge wings. Suddenly Jackie's voice rose above the whirlwind, and I realized that the beast wasn't coming *for* her; it was coming *to* her. The dragon pulled its dive sharply to the side and landed beside Jackie as lightly as a butterfly. This huge reptilian butterfly craned its neck toward the heavens and once again spouted fire and dark smoke toward the clouds.

As I watched, Jackie stepped lightly in front of the creature, the candle held before her. The dragon reared its head like a snake about to strike, opening dripping jaws the size of a small car. But instead of the jaws lunging out to crush and tear, the dragon's head leaned forward daintily. I could see its chest expand as it sniffed the candle sharply, and only at that instant did the flame go out, sucked into the nostrils of the huge red creature.

It lowered its huge horned, scaly head. Jackie stroked the armored forehead as a rider might pet a gentle old mare. The dragon knelt to the grass like an elephant stooping to accept a rider. I watched Jackie place one bare foot into the crease of a gigantic wing and realized she was going to climb onto it's back. In my dream, I again began to scream for her to stop, to run. I was certain that if she got on the dragon, it would carry her off to be devoured in some strange place. I was twisting and turning, and later I would wake in knotted, sweat-soaked sheets.

Despite my thrashing and screaming, Jackie mounted the armored back and seated herself at the base of the muscular neck. She took the stiff scaly mane in her hand, and the dragon reared like a horse and then sprang into the sky with a single beat of the great bat-like wings. Her lips parted, and I could hear the haunting Celtic melody echoing through the sky even as the wind from the dragon's ascent blew me backward.

The monster creature mounted like a gigantic bird of prey. One instant they were hovering over the meadow, blowing the morning mist into strange shapes, and the next they were a tiny speck in the brightening sky. I saw dragon fire light the sky and the beast dropped into a spiral that slowly brought it down again over the place where I stood. Its overhead pass was so low that I could see Jackie's smiling face and read her lips as she mouthed the words, "I love you."

My hands were gripping and twisting the sheets about my body, and in the dream, the dragon again circled the little meadow. Again, I clearly saw Jackie's smiling "I love you." Then, at the end of its second pass, with a great burst of flame, the beast shot straight up into the sky and quickly vanished from sight.

I woke with a start, breath ragged and gasping, soaked in sweat, and almost crying from the force of the dream. I glanced over at the clock and saw that it read 5:46. I couldn't believe only an hour had passed. I swung my legs over the side of the bed, put my head in my hands, and just sat there for a few moments.

The image of Jackie clad in white and dancing around the meadow was as beautiful and seductive as the image of the dragon was terrifying and repulsive. I was thinking of these things when my mind made the connection. I rose from the bed and snatched the dragon-embossed pendant Jackie had given me from the place I had laid it when I had showered. I put it back around my neck with a grimace, thinking to myself, "Stupid pendant . . . this crap is probably why I'm dreaming of Jackie riding a dragon."

I climbed back between the now-chilly, sweat-damp sheets and pulled them up to my chin, determined to squeeze in a few more minutes of sleep. As my eyes drifted shut, the image of Jackie's face, hair flying in the wind,, and her smiling words "I love you" sent a chill up my spine. I smiled in spite of myself, and as I drifted off to sleep, I whispered into the darkened room, "I love you, too, Jackie."

Later in our relationship, I would learn that our commitment of love to each other, and all that surrounded it, was more than a simple dream. I had actually become spellbound. That very night, while at her family conclave, Jackie had removed the tarot cards which had been handed down to her from her grandmother and had taken a reading. After the reading, she had cast a spell on me—a love spell. I guess as spells go, a spell that made me love and be loved by Jackie White isn't such a bad thing in any way, form, or fashion.

I knew Jackie was a little different when I met her, but I didn't know that she and her family were practicing Wiccans. Now, this doesn't mean that they were broom-riding, orgy-having, goat-kissing, card-carrying, fairy-tale witches and warlocks. As a matter of fact, Jackie's parents were just plain hard-working folks who got their kicks out of dressing up, out of sight of the neighbors, of course, or at a conclave with like-minded folks, and working their rituals and festivals. The problem was that I never came to embrace the whole Wiccan thing, and that eventually cost me my relationship with Jackie.

Later that Monday morning as I pulled my '39 Ford out of the driveway and started on my way to pick up the rest of the Mag 6 for school, I wanted nothing more than to tell them about my dream, but I knew they would just laugh their collective asses off at me. So instead, when the conversation started out about our waterskiing adventure with the Washington Redskins, I just fell in stride with the rest.

Of course, sports and girls were always popular subjects with us six, and Lily steered the conversation toward our upcoming football game against St. Augustine Deaf and Dumb School. "Hey, Rollo," he quipped, "I heard your parents were going to administration today to see if they could get you transferred to St. Augustine D and D as a charter student for a new blind students' class."

"Go bite yourself, Lily," I replied, without the slightest hesitation. "Just 'cause I can't see the ball coming my way when I look up into stadium lights, it doesn't mean I'm blind as a *bat*."

The instant I said the word *bat*, the image of Jackie astride the giant bat-winged lizard flashed to my mind, and I thought to myself, "OK, get hold of yourself. You can't even say the word *bat* without getting pictures of Jackie and dragons. Careful, or it'll be unicorns and fairies next."

When we got to school, I searched the crowd for Jackie but couldn't find her. I caught myself wondering if maybe she was circling the football field looking for a safe place for her dragon to land. I finally spotted her as she got out of her parents' car on the street in front of the school. I started toward her, but just as I did, the bell rang for first classes, and she had to almost run to get to the front doors in time. I knew I'd never have time to talk to her then.

I walked into the school with the Mag 6 and the rest of a group of seniors, figuring I'd catch up with her during lunch. I wanted to tell her about the dream, about how beautiful she had been in it. I wanted to see her reaction when I told her she had been soaring through the skies on the back of a fire-breathing monster. I did *not* intend to tell her about the words "I love you."

One week into the school year, classes had already become routine: handing in homework assignments, giving oral reports in front of the class, pop quizzes on the most mundane lessons. I always believed the teachers loved to watch the students squirm in their seats when, at the beginning of their class, they loudly announced, "Pop quiz today. Clear your desk of your books. No looking on anyone else's paper."

During pop quizzes in my geometry class, Ted Dassey, the guy sitting directly behind me, would reach over my shoulder and drop a note, "Rollo, let me peek at your paper. Shift over in your desk so I can see your answers." Later in the year, the note got shortened to just, "Move!" I liked Ted, and if peeking helped him, so be it; my contribution to building and maintaining class esprit de corps.

At lunch, Jackie found me first and came up to me, appearing almost giddy. "Hi, Rob," she said with a startling smile. "This is the week we finally go out. Where do you want to go?" She said nothing about her trip with her parents, nor asked me about my weekend, nor mentioned the Lee game.

"Let's go to the 5 Points Theater. They're playing *Some Like It Hot*. Sort of describes our date," I said teasingly.

Without missing a beat, Jackie responded, "I said I'd have something special for you for waiting a week for our date. *Hot* would describe what I have in mind."

"OK, then, it's *Some Like It Hot* for Saturday night. How about I pick you up at 7:00? Early movie usually starts at 7:30. We'll be out by 9:00 and can go grab something to eat or whatever."

"Let's do the *whatever*," was Jackie's astonishingly sultry answer as she winked at me, then spun away to make her way through the lunch line with her girlfriends.

Wishful thinking got the better of me with Jackie's teasing answer. "If *whatever* is going to be more than a first-date kiss, then I'd better get over to the Burger King on Kings Highway and buy a new condom out of the vending machine in the men's room." Of course, these words were whispered so low that even I couldn't hear my own voice. Unconsciously, I patted my wallet as I thought about the condom that had been riding there for at least a year and maybe two.

Later in the day, Oz and Star pulled me aside and confided in me the details of a prank they were in the process of pulling on Crazy. Since Crazy didn't have a current girlfriend or seem to be making any efforts to find one, Oz and Star decided they would create a girlfriend for him.

Oz and Star needed a senior girl to go along with fabricating a girlfriend for Crazy. Sandy Shirley jumped at the chance to be part of the prank. She had a crush on Crazy and wanted to get close to him, so she figured that at the end of the prank, Crazy would laugh at the whole thing and ask her out on a date. Boy, she couldn't have been more wrong in judging what Crazy's reaction would be.

Daily, under the pseudonym of "PB," Sandy wrote Crazy an anonymous little love note. On some notes she sprayed a little perfume, and on some she planted a big kiss, leaving a perfect lip imprint in bright red lipstick. "PB" were initials Oz and Star had picked out of the air, though there were a couple of cute sophomore and junior girls with those initials. Maybe Crazy thought PB was one of them.

Each day, a love note was secretly dropped in Crazy's locker. (In the 1950s, high school lockers were never locked, as students did not bring guns or drugs to school. The most harmful substance you would find in someone's locker was a pack of unfiltered Camel cigarettes.) Each of Sandy's notes built on the previous ones, and the plan was to get Crazy to a secretive meeting with the anonymous admirer.

The first note was simple: "Hi, you're cute! PB." Oz and Star strategically positioned themselves to watch Crazy's reaction to discovering it. He looked at the note half-heartedly, read it, threw it back in his locker, and slammed the door.

"Crazy, what's the problem? You seem pissed at something," said Star, standing nearby.

"Oh, someone put a stupid note in my locker that was meant for someone else. You'd think they'd know this is my locker."

Star and Oz couldn't believe what Crazy had told them; he thought the note was meant for someone else! For the next love note Sandy wrote, they had her put Crazy's name on it. The next day when he opened his locker, there was another love note from PB: "Dave, don't be mad at me for writing these notes. I am very shy, especially with a cute senior. Good luck in this Friday's football game. You're the team's best player. PB."

This time, upon seeing and reading the love note, Crazy didn't throw it away but put it in his notebook. For Crazy, the challenge began of finding out who the mysterious "PB" was.

This secret note routine continued, note after note, day after day, for several weeks, till the killer note hit Crazy's locker.

"Dave, I need to know if you really want to meet me. Wear a red sweater to school tomorrow if you do. Then I will tell you who I am. Love, PB." Well, that cinched it for Crazy; PB was coming out of the shadows to reveal herself, and the word "Love" was a nice touch to rev up Crazy's emotional engine.

When I pulled up at Crazy's house the next day to pick him up for school, I had a very difficult time keeping from laughing at him. Since Lily and Spiff weren't in on the secret love note caper, and Star and Oz had yet to be picked up, I was the only one in my car who knew what was going on with Crazy and "PB." Coming down the walkway to my car came Crazy in the brightest red sweater mankind ever wove from lamb's wool and sold at JCPenney. Rudolph the Red-Nosed Reindeer should have a snoot that bright.

I could only comment to Crazy, "Hey, nice sweater. Practicing to be a stop sign for Halloween?"

"Naw, it's something my mother gave me for Christmas. It's a little cool today, so I thought I'd put it on." Crazy did not elaborate. I let it pass so as not to ruin it for Star and Oz when they got in the car and saw Crazy's attire.

Star was waiting out front of his house, probably in bated anticipation to see if Crazy had on a red sweater. As he got into the car and saw Crazy looking like a red-wrapped Christmas gift, it was all Star could do to hold in his laughter. "Morning, guys," he greeted everyone. "Looks like it's gonna rain."

"No," replied Lily. "Sky's perfectly blue, not a cloud in sight."

Star followed quickly with, "Red sky in the morning, sailors take warning. Oh, that's not a red *sky*—it's Crazy's red sweater I see!"

Crazy just looked at Star and replied, "Stuff it, Star."

The same scene was repeated at Oz's house. Out front of his house, Oz stood, impatiently waiting to see if Crazy would be adorned in red. Climbing into the back seat, Oz just looked at Crazy and turned away to look out the window. In my rearview mirror, I could see that Oz had tears in his eyes from holding in his laughter.

Once at school, when we had parked and had all gotten out, Oz moved discreetly behind the car, where I heard what I imagine was meant to sound like a cough, though it sure sounded like a burst of laughter to me.

That day, the love note told Crazy, "So we can have some private time together, meet me in the football bleachers after your practice. I can't wait for us to be together. PB."

Later that day, in the cool and dimming afternoon, the Mag 6, minus Crazy, sauntered across the football field. There in the football bleachers sat Crazy, unmistakable in his red sweater. "Hey, Crazy," we yelled, "what are you doing, sitting alone in the stands? Waiting for someone?" We paused as he fumbled for an answer, apparently realizing he couldn't deny it; after all, he was sitting alone in our stadium built for three hundred spectators. "You wouldn't be waiting for someone with the initials 'PB,' would you?" laughed Star.

Crazy jumped straight up as if a bolt of lightning thrown from Mt. Olympus by Zeus had just hit him squarely between the eyes. "Oh, I knew all along you assholes were behind the PB notes! I could smell the *gefilte* fish on them; paper must have come from Star's house. Who wrote the notes?"

"Sandy Shirley wrote the notes; Oz dictated them," answered Star. "Hope you're not too pissed. By the way, if it's any consolation, Sandy really got turned on with the note thing and wants to go out with you."

Crazy got up and headed to my car to go home. I could tell he was trying to be a good sport about getting his emotions jerked around by his buddies. He probably also felt like a real dumb-ass wearing that stop-sign-red sweater to school. To this day, I don't think Crazy has ever fully forgiven us for that practical joke.

The game against St. Augustine Deaf and Dumb High School on Friday night in St. Augustine proved to be another embarrassment for our football team. Even though we beat them 27–7, it was *how* they scored their seven points that was so humiliating.

Winning the coin toss, they elected to receive the ball. From their 22-yard line, they came out to run their first play. From my new position as defensive linebacker, I could see that they used sign language in the huddle to call their play.

At the line of scrimmage, all their players started clapping. Thinking they were clapping in respect for our team, maybe some sort of new sportsmanship routine, our players also started clapping, believing we were returning the show of sportsmanship. We found out, to our embarrassment, that the deaf players used the vibration of the clapping to count the hike signal. On the fourth clap, their quarterback took the football and ran for seventy-eight yards, scoring a touchdown while eleven dumb-ass DuPont High football players were standing and clapping for *their* team. Coach threw his clipboard into the stands out of sheer frustration with our stupidity. Well, we did win.

All day Saturday, all I could think about was my date that night with Jackie and *whatever* was going to happen sometime during the evening. I made my quick trip to Burger King to refresh my condom stash. I told Mom I was going up to the local Thrifty gas station to buy some of their inflated-price (twenty-five cents per gallon!) gasoline.

I took a long hot shower—probably should have taken a really cold one to quell my building sexual expectations. To shave the few stubbles of beard I proudly sported on my chin, I used my Gillette double-edge razor with a rusty blade that should have been changed, then splashed some "oh, shit!" stinging Mennen's After Shave on my face.

My dress for this special evening was my favorite Lacoste blue pullover shirt, tan sweater-vest, and blue slacks with penny loafers, topped by my manly letterman's jacket. I was the all-American image Jackie's parents would surely approve of in a heartbeat.

The drive to Jackie's house took only about fifteen minutes, which was a real treat and gas saver compared to the forty-five-minute trek out to Stacey's. Plus, the streets were paved and lighted all the way, quite unlike the pitch black of the drive on the pitted gravel to the Purcells'.

I hated that drive to Stacey's, but what I really detested was the drive home, especially late at night after an extended date. One night, going home tired and half-asleep, I hit the brakes on the main highway upon seeing a flashing railroad-crossing signal. I sat for several minutes in my car, stopped dead on the highway, just watching the flashing red lights. After sitting there long enough to wonder why the signal was flashing with no train in sight, I finally woke with a jerk, came to my senses, and recalled that there *was* no railroad crossing leading out to her house. *Poof*—the flashing signal light disappeared. I said to myself, "That's it, no more; I am going to kill myself driving out here and trying to drive home."

The flashing railroad-crossing experience was yet another factor that contributed to why Stacey and I split up.

As I pulled my dad's Cadillac into Jackie's driveway, it dawned on me that breaking up with Stacey had probably saved my life. I was *destined* to nod off *some* night driving home from her place, wrap myself around a tree, and come to a sudden and deadly stop. At least with Jackie, it would be hard to fall asleep on a short fifteen-minute drive home.

While waiting on Jackie to finish dressing, I made small talk with her parents about their previous week's trip to their camp. They offered me an invitation to join them the next time. I agreed, if only to get out of the house with Jackie as quickly as possible and on to *whatever*.

Jackie appeared from her bedroom in a long white dress, a wide studded black belt, and a black scarf in her hair, which provided an alluring contrast to the gossamer platinum strands. A necklace hung around her neck, but it disappeared under the neckline of her dress, so I couldn't see the pendant.

My impression of her as she joined her parents and me was that she looked unbelievable, much different than how she looked standing out in front of the school each day. I felt like I was taking a grown woman out on a date—and me looking like your basic high school jock, standing there like a real *goofus* in my letterman's jacket and penny loafers.

In my dad's Caddy, Jackie slid up next to me as if we had been going together for some time. I caught a whiff of her perfume. "Wow, what are you wearing? Smells different from anything I've ever smelled before. Expensive French perfume? Oh, and your white dress tonight—it looks familiar; have you worn it to school this year?"

I knew I was babbling, but with her sitting so close, and so fresh and feminine, I couldn't help myself.

Jackie giggled and said to me, "The perfume is something I bought today, just for tonight. It's made of exotic oils, with a musk scent. It's supposed to drive your date crazy. Do you feel crazy yet, Rob?" She smiled flirtatiously. "Oh, and the dress—I'm pretty sure you *have* seen it before."

Not expanding further on the dress, Jackie started talking about how she loved movies and was really looking forward to seeing tonight's show, *Some Like It Hot*, with Marilyn Monroe, Tony Curtis, and Jack Lemmon. Jackie blurted, "I'm a big fan of Marilyn Monroe, and I think she's much smarter than she lets on. Don't you, Rob? Don't you think Marilyn's smart, and that she's sort of pretending to be a little daffy? Playing the dumb role? She is an actress, after all."

Not wanting to disagree with Jackie, I played along. "Yeah, I think she's getting a bum rap. Hell, Joe DiMaggio and Arthur Miller, two famous Americans, married her. They wouldn't have married her if she were a bimbo."

I was thinking to myself, "Hell, she probably has the IQ of a turnip, but with a body that would stop an out-of-control, sixteen-wheel semi-truck in its tracks. Joe and Arthur didn't want to get inside her brain; they wanted to get inside her bra and panties." But I figured that wouldn't quite be what I should say on a first date, so I kept my thoughts to myself.

"Rob, you and I think alike. That's what I love about you. I want to ask you something. . . . Do you believe in the supernatural, like spirits of the dead that are still on earth, needing to finish something before departing to the beyond? Do you believe in life after death?"

"Uh, that's quite a leap, from Marilyn Monroe to life after death," I said, trying to figure out where Jackie was heading with our conversation. "Yes, I believe in God, Jesus, and heaven, if that's what you're asking. I believe there are people who die that hang around to take care of what you said, unfinished business. Some people might even have the ability to actually communicate with these spirits through a, what do you call it, a séance?"

Nodding slightly in agreement, Jackie responded, "Yes, yes, that's it, the ability to talk with spirits that are still here on earth. What if I told you I frequently communicate with my grandmother, who died in a horrible car wreck about a year ago?"

Chuckling nervously, I replied, "Well, I would say that's really spooky. How do you talk with your grandmother? Long-distance call through Bell Telephone or though a Ouija board?"

In a very serious and very sexy voice, Jackie took hold of my free hand and said, "Tarot cards. Grandma tells me what she wants me to do through the tarot cards. She told me you were a great match for me, or should I say, the cards lined up to indicate you and I would make a great couple."

"Tarot cards? What are tarot cards? Can you play poker with them?" I asked in a tone I hoped she'd hear as sincere because I truly wanted to know more.

"Tarot cards can predict the future. They've been around for hundreds of years. Some of the more important cards relate to the devil, death, the sun and the moon, strength and justice, things like that. Two of the cards are called The Fool and The Lovers. If you get the Fool card, you could be in for changes in your life. The Lovers card is for finding a new partner, a lover, a new relationship. Getting both cards means you need to be very careful in picking your partner, not to rush into a relationship."

Jackie paused for a minute, and though I never took my eyes off the road, I knew she had turned in the seat and was studying my face as she spoke.

"This weekend at the camp," she continued, "I took the tarot cards that have been in the family for almost seventy years. I asked Grandma about us, and the two cards she dealt through me were The Fool and The Lovers. So, see, we are meant for each other, but we must proceed carefully and not do anything stupid to ruin our relationship."

Jackie, somewhat winded from her dissertation on tarot cards and her grandmother, stopped talking and got real quiet and reflective. She turned to stare out the passenger-side window. Hoping to pull her out of her mood, I proclaimed, "Well, if you grandma says it, then it must be so. If she dealt the Fool and Lover cards, then we can declare to the world we are lovers, in the figurative sense."

I figured the condom in my pocket was going to have to go into deep storage. Jackie, as seductive as she was, seemed childlike in her reliance on a deck of cards to guide her through life's decisions. The Fool card told her to go slowly with her new Lover. That meant for Rollo, no sex tonight.

The movie was great; Jackie and I laughed at all the scenes everyone in the theatre thought were funny. From the very outset, Jackie curled up in her seat and put her head on my shoulder and took my hand in hers. Her hand was soft and warm, her fingers long and slender. "She'd make a good piano player," I thought. "Likely a fabulous lover, too."

The portion of my brain (an extremely large portion in any normal teenaged male) devoted to sexual fantasies visualized those warm hands on my back, stroking my neck, and digging into my shoulders in a hot, passionate embrace. My sexual-fantasy interlude was snapped when Jackie asked for our shared box of buttered popcorn and soft drink.

Jackie was into the movie and was eating up Marilyn Monroe, playing the part of Sugar Kane, a ukulele player in an all-woman band. Jackie was mesmerized by Marilyn's interaction with Lemmon and Curtis; she seemed to be studying Marilyn's mannerisms as if she wanted to imitate them and incorporate them into her own personality.

Leaning toward her, I said, "Going to go blonde and become the next Sugar Kane?"

Jackie squeezed my hand hard and leaned in my direction with her catty reply: "Only if you start looking like Tony Curtis."

After the movie, we headed back across the river to San Jose. Now I began testing the water to see what was next on our date agenda. I asked Jackie, "Want to go to the Texas Drive-In to see who's there, get something to eat?"

Staring straight ahead, as if transfixed by the headlights of oncoming cars, she said simply and straightforwardly, "It's time for the *whatever* I promised you. Do you know where the St. John's River Park is, by the DuPont estate? Go there."

My breathing shortened and I fought to not let it be too obvious as I visualized what she had planned for us. Maybe she wanted me to find a secluded area to park so we could make out, which, for a first date, would be more than what I normally would have expected. I found myself thinking, "Her grandmother and the tarot cards would be OK with us just parking. Making out would be within the boundaries of two lovers going slow, no trying to get to 'first base.'"

As we entered the park, Jackie started giving me driving directions. "Turn right here . . . turn left . . . OK, keep going straight." Then she said, "Pull over to that parking area near that big oak tree." Once parked, I started to turn toward her to lean into our very first passionate kiss, but I got a surprise when Jackie opened the passenger door and quickly got out of the car, then turned to me and said through the open door, "Come on, get out, and follow me."

Jackie started into an area of the park, somewhat lighted by a street lamp near the parking area. I followed her, wondering to myself, "Hope Jackie isn't some sort of freaky killer, luring me to a secluded park and then killing me. It could be some time before they would find my poor decomposed body."

Jackie was now down to a section of the park that opened to the river near some playground equipment. She motioned me to come to an area bordered by bushes, near the playground. Then she disappeared into the shrubbery. "OK, this is not what I had in mind for our *whatever*," I thought to myself. "I wish we were back in the front seat of my car swapping spit."

Suddenly, Jackie reappeared from the bushes with a small basket in her hands. She called to me, "Come on, scaredy-cat, I won't hurt you . . . much." Then she giggled like a little girl and beckoned me toward her.

As I approached, she opened the basket, pulled out a small blanket, and spread it on the ground. She positioned herself on the blanket, and by the time I got to her, she was taking from the basket some food containers and a thermos. "Uh, are we doing a picnic in the park, in the dark? Can't say I have ever done that before."

"Sit down," Jackie commanded me in a soft, seductive tone. "I have some surprises for you."

Once on the blanket, I looked around and saw, to my surprise, that Jackie had picked a spot with a great view of the river and Jacksonville's skyline with all its twinkling lights. Plus, there was a grassy knoll above us, so we were out of the line of sight of anyone else parking near my car. "Great spot. Did you come here earlier and hide the basket in the bushes? How did you find this place?" Now I got a little bit jealous, but tried not to let it show as I said, "Jackie, have you been here before with someone else?"

"No, silly, only with you. Something I want to do for just you . . . just us. Here, eat one of these little sweet-cakes I made this afternoon. There is a juice drink in the thermos to wash down the sweet-cake."

Taking the sweet-cake from her, I bit into it, not really knowing what to expect. The texture was soft and surprisingly sweet, like a bran muffin. There was a nutty undertone, and I questioned, "What kind of nuts are in the cake? Tastes like pecans."

"It's fragments of walnut husks and willow leaves. Try the juice drink and tell me what you think."

Picking up the thermos, I took a big gulp of what tasted a little like orange juice, but with somewhat of a bitter aftertaste. "Yuck, sorry, this is a little hard to take. What's in it, 100-proof vodka?"

Jackie looked at me directly and said, "Not quite, it's 80-proof vodka from my dad's liquor cabinet."

"Shit, man," I thought. "This girl is unbelievable. She's feeding me screwdrivers in a park in the dark of night, while we gaze at the beautiful skyline. What could be next?" I was almost scared to find out.

Well, the next surprise was a pair of finger cymbals that she put on her hand, and then I almost lost it. From the basket came a black candle, just like the one she'd been holding in my dream. She drew a matchbook from the basket, pulled a match, and lit the candle. Looking at me with her smoky gray eyes, she said, "Take another drink and relax. I've made up a little something for you."

Jackie stood up and, with one hand, took the scarf from her hair, then shook her head so the platinum waves fell freely onto her shoulders. Blood started to shoot through my "Mr. Willy" on the way to a five-gun salute.

As I took another gulp from the thermos, my whole body started to melt into the blanket, every muscle relaxing—well, *almost* every one. Jackie kicked off her shoes and was now barefoot in the grass. She began to tap the finger cymbals and hum a song. Now I was thinking, "If I see a dragon flying overhead, I'm going to crap in my pants. This is looking more and more like my dream on Monday."

Jackie began to sway, and then to dance, turning in small circles, singing to me. I couldn't understand the words. She pulled the necklace from her dress, a pendant with an image of a five-pointed star. The vodka was doing its duty, I was getting plastered, and now the whole scene became surreal.

I closed my eyes, and when I opened them again, Jackie wasn't in front of me. I turned my head quickly toward her voice. She had gone over to a swing in the nearby playground area and was swinging and singing, all the while holding her black candle, which remained lit, even though the flame flickered just the tiniest bit. The replication of the image of Jackie on the dragon flying through the air, black candle in hand, virtually floored me. I couldn't handle the déjà vu of Jackie swinging, as if she were on the fire-breathing, red-scaled dragon.

Then Jackie stopped swinging, came over to me, blew out the candle, and dropped down on top of me. She took my head in her hands and kissed me more passionately than I had ever been kissed, her tongue sliding into my mouth and dancing around my tongue. Well, with Jackie lying on top of me and giving me the most incredible French kiss, Mr. Willy exploded with joy.

Jackie pulled her tongue from my mouth, pulled back, and, looking passionately into my eyes, said in her soft, throaty voice, "*Whatever.*"

Then she laughed, got up, and started to fix herself, putting the scarf back in her hair, the pendant back in her dress, her feet back into her flat shoes. "We have to go. Put the thermos and container in the basket. Fold the blanket and put it in there, too. I'll put the basket back in the bushes and come get it tomorrow."

I could barely walk; I was intoxicated not only by the liquor but by the last forty minutes of Jackie dancing, singing, and kissing me with what must have been her patented French kiss. I swear her tongue almost touched my brainstem. With a little wobble in my legs and Mr. Willy proud but limping along with me now, I felt completely exhausted and a little woozy. Getting to the car and getting Jackie back home was almost as much a thrill as driving home from Stacey's half-asleep.

As I parked in Jackie's driveway, I said to her, "I had a dream earlier this week, and you know what? Tonight was very much like the dream. Is there something about you and your extra little powers I should know?"

"Rob, I'm like any other girl. No special powers. No magic. My family loves having fun playing pretend with their friends, doing nothing different than kids playing cowboys and Indians, cops and robbers. Nothing harmful."

Jackie winked at me and got out of the car, but leaned in and said, "Well, maybe a spell or two just to liven it up. Oh, the dream was something I cooked up while at the camp. There is one thing in the dream that was missing tonight."

Looking into those beautiful gray eyes, I had to ask, "What's missing?"

"I love you." Jackie looked long and hard at me for several seconds, then shut the car door and walked matter-of-factly into her house.

I was dumbfounded. Jackie had willed a dream that she then played out on our date. Her "I love you" put the cork in the bottle. I put the car in reverse and began to back up. Then I hit the brakes, looked back at the house, and mouthed, "I love you, too." The lights in the house went black as I made my commitment to Jackie. For just a second, I thought I saw her silhouette in the darkened window, and then she disappeared.

Tonight, the fifteen-minute drive home from Jackie's house took longer than the drive from Stacey's Ponderosa. About ten minutes from home, I pulled into the San Jose shopping center, which was closed for the night, turned off the car, and, in the dark of the center's parking lot, opened the car door and puked my guts out.

My nerves had gotten the best of me, what with the real roller-coaster emotional ride from Jackie's *whatever* surprise that replicated my earlier dream, and her admission that she had created it through a spell. On top of frayed nerves, my stomach was turning from the combination of sweet-cakes, spiked orange juice, and slimy buttered popcorn from the movies. Puking helped relieve the nausea, but my nerves were still popping like a shorted-out, sparking power-pole transformer.

I thought I loved Jackie, even with her quirky, refreshing, but scary beliefs. She was tantalizing and seductive, much different than Stacey. But I also felt a bit like a pawn in her own weird world and that of her family who thought they were witches and warlocks. I would have to decide whether Jackie's uniqueness and passion were worth the trade-off for the loss of my "self." Someday, would she and Granny play the Devil tarot card for my soul?

After a period of time sitting in the deserted parking lot, I felt a little better. I started the car and pulled out onto San Jose Boulevard and drove home. On the way, I rolled down the driver-side window to let the fresh night air punch me in the face, clearing my addled brain at least a bit. Just as I turned into my own driveway and killed the engine, I decided I would give Jackie the benefit of the doubt about her beliefs. But in a few months, if I still felt like I was being used for her amusement, I would deal our relationship the Death card from my own deck of cards.

Chapter 9

Fall

*T*he fall of 1959, all the way up until Christmas, my personal life seemed to parallel many history-making events. On October 2, 1959, CBS-TV launched a trend-setting show, Rod Serling's *The Twilight Zone*. The weekly, half-hour show told fictional stories of supernatural, sci-fi events and how they impacted the lives of those caught unaware.

Usually the show's storyline featured how some poor slob's life was suddenly turned upside down by some unexplainable and eldritch happening. The whole point of the show was to scare the living crap out of the viewer, with the notion that the same sort of unexplained event could befall them. Viewers often had nightmares in which some type of strange tragedy suddenly descended upon them with a vengeance.

My dates with Jackie could have played as shows for *The Twilight Zone's* entire season. With each passing week, our outings became more surreal and unexplainable. During a bye week on our football schedule in October, my trip to Jackie's parents' fishing camp fulfilled my obligation to their invitation to spend a weekend there with Jackie. The events during that trip looked like good old Rod Serling himself had scripted everything; it turned out to be a real sci-fi–like happening.

Jackie's parents' fishing camp was about forty miles south of Jacksonville, on about two acres on the river, with a small house about fifty feet from the water's edge. A beat-up sixteen-foot aluminum fishing boat with an outboard engine, secured to an aging dock, completed the scene. After all, what fishing camp would be complete without a rugged old dock and a run-down boat?

The camp was not exactly easy to get to, about a mile off the main highway down a dusty bumpy-ass dirt road that rapidly became a *muddy* bumpy-ass dirt road with the slightest rain. At night there were no lights, just the moon to help light the road, and out in the Florida dark, it was easy to imagine that all kinds of eerie things were crouching just beyond the headlight beams.

That Friday night, I met Jackie at her house and she rode with me, following her parents to the camp. In the car, we talked about all the things two teenagers who were going together would talk about: mostly what our friends were doing, who was dating whom, which couples had broken up, the teachers we hated, and the football games we had lost.

I purposely stayed away from talking about tarot cards, her dead grandmother, and anything to do with witches and warlocks. Even with Halloween coming up, I didn't have the balls to ask Jackie what she was going to dress up as for our high school Halloween dance, fearing she would say, "Why, a witch, naturally; what else?" My suggestion to Jackie would have been to go 180 degrees in the other direction and go as a Catholic nun, complete with habit and rosary beads. Of course, that would never happen and I knew it, so I just tried to avoid the subject as best I could.

At the camp, I was shown to a small guest room where I would be sleeping. Jackie had a second bedroom, and her parents took the third; we all shared one bathroom. Conversation with her family was fairly normal, the kind of small talk that was polite at the time. Our topics were pretty much limited to my family, where I was planning to go to college, and then the obvious—did I like fishing, had I ever been bass fishing.

I told them my family had a boat and we went deep-sea fishing off Jacksonville Beach, or sometimes fished in the Intracoastal Canal, but that I had never been bass fishing. Jackie's dad, Bill White, said he would wake me early so we could go and see if we could catch something. I said, "Great, see you in the morning," and nodded goodnight to Jackie. I was pretty sure that kissing her in front of her parents would not be a good idea, and I toddled off to my little bedroom.

I woke suddenly about 2:30 a.m. to what I thought was rustling in the bushes outside my window, and for some reason all my senses were on full alert. I slowly moved to the window to peek out. There, in the light of the full moon, were good old Bill, his wife Betty, and Jackie, in dark-hooded smocks holding lit candles and chanting some unintelligible garble.

Somehow I didn't think Bill was casting a spell that would cause us to catch our limit of bass in the morning. As I watched, barely breathing, they suddenly stopped chanting and looked directly toward my window. I ducked below the window sill like someone had been pointing a gun at me, hoping like hell they hadn't seen me. I crawled on the floor back to bed, slid back in, and almost covered my head like a scared toddler before I caught myself at it. I did know that I didn't want them to see my shadow moving around in the room since I didn't want them to know I had been watching their little middle-of-the-night candlelight marshmallow roast.

The next morning at 5:00 found Bill rapping on my door, announcing, "Early bird gets the worm," which had nothing to do with fishing, but I guess it was the only cliché he could think of after being up so late playing warlock. The two of us left the house with coffee and a doughnut each and went down to the dock, Jackie and her mom still asleep.

Bill and I fished for an hour or so. He caught a couple of nice bass, and I managed to catch a large weeping-willow tree and a neighboring dock with my highly inaccurate casting. Finally, I hooked a small bass that we had to throw back in, which was understandable since the lure I was using was almost as big as the fish that had bitten it.

After about two hours of rod-and-reel fishing, Bill said he wanted to do some bow fishing for catfish. Reaching into a bag he had stowed in the front of the boat, Bill pulled out a crossbow and several menacing-looking arrows with fishing line attached. With the outboard engine off and the boat just drifting, Bill stood like a Viking explorer in the bow with his crossbow and, within a few moments, let fly an arrow into the water. With the reel attached to the crossbow, Bill reeled in his fish, an act that was really more like dragging in a waterlogged stick than catching a fish. I easily understood why when I saw that the catfish he pulled over the side of the boat had been impaled through the head by the barbed arrow.

Even though an arrow through the eye *should* convince even the most stubborn catfish that he is, in fact, very, very dead, this one was still flopping around a bit until Bill finished the convincing with a blow of a ball-peen hammer. Bill grinned and matter-of-factly yanked the arrow free, leaving the eyeball stuck on the barb.

Bill was still grinning when he looked at me and said laughingly, "Fun way to catch fish. Want to shoot one yourself? It's a real charge."

"No, thanks, Bill, I'll let you do the bow fishing. I'd probably shoot myself in the foot and there'd go my football career."

Bill looked at me with his piercing black eyes and said, "Don't like killing things, do you?"

I couldn't decide whether to pee in my pants or throw up in the boat, because at that second, the impression I got of the father of my girlfriend was of a very, very scary guy. I wondered if he would shoot *me* with that crossbow contraption, put an arrow through my eye, and hit me in the head with his hammer.

I answered him in what I hoped would be a satisfactory amount of false bravado. "Naw, doesn't bother me. Hell, my dad and I shoot sharks with a .357 Smith and Wesson when we go fishing."

Old Bill's eyes lit up on hearing that, and he replied with an even bigger grin, "Must create a real feeding frenzy, other sharks attacking the one shot and all that blood. Must be fun to watch?"

"Yeah, we get a charge out of it, my dad and me." Truth was that we had never shot a shark with Dad's gun, especially since we couldn't hit the broad side of a barn shooting that cannon. Why waste .357 bullets on a pea-brain shark?

The whole experience with Jackie's dad that day shooting catfish and beating them to death with a hammer, on top of the dancing in the moonlight I had witnessed the night before, pretty well did it for me and my future with Jackie. That night, she and I went to a B movie in town, something about a flatfoot detective searching for a one-armed bank robber. On the way back to the camp, we stopped and parked on the dirt road and made out for a while. Clearly, the passion wasn't there as it had been on our earlier dates.

Jackie asked me if I felt OK. Of course, I told her a huge lie: "No, I think getting up at 5:00 and the coffee and doughnuts and the smell of fish sort of did me in today. I'm sorry I'm a bum date tonight."

Jackie just looked at me without saying anything. I could tell the

Death card for our relationship was moving toward the top of both of our decks. After a long, awkward silence (the kind that always precedes such things), Jackie said, "Let's take a little break from dating so much and sort of recharge our batteries. I really love you and don't want to lose you by being together too much. What do they say, absence makes the heart grow fonder?"

"Yeah, that's a good idea," I replied, doing everything in my power to keep any sound of relief from my voice. "A little break is good. We can go to the Halloween dance next week with some of my buddies; Star's looking to double-date."

Jackie seemed to perk up at that suggestion. I asked her a question I had been putting off for too long: "What are you going to the dance as?"

Those sultry eyes sparkled in the moonlight and she almost giggled as she said, "I was thinking of the usual Halloween costume, a witch maybe. Then I thought, maybe it would be funny to go to the dance as a nun. Would you like that, Rob?"

"Shit, she read my mind, just like the first day I met her," I thought. "Probably reading it now, too." But I answered her the best I could: "Hey, that would be funny; everyone will get a kick out of that."

As it turned out, Jackie did go to the Halloween dance as a nun, and I went as a mummy wrapped head to toe in gauze. I've never kissed a nun before or since, so kissing Jackie that night was a little strange. Plus, the gauze wrap around my head kept getting in my mouth and giving me the worst case of "cotton mouth" (literally!) that I've ever had to this day.

The first week of November, I found I had something in common with the auto industry, and the parallel continued. The Ford Motor Company pulled the plug on its controversial Edsel car line, which was destined to be a colossal failure from the car's inception. That same week my relationship with Jackie, which had also been destined for failure since the beginning, ended just as suddenly.

At school the week after Halloween, I opened my locker to find that Jackie had left me a "Dear John" letter, along with my framed "To the One I Love" photo and my class ring. Her letter was short and sweet: "Dear Rob, I guess both of us knew that this day would come. I love you so much, but I must find someone who shares my spirit and beliefs. You will always

114

be in my heart. Good luck in your athletics. Maybe someday I'll see you in the Olympics. Love, Jackie."

That same day, I dropped the dragon pendant and chain in her locker—no note. Why bother? What would I say? "Guess our love wasn't really in the *cards*"? "I can't hold a *candle* to your level of caring and love"? "*Whatever* you want from me I couldn't give back to you"? As I shut her locker, I put my hand on the door and whispered, "Adiós, my beautiful Kim Novak. It was great while it lasted."

Through the grapevine the next week, I heard that Jackie was going out with some hotshot junior named Reginald Bradley III, whose parents had become rich off their business, a major urinal-production company. They lived in a big house on the river with a urinal, word had it, in each bathroom. Reginald's mother must have detested seeing a toilet seat up, so she had her company install their urinals in all her bathrooms and, *voilà!*, pisser problem solved, no muss, no fuss. I imagine when you can afford a urinal in each bathroom, you can afford someone to clean them, too.

As I thought about Reginald, I hoped he loved shooting catfish through the head with a steel-tipped arrow and then bashing their brains in with a ball-peen hammer. Or better yet, I hoped Reginald would love standing out in the dark in the middle of the night, holding a wax-dripping candle in a fake monk's habit and chanting weird Celtic songs. Most of all, I hoped he would enjoy talking to Jackie's dead grandmother through a deck of tarot cards while sipping a steamy cup of freshly made witch's brew. If urinal boy was the type of guy to like those things, I figured he'd be a perfect fit for Jackie, my Kim Novak, and her wacky fun-loving little family coven.

I stopped by Spiff's house later that night to talk about Jackie putting the dumps on me. Among all the Mag 6, Spiff was the best listener, always sympathetic to your side of the argument or situation. Though Baptist in his religious convictions, Spiff really should have been a priest. After listening to your confessions of the heart and your stories (sometimes outright exaggerations, if not lies) of front-seat sexual escapades, Spiff would forgive you, bless you, or provide you with an astounding amount of moral support—and sometimes all three at once.

That night after getting Jackie's "Dear John" letter, I found Spiff and

Oz holed up in Spiff's room, playing a wild prank on unsuspecting persons randomly picked from the Jacksonville Southern Bell Telephone book.

Oz was arbitrarily calling some poor schmuck he had picked as a mark from the phone book and starting a conversation: "Hello, this is William Wilson from the law firm of Wilson and Wilson Attorneys, calling from our new offices in the Prudential Building. Is this Mr.—?" (or Mrs., and he'd insert a name from the phone book).

After getting a positive answer, Oz would continue: "I am very sorry to have to call you with some bad news, but your estranged aunt Cora May Whittaker in Rhodesia, Africa, died last month and named your family in her will. Our law firm represents Ms. Whittaker's estate and distribution of her money and assets. Do you know Cora May Whittaker?"

Normally, the mark would pause and roll around in their brain what they had just heard, especially "named your family in her will." "If I say no," the mark was surely thinking, "it might mean, there goes millions of dollars; if I say yes, maybe the lawyer will quiz me about what I knew about Cora May Whittaker, and I could lose the millions of dollars." So the mark usually just played dumb: "Well, I sort of remember my dad talking about his estranged Aunt Cora, but Dad passed years ago, so we haven't heard anything about Cora for some time." Bingo, the hook was set!

Oz would grin and continue with a surprising amount of feigned sincerity: "So, you *do* remember your dad talking about his estranged aunt Cora May Whittaker?"

"Yeah, there was some mention of her. Could you tell me what happened to Cora?" would be the general direction of the reply.

"Yes, Ms. Whittaker was a spinster, no family, no offspring, so after much research, it appears your father was her only direct heir, but with your father gone—and let me offer my condolences—you would be the next in line for the inheritance."

Usually, there would be a long pause on the phone while the mark took in "next in line for the inheritance."

The mark would say, "Thank you for your sympathy on my dad's death. What is the inheritance you are talking about?"

Oz would roll his eyes comically as the hook sank deeper into the mark's unsuspecting jaw.

"Unfortunately, we cannot discuss this any further on the phone due to the sensitivity of the matter. You will have to come to our offices to verify who you are and then discuss Ms. Whittaker's estate in Rhodesia. Are you familiar with Rhodesia and its wealth of copper mines?"

Oz would put his hands over the phone and laughingly make some smart-ass comment at this point, usually something like, "This dumb-ass couldn't find Rhodesia on a map even if I stuck a blue pin in it and told him to look for the pin." Spiff never failed to crack up at Oz's side comments.

The mark would usually think for a long minute before replying slowly, "Yes, our globe in our living room has Rhodesia. It is a long way away. Would we have to travel there to claim the inheritance?"

Oz would laugh as if he were Lawyer Wilson. "No, no, fortunately, Ms Whittaker cashed out her copper mine holdings before she died. Everything she owned is in cash in the estate. Can you come to our offices next week to settle the estate?"

The mark would almost always nearly jump through the phone to reply, "Can't we meet tomorrow morning?"

Oz reeled them in with, "We're busy in the morning. How about tomorrow at 4:00 p.m. sharp?" Oz would then give the mark a bogus suite number in the Prudential Building and ask for a general physical description so he could tell the receptionist to keep an eye out for them when they arrived for their appointment.

The next day after school, Spiff and Oz would be strategically positioned outside the Prudential Building, where they could identify the mark from the description as he or she rushed to find the bogus suite and get their inheritance money. Within thirty minutes, the mark would be back in front of the Prudential, shaking their head because the office address was, of course, not in the Prudential Building, or any other building in Jacksonville. Slowly, the mark would realize that a cruel practical joke had been played on them and their greed, for someone pretending to be an unknown relative had gotten the best of them.

From a distance and hidden from the mark's view, Spiff and Oz would watch the mark's interactions play out with his or her other family members. Usually, the mark left the Prudential Building laughing, understanding they had been had. Some of the marks were really pissed off and probably called the Jacksonville police to complain, but the technology for tracing phone calls wasn't great in 1959, so no cops came knocking on Spiff's door. Plus, the mark was never out any money, except the price of gas to drive to the Prudential Building to cash in on a nonexistent Cora May Whittaker's estate.

Cora May Whittaker, a great Rhodesian copper-mine heiress, and benefactor to many unwitting Jacksonville citizens. God rest her soul.

The week of Thanksgiving, the senior girls played the junior girls in DuPont's traditional Buttons and Bows touch football game. Crazy and Lily worked with the senior girls, assigned them positions, and rehearsed four or five basic plays. The best play was a reverse that was a real sucker play. One of the faster senior girls, Susie Prince, was hiked the football and took off running like a bat out of hell to the right side of the field. All the junior girls would haul ass to the right side of the field, trying to catch her. Susie would then hand off the ball to another fast senior, Gail Gross, who would shag ass to the left side of the field and cut up to the goal line. The reverse was a slam-dunk scoring play, and the senior girls won by a lopsided score, 48–0 or something like that.

The highlight of the Buttons and Bows game was when Linda Wills, a ballet dancer in the making, punted the ball from around the 20-yard line. Linda got her ballet-trained leg into the ball, it sailed over the head of the junior girl receiver to the 50-yard line, then bounced end over end to the 10-yard line—a 70-yard kick.

Somehow, when the local paper reviewed the game, and the headline was, "70-Yard Punt by Senior." That got picked up by the wire services, and the next week, a letter from Notre Dame came to the Athletic Director inquiring about the school's punter and "his" statistics. I bet Linda Wills still has that letter from Notre Dame framed and hanging in her den, wherever she lives. Too bad the Irish didn't offer her a scholarship. "Touchdown Jesus" would have been proud of the college.

Our own football team finished the season on a down note. On Thanksgiving Day, we played a new local high school and got our butts kicked. I think collectively our team was really more interested in eating turkey and stuffing than in scoring touchdowns. Our competitor was obviously more interested in stuffing a football up our collective ass and making us *look* like turkeys, which they did with almost military speed and efficiency.

They clearly had a different perspective on turkey and stuffing than we did. Our claim to a successful season centered on the fact that we had won one more game than last year's team, which was enough to make Coach happy, as he had predicted improvement from the opening pep rally. By the next year he had taken a vice-principal job at an out-of-state middle school. If the middle school had a midget football team, Coach would probably have a losing season coaching them, too. Winners win, losers lose; life never changes, even for football coaches.

Chapter 10

Christmas

*D*ecember has always been a real emotional roller-coaster month for me, as it is for many people. While I enjoy the *good* about Christmas, I try to tuck whatever *bad* emotions I happen to be experiencing at the moment in a spot in the back of my mind which I try to flush out daily. I really do love the holiday season, both for its religious meaning and for the fun of the decorations and gifts and the fellowship with friends and family. This Christmas was even more fun than usual because I was running with my Mag 6 buddies and experiencing the beginning of a new love interest, a girl named Ginny.

It was Saturday, December 12, when I went to a Christmas party at the home of Mary Ramus, who happened to live on the same block I did, which was great because it was easy to just walk a few houses down and join the festivities. Mary Ramus, a sophomore, had asked me to the Christmas party she threw every year for a few of her friends.

Of the rest of the Mag 6 gang, only Lily was invited, since his sister Sarah was friends with Mary and Lily had to drive Sarah to the party. Lily and I parked ourselves in a corner and swapped stories about the antics of our other Mag 6 buddies. At some point, I went into the kitchen to get a fresh soft drink. (Mary's parents totally forbade beer in the house, so teeth-rotting soft drinks were the beverage of the night.)

On the way back to my place in the corner, I accidentally bumped into a couple standing in the kitchen doorway. "Sorry," I said as I narrowly missed dousing them both with my drink. Then I simply continued across the room without another word, not paying much attention to either of them. I told Lily, "I almost walked over a couple over there by the kitchen," and fate struck as I glanced back in their direction.

At that second glance into the kitchen, I locked eyes with the girl I had bumped into, and it was like lightning struck us both. It was like one of those scenes from a movie where, in a split second, I envisioned the two of us dating, attending law school, both passing the law exam, getting married, having children, running a successful law firm, becoming grandparents, and growing old together.

They say people who are dying see their life pass before them. I'm not sure if that means their entire life or snippets of the best parts of their life, but whatever it is they visualize, it supposedly happens instantaneously. Well, that's pretty much what I experienced when Ginny and I looked at each other. I don't know if she experienced the same movie-reel highlights, but she must have experienced something, judging from the way she smiled at me. It was as if she also had caught an image of us together in our old age, sharing the experience of rocking on the front porch of life.

Ginny's date caught the two of us doing the eye-contact, falling-for-each-other thing and instinctively moved between us to cut off the electric flow of emotions. I turned to Lily and said, "I'm in love. Who's that girl?"

Lily followed my gaze and answered, "I think her name's Ginny Vaughn. My sister would know; do you want me to ask her?"

"Yeah, find out who she is. I want to call her and ask her out before someone else scoops her up. I wonder why I never saw her in school, but then, I guess I probably haven't been paying too much attention to anyone else, what with Jackie in my face for the last four months."

In the 1950s version of social networking, I got Ginny's phone number from Lily, who got it from his sister, and the next day, Sunday, I called her. "Hi, is Ginny home? This is Robert Strand; I am a friend of Sarah Smith's brother. Sarah gave me this number for Ginny."

After letting me babble for what seemed like several minutes, Ginny's mother said, "I'm sorry, Ginny's at the library for the day, working on a writing assignment for school. She won't be home till dinner time, and we plan to go to evening services at our church. You'll have to call again sometime. Sorry. Goodbye."

Sitting there holding the dead phone receiver, I pondered things a bit. "Well, my plans for rocking together in our old age just got set back by a writing assignment. I'll just have to run her down in school on Monday and ask her for a date. Her mother said they are going to an evening service; they must be a religious family. That's great. No need to worry about Ginny and her parents dancing around in the moonlight in the middle of the night, with black candles and monk-like smocks. I like that, finally a *normal* family after all the nuts."

When I finally ran into Ginny in the school hallway the next day, I made a smooth opening move with the brilliant line, "Hi, remember me from Mary's party? I'm the guy that ran into you in the kitchen?" As soon as the words left my mouth, I was thinking to myself, "Really dumb opening line, Rollo. You sound like a nerd looking for a date."

Ginny answered in a very straightforward fashion, which I soon learned was her style—direct, to the point, and no bullshit. "Yes. It's kind of hard to forget some bull in a china shop running over you in his quest for a bottle of soda pop. It was like you had never had a soda in your life."

I was about to retort, "Look, sister, I'm sorry I bumped into your sweet ass. I was thirsty and the hostess only had gut-rotting sodas instead of the real thing. So shove it," when she looked at me and continued, "You called Sunday. I presume your intention was to ask me out. How about this Saturday night? We can go to the Christmas pageant at our church with my parents?"

I quickly thought over Ginny's offer. "Hmmm, that's pretty direct. A first date with her parents to go to church to celebrate Christ's birthday. Yeah, I'd like that. I need a big change in my love life. Maybe this one has no bitchy mother or kill-crazy dad, a girl without any issues."

"Ginny," I answered with a genuine smile, "I'd love to go to church with you and your parents on our first date. Thanks for the invitation." My assumption was that she understood there would definitely be a second date.

"We're on," she answered immediately. "Come by the house around 6:00. We can ride with Mom and Dad." She penciled her address on a sheet of paper, and I quickly noted that her house was on the route I drove each school day to pick up the Mag 6. Every day I had been driving past her house and never knew she even lived there. Man, I had been wasting time with Jackie.

During the week, the Mag 6 decided that on Saturday we'd go to JCPenney to buy some Christmas gifts—or at least that was our excuse. We actually wanted to have a group photo made with Santa Claus and whisper in his ear what we wanted for Christmas. As seniors in high school, we were well aware who the real Santa Claus was, but just to cover our bases, we decided to tell JCPenney's Santa Claus all about our Christmas wish lists anyway. And why not? Nothing wrong with a little added insurance, is there?

That day at the department store, some of us got on the escalator for the second floor, looking for Santa. Then when we got to the second floor, we discovered he was actually on the first floor, so we immediately started back down the parallel escalator. Crazy and Star were coming up the other one, and I yelled to them to come back downstairs since that was where Santa's North Pole Shop and photographer were located.

For some unexplained reason, Crazy leaned over the handrail of the up escalator and started giving us his "Chee-vee-vee" routine. While entertaining us with his antics, Crazy failed to notice that his head was about to meet the second floor. When it did, Crazy almost decapitated himself. We watched in horror as he was pulled off his feet and fell back down the escalator. Crazy disappeared below the escalator railing so we couldn't see him for several seconds, and then suddenly appeared back on his feet, flashing a big embarrassed grin and yelling, "Whoa, I'm OK, I'm OK, that was close. See you on the first floor at Santa's shop."

The JCPenney Santa Claus was what you'd expect, a rent-a-Santa in a cheap Santa outfit, fake white beard and hair, something left over from Halloween from a monk or pirate or Gabby Hayes cowboy outfit. The instant he spotted the six of us big teenagers standing in line to have their photo made with Santa, you could see his brain working as he tried to decide whether to leave early for lunch and just let the photo elves deal with us. My eye contact with him was pretty clear: "Don't even think about bailing on us, Santa."

We all gathered around him and had our group photo made. Then each of us got an individual photo, complete with a gift-card envelope for an extra twenty-five cents. I gave my Santa photo to my mother for Christmas; she kept it in her family photo album till she passed away at the age of ninety. Mom said it was one of her favorite photos of me. Dad just shook his head in disbelief and probably wondered how his son, about to graduate from high school and go to a major university, could end up on Santa's lap at JCPenney.

On Saturday night, my first date with Ginny was just "nice," and I mean that in the nicest possible way—*nice* dinner, *nice* conversation with the parents, *nice* Christmas pageant, *nice* ice cream at the coffee shop afterward, and a *nice* friendly handshake from Ginny and her dad as I left her house and went home. I had never had a "nice" date, ever. There had always been some wrinkle to the date, some trauma: mother hates me, daughter lives in the third dimension, dad's a sportsman who loves killing God's creatures with a 12-gauge shotgun or a crossbow and steel-tipped arrows. In fact, Ginny's dad was a *nice*, friendly, 8-to-5 civil servant who subscribed to *Life* and *National Geographic* magazines, not even a sports magazine of trophy-killed fish, birds, deer, or mountain lions in the house. And her mom was very pleasant to me, too.

When I didn't hear anything on Sunday, I was tempted to give up on the presumed future mother of my children. But then Ginny called me on Monday, the first day of Christmas vacation, to tell me thanks for the date. She said she really enjoyed going out with me, and could we do so again soon? I told her that a few of my friends were going camping for a couple of days on our family boat, and then it would be Christmas, so maybe the weekend after Christmas we could go out? Ginny agreed, and we set a date for the next Saturday. She wished me a merry Christmas, I returned the good wishes, and we simply ended the call with no further ado.

"Boring, boring, boring. This Ginny is going to be b-o-r-i-n-g!" was my immediate thought. Boy, I later found out how wrong that assumption was, as beneath that egghead, straightforward, straight-laced demeanor was a young woman full of pent-up p-a-s-s-i-o-n! She gave me hope that my condom stash might be able to come out of deep storage in a shoe box on the top shelf of my closet under an old pair of tennis shoes. (I sure prayed my mother would never take the smelly tennis shoes out of the shoe box to discover what was hidden underneath, as she would surely be very disappointed in her son's moral intentions with the girls he was dating. But what can I say; I was a normal teenager, after all.)

On Tuesday, Oz, Star, and I set out on our overnight camping trip on the family boat out on the St. John's River. We told our parents we would be back on Wednesday afternoon, the day before Christmas Eve and my family's traditional day to attend Christmas church. Star, being Jewish, didn't care so much about the Christmas thing and church; he would have been happy to stay out camping for days.

On the way to the boat launch on the river, we made the split-second decision to change our destination. We did a 180-degree turn on the highway, choosing the Intracoastal Canal for our camping trip instead—our first mistake. And we made the change in destination without telling any of our parents, which turned out to be our second mistake.

For those not familiar with the area, the Intracoastal Canal or Intracoastal Waterway is a three-thousand-mile network of waterways and canals that are partly manmade and partly natural. The whole waterway runs along the Eastern seaboard so that ships and boats can make the journey north or south without risking the hazards of the open seas.

Often, when we were riding on the Canal, we saw luxurious yachts with New York and New Jersey markings going south toward Miami. With a zillion inlets, the canal is a great place to find a secluded spot for camping, but it does have the major drawback of being just a few miles from the ocean. This means that any storms that churn up the ocean have a similar effect on a boat on the canal. Unfortunately, we learned this major drawback the hard way that Christmas week as, unknown to us, a major gale was racing up the coast heading straight toward us novice boatmen.

On the canal, the water was at first as smooth as silk as we motored south toward a spot marked on our waterway map as Pine Island. The island lay just ten miles from where we had launched; we thought this would be close enough to get back home in a couple of days, yet far enough to provide a spirit of adventure. On the ride out, Star begged to take the wheel. He wanted the prestige of waving to the boats anchored along the shore for a little fishing. Star wanted everyone to see him as Captain of the *Miss Marian*, not just a deck hand manning the ropes.

I couldn't help but tease him. "Hey, Star, take off your yarmulke and put on my dad's captain hat. Not many Jewish sea captains in this area."

"Stuff it, Rollo. Someday I'll own a yacht five times the size of this tug boat," Star shot back. "Besides, I don't have my yarmulke with me."

"You should've brought it along to cover that bald spot you're already getting. Looking a little more like your dad every day, bald as a billiard ball," I laughed. There was some truth to it; Star's dad had only fuzz for hair. Star knew that someday he'd look in the bathroom mirror and see the spitting image of his bald dad.

About a mile from Pine Island, the wind started to pick up and the water began to get some real chop to it. By the time we had turned the last bend and had the island in sight, a cross-wind was really blowing, making it difficult to navigate the water. The gale had come upon us without any warning.

Oz looked at me and I looked at Star, who was still behind the wheel, and collectively we said, "We are in deep shit. Got to get off the canal and find shelter." We made for the island very slowly to buffer the churning canal water and not hit anything, like the tree limbs and other flotsam that the winds had already snagged and dropped into the canal.

At the island, we pulled around to the lee (a smart-ass nautical term for "sheltered from the wind") side of the island and almost out of sight of the canal. That's when the boat stopped—I mean, literally stopped dead in the water—as we hit an unmarked sandbar. Now, with the winds really howling, we threw the anchors out the front and the back of the boat so as not to get blown into the island's rocky shoreline and rip open *Miss Marian's* hull, leaving us all in for a rough swim. By now, a cold, pelting rain had also started and we were drenched, so we jumped down into the cabin to dry off and find some warmer clothes.

"OK, now we are really stuck. That sandbar should've been on the map," I griped. "No one can see us from the canal. How in the hell are we going to get out of here?" I was worried not only about our well-being, but about the boat as well. I could visualize the *Miss Marian*, my dad's pride and joy, crushed against the rocks, and me showing up with just the only salvageable piece, the boat's hull where its name was etched, saying, "Oops, sorry, Dad, here's your boat back."

I looked in the cabin for some flares, which I had seen my dad put in one day in case of some emergency. I reckoned our present situation was rapidly escalating to a red-alert emergency. I finally found three bright orange flares—in a box marked "FLARES," which, for some reason, I hadn't seen the first four times I looked.

I turned to Oz and Star and said, "We're in luck, we've got flares. I can stand on the top of the cabin and, when a ship goes by, light this sucker, and maybe they will see us and offer help."

Oz looked at me as if I had lost my mind in the peril we were in. "Uh, Rollo, shouldn't we wait till the gale stops? What if they don't see the smoke from the flare? We only have three to use to call for help."

"Look, Oz, we may not be able to use any of these flares if the anchors don't hold and we end up on the rocks. I don't want some coroner looking at my dead body with the unused flares still in my hand and saying, 'Wonder why the dumb shit didn't fire them off for help.'"

I went outside the cabin into the storm and was immediately soaked again to my skin. It was cold, penetrating rain, and it stung my face like a thousand needles punching into me all at once. I climbed to the top of the cabin, which exposed me even more to the elements, while Oz and Star stood partially sheltered on the back deck, looking up at me. It was twilight, and I guessed we only had another ten or twenty minutes before it would be pitch black.

I had no more than gotten to the top of the cabin when what should appear coming down the canal but a sleek, mammoth luxury yacht. I yelled to Oz and Star that we were in luck, there was a yacht on the canal. I took a flare, held it away from my body, and, pointing it straight into the wind, I pulled the ignition string. A billow of orange smoke poured out, but not toward the canal where someone on the yacht would see it. Instead, due to the vagaries of nature, the wind shifted, and the smoke blew directly into my face, up my nose, in my eyes, and onto my wet hair.

The wind-driven smoke proceeded down onto the deck area where Oz and Star were standing, and, like me, they were soon covered with its sulfurous stench. We all began coughing. With orange residue all over me, I looked more like a giant pumpkin fit for Halloween than a kid out for a pre-Christmas cruise.

"Throw the damn thing in the water before if kills us!" yelled Star.

I threw the flare into the water and watched it continue to billow smoke as it floated away. I looked toward the canal to see if anyone on the yacht had seen our smoke. Even at the distance we were from the main canal, and tucked in behind the island, I could see its main cabin. I could see through the windows that the lights were ablaze and three absolutely gorgeous women were standing inside, champagne glasses in hand, totally engrossed in conversation with some short, fat, old man who appeared to be the center of their attention.

The captain of the yacht, presumably high above in the wheelhouse, had apparently not seen the orange smoke. Even if he had, I wondered if the old geezer below would have allowed him to stop the yacht and thereby interrupt his tête-à-tête with the three lovelies.

The large yacht could maneuver easily through the gale, which, by contrast, had shoved the *Miss Marian* around like a rubber ducky in a draining bathtub. As the yacht passed Pine Island and continued south, I shot the geezer and the invisible captain the middle finger. The girls were too cute to get "the bird" for just being along for the ride.

I was soon back in the cabin, wiping the smell of sulfur smoke off my face and out of my hair. I looked at Oz and Star, who were doing the same, and said laughingly, "Well, that was a lot of fun. Anyone want to give it a go with the next passing ship?"

Star looked at me and said seriously, "Put the flares away. Let's just hunker down till this storm passes. By the way, where is the ship-to-shore radio? Did you bring it? We can call for help, call the Coast Guard."

"Uh, know that box in the back of the car that I asked you to bring when we were loading the boat at the launch?" I said, looking at Star.

"Yeah, what about it?" he replied before realization dawned on his face.

"Ship-to-shore radio is in the box," I stated flatly. "I guess you forgot to take it out of the car in your hurry to get on the boat and put on the captain's hat. Good going, asshole." I was pissed.

"Look, you should have thought to hook it up before we left the dock. I was helping Oz load the beer and sandwiches and the fishing gear. It's your boat; you're a bigger asshole than I am." Now Star was pissed at me for jumping on him.

"OK, guys, cool off. We'll get through this without the radio," said Oz. "Even if we had the radio, who are we going to call? Mom? Dad? Scare the shit out of them a couple of days before Christmas? They'd be pissed we came out here on the canal instead of going on the river, where we probably wouldn't have caught the teeth of this gale. Maybe a miracle will happen, someone will help us."

"In your wet dreams, Oz," said Star. "No one's going to find us behind this island."

"Look, let's drink a few beers and relax. We're not going anywhere," I said, trying to find some courage and calm in the midst of our situation.

After beers and a round of friendly kidding with each other, we decided that in the spirit of Christmas and Hanukah, we would give each other a gift. Later that night, I gave Star a toilet paper–wrapped, rusty pocket knife I had in the bottom of our boat's fishing-gear box. Star gave Oz his snot-caked handkerchief wrapped in one of our sandwich bags. Oz gave a gift that was more traditional: He crushed an empty beer can flat, tied some fishing line through the tab, and told me it was a Christmas tree ornament. It was wrapped in an extra pair of underwear he had brought along. While we got a kick out of the silly gift-giving, the symbolism of giving something that belongs to you to your friends wasn't lost on us. That's probably why we are such great friends, even today.

Sleeping was almost impossible. The howling wind didn't let up much, and the boat shuddered and creaked with the harder gusts. I went out once during the middle of the night to make sure the anchors were still holding, and the water was so shallow that you could almost see the sandbar underneath the boat. I didn't stay out of the cabin very long as it was cold and wet and there wasn't a damn thing I could do about getting us unstuck.

By dawn, the rain had decreased to a steady drizzle and the wind had finally almost quit. Lying in the cabin bunk beds, the three of us wondered if our parents were worried about us being out on the river in the gale. Maybe they had called the Coast Guard when we didn't answer the ship-to-shore radio, except the Coast Guard would be looking for us on the river, not here. We started to verbally kick our asses for the dumb decision to come to the canal. Three hotshot teenagers were each saying to ourselves, almost literally, "I want my mommy. I want to go home."

Then it happened—the miracle! We could feel the boat moving! The three of us leaped out of the cabin to discover that the boat had somehow been dislodged from the sandbar and was now a good thirty yards from the island, anchors hanging straight down in the deep channel. Instantaneously, we all screamed with joy. "Thank you, God!" I yelled. We pulled up the anchors, fired up the outboards, and quickly got back into the Intracoastal Canal, and back to the boat launch facility where I had parked with the boat trailer.

On the way home, boat in tow, we were quiet. We knew we had dodged a huge bullet, surviving a major, life-threatening gale in our little cabin cruiser. I finally very carefully backed the *Miss Marian* into its usual spot in the driveway, with Star and Oz directing me. They had parked their cars at my house, so, thankfully, I didn't have to take anyone home. The afternoon was now sunny but still cool, and we stood in the driveway, looking at each other without saying a word. Then I said, "Merry Christmas, Oz. Happy Hanukah, Star."

"Yeah, Merry Christmas, Rollo," Oz and Star said in unison. Then they turned and walked to their cars, and left.

I went into the house, expecting to see my parents sitting at the kitchen table on the phone to the Coast Guard, local police, or anyone who might be able to find us. Instead, Mom was in the kitchen doing some Christmas baking, Dad was back in his workroom starting on a new painting, and my sister was in her room, door shut, doing whatever sisters do in their room with the door shut.

Mom looked at me and said, "Clean up, Robert; we're going to have an early dinner and go to church for their Christmas pageant." Not even a question as to "How was your camping trip? Did you have a good time?" Nothing, *nada*. Such was a conversation with Mom.

Standing in the family room, in the warmth of the house, overwhelmed by the intertwining smells of the Christmas tree and the pumpkin pie Mom was baking, I wanted to cry. God, it was great to be home. I wanted to drop down and kiss the floor. Later that night at church, I said a special prayer to God, thanking Him for getting Oz, Star, and me back home safely and for giving us the miracle of Pine Island.

Christmas Day was as wonderful as any Christmas I could remember. Our family loved the spirit of the day, Jesus' birthday, the gift-giving, the cookies and Christmas candy. The living room was soon littered with Santa Claus–themed wrapping paper and colorful ribbon.

At one point, the phone rang. It was Oz, wishing me a merry Christmas, and then he complained that all he got for Christmas was underwear and socks—no radio, no records, no play things. He asked me what I got for Christmas gifts, and I told him mostly the same but that one of my uncles had sent me a toy rocket launcher, the kind where you stomp on a rubber ball to send it soaring into the air. I think my uncle forgot how old I was. Anyway, I agreed to meet Oz in an hour at the football field so we could give the rocket launcher a try.

Christmas Day was cold, maybe in the mid-forties, overcast and hazy—not too unusual for Jacksonville in December. After we had launched the rocket several times, just generally acting like grade-school kids, yelling and whooping as the rocket flew up in the air, Oz said he was going to go over to Spiff's to see what he was up to. I could tell that Oz was killing the day, not wanting to hang around his house for whatever reason.

When Oz left the field, I also started to leave. But just then, some unexplained force caused me to go over to the stadium bleachers and sit down. The afternoon was getting colder, so I pulled my jacket up around my neck and shoved my hands deeper into my pockets. There was a bite to the air each time I took a breath. I could see the back of the school, gray through the haze and looking like a giant mausoleum. The football field grass was winter-dead, the chalk lines on the field almost not visible anymore. I looked at the cinder track that ran in front of the bleachers on the far side of the security fence and realized that in a month or so, I would be working out there for the spring track season. I hoped I could break a few of the school's sprinting records and maybe even get a track scholarship to some college. Dad would love that.

As I looked at the back of the school and football field, and then at the empty bleachers around me, I thought to myself, "It's been a helluva a year so far. Stacey ending our relationship, Jackie and her craziness, now maybe Ginny. Football was a bust; I should have done much better, and I'm sure Dad is very disappointed. My grades suck; I'll be sacking groceries at Winn-Dixie if I don't improve my grades and get into a college. Only a few more months and this school will be history. I want to stay in high school forever, but I also want to go to college and get out of Jacksonville."

I sat in the bleachers for more than an hour, just looking at the school and the field and the track and reflecting on the last four months. Then, a few young kids walked onto the field and started throwing a football around. One of them yelled at me, "Hey, want to play touch football with us?"

I climbed out of the bleachers and, looking back at them, I yelled back, "No, thanks for asking. Gotta go home. Besides, I suck at football." I walked back to my ambulance-white '39 Ford and went home to be with my family.

That Saturday, Ginny and I had our first date without parents along. She was fantastic, another miracle in my life. Two miracles in the same week! How much better could God treat me?

Chapter 11

Ginny

Annette Funicello was the most popular cast member of *The Mickey Mouse Club* television show, which ran from 1955 to 1959. The show was extremely popular with preteens and teenagers, and maybe even some adult male perverts, mainly because of Annette. Annette was high-energy, talented, and very attractive with Italian features, dark hair, dark eyes, and a simply beautiful olive skin tone. She could sing, dance, and act with the best of them, and on those merits alone she had everything going to make her a television star.

But her real secret weapons, the ones that kept millions of teen male fans coming back every week to tune in to *The Mickey Mouse Club*, even though most would never admit they watched the show, were her breasts. For a young teenager, Annette had a beautiful pair of budding breasts. Old Walt Disney saw Annette's emerging assets and put her in the singing and dancing numbers that would show off those breasts in the most enticing, and yet arguably innocent, ways possible. I, for one, would stop and watch Annette, if by chance my sister was watching *The Mickey Mouse Club*, just to catch a glimpse of those puppies. By the end of 1959, the show was off the air and Annette went on to maximize her now fully mature 36Cs in bikini movies such as *Beach Blanket Bingo* and *How to Stuff a Wild Bikini* with co-star Frankie Avalon, though I never understood why anyone would want to look at him.

In high school, Ginny was Annette Funicello's twin sister—or could have been. Like Annette, she was talented, maybe not in song and dance, but in athletics, lettering on the swim team. She was smart, but not like

Annette, who had to memorize dialog for the show; Ginny's smarts were in the classroom, where she ranked at the top of her class in grades. Ginny had many of the other characteristics of Annette Funicello as well. She was fun, attractive, about 5'4" with dark hair and eyes, and she was a real boy killer with her magnetic personality.

Ginny also had Annette's secret weapon. Most boys in her class didn't realize she was carrying the rack of the century because she mostly wore blousy tops that minimized her voluptuous breasts. Most of the boys missed seeing Ginny in her Speedo swimsuit since no one went to the girls' swim meets except the parents of the swimmers. I also missed Ginny's swim meets, because I was running in track meets on the same days that she was swimming.

On our first date without her parents, Ginny and I went to the Florida Theatre in downtown Jacksonville to see the movie *The Nun's Story* with Audrey Hepburn. I wasn't really interested in that movie—it was way too dramatic for me—but hell, what teenage boy ever wanted to sit through a drama anyway? I was more of an action movie kind of guy, but Ginny was more on the brainy side and she was all for *The Nun's Story*. I think my fear was that somehow Ginny related to Audrey Hepburn as a nun. I could see this relationship going nowhere unless I became a priest. I later learned I was completely wrong about Ginny and the nun thing.

I went through the usual arm-around-the-back-of-her-seat thing, then sliding my arm down the seat and draping it around her shoulders. At some point during the movie, Ginny turned to me and said, "If you want to put your arm around me, don't give me a wimpy wet noodle of an arm. Put it around my shoulder and hold me." OK, that was pretty direct, and yes, I was doing the wet-noodle arm routine, and even I couldn't stand myself being wimpy.

I whispered, "Sorry, not sure how you like to be treated on our second date, or on any date. I don't want to be too forward with you. I really like you."

Ginny turned to me and said in a low, direct voice, "You want to get in my panties? Show me some macho."

My poor brain exploded with that statement. Mr. Willy started to pump iron. My brainy, athletic, "Wonder Woman" was also sexy to the point of being hotter than anyone I had ever dated. My reaction to her was pretty lame: "You ain't seen macho till you seen me in action."

Ginny started laughing almost uncontrollably. "Oh, my God, that's the worst line I've ever heard: 'You ain't seen macho till you seen me in action.' Besides, your grammar is awful, and I really doubt you even know how to spell macho or what the word means." She laughed some more and repeated, "'Ain't seen macho till you seen me in action!'" Ginny bent over laughing and started coughing from the spasms of trying to stifle her laughter and not disturb the other moviegoers.

She wasn't very successful. Only minutes later some audience members started whispering, "Quiet, shhhhhh."

Other theatre-goers strained to look in our direction. I hunkered down in my seat and tried not to look conspicuous, but it was impossible because Ginny was convulsing with laughter and muttering loud enough so others could hear, "'Ain't seen macho . . .'"

I was also embarrassed to be watching *The Nun's Story* while Ginny was hinting that I might have a shot to get inside her panties. I hoped God wouldn't strike us dead in the middle of the movie for indulging in a discussion about the possibility of premarital sex in front of Audrey Hepburn the nun. I wondered briefly if lightning could actually penetrate the roof of the theatre and hit Ginny and me sitting in the balcony.

Ginny finally got up and went out to the lobby, still laughing but at least, finally, a bit more under control. I followed her out, apologizing to the patrons around us who were looking at me. "She isn't well. Her mother was a nun, and the movie hits too close to home." The "mother was a nun" line put puzzled looks on their faces; they apparently didn't know how to interpret that statement, and I was too ignorant to realize what I had actually said.

I finally caught up to Ginny in the lobby as she was wiping tears of laughter from her eyes, and she said, "I'm going in the bathroom to fix my mascara. Don't let anyone steal my Macho Man." Of course, her statement brought on new fits of laughter, which I could hear even after she had gone into the women's room.

I went into the men's room to relieve myself from the pressure of Ginny making a spectacle of me in front of dozens of people sitting in the balcony of the Florida Theatre. Well, that and the simple fact that Mr. Willy needed a respite from mulling over the possibility of having sex with Ginny tonight.

Ginny and I reappeared in the lobby at the same time. She was in control of herself again, for the moment at least, and she had reapplied her makeup and was looking as beautiful as ever. Without saying a word, Ginny came up to me, put her arms around my neck, and pulled me to her, giving me a tongue-sucking kiss that almost vacuumed my brains out of my head.

When she finished kissing me, she pulled back slightly and said, "I'm sorry if I offended you, but it was funny." Then she went on, "I won't forget the panties promise—someday. Let's go. The nun movie isn't what I thought it would be. Besides, I need a macho man like you, not a priest." This time we both started laughing, and laughed our way out of the theatre and down to the Texas Drive-In to get something to eat.

Located in the Landon area of Jacksonville, off Hendricks Avenue, the Texas Drive-In was a classic hole-in-the-wall drive-in restaurant. The last time it had been painted was probably when it was built twenty years before Ginny and I first went there. The parking lot was a pothole-ridden, unpaved space primarily lit by the lighting that emanated from inside the restaurant.

The menu was composed of heartburn-guaranteeing selections such as their classic greasy hamburger and fries. Rounding out the sub-quality food was the sub-quality service of their lousy waitresses who were obviously trained in food service at the state prison. With all that going for the Texas Drive-In, it was the most popular place in Jacksonville for teenagers to see who was with whom and to be seen with your date for the night. Some cars would just slowly cruise through the Texas to check everyone out, while the more adventurous, daredevil types would actually stop to challenge their stomachs to a burger and fries. If you had a date on Friday or Saturday night, you *had* to take her to the Texas Drive-In; it was a requirement.

Ginny and I pulled into the pocked dirt lot and parked in one of the service areas, hoping we would get a waitress who would take our order and reappear with the food within some reasonable amount of time. Sometimes you'd give an order to one of the waitresses and never see her again. It was like some alien from outer space had beamed her up to their spaceship with your order in her hot little hand. Our only other option for food was to get out of the car and actually go into the Texas, which was totally not cool. After all, who would see you in your car if you were in the restaurant grabbling for a burger?

Just a few moments shy of eternity, a waitress appeared at our window, and we quickly ordered something to eat. Then we settled in for a long wait and began to look around to see who we could see.

Before long Ginny said, "There's my old boyfriend over there in his hot Chevy ragtop. What a jerk. Not sure who he's with now, some girl with platinum hair. I think she's in my class at DuPont."

I almost wrenched my neck whipping around to see who was in the Chevy ragtop. I could see directly into the front seat of the car, and there, with her arm around the neck of her date, sat my ex-girlfriend. I said out loud, "My God, it's Jackie! Who's that guy she's with?"

"Wow, who's Jackie? You seem shocked," Ginny responded.

"I dated her the first several months of the school year. Who's she with?"

Ginny looked at me and said, "Reginald Bradley III. I dated him the first several months of the school year, and we just broke up, same as you and Jackie. Well, breaking up implies we were dating on a steady basis. I just went out with him a couple of times, until I found out that he's a very shallow person. The jerk only wanted to talk about how much money his parents make selling urinals. I *flushed* old Reginald from my life just before I met you. He was my date at Mary's party when we first met. You remember that night; it was when you ran over me to get a Coca Cola." Ginny started laughing.

"OK, my turn. Jackie and I were pretty serious for several months. She has an unusual perspective on life—I mean, *unusual* to the extent that she uses tarot cards to help her make her decisions. Her family's really strange, too; it's Halloween every night at their house. I threw in the towel with Jackie before Mary's party. No, that's not right. *I* didn't call it quits; she did, and she dumped me because I didn't believe in her black magic."

Ginny took a long look at Jackie and said, "She's very pretty, got kind of an unusual look, like someone I've seen before, not sure who."

"Kim Novak. She looks like Kim Novak," I said, somewhat forcefully. The venom in my answer took Ginny aback.

"Wow, touchy. You still carrying a torch for her?" Ginny pulled back away from me a bit.

"No more than any torch you have for the Urinal King. Hey, let's not let these two come between us. Besides, they seem perfect for each other. Maybe Reginald can create a little *yellow* magic for Jackie." I laughed at my own joke, but Ginny just grimaced and shook her head.

"Yeah, let's let them be happy with each other. We'll make our own happiness." Ginny slid back to me and leaned up and kissed me with one of her passionate, tongue-sucked-out-of-your-throat kisses.

Our embrace was rudely and all too quickly interrupted by "Which one of you love birds had no onions, no pickles, light on the mayo?"

Later on, parked in the driveway at Ginny's house, we sat for a few minutes and swapped a few light kisses, and I asked her, "Want to go to the beach tomorrow? Just walk on the sand? Should be warm, in the 60s."

"No, I've got studies all day tomorrow; big quiz in algebra and a paper due in English class when we get back to school. I need Sunday afternoon quiet time to study. Don't you ever study?" Ginny appeared concerned for my shortfall in educational commitment, as if choosing the beach over studying would somehow warp me for life.

"Yeah, my dad makes me put in two hours of studying every night, except Fridays and Saturdays, before I can go out or get on the phone. Sundays it's only an hour, anytime during the day or evening. In my room, on the wall, Dad put a poster chart with little boxes for each day of the week where I have to put the times I start and stop studying. Next thing he'll put on my wall is a time clock to check in and out so I don't fudge on the wall chart. Guess he doesn't trust me. So anyway, on Sunday, all I need is the one hour of studying, which I can do after we go to the beach."

"Sorry, Rob, I have church, the family dinner, and then all afternoon studying. By seven, I'm ready for bed. After a hot bath, I get in bed and read a novel till I fall asleep. Do you read novels? What's your favorite?" Ginny asked, probably to get a scope on my intellectual curiosity, which was zip.

"Yeah, I read a lot of books, mostly classics like *Tale of Two Cities* and

War and Peace. Actually, the book I am reading right now is a combination of the two; it's called *A Piece of Tail*." I started to laugh, and Ginny just looked at me as if I were totally illiterate.

"*A Piece of Tail*? Is that what you have on your mind all the time? Boy, are *we* on the wrong intellectual train together."

So Ginny was disappointed in my little pun, even though I thought it was pretty cute and would be sure to tell it to the Mag 6 when I saw them next week. I knew Lily and Crazy would get a kick out of it.

Abruptly, Ginny got out of the car, turned, and said to me, "Look, Macho Man, if you want to have a future with me, then you need to stick your face in the books more and spend less time thinking about sticking your face between some girl's legs, especially mine." She slammed the car door and walked into her house.

"OK, not a great way to end our first night alone together," I mused. "Maybe the *Piece of Tail* pun was a little over the top. I'll call her tomorrow and apologize and promise to work harder in school, study more, and become an 'A' student. If those are the keys to making her happy and wanting me as her boyfriend, then I'll be a better student. Plus, if those are the keys to getting into her 'magic kingdom' south of her belly button and north of her knees, then I am *really* for it!" I thought happily to myself as I pulled away from Ginny's home. I had barely gotten down the street when I started to giggle like a little girl at the thought of her "magic kingdom."

The week before school resumed, our Mag 6 group went surf-fishing off Fort Matanzas Beach, south of St. Augustine. There's a bridge there that spans the Matanzas River where it dumps into the Atlantic Ocean. Where the river and ocean meet, the tarpon fishing is spectacular. Tarpons can get to five feet or longer, are bright white and silver, and have more fight in them than any other fish in the sea, which is why they're known as "silver kings."

At the time, I was still moving a little slowly from the game against Jackson High that had earned me a broken leg, so I limped into the surf up to my knees to cast my line into the river. About the third cast, a monster tarpon hit my lure and jumped maybe four feet straight out of the water, shaking its head to try to free itself and sending spray upwards like a fountain.

I just stood there, frozen, at the spectacular size and beauty of the tarpon. Nearly speechless, I turned to the others, who were either in the surf or on the beach getting their lines ready, and mumbled, "Shiiiiiitttttt." The tarpon shook the lure from its mouth, and I was left standing in the surf, ecstatic and dumbfounded. None of the guys had even seen what had just happened to me. The thrill of hooking the tarpon lasted three or four seconds, which, coincidentally, turned out to be about as long as my first intercourse experience—three to four seconds—well, maybe five seconds, tops.

Suddenly, as the tarpon disappeared in the surf, a huge, six-foot, white-sand shark broke the surface, its dorsal fin cutting the water only about six inches from my legs. One of my favorite passages in the Bible is when Jesus walked on water in a raging storm, chiding his disciples that if they were true believers, they could also walk on water. When the shark broke the water, I swear I became like Jesus. Even with my broken leg, I believe my feet never dipped below the surface of the water as I walked—or rather, hauled ass—from where I was in the high surf back to the beach, yelling all the way, "Sharrrrrrrrk!"

Jesus would have been proud of me for the way I negotiated the surf to the beach. Everyone else in the surf, who had previously been occupied with fishing, suddenly duplicated my miracle and got back on the beach without stopping to see if I was bullshitting them. "Shark" is nothing you hang around to see if someone is kidding about unless you want a stump for a leg the rest of your life.

None of us dared go back into the surf to fish, so we decided to have some fun and attack Fort Matanzas, a federal and state park and the site of a historical fort built in 1740, located just up the sand from where we had started fishing. Pretending we were Spanish invaders, we climbed all over the fort until one of the park rangers decided we were being too unruly and were bothering the other guests, all two of them. On the park ranger's command, we all left the fort's grounds, except for Crazy, who thought it would be fun to play a little "hide and go seek" with the park ranger.

Crazy found a spot in the Officers' Quarters room where there were two entrances, one being a small opening in the ceiling that led out onto the observation deck. The acoustics were such that sounds within the room created an echo throughout the fort, so we started laughing when we heard the echo of "Chee-vee-vee" bouncing off the fort's old walls. The more "Chee-vee-vees" we heard, the more pissed the park ranger became because he couldn't pinpoint where Crazy was hiding.

At some point, the park ranger called in reinforcements, another park ranger who was easily forty pounds overweight and so out of shape that a two-year-old could have outrun him. The two rangers started scouring each of the fort's rooms, save the one Crazy was in. I'm pretty sure that was because neither of them wanted to scale down the shaky ladder from the observation deck to get into it.

Crazy, sensing it was a good time to leave before getting caught and arrested by a federal park ranger, slipped out a side door of the Officers' Quarters, which the rangers had yet to enter. He met us outside the fort's entrance, and we quickly left the park. At the gate leading into the park, Crazy leaned out of my car window and yelled back to the rangers now standing at the entrance to Fort Matanzas, "Chee-vee-vee"—sort of like the Lone Ranger's "Hi ho, Silver, away!" on television each week.

As we left the parking lot for the main highway, I happened to glance in the rearview mirror, and I could swear I saw the fat park ranger give us the middle finger. I assumed his gesture was *not* to say, "Come back and visit us again real soon, y'all hear?"

Early in the week after our Saturday night date, I called Ginny to apologize for my rudeness in not taking seriously her belief that I should study more, read more, and be less of an oversexed, testosterone-charged, typical teenager. I was honest with her when I told her I was committed to working harder on my schoolwork, especially since I really needed to have a great last half of the year to bring up my grades so I could get into a decent college. Otherwise, I told her, I didn't think she would want to marry a guy whose sole career choice was sacking groceries at the local Winn-Dixie grocery store. Ginny didn't quite understand what I was talking about with that reference, but she did warm to my commitment to study more and get better grades.

I asked Ginny if she had a date for New Year's Eve, and I was surprised to find out that she did have a date . . . with her parents and her brother, to go to see *The Nutcracker* ballet, which was still playing in town, and then out to dinner as a family. She didn't even hint that I could go along with them, and I assumed this was because they had already purchased the tickets. When I asked her about it, she said something like "four is family; five is someone along for the ride," but I just shrugged the comment off and said I'd see her in school next week and hung up the phone. So, "What is Rollo going to do for New Year's Eve?" suddenly became the big question I was asking myself. "Can't be alone on the big night, need someone to kiss and welcome the New Year with," I thought.

As it turned out, on New Year's Eve, I ended up in bed with a wicked cold, which I attributed to our surfing outing and getting hot and sweaty running around Fort Matanzas. Lying in bed with my little terrier Tippy, at the stroke of midnight I grabbed her and gave her a kiss on the head. She reciprocated with a big lick on the side of my face. I laughed to myself, "My love life has really gone to the dogs! Oh, well, at least my Tippy loves me for who I am, brain-dead and oversexed." I felt like a truckload of cold crap physically and was having a big self-pity party emotionally. So, rolling over on my side, I stared at the study chart on the wall, and as I drifted off to sleep, I thought of Ginny and said to myself, "I'll show you who can get 'A's.'"

My very last (and supremely teenaged-male) thought before the sandman put me out for the night was "I wonder if she'll let me get in her pants if I get the 'A's'?"

Ginny and I dated steadily for the rest of the school year and into the summer. Our dates evolved into a once-a-week routine, usually on a Saturday night and usually to a movie somewhere around town. During the week, we didn't see other outside of school. Our infrequent getting together was due to studying and the fact that I belonged to a number of senior social clubs that I attended—not the academic groups I had signed up for, but fun groups like the Letterman Club and Senior Boys. Ginny belonged to several sophomore clubs, although there were fewer for the sophomores than for the seniors.

I joined a bunch of geeky clubs to beef up my resume for college, although I never went to any of the meetings. I found out you could list all your clubs in the yearbook, have your photo made with each of the clubs for the yearbook, then when the yearbook went to press, drop out of the club meetings. Your listing and photo would be forever memorialized. Then ten, fifteen years later, when showing your yearbook to your children, they could say, "Wow, Dad, you were really popular in high school. Look at all the clubs you were in!" And I imagined that I would reply with somewhat of a straight face, "Yeah, your pop was in all the clubs. All the girls were fighting over me to be in their club. What can I say? I couldn't disappoint them."

Friday night dates with Ginny were a rarity since both of us were usually too pooped from study and our social schedule to be of any fun on a date. Besides, Ginny did have a little bit of a vain streak in her and wanted to have her hair fixed just right when we went out. She said she needed all of Saturday to get ready for our big date. So for Friday nights, I usually took off with some or all of the Mag 6 to see what kind of trouble we could get into without getting arrested.

During the spring, both Ginny and I were involved in sports. Ginny was on the swim team and I was running track. The swim team was the only girls' sports team the high school sponsored; there was no girls' basketball, no tennis, no golf. If you were a girl and wanted a DuPont athletic letter, you'd better swim like a fish or dive from a diving board like Tarzan from a cliff. Ginny was a diver and, from what I heard, a good one, although I never got a chance to attend a single one of her swim meets.

I had track meets in the afternoon, or at night under the lights, at high schools all over the county. At the end of the regular meet season, Lily and I and several others qualified for the state track meet held at the University of Florida's track stadium. Our relay teams medaled at the meet, but I got mopped in the 100 and 220. In the 220 trials, I split the bottom of my foot wide open from the pressure of running on the curved track. That injury pretty much wiped me out in the sprints.

Ginny did come to one of my nighttime track meets at Fletcher High School, which was located in Jacksonville Beach. The parents of one of her girlfriends drove her out to the meet since the girlfriend's brother was also on the track team and the whole family came to watch him run. I made arrangements with Ginny's parents to drive her back from the meet myself.

I proudly won the 100- and 220-yard sprints. (Everything was

143

measured in yards in those days; there was no use of meters. In fact, the metric system was unheard of in schools; the good old American standard system of measurement was good enough for everybody.) After my wins, I took Ginny for a quick walk on the nearby beach. We waded in the surf, but only up to our ankles since we didn't want to go home drenched. The little stroll through the surf was a bit anticlimactic after my big track wins, but we did stop several times for some great kissing and hugging, though nothing more, not even light petting.

On the way home that night, Ginny positioned herself so she was in my arms, lying sideways in the front seat. I actually had my arms around her *and* my hands on the steering wheel, which was a great arrangement because this little maneuver allowed me to drive *and* kiss Ginny without taking my eyes off the highway—well, at least not for very long.

The only problem with driving and kissing is that it's against the law, which I had to discover the hard and expensive way. We had just finished a particularly crotch-tightening kiss when I sensed a car alongside me, keeping pace with me rather than trying to pass me. I glanced quickly to my left and looked directly into the eyes of a couple of pissed-off Florida Highway Patrolmen, who were trying to figure out how I was driving sixty miles per hour while tangled in a lip-locking embrace with my girlfriend.

I knew that trying to run would be useless, and minutes later, we were standing alongside the highway outside my car while the cops read us the "riot act" and threatened to arrest us and take us to jail. I told them I had been in a track meet at Fletcher, as evidenced by my sweat outfit over my track shorts and top, and that I had won the 100 and 220 and Ginny was *just* giving me a congratulations kiss when they had driven up alongside my car.

They seemed to buy my lie. Plus, one of the cops said he had run track in high school and was impressed with my winning times. The highway patrolmen eventually gave me a ticket, but they wrote it up as making an illegal u-turn, which I explained away to my dad by saying that the route was unfamiliar and the street signs weren't clear and it was dark.

I paid my dad back the twenty dollars I owed for the ticket by painting the swimming pool fence. Painting the fence was worth it compared to the trauma Ginny and I would've gone through if both sets of parents had been forced to make a late-night trip to the Jacksonville Beach jail to bail us out. I'm sure any hopes I might have had of a future with Ginny would have ended at the jail steps.

The last day of the school year, which was also, of course, the last day of my high school career, was almost surreal for me. Each class was a blur as teachers tried to keep the students in control of their emotions over the imminent great leap into adulthood. I remember that some of the teachers were actually crying, too, that the school year was over. As for me, I barely remember telling each teacher how much they meant to me, which was a big lie, as none of them had actually done anything to motivate me to want to do better.

A couple of the teachers were absolutely confident that they had achieved great successes in shaping our young lives. In particular, Miss Hamilton, senior English teacher, seemed all caught up in herself and her perception that all her English students were better prepared for the challenges of the outside world because she had made them read and memorize lines from Samuel Taylor Coleridge's *The Rime of the Ancient Mariner*. The only thing I took away from that particular battle-axe's course was the fun of having Freddie the Farter deliver his signature explosions during her class.

Somehow, most of us seniors ended up in the main hallway just before the final bell rang for the final day of the school year. I remember standing by DuPont's pathetic sports trophy case and looking at the last football trophy the school had gotten. I did the math and figured out that I had been in grade school when DuPont had won its conference title and gotten the cheesy, plastic, six-inch trophy to commemorate the team's accomplishment.

Unknown to me at the time, Alfred I. DuPont High would, within a few years, be decommissioned as a senior high and relegated to rebirth as a middle school. But I figured that, *someday*, though I didn't know when, the few tiny plastic trophies that Alfred I. DuPont had earned would end up in the school's Dempsey Dumpster. Standing there in the main hallway by the trophy case of worthless plastic statues, I realized for the first time that athletic achievements are fleeting and soon forgotten. Ginny was right: Your education and brain will take you further in life than a shelf full of plastic trophies, unless you become a hotshot professional player making zillions of dollars.

Moments before the final bell, the seniors, almost as one, broke into singing the schools alma mater. Some sang with tears streaming from their eyes in the sudden, stark realization that their high school days would be over in about fifteen seconds. I just stood there and laughed. My limited number of friends, my girlfriends Stacey and Jackie and now Ginny, and, most important of all, my Mag 6 buddies would be the only cherished memories I would have of DuPont High School. Wait, I take that back; Coaches Luck and Mahoney were like fathers to me and mentored me through difficult times, both in sports and in my personal life. I'll always remember them and love them for their contributions to my young adulthood.

I couldn't take the mass weeping that was going on in the hallway, so I opened the front door and stepped outside. I was by myself for just a few moments, but I can still remember how the sun's rays sliced through the tall pine trees dotting the school's grounds and warmed my tear-free face. The air was a heady and exquisite atmosphere filled with the scents of pine needles, freshly cut grass, and a mixture of the smells an old school building emits, mostly the slow decomposing of its structure, bricks, mortar, and shingle roofing.

I looked to the spot on the school's lawn where, on the first day of my senior year, I first saw Jackie. Somehow, I could still visualize her standing there, looking back at me with those smoky gray eyes and that platinum hair and that mysterious and sultry look that made me think of Kim Novak. I said to my imaginary vision, "Good luck the next couple of years, Jackie. Before you know it, you'll stand here on these steps, and maybe, just maybe, you'll be thinking about me."

"Hey, Macho Man!" My daydreaming was interrupted by Ginny, who was standing in the shadows very close to where I had first seen Jackie. "How come you're not inside with your classmates for a final goodbye? Too macho to shed a final tear for good old DuPont High?"

Somewhat annoyed that she had interrupted my thoughtful and reflective mood brought on by the last few seconds of my years in high school, I said, "Ginny, what're you doing out here, hiding in the shadows?"

"Not hiding in the shadows; getting out of the sun. I was waiting on you to come out those doors. I have something for you." She walked to the steps where I was standing, and I stepped slowly down to the sidewalk to meet her.

She handed me a little box wrapped in silver paper and a silver ribbon. "It's a little graduation gift for you. I wanted to be the first to give you something, especially since you worked so hard these last few months to get good grades. I also have another little something for you, but I couldn't gift-wrap it."

I looked at the little box in my hand and said, "I am floored and embarrassed. Sorry I jumped at you. Yeah, I guess it is a little emotional inside the school, and maybe inside me, too. Maybe I am feeling like a big chapter of my life's closing. At least I have you to help me start a new chapter."

I laughed a little nervously, hoping to hide the emotion that was starting to well up as the reality of graduation day hit home. "Do you like my analogy with books and chapters? Could have been about sex."

"You're so cute; that's why I love you." Ginny put her hand around the back of my head and pulled me to her and gave me a beautiful, warm, sincere kiss, the kind that really says "I love you."

"Open your gift." Ginny was suddenly excited, acting almost like a kid in a candy store.

Within seconds I tore the paper and ribbon off the box and lifted the lid. Inside was a silver pendant and chain. Picking the pendant out of the box, I could see that the figure engraved on it was of a biblical-looking old man with a child on his shoulders. I loved it even though I wasn't sure what it was, so with a questioning look, I said, "It's beautiful."

"The fellow on the pendant is St. Christopher, who protects you from harm. I want you to always think of me when you wear the chain and pendant. I want St. Christopher to take care of you. I don't want to lose you, ever." Ginny had real tears in her eyes and her voice trembled just a tiny bit as she proclaimed her affection for me.

"Wow, Ginny, I love it, and I love you." I put the chain and pendant on. Then, holding up the pendant toward the sky, I said proudly, "Well, St. Christopher, make sure nothing ever happens to Ginny and me."

Ginny laughed and then looked at me and said, "There's another way I want to show you my love, but we have to wait till we're alone. I think it's time we share each other in a more physical way."

I just stood and looked at her. As she stood there on the sidewalk, her beauty was radiating, almost outshining the rays of sunlight filtering through the pines. The tears that had just spilled down her smooth cheeks shone like diamonds, and the love I felt in that instant was as real and true and pure as any I've ever felt in my life.

Suddenly, the school's doors flew open and hundreds of students dashed outside, heading toward home and a long summer. But in that moment, my reality had narrowed to just the two of us. Ginny and I just stood in the middle of the streaming crowd, now holding hands, just looking at each other, and ignoring it when we occasionally got bumped by a student running to a waiting car or school bus.

"Let's go and get out of here," I said to Ginny in a voice hoarse with restrained emotion.

"Where do you want to go?" Ginny asked with the same emotion inflected into her simple question.

"How about we go to the Texas for a grease burger and fries?" I said laughingly, trying to shake the tightness in my love-strained chest.

Ginny looked at me with a big smile that far outshone the sun and replied in a simple and wonderful fashion with a single word: "Perfect."

Chapter 12

Summer of '60

little known fact in American history is that in 1620, the *Mayflower* pilgrims landed first in Jacksonville, Florida, then went up the coast to Plymouth Rock. While in Jacksonville, they built a hotel and named it after their ship. The Mayflower Hotel, as it is called, is where Alfred I. DuPont's Class of 1960 graduation ceremonies were held—right there in the convention hall of the very ancient and historical Mayflower Hotel. My guess is that the hotel was built by the pilgrims to honor their newfound Indian friends. The pilgrims and Indians held their first wampum exchange there in the very same Mayflower ballroom where our graduation celebration took place. The ballroom carpet looked and smelled like a few teepees had been set up on it over the years.

Well, actually, that's a slight exaggeration about the age and condition of the Mayflower Hotel, but not by too much.

The featured speaker for the graduation ceremony was Congressman Bob Sikes, who looked very much like a member of an amateur barbershop quartet dressed in his bow tie and plaid jacket, and with his flat-top hairstyle and high-pitched weasel voice. His speech for our class was straight out of the graduation ceremony textbook: "How the 1960 Graduating Class of Alfred I. DuPont Will Be the *Future* of America." Sitting there with my classmates and looking around, it was a terrifying thought that Freddie the Farter was America's future. Or that future America might depend on someone like Lily, who graduated from high school never learning to write a simple sentence in longhand. If Lily had been around to take part in drafting the Declaration of Independence, guess what? It would have been printed, including his signature. No "*John Hancock*" in bold handwriting, just a scrawled "Lily" in unreadable printing.

Even worse was Crazy, communicating his "Chee-vee-vee." I imagined Crazy sitting at the negotiating table across from the feared, irrational Russian president Nikita Khrushchev, desperately trying to prevent the start of World War III. The Russian leader would be pounding on the table with his scruffy, brown shoe, would be demanding to know what America was going to do to stave off the impending war, and Crazy would look into Nikita's cold, Russian eyes and say flatly, "Chee-vee-vee." Almost immediately the H-bombs would be raining down on the United States, as Nikita would probably think "Chee-vee-vee" was some sort of code word for "Go f*** yourself." Yeah, I was convinced that America was in deep shit if its future relied on the 1960 graduating class of Alfred I. DuPont High School.

At the conclusion of the graduation ceremony, a number of senior boys, myself included, and a few "ready to lose their virginity" senior girls headed straight to Jacksonville Beach to various rental cottages for an all-night celebration and whatever the mixture of passion and booze would produce. What happened early in the evening was predictable: The senior girls partied without the senior boys; no senior girl was willing to give herself up to Qetesh, the Goddess of Ecstasy and Sexual Pleasure. For the weekend, the girls got their thrills drinking Southern Comfort from three-ounce Dixie cups. A sickening thought—sucking down the sweet, syrupy liquor three ounces per gulp.

The senior boys were obsessed with seeing who could drink the most cans of Budweiser beer. Contests soon evolved (of course, teenage boys will make a contest out of everything, from farting to who can burp the loudest) as to who could hold the most beer without taking a piss and who took the longest piss. From the start, it looked like Darrell Jones, a good old country boy who played offensive tackle on our football team, was going to win both contests hands down.

On his second six-pack, somewhere at the tenth beer, Darrell let out a beer fart that literally shook the cottage's creaky windows and doors, then bolted to the bathroom. Four of us with watches with second hands crowded into the small, one-person bathroom and watched with somewhat bated admiration as Darrell filled the toilet with what appeared to be a gallon of beer. Darrell's pissing time came in at 144 seconds, capped off with a second beer fart, which prompted us to make a quick exit before we got asphyxiated.

The senior boys' cottages had the very macho name "Pink Queen Conch Cottages." The cottages were normally rented to one-night honeymooners, usually a sailor on leave who just had time to get married and spend one blissful night with his new bride. Sometime in the next three months, the lucky sailor would get a letter from his wife telling him he was going to be a proud father, thanks to their one-nighter at the Pink Queen Conch Cottages. I always wondered if the rock stars "Pink" and "Queen" were affectionately named after the cottage where mom and dad got it on during their honeymoon night.

The manager of the Pink Queen Conch Cottages sensed right off the bat that our senior guys were going to get drunk and break up the cottages' furniture. We assured him that nothing like that would ever happen and that we were there at the beach to swim and lie in the sun and enjoy the fellowship of our fellow students. This was, of course, nothing but pure bullshit, but he bought it.

Just to demonstrate our intent of a quiet weekend of fellowship, we gave the gullible manager an extra $50 deposit for any scratches we might leave on the furniture. Of course, the extra $50 didn't even begin to cover the several beds that magically collapsed from fifteen fun-loving teenagers playing "pile on" during the drunken party that started shortly after we all arrived and lasted well into the morning.

On Saturday morning, I rolled over in what little section of bed I had and opened my eyes. I found myself staring straight at Star's closed eyes. There was a slimy piece of lettuce protruding from the corner of his drooling mouth, probably a leftover from the hamburgers we had picked up on our way to the beach. Lying in an opposite direction on the bed, just below Star's disgusting mouth was Lily's left foot, wearing a sock with a hole from which Lily's big toe emerged. This was quite disturbing in my too-close view since the big toenail was blackened and oozing bloody pus, probably from someone dropping onto it a brick we drunken revelers had pried loose from the cottage's fireplace. The sight of Lily's black, bloody big toe and the lettuce hanging out of the corner of Star's mouth made my stomach churn. Plus, the entire room reeked of the bile and Budweiser beer that someone had puked under the bed during the group pile-on.

I rolled out of the beer-soaked bed and staggered, bleary-eyed and weak-kneed, into the bathroom. The sight in the mirror was most disturbing: My eyes were twin pools of blood-red, and both were puffy, as if I had been on the losing end of a fistfight. I did slightly remember that at some point during the pile-on I had been kicked in the face by Darrell, who I vaguely remembered was stark naked when he pounced on our pile of classmates. I think I was trying to pull Darrell off the pile when someone at the bottom accidently grabbed Darrell's balls and gave them a real pull.

The fun of "pile on" quickly turned ugly as Darrell's balls were suddenly squeezed till they turned a bright shade of purple. He started screaming and kicking, my face being the first place his naked size-13 foot landed. It was a wonder Darrell didn't break my nose. I think at that point I had beaten a hasty retreat and let Darrell deal with his balls being pulled from his fat-ass body.

In the bathroom where Darrell had won the pissing contest the night before, I threw water on my face and combed my hair with my fingers. After searching high and low in the main room of the cottage, I finally found my jeans in the corner. I virtually wobbled outside to the sidewalk that ran along the main street in front of the cottages. Halfway down the block, I found a pay phone. Luckily, I also found enough change in my pocket to make a call, so I called Ginny. Thank God she picked up on the second ring.

"Hi, I miss you. Want to go out tonight?" I said, feigning an air of cool nonchalance.

"I guess you're not having a sex orgy at the beach, to want to go out with me? Did all the senior girls go home after the orgy, or are they still there? Or have you run out of condoms?" Ginny giggled.

"No, smart-ass, we discovered that Budweiser can produce beer faster than fourteen 'pop me another Bud' seniors in this flea-infested cottage can consume in one night. My bed is probably 3 percent alcohol from the beer that got spilled on it. I'm coming home, no second night for me. Besides, I want to see you."

"Will you be dried out by tonight or smelling like a beer keg?" There was a little bit of sarcasm in Ginny's reply.

"I'll drink a gallon of Listerine and pour a bottle of Canoe over my body if that would make you happy." Now I was honestly starting to get a little testy, thinking that Ginny should be a little more excited to see me, especially after our last-day-of-school love-sharing moment.

"I just think you need to slow down on the beer blast you've been on in the last few weeks of school winding down. I feel you need a beer to get in the mood to have fun, be happy, make me laugh at your one-liners. Just cool it with the beer before your liver drops out of your body onto your bathroom floor. I don't want a boyfriend on a pump the rest of his life."

Looking into the glass of the phone booth, I could see that my face was disgustingly swollen from too much beer and so-called fun, and I decided Ginny would end our relationship if she saw me in my current condition. Quickly, I said, "Ginny, you are, as always, 110 percent correct. I need to slow down and smell the roses; otherwise they—you—will be putting roses on my coffin."

Ginny yelled into the phone, "Don't talk about coffins and dying! Just cut down on the beer! I know when you go to Tech in a few months, with the fraternity parties, you'll be there with the best of them around the keg of cold beer. But for now, with me, no more beer! Can you do that? If you can't, then I'm not sure we can be a couple."

"OK, Ginny, where is the 'no beer' coming from? I've never been drunk, not even a little bit tipsy with you from any beer I've had with the Mag 6 or any of my friends. What's the big deal?"

After a long silence, Ginny said in a very adult voice, "My dad is an alcoholic and goes to Alcoholics Anonymous. I don't want you sitting with him at one of their meetings sometime in the future."

I was stunned and speechless. I had never known about Ginny's dad being an alcoholic, but of course, how would I know? It wasn't my business to know what went on in her family. Thinking quickly, it dawned on me that I had never seen her dad with an alcoholic drink, just iced tea or a soft drink. Now, much of Ginny's demeanor and personality made sense to me—her being so adult for her age, driven to excel so her parents would be proud of her, and maybe she was even trying to set an example for her dad to stay sober so she would be proud of him.

"Ginny, I feel like a major shmuck right now. I've embarrassed myself in your eyes. Thank God you can't see me now, but I think you know what I must look like after drinking and partying all night. I can't even stand myself as I am looking at a reflection in the glass in this phone booth. Let's cool it for the next week. I got to go do some 'get ready for college' shopping with my mom. How about we see each other a week from today and talk about our future?"

"I love you," Ginny replied. "You can see what you have to do to keep us together. It's way too important to me, and I feel you understand my sensitivity to alcohol. One week. We can talk on the phone this next week, but a week from today we can be together and maybe really get to know each other." Ginny giggled at her final words, which in turn made my heart start to race, which was not necessarily a good thing as it intensified the pounding hangover already going on in my head.

"One week, really get to know each other. We're on. Oh, something else I need to tell you," I said very coyly.

"What?" Ginny seemed puzzled.

"I love you." I hung up the phone so she could dwell on those words. Plus, my mouth and brain were not working together very well, so I headed back to the cottage to try to find some aspirin for my raging headache.

I cut back my beer intake over the weekend to see if I was able to control my desire for the foamy wonder of life. On Saturday afternoon, at our combined senior boys and girls barbeque, I had a big plastic cup of Lipton iced tea, which left me feeling that mule piss would have been more thirst-quenching. I missed having my beer with a burger.

Oz and Spiff asked me if I was feeling OK, and I told them that I had to cool it with the beer since I was going to run in a Junior Olympic track meet in a few weeks in Tampa and then an open college meet in Atlanta, which was the truth. I needed to get back in some type of reasonable shape to participate in the meets, especially the open college meets, since I would be going up against top-notch college sprinters.

I left the senior getaway after the barbeque and went home to be by myself and try to get my mind together. After my talk with Ginny about her dad being in AA and Ginny's insistence about what it would take for us to have a future, I knew I needed to become a borderline teetotaler. I knew that the summer was going to be loaded with parties; the Mag 6 and practically every other senior in Florida would be celebrating getting out of high school and going on to college. I was already getting invitations to fraternity rush parties for Jacksonville chapters of Tech fraternities.

I sensed there were dark clouds gathering on the horizon for Ginny and me, what with the upcoming stress of me transitioning to college life and Ginny with two years still left in high school.

Within a couple weeks of being out of school, all of the Mag 6 had summer jobs ranging from construction and Bell Telephone lineman work, to loading plumbing pipes onto tractor trailers and unloading other plumbing pipes from other tractor trailers, to clerical work and my job. I worked at a manufacturing plant for Winn-Dixie, roasting coffee and packing it into cans, and packaging spices into the little boxes and bottles that were sold in the Winn-Dixie stores.

I also did janitor work, opening the plant in the morning and cleaning the men's and women's bathrooms before all the employees showed up for the work day. I found the men's bathroom was constantly dirty from handling the filthy coffee bags unloaded from train boxcars alongside the warehouse, but the women's bathrooms were worse—a gagging mess from hair on the floor, in the sinks, around the toilet. It was as if the women were shedding their hair like a St. Bernard dog in the middle of summer.

Of all the Mag 6, I was the one who came home every night totally exhausted from the physical labor and having to drive clear across Jacksonville each morning to the manufacturing section to open the plant at 7:00 a.m. The working hours and hard work resulted in the sad fact that Ginny and I only saw each other on the weekend; of course, this meant that it wasn't exactly a love feast every day of the summer. I also didn't see much of any of my friends that often. Summer was slipping by quickly, and soon I would be on my way to college.

One particular evening, a Friday night after work, six of us met at the Huddle House restaurant in the Lakewood Center near our homes and started shooting the breeze and eating hamburgers, splurging a little of our weekly pay on food. The group included four of the Mag 6—Oz, Star, Lily, and me—and Ted and Todd, two of our other buddies.

As it happened, a perfect storm was in play for us this evening. Our conversation turned to the music of the day and a new dance craze, the Twist, that was starting to catch on with the teenagers, replacing the traditional bop dancing. The Twist also was a little more erotic with the girl's hips swaying frantically as if she were throwing her hips in her dance partner's face, insinuating, "I've got it, you want it . . . forget it."

How the idea actually started is buried in the lore of the event, but someone suggested that there must be a Guinness world record for how many hours a couple could twist, sort of like the old 1920s marathon dance contests. The idea of marathon dancing led to talk about dancing for distance. Then, with our collective genius, we six high school graduates with a combined IQ of 150 decided that maybe we could set the Guinness world record for doing the Twist for the longest distance. But we wanted recognition for it, so we would need the *Jacksonville Journal* to cover the event.

Since it was Huddle's closing time, we went to Ted's house nearby to plan our strategy. Also, Ted's parents weren't home, so we scored a couple of six-packs of Pabst Blue at the local liquor store, and once at Ted's house, each of us had a couple of the Blues to liven up the excitement of pulling off a scam on the local media.

Oz, who is the master of phone bullshitting, was elected to call the *Jacksonville Journal* to get some reporter to come take pictures of our group setting the twisting-distance Guinness world record. A couple of circumstances added to the perfect storm of pulling off this con story. First, there was zero news happening in America that July day of 1960; thus, the night reporter for the *Journal* was bored and wanted to get out of the office and maybe knock down a shot or two of Jack Daniels while out on a story—any story. Oz was spectacular in selling the reporter on the fact that our group was out to shatter the world twisting record held by a group of students from LSU. The final happenstance that made the night successful was the fact that the night desk reporter was too lazy to check out the story or even call to verify that there was a twisting Guinness world record held by LSU students in the first place.

The reporter asked Oz where we were starting and ending our twisting record-breaking attempt, and without missing a beat, Oz said we would start in the parking lot of the Lakewood shopping center and end at the foot of the Warren Street Bridge. The reporter asked when the group would start, and Oz told him 11:00 p.m. or so, which gave us and the reporter twenty minutes to get to the Lakewood Center and get ready in the parking lot. From Ted's house, we were back at the Lakewood Center in about ten minutes, and to our amazement, at 11:00 p.m., a beat-up Ford Fairlane pulled into the parking lot and out popped the *Jacksonville Journal* reporter with his pad and pencil in hand.

Oz was our spokesman since he was the one who had originally talked with the reporter. "Hi, we're a group of recent DuPont High School graduates. My name is . . ." And Oz proceeded to give the names and spellings for each of us to the reporter, who meticulously took down the information, even though I could detect a hint of bourbon on his breath.

Oz continued, "We all work summer jobs, all of us are going off to college in a month or so, and we had heard that some students at LSU had set a record for twisting around the campus's perimeter. That's something like 2.5 miles. We said, 'Shit, we can top that.'" Oz paused as he watched the reporter take down every word he was saying. He asked the reporter, "Can you print 'shit' in the newspaper?"

"Nope, but I'll clean it up. If we run the story," the reporter quipped and looked at each of us as if to say, "You better do this twisting thing or no story." Then he asked, "So, how long will it take you to twist the five miles?"

Oz told him, "We should be at the bridge about 5:00 a.m."

The reporter turned to all of us and asked, "So, when are you going to start this twisting?"

We all looked at each other and said in unison, "Now!" With that, the six of us formed a snake-like line and started twisting from side to side while walking forward. We got to the street and started down San Jose Boulevard toward town and the Warren Street Bridge, some five miles away. Fortunately, the traffic on San Jose Boulevard was light for a Friday night, even though it was now close to 11:30. As we twisted and walked, the reporter in the Ford Fairlane followed behind us to capture the insanity of what we were doing.

Prior to starting this hoax, each of us had cleared with our parents that we were spending the night at Ted's house. We certainly weren't telling them what we were up to with the *Jacksonville Journal*. We also calculated that walking slowly for five miles would take us five hours, give or take thirty minutes. So, by leaving the Lakewood Center area after 11:00 p.m., we would be at the Warren Bridge around 5:00 a.m.

The reporter pulled alongside us and told us he'd be checking up on us to make sure we were twisting the entire distance, and then he hit the gas and sped away. We watched as his car disappeared down the street, and the instant his taillights were gone, we stopped twisting and started to walk, keeping an eye out for car lights in either direction. Sure enough, in a few minutes we saw lights coming back toward us, so I yelled, "Bandits coming, start twisting!" Within a few minutes, the Ford Fairlane came down San Jose Boulevard in the opposite direction, and our reporter slowed it as he went by to be sure that we were still twisting. Once he was satisfied that we were still giving it our all, the Fairlane took off, and once it was out of sight, we stopped and gathered as a group, and I said, "Do you think this asshole is going to shadow us till 5:00 in the morning?"

The consensus was that we weren't worth five hours of his time to make sure we did what we claimed we were going to do and twisted all the way down San Jose Boulevard in the middle of the night. My suspicions were that he was going to go back to the office and then reappear in the morning at the foot of the Warren Bridge. Since we had only gone a quarter of a mile down San Jose, I ran back to the shopping center and got my car and came back, and all of us piled in the car and went to Ted's house to catch a little sleep before getting back up and driving to an area near the bridge to resume our twisting.

At 4:00 a.m., most of us were still awake, too pumped up to really get any sleep after all, so we piled into my car and drove to a parking area about a quarter mile from the Warren Bridge. No cars were on the road, so we made our way to the side of San Jose Boulevard and started walking very slowly to the foot of the bridge. At 4:45, almost at the foot of the bridge, some of the group started bitching about the whole idea.

Ted yelled at Oz and me, "Rollo, Oz, whose dumb-ass idea was this? Here we are, standing in the middle of San Jose Boulevard at the crack of dawn, cold, tired, hungry! My feet are killing me! Shit! Let's go home. That reporter isn't coming back."

Todd also piped in: "Come on, let's go. I got to go to work this afternoon. I'll be dragging ass during my shift. Besides, I got to take a piss. I didn't go before we left Ted's house."

I turned to Todd and almost yelled, "Piss in the street—there's no one to see you. You can even take a dump if you need to, we won't watch. Geez, what a quitter." I turned away, shaking my head in disgust.

Todd had turned to some nearby shrubs along the road and started to pee when Oz yelled, "Car coming over the bridge, start twisting!"

Todd stopped in the middle of his peeing and started groaning, "It hurts to stop pissing."

"Shut up! Your schwantz isn't going to fall off!" I yelled at him. "Start twisting!"

The car approached slowly from over the Warren Bridge, and there it was, the Ford Fairlaine, which I now noticed had rusty fenders and a broken-off side mirror. The car pulled off the bridge to a parking area for people who want to walk over the bridge. Out of the car stepped the reporter, but now he carried a camera in his hand, one of those you see in the movies with a big flash attachment.

Oz and I looked at each other and the mental message was clear: "Be the first one in line for the photo—screw everyone else!" I moved toward the reporter, but Oz had already gotten to him. "Hey, we made it, we broke the record! We're world champions! Going to take our photo?"

"Congratulations, you guys. I put something in the paper. Line up here on the curb for a photo. Pretend you're twisting," the reporter said as he was looking at his camera and setting the light meter since it was still dark out.

Oz got his ass first in line, I muscled my way in ahead of Star and Lily, but Lily pushed Star out of the way to get third position. Star ended up fourth in the line. Ted and Todd were too slow on the uptake to understand what was going on, so they politely took fifth and sixth position, Todd bringing up the rear of the line. The reporter took several photos, recorded a little more of our thoughts about breaking the bogus LSU twisting record, thanked us, then got in the Fairlane and disappeared back over the Warren Bridge, probably headed back to the *Jacksonville Journal* office.

Once we were sure the reporter was gone, we piled back into my car, and I drove everyone to their respective homes or parked cars in the Lakewood Center. I went home, quietly got in bed without waking anyone, and slept till noon.

That Saturday night, Ginny and I had a pretty vanilla date of a movie at the Florida Theatre, soft drinks and fries at the Texas Drive-In, and a few minutes of parking and making out at a dark, private side street just newly constructed off DuPont Street, near our houses. We exchanged the typical "You mean so much to me" and "We are so good for each other."

I did not tell Ginny about the previous night's events, especially about drinking the beer. I didn't want to ruin what pleasures I could garner from my date by upsetting her. At Ginny's house, as I dropped her off, I turned to her and said, "Ginny, I really love you and am going to miss you terribly when I go to Tech next month. I hope we make the most of the time we have together."

I wasn't sure she got what I was referring to, till she looked at me and said, "I promised we would get to know each other better. Let's spend some private time next weekend—no movie, no Texas, just us, somewhere private."

My brain was screaming, "Where private? What does she mean 'get to know each other better'? Could Mr. Willy finally get to meet Miss Kitty?" I kissed Ginny very passionately and said to her, "I will find us someplace private. I do want to be with you."

Ginny kissed me back and ran into the house.

On Monday, at the packing plant, I had another shitty day of milling and packing spices into little boxes so that women throughout Winn-Dixie's service area could bake pies and cakes and dinners for their families using the spices I jammed into the boxes. Of all the spices we packaged, cinnamon burns like crazy when it comes in contact with your bare skin. Often I would be crying in my shower at home with the pain of having to wash cinnamon powder off my face, arms, and hair. Still today, I can't eat any baked goods with cinnamon in them.

When I got home, my mom said I had an emergency call from Oz. I called him, hoping nothing serious had happened to him, any of the Mag 6, or any of their families. "Hey, Oz, what's the emergency? My mom said to call you when I got home."

Oz was laughing and said, "Have you seen this afternoon's *Jacksonville Journal*? You may want to go get a copy, or many copies. Our twisting photo is in the paper."

"You're kidding! The reporter actually put our photo in the paper?" I was excited that our little stunt had actually paid some dividends.

"Rollo, go get the paper" was all Oz would tell me.

Since we didn't take the evening paper, I went down to the local convenience store and picked up a copy of the *Journal* from the stack near the door. I paid for the paper and, as usual, started flipping from the back section to the front.

"Nothing, nothing, nothing." I wondered to myself, "What in the hell was Oz talking about?"

I was about to trash the newspaper, thinking Oz had pulled a trick on me to get me to go spend my money on a paper with nothing in it, when I finally noticed the half-page photo on the *front page*. There we were, the Twisting Champions of the World, Guinness Book and all. The reporter from the *Jacksonville Journal* had done a huge article on us and put the photo of us on the curb at the foot of the Warren Street Bridge on the front page as leading news of the day.

The photo wasn't very well done. Oz led off the photo, then there was a nice picture of me and Lily and Star, then a half-photo of Ted. Todd got cut out of the photo, all except one foot, but he did get his name in the caption below. I knew when the reporter was about to take the photo that it would be a case of getting in front or getting cut out. Sure enough, Todd didn't make the front page of the *Jacksonville Journal*, even though he suffered through the long night on San Jose Boulevard along with the rest of us. If Todd hadn't taken a piss before the reporter shot the photo, more than his left foot would have been in it.

I bought twenty copies of the *Journal* and took them home to show my parents and sister. They thought the whole stunt was really funny. Oz's dad, while stopped at a light on the way home from work, saw the photo on the paper at a curbside newsstand and started to crack up with laughter.

I took a copy of the *Journal* to Ginny and briefly told her what we had done with the twisting and the reporter. I hadn't wanted to tell her about our twisting stunt until I saw what, if any, press we got so I could surprise her. I didn't tell her the guys had a date with a couple six-packs of Pabst Blue Ribbon that night. Ginny really thought the whole newspaper photo and article was the type of stunt Oz and I would pull off. Since I was still in my smelly work clothes, Ginny pushed me out the door and said she would see me on Saturday for our private time alone.

In fact, the photo and article got picked up by the Associated Press and went all over America. Years later, we had people recognize us, and most thought it was a pretty cool stunt we pulled off.

We did run into some older persons from time to time who didn't hesitate to give us a piece of their minds and accuse us of trying to bring down America with the wicked Twist dancing and rock and roll music.

Chapter 13

Alone

The pressure was now on for me to come up with the private place for Ginny and me to be alone and begin to explore our physical love for each other. My first thought was the Horne Motel. So I called and asked what the room rate was, and it turned out to be pretty reasonable for my first tryst (of course, a teenager is willing to shell out nearly anything if there's a chance for some hot sex). But I wasn't sure Ginny was going to go for a seedy motel complete with a bed that vibrated for a full ten minutes when you dropped a quarter in the slot.

I thought about doing the Jackie routine in the park with the hidden basket with a blanket inside. This seemed like a good, economical, and romantic solution until the thought crossed my mind about what would happen if we were spread out on a blanket and Jackie and Reginald came swooping down on her broomstick or fire-breathing dragon. That would be embarrassing for all of us—well, except maybe the dragon, whom I was sure wouldn't be the least bit embarrassed.

On Wednesday after a long day at work at the plant packaging a thousand cans of drip coffee, I stood in the shower and let the hot water massage my back. My mother opened the bathroom door slightly and said, "Your dad and I are going to Hilton Head, South Carolina, for the weekend and your sister is staying with her friend Carolyn, so you're on your own. I'll have some food made up for you. You don't mind if you're alone for the weekend, do you?"

I almost fell out of the shower doing a dance under the pelting water. Calmly, I replied, "Oh, no, Mom, I don't mind holding down the fort this weekend. You guys have a great time." But inside, I was screaming to myself, "Yes, yes, yes! The house, the pool, the beds—all to myself and Ginny! Thank you, thank you, and thank you!" I wasn't sure and didn't care whom I was thanking—maybe the Gods of Love and Lust and rampant teenage male hormones.

I thought I would surprise Ginny with the news as we drove to my house on Saturday night. I couldn't sleep the next several nights, tossing and turning and visualizing Saturday night and what Ginny and I would do with our private time together. I would have to have extra protection ready to use. The cheap condoms under my smelly tennis shoes in the shoe box in my closet needed to be replaced with a top-of-the-line, brand-name variety, maybe a Trojan, advertised as extra-sensitive and slightly lubricated. I frowned when I realized I would have to go to the drug store to find this quality of condom since the Burger King only sold the cheapie brands. I couldn't tell my Mag 6 buddies of my pending pleasure evening with Ginny; otherwise, one of the smart-ass friends would try to scuttle the evening for laughs.

On Saturday, everything was going according to my well-laid plans for getting well-laid. Mom and Dad left early for Hilton Head, dropping off my sister at her friend's house on their way. I made a trip to the local drug store, where, even though I tried to act mature and cool, I was sweating bullets when I asked the balding, seventy-something druggist for a box of Trojan condoms.

He just looked smugly over the top of the bifocal glasses perched at the end of his pock-marked nose and asked, "Do you want the box of six, twelve, or twenty-four?"

I knew he was playing with my mind, as no teenager had need of twenty-four condoms for a weekend, a month, or even a year. Teenager sex in the early 1960s was more wishful thinking than ever a reality. I told him the box of six Trojans was what my dad wanted me to buy, hoping to make the druggist think the condoms were not for me.

The druggist started laughing, knowing it was a lie because no father in his right mind would send his son to buy his condoms. I pushed my condom purchase deep into my pocket so if I ran into anyone I knew, it wouldn't be out in the open in front of God and everybody. I could just imagine running into Ginny's mother shopping at the drug store and her asking, "Hi, Rob. What are you here for? What's in the bag?"

I had no idea how I would respond to that, but I was pretty certain I wouldn't say "Oh, it's a box of Trojan condoms for my date tonight with your daughter. Have a nice day."

Once in my car, I pulled the condoms out of my pocket and put them under the seat just in case I got stopped on the way home for speeding, or got hit by another car and the cop on the scene asked me, "What's that bulging in your pocket? A knife? A gun? Carefully remove what you have in your pocket. No sudden moves." I could just see his tense face and his hand on the revolver.

"Sorry, Officer, it's just a box of Trojans for my dad." I imagined that any cop faced with that scenario would laugh at me just like the druggist had. I also didn't want to get into a crash and get killed on the way home and have the sad-eyed cop tell my mother, "Here are your son's belongings, watch, wallet, box of six Trojan condoms." My mother would never understand why I died with a box of Trojans under the front seat of my car.

I called Ginny and told her to bring a bathing suit because our date would be at a place where we could swim, maybe a pool, maybe the beach. I wanted to surprise her about our date being just minutes away at my house and the swimming being in my very own private swimming pool. My thought was that sometime during our night, maybe we would take a swim to wash off the residue of passion from earlier in the evening.

When she got into my car, Ginny was already in a loving mood and kissed me on my neck and ear. "So, do we have somewhere we can go to be alone? I've been thinking about this night for the entire week."

"Yes, I have the perfect place for us to be alone: my place. Parents and sister are gone for the weekend and we have the entire house and pool to ourselves. No one knows we are there—no Mag 6, no one."

"That's wonderful. I can relax and not worry about someone seeing me somewhere I shouldn't be." Then Ginny giggled and said, "Like at a motel or at Hill 13 at the beach."

"OK, my home it is," I said with my most virile and lecherous grin.

Within minutes, we were in my house. I had turned on the stereo, put on some well-selected records, including the Platters and Johnny Mathis, certainly not rock and roll. Elvis or Buddy Holly just wouldn't set the mood quite right, although a little "roll in the hay" would be great. I dimmed the lights so the neighbors couldn't see who or what was going on in the house. The air-conditioner was humming along at a cool seventy degrees; the atmosphere was perfect.

I said to Ginny, "Want to take a swim, listen to the music, and stretch out on the couch?" I needed to build the mood for the both of us, not wanting to go right to the closing line, which would have been something like, "Let's go back to my room and make mad, passionate love."

We got comfortable on the couch and began to kiss and really get into it when fate dealt the night a near-fatal blow with the ringing of the phone. I had to answer in case something had happened to my parents, even though what I really wanted to do was yank the cord out of the wall and get back down to business with Ginny.

When I picked up, it was Oz on the other end of the phone. "Rollo, I'm desperate! I'll give you anything to come get me now! Please, man, come on, I'm begging you!" This came pouring from a buddy of mine I had never heard or seen so shaken. Oz was clear across town, hiding in a drug store from the aftermath of getting chased by the angry patrons of a theatre where his buddy Danny had thrown eggs at the moviegoers and earned their ire.

So, there went my dream night with Ginny. Both of us jumped into my car and headed off to pick up Oz and bring him back to his house before he suffered a fate worse than death. Oz was still shaking when we dropped him off outside his house because he realized he had almost gotten arrested for egg-throwing with his idiot dying buddy, Danny.

Once we got back to my house, Ginny and I only had about an hour to kill before she had to be home, so I tried to salvage the evening the best I could. "Ginny," I said with the most sorrowful and thoughtful expression I could manage, "I'm so sorry we lost our special night together. Want to take a quick swim, then head home?'

"Sure," Ginny answered, sounding a bit disappointed herself. "I'll just go change and meet you at the pool."

Ginny went into my parents' bathroom to get into her bathing suit, and I changed in my bathroom, then went out the back door to the pool. I turned on the pool lights and dove into the water. It was great, not cold and not warm, just perfect.

I was floating around and killing time when Ginny came out of the house dressed in a beautiful two-piece bikini the likes of which I had never seen on her. Thank God she didn't put on her ugly black Speedo from her swim meets.

The bikini pushed her beautiful breasts up and showed off her flat, tan stomach, making her body a breathtaking vision. While grinning outwardly, I cursed Oz silently for ruining my big plans for our first sexual interlude. My six Trojans would stay in the box, and I was suddenly hopeful that on Monday I could take them back for a refund.

Ginny asked me, "Can I turn off the pool lights? They're a little bright. We can swim by the light of the full moon; it's much more romantic that way."

"Sure, switch is over by the wall," I replied, and I watched Ginny as she turned off the lights, then walked to the diving board.

I was getting ready to make some wise-ass remark about her diving abilities, which were actually excellent since she was, after all, a diver on the swim team. Then, lightning struck me from the God of Passion and Lust, and the most unbelievable thing happened. What came next left me absolutely dumbstruck. What I saw before me was an image that would be burned permanently into my brain.

Ginny was standing in the moonlight, at the foot of the diving board, when she slowly undid the strings on her bikini top and dropped it onto the deck beside the diving board. There she stood in the illuminating rays of the full moon, exposing the most fantastic, beautiful pair of breasts God ever blessed a young girl with. Even Michelangelo, with the finest marble in all of Italy at his disposal, could not have carved a more perfect pair of breasts. I had to move to the side of the pool to brace myself as the sight of Ginny with her breasts exposed was more than I could comprehend, and suddenly my brain threatened to shut itself down in pure erotic overload. She hadn't said a single word to me to hint at what she was going to do, and the visual experience left me babbling to myself like an idiot.

Ginny stepped lightly out onto the diving board, then, with a single perfect bounce, pushed her unbelievable body into the air at least a full three feet off the board. Her breasts didn't move even a tenth of an inch in any direction, but merely followed the rest of her flowing form as she arched her back and went into a perfect swan dive. At the apex of the dive, I lost it. My heart stopped beating, I suddenly couldn't breathe, and I felt like I was dying, yet never more alive, all at the same time.

As if in slow motion, Ginny's body found the perfect form for her descent: Her arms extended like a swan in flight, her back arched as if she were trying to touch the back of her head to her butt, and her legs were together without the slightest bit of separation—I mean, during that dive you couldn't have put a dime between her legs.

Ginny slid into the water with almost no splash at all. Any judge in his right mind would have scored her dive a perfect 10. She resurfaced and glided effortlessly up to where I was holding onto the edge of the pool with a death grip. She flipped her head in the water, then threw it back, which flattened her hair against her scalp. She looked at me with her big brown eyes, water in her face, her perfect breasts slightly below the water line, and said ever so quietly, "I want you to hold me."

I came up to Ginny, who immediately put her hands around the back of my head and pulled her body to mine, pressing her warm, soft breasts against my chest. She kissed me then, pushing her tongue into my mouth, and I reciprocated with a French kiss more mind-blowing than any we had ever achieved in all our hours of making out. I reached up and began to touch her breasts, which caused Ginny to gasp and push her tongue even deeper into my mouth.

I said to her, my voice husky with rising passion, "I love you and want to make love to you."

Ginny almost instantly pulled back and looked at me with a mixed expression, as if to say both, "Oh, yes, I want you, too," and "Not here, not in the swimming pool." Then she said softly, "I love you, too, but we're a long way from making love. We have to take it slow; making love is a major commitment for both of us. Is that OK with you?"

The question was one of "damned if you do and damned if you don't." If I had answered, "No, it's not OK. I want to make love *now*," the night, and maybe our relationship, would have flamed out like a Roman candle.

If I had said, "I can wait forever for sex with you, Ginny," I *could* have been left waiting forever. I went for the bird-in-the-hand answer—in this case, the bird just happening to be a beautifully formed breast I was holding. "Ginny, I can and will wait for making love till we both know it's the right time."

"Oh, Rob, I knew you'd understand!" She kissed me again and said, "Our time will come." I would have to be patient if I wanted to make love with Ginny, and there in the cool water, with her warm breasts against my chest, I figured it would be well worth the wait.

We splashed and played for several minutes, then Ginny got out of the pool and went to the diving board, put her bikini top back on, and started for the house. "I have to dry my hair and we have to go home. Get dressed."

Ginny disappeared into the house, and within twenty minutes she was dressed and ready to head home. I was still getting dressed, probably due to the fact that after seeing Ginny's beautiful half-naked body silhouetted against the full moon, my brain was shorted out and I was having difficulty even getting my shoes on, which, considering that they were loafers, shouldn't have been that difficult.

Once I finally managed to get dressed, we hopped into my car and drove back to her house. After a couple quick kisses, she got out of the car, turned, and said to me, "Tonight was very special for us. We can only do what we did when the time is right, not every time we go out on a date. Is that OK with you?"

"Yes, Ginny, I only want to do what we did when it is special for both of us. I love you." The truth of the matter was that I wanted to do what we did and *more every* time, but I knew if I said something to that effect, I would be shooting myself in the foot.

Ginny just smiled and went into her house, leaving me to bang my head against my steering wheel and say to myself, "Shit, only on special occasions? Birthdays? Valentine's Day? Thanksgiving? I'm gonna be the horniest teenager on earth—no, in the *universe*—waiting for the time when it will be special for both of us!"

I went home to an empty house. The Johnny Mathis records were still playing, but I wasn't in the mood for mood music anymore, so I shut them off and put them away. I went into my bedroom and took the new condoms out of their hiding place. I sighed as I figured the old druggist would laugh at me if I tried to get a refund on the box of Trojans, so I just hid them in my smelly sneakers. Even though Mom wasn't home to remind me, I dutifully brushed my teeth and went to bed—alone. Well, not totally true; my faithful dog, good old Tippy, jumped in bed with me and gave me a look as if to say, "I love you." Then she proceeded to lick my face.

Dogs are man's best friend, especially when you think you are going to make love to your girlfriend and it doesn't happen. They're always there for you and will always give you a big lick on your face to heal your emotional wounds and make you feel better. I grabbed Tippy and gave her a big kiss and said, "I love you, too, my beautiful dog."

"Crash and Burn"

With the summer winding down, my relationship with Ginny was on the same track, just like two freight trains fixing to collide head-on. It certainly wasn't that I *wanted* to lose Ginny, but physics was soon to come into play with the mathematical formula of time and distance multiplied by the ages of the lovers making for an imploding love universe. I had decided to play football at Tech as a walk-on, which meant I would start college three weeks before the rest of my buddies. Lily also decided to go for it with football at his college of choice, so he would be leaving the same time I would.

It didn't take long before the fraternity parties became more frequent and, quite honestly, more fun than hanging out at the Texas Drive-In on Saturday night. I kept coming up with more and more excuses why Ginny and I couldn't go out on this or that weekend. My problem was, I couldn't bring Ginny to the parties because they were basically drink-a-thons and I didn't want her to know I was moving beyond the beer blasts into cocktails with key Tech alumni.

With Ginny's aversion to alcohol, I tried to conceal my socializing on the cocktail circuit, but soon I decided I simply couldn't hide my transgressions, and quite honestly, I wanted to come out of the closet and tell her what I was up to.

It was nearly the end of the summer, just before I was to leave for college, when everything came to a head. I was leaving work for one of several goodbye dates I had with Ginny before college when one of my co-workers, Buzz, asked me to drop him off at a vendor-sponsored catfish and beer party.

One of Winn-Dixie's trucking vendors was throwing an end-of-summer party for the companies that used their semis to ship product. The party was at a local fish restaurant that had an outside cooking grill, but the real attraction was the beer flowing from five ice-cold kegs. Buzz invited me to have a catfish dinner and a beer before heading home to clean up and meet Ginny. Mind you, I wasn't one to say no to a good grilled catfish washed down with a super-cold beer, and I had every intention of doing no more than having dinner and a beer and hanging out with Buzz for absolutely no more than thirty to forty-five minutes, tops.

After more than an hour and a half of beer-drinking with Buzz, I realized in bleary-eyed horror that I only had thirty minutes to pick up Ginny for our date. Buzz had missed his ride to his house and imposed on me to take him home. Not having time to take Buzz home *and* be at Ginny's on time, I made the most stupid decision I'd made since graduation: I decided to take Buzz with me to pick up Ginny, then afterward go to my house to clean up, and then the three of us would drive back across town to drop Buzz off and Ginny and I would go on to our date. Of course, in the telling, this all boils down to one long, confusing sentence and one dumb, dumb, dumb-assed idea.

Ginny, being who she was, was appalled at our dirty work apparel, our foul, stale beer breath, and just the general unacceptability of our demeanor. Not to mention the fact that she took an immediate dislike to Buzz, possibly because his name implied the condition the two of us were in when we picked her up: "Beer Buzz."

Ginny jumped to the conclusion that Buzz was the instigator of getting me to the catfish and beer party and of me subsequently showing up at her door in a not-so-great condition in terms of appearance or sobriety. Ginny told us immediately to go sit in the car because she knew that if her dad caught sight or smell of us, he would never allow her to go out with me again. She also knew he would probably try to kill me, and most likely succeed, for my showing up drunk at his home and thereby showing disrespect for Ginny and the rest of his family—all of which, on retrospect, he would have had every right to do.

We drove quietly to my house and I cleaned up while Ginny and my mother entertained a buzzing Buzz, who spent the entire time commenting on how rich my family must be to have our own swimming pool. I kind of thought the conversation was a little out of line, but I would have been happy for *any* conversation during the ride back across town with Ginny to drop Buzz off at his house. Instead, the silence was truly deafening; you could have cut the tension with a dull spoon, let alone a knife.

After we had dropped Buzz off and were heading back across the river to start our official goodbye date, I finally got tired of the cold silence and said to Ginny, "I know you're really pissed at me, and I don't blame you, seeing as how I was a real jerk tonight. Is there any way I can make it up to you?" I figured she would cut me some slack since it was one of our last dates, and for a long moment I lived in the hopes that maybe she'd offer me a "get out of jail free" pass. Wrong again, Robby boy!

"Rob, I want you to take me home right now, and I don't want to ever see you again. I told you I didn't want a boyfriend going to AA meetings with my dad. You're a borderline drunk, and I can find a boyfriend who respects me and my family." Ginny was more than pissed—she was livid with me. She had dug in her heels and thrown down the "our relationship is kaput" gauntlet.

I had one shot to try and save our future, to throw myself on the mercy of the court, to beg my way back into her good graces. Just before I started to grovel for forgiveness, I realized that the whole reason I had showed up at her house high from drinking too many beers was that I simply didn't care about trying to keep up my façade of being a teetotaler on dates with Ginny. I suddenly realized that I much preferred going out and having good, honest fun with my future college colleagues. They won out over Ginny in that brief instant. After all, college was where I was going to be for the next four or five years of my life, not at the Texas Drive-In or sitting in DuPont High's football stadium cheering on the high school team.

It was clear to Ginny before it was clear to me that it was time for both of us to move on. Ginny would be a junior in high school and I would be a freshman in college. That amounted to us being not only worlds, but whole universes, apart. Our friends would soon change, my Mag 6 buddies would also be moving on to a new life and new experiences with different people, and it was sad in many respects, but also exciting and exhilarating with so many unknown future opportunities just around the corner.

At length I said to Ginny, "I can honestly say you've meant more to me than anyone I've ever loved. I'll never forget what we meant to each other, and I'll always love you. In the end, I'm truly sorry it ends this way, but maybe it's best for you, since you can always blame me and how I treated you for our breakup. All I ask is that you please do try and remember our good times together."

Ginny cried all the way to her house. She got out of the car and, without saying a word, went inside without looking back a single time. She never called or made any attempt to see me again.

The next morning when I got into my car to go up to the corner convenience store for milk, I found that during the night someone had been in my car. There, in the front seat, was my class ring and my framed photo, declaring, "To the One I Love, Rob." That day, I found a pen that matched the one I had used to inscribe the photo, and with a little overwriting, I changed the inscription: "To the One I Love, Mom." I gave the photo to my mother, who kept it in her bedroom till the day she passed away.

Chapter 14

Last Lap

On Friday, August 26, I called each of the Mag 6 and asked them to meet me the following Sunday at 4:00 in the afternoon in the stadium at the high school. I was due to leave for college the very next day, and I wanted to spend a few minutes with all of us together as a group, get in a few last laughs, and maybe get a little misty-eyed knowing the glorious past couple of years with them as my closest friends and confidants were coming to a close. Somehow, even though we would give each other the "promise to stay in touch" and "get together over the Christmas holidays," I instinctively knew that those moments could never replace the camaraderie I had shared with them on a daily basis for the last two years of high school.

Breaking up with a girlfriend is a gut-wrenching experience; the emotions go on for days and weeks as you feel as if you have lost the one and only love of your life. But losing a buddy, not to death, but to time and distance, is like the Chinese torture of a constant dripping of water on the forehead. Every day of your life something reminds you of your past friendship, such as having a beer and talking with new friends but trying to tell them the funny stories of adventures with your old buddies. The stories bring tears to your eyes while they bore the living crap out of your new friends. Oh, they may laugh at the right spots when you laugh, but they didn't experience the emotion of the event that you and your friends did. When replaying the memory of twisting down San Jose Boulevard or of the scary, stormy night stranded on a sandbar in my dad's boat just days before Christmas, I knew it would be only me, and those of the Mag 6 who were there with me, who could truly appreciate the fun and excitement of the adventures. Losing the day-to-day contact of a close buddy is definitely harder on one's emotional fabric than getting dumped by a girl.

The last meeting with our group would work great for Lily since he also was leaving for college and football camp, which would begin the first of the week. The others in our group didn't have to leave for college till after Labor Day, so they had a few more days to pal around and maybe get themselves into one last adventure before heading out for their chosen school of higher learning.

Lily and I were facing the shared unknown of playing football at the college level and whatever else might lie ahead of us. In our garages during the summer, both of us had tried to bulk up by doing weight lifting. Neither one of us gained much from pumping the iron, however. I actually *lost* a few pounds since I was still running in some summer track meets. Going off to Tech to play in the big league while weighing in on the lighter side for my playing position, I was destined to be slaughtered by bigger, faster, tougher senior players.

In the 1960s, freshman college football players had their own teams and played other freshman college teams on a shortened schedule. But for most all college football programs, the freshman team was referred to as "the meat squad," which is basically what we were—some live meat for the senior players to scrimmage and have fun beating to a pulp.

Lily and I had bonded more during the past track season since both of us were sprinters and ran together on DuPont's medal-winning relay teams. We had been elected co-captains of the track team, although to this day, I still kid Lily that I was the captain and he was the co-captain, kind of like airplane pilots—one is the pilot and one is the co-pilot, not both co-captains or co-pilots. Lily is still pissed that I try to make a distinction in our captain status.

As we prepared to start college, we all thought our big adventures were ahead of us, that we had filled our memory buckets with all the great times of our pre-college years and that there were no more adventures for the Mag 6, especially Lily and me, leaving town in just a scant couple of days. Boy, was I wrong on that assumption!

"*Axe Handle Saturday*"

Lily and I got together the Saturday before leaving for college and headed off to downtown Jacksonville to do some last-minute shopping and errands, picking up some clothes for college and the typewriter I had dropped off for repair earlier in the week. My vintage 1930s Smith Corona typewriter had badly needed repairs because the "L" key kept sticking, probably from various and sundry food particles and drips of sticky drinks that accidently fell between the keys while I was eating and typing.

I loved the typewriter and how I could rest my fingers on the keys without it typing. The new IBM Selectric typewriters that were the rage of the business community had one flaw: For a novice typist like me, one slight touch on the keys would give you more letters than you wanted— "ZZZZZZZZZ." Plus, it was a pain to undo mistakes.

With my Corona, I never made a mistake by pushing the wrong key, because you really had to *push* the key to make the letter appear on the paper. If you did make a mistake, you could simply erase it with a rubber ink eraser.

After picking up my typewriter from the repair shop several blocks from the center of town, we headed on to our destination of the day, Hemming Park, which was in the center of downtown Jacksonville and surrounded by quite a few of the local retail stores. One of the surrounding stores was Woolworths, and Lily and I headed there to get something to drink from the lunch counter and to pick up some basic school supplies, like pens, pencils, notebooks, paper, and, of course, a stapler.

As we neared the store, we could see a mob of men of all ages in Hemming Park, carrying axe handles and baseball bats. Not only was the sight of this many men, armed as they were, odd and terrifying, but their overall appearance was that of country or rural folk, not the type of people who lived or worked in the nearby suburbs. To top it off, you could see from the looks in their eyes that they were pissed off about something and were looking to make trouble. I could hear the mob yelling unintelligible threats which seemed directed toward the Woolworths store. We soon found out that every member of the mob in Hemming Park was a dues-paying member of the Ku Klux Klan.

When I first spotted the crowd, I said, "Hey, Lily, check out the park. Look at that, a bunch of rednecks with axe handles and ball bats. What's going on?"

"Don't know, Rollo. These guys look like they're spoiling for a fight. Maybe we should haul ass out of here."

Lily was rightly concerned, as rednecks sometimes didn't differentiate between beating the shit out of white guys, especially college-looking guys, and their primary target, black folks.

"Let's just run into Woolworths and grab our school supplies and get out before anything happens. It looks like they're just milling around, maybe waiting for someone to start something. Besides, maybe the cops will stop anything that gets started. Come on, let's hit Woolworths and then go."

I nudged Lily up the street and we ducked into Woolworths, which turned out *not* to be such a bright move because when we walked through the store's front doors, so did a number of the pissed-off rednecks with their axe handles.

Inside, we immediately spotted what was making the redneck KKK members go insane. There at the lunch counter sat a handful of young, college-age, black men and women. Jacksonville in 1960 was a segregated city, and the Woolworths definitely had a "whites only" food service policy. So, well, the black college students were definitely looking to make a statement, but by doing so, they were destined to get the shit beat out of them by the KKK. Within a few seconds of Lily and me entering Woolworths, the black students got their wish for a confrontation with the KKK; the rednecks came pouring through the doors and started swinging their axe handles at the black students.

"Holy shit, Lily! We gotta get out of here, get back to the car, and get the hell out of downtown!" I shouted. "This place is erupting and, shit, who knows, maybe they all got guns and are going to start shooting anything that moves, which could be you and me!" I grabbed Lily by the shirt and started pulling him toward the nearest emergency exit.

We had just started trying to make our escape when four very big white men grabbed one of the black male students, picked him up like a sack of potatoes, and threw the college kid screaming into the display window near the lunch counter. The black student hit the window, but, being plate-glass, the window thumped and shook with the blow but didn't shatter into flesh-shredding fragments. The impact of hitting the window must have been much like being thrown hard against a brick wall; the student was knocked cold and fell into the mannequins, where he lay looking like one of them, grossly contorted, in the window display space, legs and arms twisted in multiple directions.

Lily and I made our retreat through the emergency exit and out to the side street. My car, though, was on the other side of the building, which meant we had to make our way around the block to get there. We got to the street in front of Woolworths and saw that none of the rednecks were out on the sidewalk; most were inside the store and some still in Hemming Park.

"Lily, let's make a dash for the corner, then cut down the side street and jump in the car." Lily looked at me with an expression of terrified agreement, so I yelled, "Run!" We made a mad dash for safety before the sound of my word had faded.

We both made it to the corner without interference and were just starting to feel a little safer when we turned the corner and ran headlong into a bunch of the redneck Klansmen, who were advancing up the side street in search of targets.

Lily grabbed one of the men to catch his balance and, looking square into the fellow's eyes, was suddenly shocked to recognize him.

"Hey, I know you. Aren't you Melvin? We went to grade school together in Ocala?"

I suddenly found myself staring straight into the eyes of the other Klansmen who were obviously just spoiling to beat someone with their axe handles. You could tell these guys didn't want to go home without their prized axe handle being stained with some poor bastard's blood, but I most assuredly did not want my Type A blood to be the blood on the end of one of these asshole's axe handles.

I also found myself looking at Lily, still holding one of the men by his shirt, carrying on a conversation with him, and calling him by name. I said to myself, "I am going to have my brains spilled all over this street, and Lily is having old-home week with one of these animals. What the shit is going on?"

Melvin yelled to the other men, "These guys are OK, leave 'em alone. Let's go to the park." And with that, Melvin and his axe handle–wielding buddies took off.

I looked at Lily and said, "You *know* that asshole?"

Lily, with one of the most wild-eyed expressions I have ever seen, gasped, "I went to grade school with Melvin in Ocala. Unbelievable! Melvin is here at this race riot! He's in the Klan! He saved our asses! God's definitely watching over us."

"Run to the car, Lily! You can send Melvin a thank-you note tomorrow."

We got to my car and headed toward the bridge back across the river. We hadn't gone a block when we were stopped at a street barricade by four of the largest humans I have ever seen, all four in police uniforms and all four carrying shotguns. I wanted to pee in my pants since I thought the cops might think we belonged to the race riot and were somehow connected to the Klan.

One of the cops leaned in through my car window and took a long look at us. Then he said to the others, "Not Klan. Let them through."

I'm guessing that our Lacoste shirts with the little alligator embossed on them were not KKK-issue, nor did we have the appearance of those who would run around in the woods at night wearing white sheets, carrying torches, and setting big wooden crosses ablaze. I'm also reasonably sure that my pathetic look of "Please don't mess with us; we're the good guys" helped get us through that police barricade and back on our way home.

That riot evolved into the worst race riot in Jacksonville's history, and one of the largest and most bloody riots in the civil rights movement. The media appropriately termed the day "Axe Handle Saturday." Unfortunately, as Lily and I had witnessed, the five or six African Americans who had been in Woolworths trying to get counter service were not equally equipped with weapons when the riot began. Over fifty African Americans ended up seriously injured in the riot and forty-eight arrested. As it turned out, only fourteen of the Klan were arrested.

My mother was frantic when I finally got to my house after dropping

Lily off. The radio was blasting the news of the race riot, and my mom knew Lily and I were somewhere downtown. I told her what happened and I had to promise not to go back downtown for any reason till I left for college. I assured her most honestly that I had no desire to get my head bashed in by some toothless redneck. Besides, in a couple of days, at football camp, some toothless 280-pound offensive lineman would be *legally* bashing my head.

On Sunday afternoon, a warm and breezy day, I walked over to the high school to meet my Mag 6 buddies. The walk took me by the home of a senior from the previous year with whom I had played football. As I passed by, I caught myself glancing up at his house and thinking to myself, "Wonder what Buster's doing these days? Never saw him all summer. Maybe he's going to college full-time?" I found out later that Buster had come down with mono at college and had to drop out his second semester. Well, maybe mono was better than other social diseases he could have gotten at college.

Across the street from Buster's house lived Mary, a good friend of Ginny's—yes, that ex-girlfriend of mine. Mary was a real looker, so good-looking that most boys in her class were scared to ask her for a date. Mary sat home on many a Friday and Saturday night due to being *too* pretty. I made a mental note to explore Mary as an option when I came home during college break.

I never got around to asking Mary on a date, but a couple of years into college, when Georgia Tech played Penn State in the Gator Bowl, I threw a party for my Mag 6 buddies and some of the starting Tech football players who were good friends of mine, and I invited Mary and several of her friends. Mary had only gotten more beautiful in the two years since high school. As she plopped herself on a barstool in my rec room, Mary quickly became the center of attention for my football friends, especially Bill, the starting quarterback. After much beer and dancing, Mary accepted a date with Bill, who eventually broke curfew several times before the Gator Bowl game to be with her. Unfortunately, Tech got creamed by Penn State in the Gator Bowl, thanks in part to my having introduced Mary to Bill. I often believe that the Vegas odds makers would have tacked fourteen more points on Tech's underdog point spread if they had known about Mary.

That Sunday afternoon, my last Sunday before leaving for college, I walked slowly into the stadium and sat at the 50-yard line. I wanted the image of the entire track and field, with the school in the distance, seared into my memory forever.

The football field was being groomed for the upcoming season, and most of the bare spots had been filled in with new grass. Unlike the new plastic-grass turf, the football fields of the '60s were natural grass, which in my opinion is the only proper grass for a high school football field.

As I sat in the stands, the smell of freshly cut grass combined with the scent of the cinder track and the warm breeze to make for an almost aphrodisiac aroma. Some athletes love the smell of the gymnasium and locker room, especially the basketball jocks. I, personally, love the outdoors—mowed grass, wet cinders after a quick downpour, the pending night air with a cornucopia of smells and scents from the wind rolling across the fields, cement pavements, homes cooking dinners, the nearby river—all of the olfactory ingredients for an almost mind-numbing sensation.

Lily was the first of the Mag 6 to arrive. This wasn't unusual, as he saw the Mag 6 as an extension of his family and not even Satan himself was going to come between getting together with us on our final day before going separate ways. He and I sensed the ending of an era of fun and excitement with our gang. Lily would be at college playing football for the next four years, and like any football program, you have to commit your life and soul if it's going to be successful. Christmas vacations would be a flash in the eye, summer vacations even quicker, and junior and senior years, you stayed at college for summer classes to stay eligible for the next season.

"Lily, some day yesterday, huh? It's a wonder we're alive today. Did you see the riot on television last night?"

Lily responded, "My parents were really pissed off that we went downtown yesterday. They said we could've been beaten to death by the Klan or arrested or even killed by the cops in all that confusion. They blamed it on you that we were down there."

"Well, did you tell them you ran into your old grade school buddy and Klan member, Melvin? Maybe you're going to invite him to your house this November for Thanksgiving dinner?" I replied, poking a little fun at Lily, who hated being teased.

Lily shot back, "Melvin kept us alive! Otherwise you and I would be wearing big gauze bandages around our heads today from getting whacked by those axe handles."

"Hey, here come Oz and Star," I said. Lily looked down the track as the two sauntered up to where we were sitting. I yelled to them, "Down here. Where's Crazy and Spiff?"

Oz yelled back, "Spiff's picking up Crazy, probably be late with Crazy counting his pennies."

But right behind Oz and Star, I could see Spiff and Crazy coming to join the group. So I yelled out again, "Spiff, Crazy, down here."

We were all together and making small talk when I said, "I wanted us to get together before Lily and I blast out of here. Probably the last time we'll all see each other before Christmas. I, for one, just want to say goodbye and let you know it has been great knowing you."

Oz looked at me and said, "Rollo, you sound like you're moving away and this is it for the Mag 6."

"No, Oz, just wanted to see all of you before tomorrow and maybe have a few laughs. I'm not moving anywhere!"

Little did I know that within a couple of years, my parents would be in California and I would no longer be coming back to Jacksonville for Christmas or summer vacation. When my parents moved during my junior year at Tech, I stayed in Atlanta during vacations since I had no place in Jacksonville to go home to anymore. I also put myself on a fast track to graduate from Tech within four years after losing credit hours during my first year due to the time commitment football required.

"Hey, Spiff, remember 'Not too good, Og'?" I was referring to a track meet we had had here at Alfred I. DuPont just a few months before. Spiff, a good 880-yard runner, was standing near Ogden Jones, a miler who had just finished running the mile only to be embarrassingly lapped by the other runners. Ogden was in terrible physical condition, so besides being lapped by his competitors, Ogden was lying on the ground throwing up when our beloved track coach, Felton Luck, walked up to him and, trying to say something nice, made the quote the Mag 6 still use today: "Not too good, Og." When we exchange that line today, it can mean anything from, "Nice try, but you were quite a bit short of winning" to "You got your clock cleaned by your competitor."

Spiff responded, "Yeah, that will live with me forever. I'll never forget Coach Luck looking down at Ogden and shaking his head when he made his offhand comment, 'Not too good, Og.' I felt sorry for Ogden, getting lapped and puking. But looking at him curled up on the ground, I could only think, 'Better Og than me.'"

Then Oz jumped on Lily with teasing about his famous science project: "Lily, it's a wonder you're going to college with the fraud you pulled in science class about natural gas being present in nature and your bogus swamp-gas methane project."

Lily protested Oz's challenge that the science project hadn't been entirely legit. "I almost killed myself wading in that swampy area down near the river to capture natural methane gas seeping to the surface in that glass jar. Do you know there's a shitload of snakes in that swamp? I could've been bitten by one of those mothers and died before getting to a doctor."

Oz continued to stick it to Lily without letting up: "We all know you didn't go into some dangerous-ass swamp full of snakes to capture swamp gas. The gas you got in that jar was from farting in the jar in your bathroom. What'd you do, eat a can of Campbell's baked beans for the farts? Or did you pay up for Freddie the Farter to fill your jar?"

"The gas in that jar was pure methane! I stomped around in that swamp for hours to get a jar of swamp gas!" Lily was starting to get a little hot from being teased.

Oz then closed his case before the jury: "Methane gas burns blue. When you opened the jar and put a match to it, your gas burned with a sick-looking yellow color, a pure fart color."

Lily was now seething and said through clenched teeth, "The color of the flame was bluish; it was the lighting in the science room that gave the methane gas a yellowish color. The gas in the jar was swamp gas, not bean farts!"

"OK, OK, Lily, we believe you," Oz interjected. "By the way, how many cans of baked beans did you have to eat to get that perfect yellow burning fart gas?" Oz started laughing, as did all the other members of the Mag 6, including me—all except Lily, who sat and sulked.

Spiff turned to Star and said, "I heard you and that idiot, Tim Barr from Kennedy High School, picked up your dates last night in your underwear?"

Star looked embarrassed as he replied, "True, but where'd you get your scoop from?"

"Melissa, your date, is a friend of my girlfriend Halley. Melissa called Halley this morning before church and told her that when you picked her up, you had on what appeared to be a pair of plaid Bermuda shorts and that even her mother commented to you that she thought the colors were quite attractive. Melissa went on to say that when you two got to the car, you actually had a pair of Bermuda shorts you put on, and the plaid shorts you wore to the door were your boxer underwear. Melissa told Halley she thought it was really funny, especially because her naïve mom was thinking your boxer underwear colors were quite attractive."

Star replied to Spiff's rendition, "Well, Tim and I were kidding each other that parents are more taken in by the clothes the date wears to pick up their precious daughter than by the boy's background. You could be a well-dressed slasher or rapist and the mother would love you and shove her daughter out the door on the date with you. If you're a medical school student or even a priest and showed up for the date in old, but clean, clothes and worn tennis shoes, the mom would probably not allow her daughter to go on the date. As a dare to prove our point, we decided we would both pick up our dates in our underwear, just to see the mother or dad's reaction. Both dates' mothers never guessed the shorts were really our boxer underwear. I was sweating it that my privates would accidently peep out through the opening in the underwear. I think if that had happened, old mom would have caught on to the ruse and maybe called the cops, claiming I was some sort of weird exhibitionist."

"So, the girls thought it was funny? Neither one was offended?" Spiff continued to pump Star for information.

"Actually, the dates got pretty turned on with us in our underwear, and putting our Bermuda shorts on in the car almost turned into sort of a strip tease in reverse. You should try it with Halley; you might finally get to first base with her." Star laughed, knowing Spiff and Halley were more on the fun-couple side and less on the passionate side.

"Look Star . . ." Spiff started, but then, with a splutter, let it drop since he certainly did not want to start sharing his personal endeavors with Halley. Spiff knew if he said anything, the world would know by late afternoon, since his Mag 6 buddies weren't always the most discreet about another buddy's conquests.

I looked at Oz and Crazy and said, "You two are awful quiet. Our last day together for some time. Any stories you want to tell us?"

Oz pursed his lips thoughtfully, then replied, "The only one I can think of is when we went to Daytona for the 500 and when we ran out of money at the motel we were staying at, I took some of the patio furniture down the street and sold it to another motel to pay for food."

Crazy piped in and added his story: "There was that time when my car caught on fire on San Jose Boulevard and not a single one of you would come help me. When you heard my car was a piece of burnt toast alongside the road, and me standing there looking for a ride home, Oz and Spiff drove by and threw out a bag of marshmallows at me and yelled, 'Make s'mores!'"

We all laughed at each other's screw-ups, and we all knew that these kinds of adventures would never happen to us again, ever. We had lived in the most carefree time in America's history, when one could make a fool of themselves and not get arrested or ostracized by your parents or your girlfriend's parents. Everyone enjoyed a good laugh and appreciated the fun-loving and enterprising attitude of their children. Possibly their childhoods had been restricted by war and the economy, so the parents wanted their children to have more in life than they did growing up.

The Mag 6 looked at each other and slowly, one by one, said goodbye with a "Good luck at school" or "Have fun with football" or "See you at Thanksgiving." In the '60s, hugging and high-fiving were not acceptable or even conceived of as ways to say hello and goodbye. In the '60s, a nod of the head or a handshake was the mode used, even among close friends. The Mag 6 went for the head nod and said "Take care" or "See you soon."

Once the group had left, I sat for what seemed like a long time in the stadium. It seemed to me that I was the only one of the Mag 6 who fully understood the finality of our parting. Looking across the football field at the high school, the memories flooded my mind to the point that I thought I would drown in the reliving of just half of them. Tears welled up in my eyes. I never wanted that Camelot era of my life to end.

I got out of the stadium stands and began to walk the track, taking one last lap. I would never run competitively on this track again. The track was made of cinders, a dinosaur of a track base, replaced in years to come by rubberized surfaces trademarked "Tartan Track." Cinder tracks had a wonderful scent and a crunching feel under the runner's feet. Some were hard-packed, some loose like sand on the beach. I fell once on the cinder track and swore never to do that again. The cinders were in my skin for weeks before I could get them out.

Coach Felton Luck was our track coach, a big, lumbering, soft-spoken, wonderful man and coach. At 6'2", 240 pounds, and fifty years of age, Coach looked like he had played some football in college and possibly thrown shot put and discus in track. But in the three years I knew Coach Luck, he never mentioned anything about his athletic days, spending most of his time nurturing his high school athletes by helping them grow, not only as athletes but also as people. Coach came from the old coaching school that taught that building character in a young athlete was as important as building skills.

Not a single person who ever had Coach Luck for a teacher or club chaperone, or for a coach in football, weight-lifting, or track, ever said a disparaging word about the man. My only confrontation with him was during our first track meet of my senior year on the very same track I found myself walking this warm, late-summer day.

I had been competing in the 100-yard sprint and got off to a great start, maybe too great. My Driver's Ed. teacher and buddy, Coach Mahoney, was the official starter for the meet. Coach Mahoney had never fired a starter's pistol or been informed of the rules involved in a false start, which say to fire the starter's pistol a second time in order to call back all the runners for another start.

I was a good step or two ahead of everyone at the start, and not hearing a recall pistol shot, I kept running. I just thought I had gotten a great start, but Coach Luck said it was a false start, even though he was standing a football field away from the starting line, as one of the timers. I finished the 100 yards at a school record of 9.9, which Coach Luck rounded up to 10.1, which tied the school record. I strongly disagreed with his decision, but he just smiled and said, "10.1." So much for my debate and argument with Coach Luck; besides, he outweighed me by sixty pounds.

Halfway around the track, I stopped at what was the starting line for the 220-yard dash. One warm, sunny spring day of my senior year, at just a daily practice, not a meet, I had raced Nate, who was also a sprinter and one of our 2:30 Club buddies, for a practice 220.

That spring practice day, Coach had me try some longer spikes in my shoes. Nate was wearing shorter spikes, and that was the only time he ever beat me. My long spikes dug too far into the cinders, making it feel like I was running in deep snow. Nate was proud of his achievement, and even years later, I heard from friends that Nate bragged about the day he beat Rollo in the 220.

Through the years, I've always had good intentions of writing or calling Nate just to tease him that the only reason he won the race that spring day was that I was wearing lead boots to give him an advantage. Thankfully, I never made that telephone call. Not too many years ago, I learned Nate had died at the age of forty-two from some strange disease he got while serving our country in Vietnam. I feel a little ashamed that I even considered trying to minimize Nate's victory over me. I'm glad Nate had that victory to share with his friends and maybe his kids—the day he beat the captain of the track team at Alfred I. DuPont High School in Jacksonville, Florida.

The starting line of the 100-yard dash was where the stadium seating began and about fifty feet from the sidewalk. When I reached the starting line, it signaled the end of my final lap. For a moment longer, I stood looking down the straightaway, and I remembered that day not too long ago when my famous 9.9 sprint had turned into a 10.1. I could see my dad in the stands, a big smile on his face as I sprinted past where he was sitting. I instinctively knew that, as a former sprinter, he knew what I was feeling, out in front of my competitors, really burning up the track, and, as he would say, "picking them up and laying them down."

I looked one final time at the stadium, the football field, the cinder track, and the school. In my mind, I could hear the school bell calling students to class or dismissing them for the day. Soon a new senior class would be pulling the same sort of pranks and having the same adventures as the Mag 6 did during our senior year. In a few weeks, on the first day of school, there would be a hotshot senior boy standing in the "senior area" of the front steps and spotting a cute sophomore girl and falling instantly in love like I did with Jackie. Some things, like senior boys falling in love with sophomore girls, never change.

Turning toward the sidewalk and street, from our last goodbye meeting an hour earlier I could still hear the six of us laughing. I still felt the pang in my heart as each one of my friends had left to go home, each to start on his way to college, make new friends, find new loves, and maybe even get married in the next few years and start a family. I instinctively knew it would never be the same again. The realization that Camelot was finished was overwhelming for me then, and, when I think back, it still is, even now.

My last lap was done, and I had to move on myself. I was soon on the sidewalk walking toward home. It was tempting to turn and take in yet one more look at the school and the track. I didn't. I had had my last lap; I had said my goodbye.

Chapter 15

Emails
2009–2010

Sadly, emails have largely replaced letters, personal notes, phone calls, and your basic face-to-face conversation. But emails are not personal; you cannot look into the other person's eyes and see if they are sincere in what they are telling you or basically lying through their teeth. LED screens with email messages do not show you the guilt in the eyes of your lover or the shifting blinks of a liar.

The Mag 6 grew up with typewriters, carbon paper, and Princess Phones. We then advanced to pagers and mobile phones that looked like walkie-talkies. Now we are in the electronic age of smart phones, tablets, and the impersonal email systems available on a variety of electronic devices.

After fifty years, the Mag 6 began reconnecting through emails, and today, we remain reconnected that way. Some of our group is comfortable with emailing, while for others, it is as comfortable as a two-finger prostate exam. Good, bad, or indifferent, emailing is the quick way to get a reading on what's going on or just to say "Hi, how are you doing?"

In anticipation of the fiftieth class reunion and reconnecting with each other, with the exception of Star the Mag 6 cranked up their emailing to each other. Only Star did not share our enthusiasm for reconnecting. We keep Star in our prayers, hoping he will come home to our group someday.

Emails: Reunion Committee (December 2008)
Rollo, it was good to talk with you a few minutes ago. I will keep you updated about a possible 50th class reunion.

(August 2009)

Dear Classmates: The reunion committee met at Dudley's home this past weekend. The dates for the Class of 1960 50th class reunion are May 21st and 22nd. The packets with all the pertinent information should be mailed in about 2 weeks. We look forward to seeing all of you at this momentous reunion! If you have any changes whatsoever in your contact information please email or phone me.

Email from Oz (November 2009)

Like you, I'm in total amazement that we're "old people" now. How in the hell did that happen? It seems like just yesterday we were peeking through Crazy's window watching him count his money. Or you, I & Star stranded in your boat on the Intercostal Waterway. Or getting caught at your pool during the DuPont air raid. If I recall, Mr. Dingle Berry just happened to see Spiff in the middle of a swan dive. The list is endless. Pure American Graffiti. Truly, the good old days.

The gold-toned envelope embossed with little dragon characters sat on my desk for almost a week before I opened it—unlike a letter from the IRS, which you immediately rip open to see if you are getting an unexpected refund or to brace yourself for the horrifying announcement: The IRS is planning to rip you a new asshole with a five-year, look-back field audit. I knew what was inside my envelope. It was not as horrifying, but close.

Time had disappeared somewhere in the cosmos. My life was moving quickly toward being nothing more than a little peapod of neutrons left on this earth when I pass to the next world. I knew the invitation to my fiftieth high school reunion was tucked in the envelope. With it was the typical information: directions to the hotel where it would be held and a questionnaire asking how many would be attending, how many nights I would be staying "at the special reunion rate," and what bonding activities I wished to participate in during the seventy-two hours at the reunion. Bonding activities were designed to rekindle old and maybe lost friendships and amounted to the choice of a bus trip with a tour of our old high school or just hanging out at the hotel in the reunion hospitality room.

In the last fifty years, when it came to my classmates, and even my

Mag 6 buddies, I had not made any efforts to drop an occasional note to say "Hi" or pick up the phone and talk to my old friends. My irrational reasoning for not staying in touch through even a simple family-photo Christmas card was that I wanted to keep my memories of our unbelievable high school days unspoiled by the realities of the present.

I wanted to remember the Mag 6 forever—the days when we were carefree, fun-loving Knights of the Round Table of our Camelot years. I did not want to know about marriages and divorces and business successes and failures and child-genius kids and grandkids or some dumb-shit grandkid in jail for robbing a 7-Eleven convenience store or selling dope to an undercover DEA agent. Worse, I did not want to hear of deaths and diseases, operations, and the challenges of walking or taking a pee or a crap. I only wanted to remember us as we were, and not lose that wonderment by having to deal with reality. My fear was that the fiftieth reunion would bring me dragging and screaming into the real world and what my friends have endured in their lives in the last five decades.

Living in California, I had missed my tenth, and fifteenth, and twenty-fifth high school reunions. The distance I would have had to travel to attend these reunions was one reason I did not go; the other was my fear that I would not know a single classmate. Only the classmates I never knew or never talked with in high school would show up, and it would be like being stranded on a desert island of non-English-speaking sailors from a sinking cargo ship!

I imagined the reunion would be like a reunion of Joliet ex-cons: All had spent time in the big slammer, but none actually got to know all the bros in the exercise yard. You sort of wander around at the "Reunion Get-Together Party" with a plastic cup of cheap sangria wine and pretend to actually remember the classmates you are talking with. I would rather have holes drilled in my teeth by some diabolic dentist.

"Ha, ha, ha. Yes, I remember our old science teacher Ms. Glabbershits. Is she still teaching at DuPont? Oh, I am so sorry; I didn't know she died of a respiratory infection from inhaling too much chalk dust." Or even worse, "Boy, time hasn't changed you one bit. I remember you like it was yesterday, Susie. Oh, I'm sorry, it's Beth. Well, do you remember me from school? Oh, we dated? How many dates did we go on? Wow, that many?

We did *what* in my car? God, I hope your kids are your kids by your current or deceased husband—please tell me yes!"

For several years for a measly $10, I purchased a reunion group photo. After receiving the thirtieth-reunion group photo, I called the vendor and asked for my money back because the people in the photo were old men either with gray hair or bald, some stooped over, looking like they had carried the world on their shoulders. The women all wore bright-colored Hawaiian muumuus; no chic California dressers; no Botox, face lifts, or other noticeable plastic surgery; none balding, but all with curly gray hair. I insisted the vendor had sent me the wrong class photo; it must be from another reunion, maybe the fortieth or fiftieth reunion of another class or even another high school.

The vendor replied that it was indeed my class photo and I should put on a pair of glasses and take a closer look. I screamed aloud as I put the photo under a 50x magnifying glass, "No! No! No! . . . It *is* my class!" Those old, balding men were the same guys I played sports with in high school or sat beside in Jack H's History class. I did not recognize a single girl in the group. What a difference it made, being an almost fifty-year-old woman, twice married and divorced, compared to the high school photo of a slim, seventeen-year-old in a short plaid skirt and tight sweater set off with a classic zero pin.

Now I was looking reality in the face and it scared the shit out of me. Before my shower each morning, as I stood naked looking into the bathroom mirror, I saw *not* a youthful, buff, super-charged, testosterone-overloaded teenager with no fears or phobias, but a thirty-pounds-overweight, neurotic slug just living to survive. Now in my late sixties, my sex appeal to women, especially younger ones, ranked somewhat lower than that of a homeless man hustling homeless women in the food line at the local mission. I had lost the "mojo" I had in high school and college; I realized I really *was* an old man, with wrinkles, gray hair, and a libido that barely registered in the positive on a scale of 1 to 10. Some days, I swore my prostate was bigger than my 7½" head. During the night, I had to get up and pee so many times that I was considering putting a cot in the bathroom to save me the steps from my bed to the bowl.

On the flip side of my fear and reservations about going to the reunion and reconnecting with the Mag 6 and other classmates was the desire to "go home" and see my old house, where I had had so many great times. Not having been back to Jacksonville for almost fifty years, I wondered what the old house looked like. Would I recognize it? Would the current owners let me take a quick peek inside? Almost every single adventure of the Mag 6, like the air raid swimming pool caper, Crazy going for the Guinness world record for flips off a diving board, and every girlfriend— Stacey, Jackie, Ginny—all were linked to that house. Even my first wife was connected with it; I had met her while standing in the front yard when she and her friend, who lived on my street, happened to drive by one day during my last year living there. It was the house my dad built for his retirement. Unfortunately, he never got to fulfill his dream due to his unexpected lay-off from work and their relocation to California.

Googling the house's address, I found the name of the current owners, who happened to be a senior couple who had lived there for more than thirty years and had raised their kids in the house. I sent them a letter, explained who I was and that I would be in Jacksonville for my fiftieth class reunion, enclosed a copy of the reunion program so they did not think it was some scam to rob them, and asked if I could stop by and take a few photos. The couple was most gracious and invited Lucinda and me to stop and visit with them and take all the photos I wanted. I was thrilled about the reunion now, as I would literally be able to "go home."

I began exchanging emails with the Mag 6, and surprisingly, Oz became the "switch engine house" for the emails going among us all. Some in our group were more communicative than others; health issues, family matters, laziness, or disinterest were the main reasons some didn't send many emails while others did.

Some in our group were not comfortable reliving old stories about themselves in high school more than fifty years ago, although most stories would not have put them in jail or wrecked their relationships with wife, kids, and grandkids.

My relationship with Oz is the most communicative of any of them. In all fairness to the other Mag 6, Oz has always been the most open about his feelings, past, present, and future. Oz believes, as I do, that our Camelot years were among the best years in America and that the Mag 6 were the benefactors of those years.

The first email communication between Oz and me came almost ten years before our fiftieth reunion:

<u>Email from Oz (November 2001)</u>

Great hearing from you. Tell me where you are and what's going on. Boy we had a hell of a group at ole DuPont didn't we? I've moved around so much and been so busy it's been impossible to develop those kinds of friendships again. High School is a special time.

Oz and I exchanged several emails in the early 2000s, then the emails stopped. I changed jobs, purchased a business, moved the business to a wonderful 1877 Victorian house on the National Historical Registry, and was involved in major lawsuits which, fortunately, we won, thanks to a great lawyer.

I often thought of my Mag 6 friends and wondered how they were doing, but I did nothing to find out. Then the invitation to the fiftieth reunion arrived and the emails became like an oak tree shedding its leaves in the fall—too many to keep up with.

Oz shared my emails with the other Mag 6 and forwarded me their replies, keeping everyone in the loop. Most of the members of our group were computer- and email-literate, except for Star who hated email, relying on his secretary to handle all his email communication.

<u>Emails (April 2010)</u>
<u>From Oz</u>

Never will forget riding the Ferris wheel at the beach with Crazy and my cousin. Crazy puked all over both of us. And the operator wouldn't stop the thing to let him off. . . .

It's amazing to me that we ever considered that kind of agony "FUN". Of course, we made an art form of doing insane things. It's scary to think what our blood alcohol levels were. D.U.I.'s were non-existent in those days. My 2nd car was a convertible and I thought nothing of driving around with an open 6 pack on the front seat. . . .

You mentioned great reasons why the late 50s were great for growing up. I've got another. How about growing up in Jax with its great beaches before they went commercial. What about my parents' 55 Chevy with the 4 barrel power pack? I never raced it much but very little from the factory could have kept up with it. I did however drive it into the woods on SR13 south of DuPont road with Spiff. The pavement was wet and it just got away from me. Spiff still harasses me about it. This is why we've got to have our own little personal reunion. The best days ever. Some scary, most hilarious. I'm enjoying these mini-vignettes we're having a lot. . . .

I was probably such a screw-up at DuPont; I had to date elsewhere . . . I really don't remember. That was probably true of Freddie the Farter too. Only human I've ever known to fart on command. A phenomenal talent. I wonder if he can still do that? . . .

The crescendo is really building toward May 21. It's finally almost here. Rollo and I have had so much fun swapping emails of some of our notorious happenings. It's been fun talking to Lily and Crazy too. And Freddie the Farter will be coming through my city prior to the reunion so the laughter can officially begin then. . . .

It's shocking how much I've forgotten. God probably protects us from remembering too much. . . .

Rollo, I don't remember graduation much other than it was a real goat-roping at the beach. I remember being up on the roof of some house. I wonder what the hell I was doing? . . .

Emails from Lily
I really would love to see y'all. . . .

Fifty years and I remember most of the atrocities well . . . but don't remember what I ate for breakfast or when I had my last bm . . . One adventure flashback was taking Rollo's boat about 15 miles up some creek off the river to a railroad trestle inhabited by an axe murderer. We ate sardines with him. . . . Rollo called him "Fella" . . . the good Lord did watch over us. . . .

From Spiff
This is really going to be good, . . . seeing you all together at one time. I agree that we need to slip off from the crowd on Saturday and catch up. We are going to arrive on Friday afternoon and leave Sunday, but can stay longer if I need to. The question is, "who will win the Mr. Neat Guy contest at the swimming pool?"

Note: In high school, the one who managed to stay on the pool float after others tried to take it was championed as "Mr. Neat Guy." Spiff won the contest more than any of the other Mag 6.

Emails (May 2010)
From Oz
I'll tell you: our high school experiences were always very important to me. I loved the movie *American Graffiti* as those times were our times. I think most people feel their glory days were college. For me it was high school. It was all upside; very little downside. Wonderful, carefree days. I don't recall ever studying. Thank God we all survived those days. I hope my grandchildren have a great high school experience but please don't follow in Papa's footsteps.

Remember some of our bush league shop lifting? The biggest one I remember was from a downtown store (JCPenney??) when those of us that were there decided we wanted some outrageous Hawaiian shirts. I may not be remembering this right but I think Lily already owned a shirt and had taken it off because it was too hot or something. In the meantime, I lifted 2 shirts and put them in a store bag. Some of you, who shall remain nameless, did the same.

In the meantime, the store security guy stops Lily who was carrying the shirt he legitimately owned. He told Lily that he should keep things in a store bag, like me, to avoid future suspicion. When I got outside, I set a personal speed record down the hill back to the car. . . .

BTW, since Star's email doesn't work, I tried to call him Friday. I got his voicemail but no response to date. Crazy has talked to him at length and Star finally coughed up the money for the reunion. Same old Star. He's the only human I know that would brave alligator infested waters to recover an old range ball. . . .

Dadgum Lily. I honestly don't remember how all the Penn St/GW business got started. Sounds like another one of those I'd just as soon forget! I do remember the "talent" but the rest is a blank. . . .

Remember when we were going to make a fortune by turning in litter bugs? There was a front page piece in the Jacksonville paper talking about this big reward for turning in violators. The reward was like $150 per violation and I think I'd done a spreadsheet showing where we could almost retire with the proceeds. I remember following people out of the new McDonald's on Beach Blvd hoping they'd pitch something. And when we finally did turn in some violators, the sheriff or whoever looked at us like we were crazy. Broken dreams once again. Another entrepreneurial scheme thwarted. . . .

From Spiff
While in Jax, maybe we can meet at the pool for a Mr. Neat Guy

contest. We'll need an inner tube, a blow up float, and a football. You may not recognize me at the reunion. I'll be the one with the desert boots. Can't wait to see us together again. 50 years is a lot to catch up on. . . .

From Lily

This caper [stealing Hawaiian shirts at JCPenney] is only a blur to me, but I do remember that Oz seemed to have the blue balls a lot. . . . he must have been on the threshold of a big score a lot. He didn't have this problem, however, one night at the George Washington Hotel . . . but that's another story for later. . . .

Crazy was the puker . . . Oz and another had a date at the GW with some "out of town talent" when Penn State was in the Gator Bowl . . . circa 1960 . . . Oz and the other guy referred to themselves as Bobumibich and Bluski . . . two guys from Penn State. The date could not have cared less. . . .

See y'all late Fri. afternoon . . . look for the one with a diaper bag and a gin 'n tonic. . . .

From Crazy

Talked to Star today and he said that he had not received any e-mails and I too had a hard time getting him on the phone. Finally he called me back and did not even have the right hotel. Hopefully, I set him straight and he plans to be there Saturday for our afternoon meeting. Tell Rollo that the Dupont tour will start at 10 and our meeting/lunch will follow immediately. . . .

There are only a few days left until our 50th class reunion. I'm sure excited. The Magnificent Six and Freddie will meet in the Osprey Room at the hotel at 12:00 noon on Saturday, May 22nd. . . .

<u>From Freddie the Farter, Honorary Mag 6 Member</u>

<u>Note</u>: Prior to the 50th, Freddie sent all of us one of the most poignant emails:

Damn! You guys were the photographic negative of the Keystone Cops: They were trying to serve the law but kept screwing-up; you guys were trying to break the law but kept screwing-up!

Whatever we did in those days pales when compared with today's drive-by shootings, school shootings, road-rage shootings, gang shootings, domestic shootings, Romeo & Juliet type shootings, pet shootings, misguided fun shootings, drug shootings, self-shootings, parent shootings, sibling shootings, and all the other bullshit shootings you can imagine. We fired off a few eggs now and then, wrapped some houses, shot some "red-eyes", tried some pitiful Bonnie & Clyde law infractions, got drunk and puked on someone else's carpet, cut farts and cracked-up passers-by, tried some Rebel Without a Cause night time driving, made fun of some people, now and then forgot to say our prayers, scratched our ass (because it itched) during the Flag Salute, smarted back at our parents (even though we loved and honored them), irritated the hell out of teachers we respected, maybe cheated on our girlfriends without malice, tried to "smack down" our close friends at every opportunity, probably muscled our younger siblings, put the dog out after it dumped on the floor, forgot to hug a tree, and a host of other prank-like behaviors that were just "blowing in the wind." (Bob Dylan).

We were some of the most decent kids that ever went through the Halls of DuPont: we loved our School, our Teachers and Friends . . . what's more . . . and this is paramount: WE LOVED GOD & OUR COUNTRY!

I for one have virtually no single or multiple regrets: anything that caused hesitation has been, hopefully, atoned. On a scale of 0-10, I have had a 9.9 life! It sounds like all of us have! It just doesn't get much better than this; although, I believe the BEST is yet to come! . . .

<u>From Rollo to Mag 6</u>

<u>Note</u>: Of all emails I exchanged with the Mag 6 from April 2010 till our reunion in the last week of May 2010, these are the ones I cherish most:

Yeah, Crazy and Spiff and Oz, funny to be writing those names after so long. Can't tell you how great it is for all of us to get together one more time. Since the sands of the hour glass are not quite as full as 50 years ago, we need to consider talking and emailing each other more. Too great of a bond between us to forget.

Saturday 1-3 works for me. They have that tour of DuPont at 10:30. I am going by my old house and meet the owner, they have been there 30 years. Sent a letter to them and they called me and invited me to come see the house. May either do that on Friday when I get to Jax, or early Saturday before the DuPont Tour which is probably an hour, out by 12, back to the hotel by 1:00. I will call hotel to see what we can do, maybe lunch around the pool.

Spiff, (probably hate that), the first thing that comes to mind is without fail, every Saturday morning, at 8:00ish, I'm still strung out from the night before, you'd call, munching cereal, and say, "Munch, munch, what are you doing today, munch, munch." My brain could only hear the munch, munch. Without fail, every Saturday morning, my wake up call from Spiff.

Crazy, running for second base, no need to slide, and there he is, dropping like a bag of flour not sliding into second base. The sound of the thud and the leg going I can still hear. Crazy, Crazy, what in the hell were you thinking? Hopped around on broken leg for months. Or turning around in Ms Hamilton's class and Crazy has straws suck up each nose. Of course if you laughed out loud, your ass was grass, so you just sat laughing and shaking hoping she wouldn't see you.

Oz and I have been sharing stories already, but the one of him coming over to my house on Christmas day to find a toy to play with as his stocking only had socks from JCPenney. We ended up on DuPont's field with some rocket you stomped on an air ball to get it to take off. Went up about 10 feet and flopped to earth. Maybe the socks were better.

Love you guys.

―――――――――――――――――――――――――――――――――――――

I made contact with the couple who owns our old home. I was planning to go by either Friday from the airport or early Saturday before the DuPont tour. I plan to call the owners before I go to Dallas to see if they have a preference when I come by. Have you ever been back to your old house? My mother is anxious to see photos of the old homestead. I want to see the pool where we had too many good times, especially an interlude one night in the deep end with someone you know. I almost drowned, found out I could hold my breath underwater for 5 minutes. Don't think I'll tell the current owners about that one.

Can't wait to see everyone. I am digging through a photo box looking for a couple of photos I know I have seen before. One is of Oz, Star, Crazy and self at a bar in Ft Lauderdale with a dancer named Liliani, and we all are 17 or 18 years old with fake ID's, mine was someone almost 30, and when being asked for our ID for drinks and we all having to produce our fake ID, she looks at Crazy and says, "No need for ID, I know you're over 21." Crazy at 18 looking 30, downhill all the way. I had the coolest Madras sport coat that I'd kill to own today.

Email's one saving grace is that you can file your favorite, most memorable emails in your personal email folder and pull them up for a good laugh when life has crapped in your bowl of Wheaties. The downside to emails is that the FBI can extract from your computer every single email you ever sent or received, even though you deleted the most damaging ones. Lots of folks are in prison due to emails on their computer they wished they had never sent or received. Defense lawyers hate emails!

Think about it . . . good old-fashioned, incriminating paper letters can be burned in your fireplace; good luck with the FBI retrieving the ashes and pasting them back together to put you in jail. Try burning emails on your hard drive in your fireplace. Not easy!

Chapter 16

Roots

Just before the reunion, Lucinda and I visited my mother in a nursing home where she was residing while recovering from a serious auto accident. It seems that everything really is bigger in Texas, including some of the idiots who drive big SUVs and trucks. An urban cowboy in his Cadillac Escalade, texting and not watching the traffic lights, t-boned my sister and mother, who were in my sister's car on the way to a follow-up oncology doctor appointment for my mother.

My mother had beaten breast cancer at the age of eighty-six. But it seemed even a tough and admirable old lady like my mother couldn't live forever. As it turned out later that summer, after taking a turn for the worse in the nursing home, just one month shy of her ninetieth birthday and two months after the fiftieth class reunion, Mom passed away. Urban cowboy driver wasn't even cited—not even a $35 moving-violation ticket. So much for justice, I guess.

After our couple of days in Dallas in mid-May, Lucinda and I arrived in Jacksonville. From the Jacksonville airport, we made a beeline to my old home. I had to use my GPS as a guide since so much had changed and the years had clouded my memory. The GPS sent us down streets that were only vaguely familiar to me at best, but we eventually made it to my old house. Travelling down the street where I had spent over four of the best years of my life, I was completely dumbstruck by how cookie-cutter everything looked. I could have been on any suburban street in America. I didn't recognize a single house on the block. The beeping GPS told me I had arrived. I anxiously peered out through the car window at my old home for the first time since my teenage years, almost fifty years before. The house could only be described as "butt-ass ugly," pure and simple.

"What the hell happened to my home? It looks like a giant pigeon flew over it and let loose with bird shit. It was so beautiful. Now look at it!"

The house certainly didn't appear as I remembered, or as it looked in the old photos. The house was no longer a young, virgin bride on her wedding day, fresh, youthful, not a wrinkle, hair coifed to perfection. What I saw was a decrepit, old woman in a dirty, ragged shawl. Someone with no taste in color or design had painted the entire house white, but the paint had faded in the Florida sun to a sickly, ashen, almost corpse-like color. All the beautiful brick work that had once outlined and accented the features of the house was now coated in that same sickly shade of birdshit-white.

When I lived there, the walkway to the front door had been methodically laid out by hand, cement poured to give the sidewalk a designer look. Now it was cracked and crumbling, being taken apart by both time and the intruding roots of a now mammoth maple tree I had planted as a sapling in the front yard. The sapling had grown so big that it could shade half of the southern states. My heart sank as I imagined what the inside of the house would look like. If the inside looked anything like the outside, I would be crestfallen. I was tempted to put my video camera back in its bag; I did not want photos of this crime scene.

"I'm almost scared to go inside and see what they did with the interior. Maybe we should just go. I couldn't bear to see the inside of the house painted with this bird-turd white." I looked at Lucinda, almost pouting like a three-year-old.

"Get out of the damn car. Suck it up. The house is fifty-five years old. What the hell did you expect—the Taj Mahal?" Lucinda certainly had a way with words. They were not very sympathetic or sentimental, but they were effective.

When the front door opened, I was very much astounded and delighted to find that the owners were the epitome of a Norman Rockwell all-American grandma and grandpa: sweet, cheerful, polite, gracious, open, just "wonderful"! Like many older folks, keeping the grass cut and the swimming pool clean was all they could handle, physically and probably financially. Painting the house on the outside had fallen to the bottom of the "to do" list—whether, as I suspect, it was too expensive to have some painter do the work or the owners just didn't care about the faded white paint, which I doubt.

"Lucinda and I want to thank you for your graciousness in letting us take a quick peek at my old home," I said. "It's really beautiful inside and out. I love what you did in painting the entire house white. Is that something you did recently?" I hoped fervently that God would not strike me dead for lying to this sweet old couple about the fact that their shitty bird-turd-white paint job had screwed up my beautiful home.

"Thank you for your compliments, but when we bought the house thirty years ago, the previous owner had lost his job and was cooking in the fireplace because the electric company had turned off his electricity. Well, he took white paint and covered the entire house, inside and out. I think the owner sort of lost it—divorce, no job, kids always being brought home by the police. We never had the time or money to repaint the entire house, what with raising our own kids, so we just lived with the white paint. I teased my kids that we lived in the 'White House,' like the President of the United States."

"Well, as they say, beauty is only skin-deep. It's what's inside that counts," was what came out of my mouth, though all the while I was thinking to myself how hard it was to get beyond the butt-ugly white paint to see the beauty.

"Can I look around the house?"

Grandpa said, "Sure, let me show you the rec room, then the rest of the house. You'll have to excuse the mess in the rec room."

With that, I followed Grandpa to the rec room. Lucinda stayed at the kitchen table with Grandma and talked about her kids and grandkids. I believe Lucinda couldn't possibly have given a crap less about touring my old house; fifty years ago, when I had had my glory days in the old structure, she had been just fourteen years old.

As Grandpa led me into the rec room, he mentioned that his mother had just passed away; they had converted the room into a granny suite, where she had lived out her last year. Now the room was full of junk—boxes, and an old bed frame and mattress, which had been taken apart and placed, haphazardly it seemed, in one corner. This was the room in which I had held "$5.00 per person and all the beer you can drink" parties during my senior year of high school. Of course, then a beer keg cost only $19 for umpteen gallons of beer, the deposit on the keg included. Now, the sound I heard echoing off the sorrowful walls was not the music we played at the parties—the Platters or the Everly Brothers singing of young love—but the soft whine of an air purifier, probably trying to rid the room of the smells of old age and death.

"Sorry, the place is a mess. Since Mom died, we haven't had the heart to get in here and clear all her furniture and clothes out. Did you have a lot of parties in here when you were a teenager?"

"Yeah, a few parties. See that closet where your mother kept her clothes? The next afternoon after one of the parties, I found one of our party guests drunk and asleep in that closet. Wonder if he is still there!" My humor meant to lift Grandpa's spirits went over like a turd in the punch bowl. He looked at me without a trace of a smile and said, "Let's go back inside and I'll show you the rest of the house." Now *I* felt like the turd floating in the Kool-Aid

As my tour guide, Grandpa led me toward the back of the house and into each of the rooms where I had spent my high school years. Walking down the narrow back hallway brought memories crashing in on me like a ton of bricks, crushing me into the worn, beige shag carpet.

The first room on the left was the bathroom my sister and I had shared, and it hadn't changed a bit. Same white toilet; same single-bowl, acrylic sink; same corner, glass-door shower stall. I stood and gazed for a moment at the shower, remembering when my mother had cracked the bathroom door to tell me they were going to Hilton Head for the weekend and my sister would be staying overnight with a friend. I had danced with joy in that shower since the news meant I would have the entire house to myself and what would eventually be a most wonderful night with Ginny in the swimming pool.

To my right, directly across from the bathroom, was what had once been my bedroom. My eyes started to well with tears as I walked into the room. Grandpa knew what I was feeling; maybe he had experienced the same kind of thing once or twice in his life. He stayed out in the hall, and

I just stood there, slowly taking it all in, visually examining almost every flake of white paint on the walls.

Straight in front of me was where I had my day bed, and Grandpa also had a day bed in that exact spot. On my bed at night as I readied for sleep, I would recount every adventure of the day; on that bed I dreamed of friends, sports, Stacey, Jackie, and Ginny; and on that bed, my dog Tippy slept with me every night, protecting me from a multitude of evildoers who, fortunately, never materialized.

I looked at the wall where my dad had riveted my old study charts above my desk to help me keep track of my homework assignments, trying desperately to help me to get my grades up so I could get into college. The chart was gone, but I swore I could see a faint outline where it had hung on the wall. I think that outline was probably just my imagination, but it was still a powerful experience. Last but not least of the memory grabbers was the sliding-door closet where, for years, in an old tennis shoe box, I had hidden my Trojan condoms. I was tempted to open the closet jokingly just to see if the shoe box was still there. When my family moved to California, I'm sure the box with the hidden condoms hit the trash bin; I just hope Mom didn't open it to see what was inside besides old, stinking tennis shoes.

I could barely manage to get through the tour of the rest of the bedrooms: the one where my sister stayed for years with her door closed; my parents' master bedroom, where I know they cried and held tightly to each other when they learned of my dad's fate at work and the day they realized they had to sell this dream house they had built and move to California. Each room held memories of joy and sorrow that seemed to crowd in on me, catching my breath and forming a lump in my throat.

The final small room was the one we had called the "junk room," as did the current owners. It had been a catch-all room for projects, hobbies, extra furniture; it was where my dad started to paint circus clowns the week after he was let go from work. Dad's family had been in the circus business when he was growing up, and my dad had a fascination with clowns. His first clown painting, which I have in my home to this day, was of an Emmet Kelley–type of clown, complete with big bushy eyebrows, wide red-lined lips, a shaggy red wig, and sorrowful eyes gazing out at nothing but looking contemplative and sad. I always believed my dad was painting himself.

"Wow, like stepping back in time, Jules Verne and all. Thank you so much for letting me spend a few minutes in the rooms and relive a few memories. My mother will love the video I took of the rooms, especially her master bedroom."

Grandpa looked at me with sympathetic eyes. "I can imagine it must be tough on you to see your old bedroom. My son grew up in that room, much like you did. Bet you could tell some wild stories." He was perking up now from our room visit. "Let's go outside and look at the swimming pool. God, I hate that pool. Can't seem to get the water crystal-clear."

As Grandpa took me to the back yard, my breathing returned to somewhat normal. I had thought I was starting to hyperventilate from all the crushing memories in the house, especially standing in my old bedroom. Once outside, I stood and stared at the swimming pool, now minus its diving board, but still the bane of Grandpa's existence. Almost daily, he had to clean the pool of the leaves that fell from the trees around the place, especially the monster maple in the front yard.

For me, the swimming pool was more than its present eighteen-by-twelve-foot cement and plaster hole in the ground with slightly murky water; it held the purity of a Baptist baptismal pool, the spiritual renewal of the Ganges River for the Hindus. This hole in the ground contained a zillion wonderful memories for me: the air raid drill and getting nabbed by the school principal, Crazy and his flips for the Guinness world record, and Ginny and her half-naked, brain-sizzling swan dive off the diving board, her body glowing in the beautiful rays of silvery moonlight. I certainly didn't share those memories with Grandpa, especially the one of Ginny's perfect 36Cs; I wasn't sure his heart could take it.

Grandpa and Grandma showed us photos of their kids and grandkids. I wondered if his son would someday inherit the house, move the family in, and give the grandkids a place to grow up and mature as I had done during my years in the place. Some summer night, as a senior in high school, maybe one of the grandkids will have the swimming pool all to himself and the God of Passion and Great Times will visit him as he swims with his girlfriend.

Lucinda and I realized we were almost running late for the reunion, so we said goodbye to Grandma and Grandpa. I took one final look at my former home. I had gone back to my roots, the only roots I really remembered, and it was breathtaking—literally breathtaking. Outside, looking once more at the faded, white-painted house and the Jack and the Beanstalk–style maple growing in the front yard, the old house now looked more like a painting of a beautiful old home, aging gracefully. I directed the rental car toward DuPont High School just a couple blocks away, but at the street corner, I stopped and turned in the front seat for one last, long look at my home, my roots. I knew I would probably never see the house again—never. At least I had the chance for this one last visit to dance with the spirits of fond memories.

At the high school, I stopped the car near the running track. Positioned now on the other side of an eight-foot chain-link fence, the running track was still there but had been resurfaced. The aged cinder had apparently been replaced years ago with the modern Tartan surface. On the other side of the fence and right in front of me was the new starting line for the 100-meters, but when I ran the track, it was the 100-*yard* dash. Poking the camera lens through the gaps in the fence, I took several minutes of video of the white-striped starting line. Lucinda thought I was nuts, taking a video of a starting line. I guess you have to be a track junkie to understand the sentimental value of the starting line for the 100-yard dash.

I stood there for a long time, almost mesmerized by staring at that line. I could visualize Coach Mahoney trying to figure out how to use the starter pistol. Coach's lack of experience in starting races had given me a few extra yards of a head start on my record-breaking 9.9-second dash. I wonder if Coach Mahoney's still alive. I sure hope so.

Looking across the track, I spotted a young female runner, maybe only in her early teens as the school was now a middle school. She was practicing with her track coach. I said a little prayer that upon graduating from this school and moving on to high school, the young runner would break all the records she was training to achieve. Better still, I prayed she and her coach would have the same special bond I had with my track coach, Felton Luck.

In sports, you may be blessed by God to have a coach like Coach Luck, a person dedicated to making you the best you can be and to doing it with grace and charm, not threats and intimidation. Most athletes will never have a Coach Luck. God smiled on me; I did.

I had seen all I wanted. Lucinda and I got back into the car. I set my GPS for the reunion's hotel and waited while the unit calculated our driving course. Thinking of my old house and gazing at the school and the track, I felt I had achieved my goal of going home one more time. It was a most satisfying feeling. In my heart, I had taken my dad and mother with me so they could visit their home along with me.

I was brought back to the present with the grating voice of the GPS alerting me, "Your destination is in 12.6 miles. Proceed ahead 300 feet and turn left onto DuPont Boulevard. Proceed 600 feet and turn right onto San Jose Boulevard. . . . Be careful not to hit the twisting teenagers on the street."

Chapter 17

Reconnecting

*M*y worst fears about the fiftieth reunion materialized the instant I got to the reunion's "Welcome Desk." One of my former classmates, whom I did not recognize, probably because I never bothered to notice him fifty years ago, was handing out the "Welcome Packets." Thankfully, the packet contained a name badge with my high school senior picture on it so others would know me by the name and maybe my photo, and I could do the same and hopefully recognize them. I said, "Hello, . . . [looking at the photo and name on his badge] Donald. Great seeing you again after all these years."

Donald looked at me as if he really wanted to say, "Rob, asshole, you never said two words to me when we were at DuPont fifty years ago, so don't strain yourself to try and make nice with me now." Instead, Donald actually said, "Welcome to your fiftieth reunion. The hospitality suite is down the hall and many of our classmates are there already, so do stop in and say hello."

I walked away, thinking to myself, "OK, multiply Donald times one hundred former classmates and I'm probably going to stay drunk for the next seventy-two hours. Being tipsy and a more loveable person, I will not have to deal with the same sort of 'Hi, asshole, long time no see, and guess what, don't give a shit that you're here, didn't care for you then, don't now!'"

Recalculating my mental GPS to remember exactly why I am standing in this dumpy hotel and getting kicked in the balls by Donald, I reassert to myself that I am here to reconnect with five of my closest buddies.

Hopefully, I can create new bonds between us so we can still be the Mag 6 till we all are in the next life . . . kicking ass.

Looking down the hallway, not ten feet away I spotted Spiff and Crazy with a couple of ladies I assumed were their wives. Spiff was exactly as he had looked fifty years ago: a few gray hairs, a couple of forehead wrinkles, but standing straight and erect, no osteoporosis issues with him. He was dressed as if I had just picked him up in front of his house to go to school: pleated pants, not a single wrinkle, Weejun loafers, matted belt, and plaid button-down sport shirt. I thought to myself, "God, I should look so good when they close the lid on my coffin."

Crazy looked to me just like the same person, the one I had picked up one school day wearing a bright red sweater to impress some phantom girlfriend Oz and Star had created. Crazy screamed innocence; even after all these years, he still seemed to have an almost virginal quality about him. I never heard Crazy say a single negative word about anyone. You couldn't have a better friend than Crazy: loyal, sincere, honest. Plus, Crazy had bailed my ass out of Jacksonville Municipal Jail the Sunday morning after my arrest at the Thunderbird Motel for loud partying in one of their guest rooms, and a friend who will bail you out of jail is a friend indeed.

Crazy was wearing an upscale Hawaiian-print shirt and khaki shorts. Hawaiian-print shirts never go out of style in Florida, and even fifty years after Lily got falsely accused by store security of stealing a cheaply made Hawaiian shirt, here stood Crazy in the expensive version of the same gaudy attire. With his balding head and standing there in the Hawaiian shirt, Crazy reminded me of a senior citizen bus tour guide at Leisure World Florida. If he'd been wearing a big, flowery lei around his neck, the costume would have been perfect.

"Spiff, Crazy . . . it's me, Rollo," I yelled and ran down the hallway to embrace my old friends. Spiff smiled and extended his hand to greet me, making me feel like I was at a Chamber of Commerce mixer meeting with all the other Chamber members. Crazy did give me a big hug, and as I returned his hug, I whispered to him, "Love you, Crazy. I really have missed you."

Crazy was giggling when he pushed back, and looking in my eyes, he said, "Chee-vee-vee." God, I have waited years to hear those beautiful words spoken by Mr. Chee-vee-vee himself. It was as if angels from heaven, accompanied by golden harps, were singing "Chee-vee-vee." I just held onto Crazy and didn't want to let him go. I couldn't wait another fifty years to hear the live version of "Chee-vee-vee" coming from the heart and soul of one of my best friends.

Lucinda came up to us, and I turned and introduced her to Spiff and Crazy, who then introduced their wives to us in turn. Though I knew of each wife, of course I hadn't personally met them. As we stood in the hallway, laughing about our Mag 6 adventures, other schoolmates came up to all of us to say hello. We all had to look at each other's little two-by-two-inch photo to put a face with a name. A few classmates I remembered easily, since the years had been kind to them and their features hadn't changed that much, but for most of the classmates I talked with, I had to look at the photo and their name, then have my IBM-server brain try to remember some little fact about them—especially whether I had pissed them off in high school. I didn't want a classmate who might still be carrying a grudge to tell me to "F off" in front of Lucinda.

I lived for the next seventy-two hours with a nonstop, ear-to-ear smile on my face, trying desperately to get close enough to whatever classmate I might be greeting to see their name and photo and try like hell to remember something about them. For the ones I did remember, the conversation then became pretty typical: "Can you believe fifty years has flown by? Where did it go? Remember Teacher [insert name]? Wonder if they're still alive? [Whether dead or alive] Wow, he/she was a super teacher. Great to see you, [look at name tag and state person's name]."

If there's a next reunion, I swore to myself, I would create a name badge and photo of Mick Jagger to see if some classmate would actually look at the badge and name and then at me and say, "Mick, you haven't aged a bit. What have you been doing all these years?"

"Oh, I have been *rolling* around the countryside, kicking up *stones*." The classmate would never get my attempt to poke a little fun at the hypocrisy of some aspects of high school reunions, especially fiftieth reunions.

While Lucinda and I were talking to Spiff, Crazy, and their wives in the small hallway, I suddenly realized I could hear Oz's voice in the lobby of the hotel. "Where's Rollo? Spiff? Crazy?" Oz had a unique, higher-pitched voice, not shrill, but higher, and just a bit of a monotone speaking voice. He was asking my "kick me in the balls" Donald, who was still manning the Welcome Desk, where we might be, since Donald had been the one to check us all in.

Since I was the one standing closest to the lobby, I said to the group, "Oz is here. Going to get him." I turned and almost ran to the lobby. There Oz stood with his wife, talking with Donald. I yelled loudly enough so anyone in the lobby could hear me, "Quick, someone call Security. We have a lunatic egg thrower in the hotel fixing to paste this place with yellow goo!"

As if on cue, Oz looked up from talking with Donald and yelled back, so everyone could hear, "Don't worry, they're organic eggs from only free-range hens. Only white goo!" He bounded across the lobby, laughing, and we embraced in a hug and a kiss on the cheek.

"Un-f***ing-believable! God, I've missed you," I exclaimed. Looking behind Oz and seeing that his wife had caught up with him, I quickly said, "Oops, sorry for the language. It's just been way too long since Oz and I were this close." My eyes filled with tears.

Oz looked at me, and his eyes began to well up also. "OK, Rollo, we can't stand here crying like babies, holding each other. Our classmates may start talking." Oz pulled back, turned, and introduced me to his wife. This was his second marriage; they had discovered each other on a "singles only" Caribbean cruise. Knowing Oz, where else would he find his second wife but on a cruise ship, which probably had the corny name "The Love Boat."

I gave Oz's wife a big hug and guided them to the hallway where the rest of our little group was waiting. Everyone embraced each other while laughing and slapping each other on the shoulder. Oz and Spiff had seen each other on previous occasions, having lived on different sides of the same city. Spiff gave Oz the official Chamber of Commerce handshake, but was a little more upbeat and laughing now. I think Spiff was finally letting go, relaxing, and beginning to remember the Mag 6 as we were at DuPont: fun-loving . . . fun-loving . . . fun-loving.

"Where are Lily and Star? Have they checked in?" I asked, looking at Oz, Spiff, and Crazy, believing they would have an answer.

Looking a little serious, Crazy replied, "Star may not come to the dinner tonight. Said he would more than likely come to the afternoon function tomorrow and the final dinner. He seemed kind of reluctant to come here—not sure why. Lily should be here shortly. I had to really twist his arm to come. Star is like you, Rollo, and never went to any of the other reunions, but he really wants to see us."

"OK," I thought to myself, "that may have been a little dig that I was a real prick for not getting on an airplane and flying three thousand miles to the other reunions."

I said to the group, "Crazy, thanks for working on getting Lily to the reunion. The Mag 6 wouldn't be the same without him. Star, well, Star was never a groupie; liked to travel with each of us, one at a time. Hell, I do want to see him; we had a lot of adventures together—Pine Island and almost losing our lives in the gale. Plus, we did a few things I can't say in mixed company."

Lucinda looked at me as if to say, "Wait till I get your ass back to the room and I will beat the story out of you if you don't tell me what happened."

The group started toward the hospitality suite to get some adult drinks and say hello to the other classmates holed up there, camped out on the few bar stools and chairs in the room. Once in the door, I said to the group, "Need to run to the bathroom before I have a beer. Too much excitement; got to take a whiz."

I turned to the hallway and started toward the men's room near the lobby. I was about halfway down the hall and looking down at my feet as I walked, sort of contemplating today's events, when I bumped into another classmate coming in the opposite direction.

"Sorry, wasn't paying attention." I looked at his name badge and photo as he simultaneously looked at mine. "LILY!" I yelled and grabbed him for a big hug, really excited to see my old friend.

Lily just kind of looked at me and mumbled, "Rollo, how the hell are you?"

I pulled back from Lily and just stood looking at him for several seconds, trying to find within his eyes and spirit my old high school track co-captain and co-survivor of Axe Handle Saturday. While the six of us all had great times together in high school, Lily was the one member of the Mag 6 that had the most in common with me. We had played football together, had run on the same track relay team, taking medals at the state meet, and had both committed our bodies to the tortures of college-level football. There was a special bond between us, and standing in the shadowed hallway of the hotel, I was desperately trying to find it again.

"Lily, I'm so glad to see you. I'm sorry I wasn't great on calling or writing over the years, but I've never forgotten what we had between us as friends and athletes. I hope you felt the same."

When sharing special moments with a buddy who is also an athlete, especially when saying goodbye till the next competition, I always think of the poignant scene in *Brian's Song*, when Billy Dee Williams, as Gale Sayers of the Chicago Bears, is speaking of his rookie camp roommate and competitor Brian Piccolo, played by James Caan. At Brian's memorial service following his death from cancer his first year in the pros, Gale Sayers pauses and, with tears in his eyes, whispers the famous line that all athletes have uttered in their hearts when thinking about another athlete buddy: "I loved Brian Piccolo." I loved Lily, and now, I wanted him to be the Lily of fifty years ago.

Lily looked at me and then confessed a grudge he had carried against me for the past fifty years. What he told me made me want to laugh so hard that I would fall down on the beer- and salsa-stained hotel carpet and roll around in fits of hysteria, but that would have really pissed Lily off even more.

Lily's confession to me was this: "Rollo, I'm not a co-captain and you the captain like on an airplane. Coach Luck made me and you equal co-captains of the track team."

For fifty years, Lily had been carrying around a joke I had teased him with. He thought that I really thought I was the captain of the track team and he was just the co-captain. I grabbed Lily and almost yelled in his face, "We are *both* co-captains of the track team! There never *was* a captain! I was pulling your leg all these years! Please forgive me."

Lily studied me for several seconds, then said very seriously, "So, we're both co-captains—no captain?"

"Yes, Lily, co-captains, no captain." I was trying to work through this issue between Lily and me in a very adult way while thinking to myself, "Shit, Lily, you're a grown man worrying about bullshit titles from fifty years ago." But for Lily, it was important, so we dealt with it as adults.

Soon Lily started to smile, a gleam appeared in his eyes, and he looked at me and said, "Rollo, I've missed you, too." Lily grabbed me and gave me such a tight hug that I thought he would never let me go. While Lily hugged me, I thought to myself, "I loved Brian Piccolo."

From the hospitality suite, everyone was ushered in a most cattle-like fashion into a dining room for dinner and a short program. Sitting at a table of twelve, we were squeezed in to make room for everyone. There were two empty chairs saved for Star and his wife, if they showed. Tapping on a water glass to get the group's attention, I jokingly said, "We have an empty chair saved for Mr. and Mrs. Elijah at our Seder table. Pour them a glass of wine in case they show."

I laughed at my own joke, but everyone else missed the humor; maybe only Star, our Jewish compatriot, would understand it. Lily looked at me and asked sincerely, "I thought the chairs were saved for Star and his wife. I don't remember a guy named Elijah in our class. Was he in the band?"

My head hit the table as I laughed hysterically at Lily's innocent comment, "Was he in the band?" God, I loved this guy.

I said to Crazy, "Doesn't look like Star will be with us tonight. Any reason why he's blowing off the reunion and us? Shit, he lives just thirty minutes from here." I was somewhat hurt by Star's absence since all the rest of us had to make a special effort to be here. I, for one, had left my mother at the nursing home in Dallas to fly another thousand miles east to be here.

I knew my mother would have insisted I attend. Mom knew all the Mag 6 since they all hung out at the house, especially during the summer around the swimming pool. She was also our foil for getting the beer for our "$5.00 per person and all the beer you can drink" parties. She really didn't know she could have gotten into a wee bit of trouble with those parties of half-drunken underage teenagers.

The food arrived for dinner—still no Star and his wife—so we all made the best of our Mag 6 minus one. The seating was not conducive for personal conversations between the guys, especially since all of us were sensitive about not saying anything in front of the wives that would embarrass anyone or prompt a scene at the table or back in one of our hotel rooms. The unspoken rule between guys in the presence of wives was to never talk about old girlfriends, police arrests, or family members. For instance, at the dinner table, a Mag 6 would never say, "Sorry about your granddaughter getting arrested for prostitution by Miami South Beach cops. Was she trying to pay her abortion bill or get cash to pay for extra days for her brother at the substance abuse center?" This was definitely not cool or acceptable conversation.

The discussions centered on the more innocent adventures we had at DuPont, from twisting down San Jose Boulevard to the air raid drill and getting caught in my swimming pool by Principal Dingle Berry. We all also raked over the coals the teachers we loved or hated, coaches we loved or hated, and classmates we loved or hated. I guess classmates at every other table were having the very same conversations about who they loved and hated at DuPont. I wouldn't be surprised if my name popped up in several conversations, especially on the hate side of the ledger.

I was pretty much a loner in high school and only really had the Mag 6 as my buddies, not sharing friendship with many others. Not that I didn't *want* to be more friendly, but I was a little shy around people I really didn't know, and my shyness was overlaid by the fact that I simply didn't give a shit about being loved or hated by my classmates. At DuPont, I was never an elected officer of a club, just a joiner, primarily to get my photo in more places in the DuPont yearbook. The only "honor" I had at DuPont was being the Assistant Principal's office helper and keeper of the oak paddle that he, the Executioner, used to swat the crap out of the male students. Maybe I had a sadistic thread running through me in high school, considering the kick I got out of watching some schmuck getting whacked on his ass till it was surely bright red.

After dinner, the evening was wrapped up by a short speech by the head of the reunion committee, announcing that the bus trip to DuPont for a tour of the school would leave the hotel at 9:00 the next morning. I'd planned to go on the tour, maybe even leaving Lucinda at the hotel to hang out. After we had driven by the old high school earlier in the day, she had expressed having no desire to take a bus there and wander around for more than an hour as some of the Mag 6 and I relived old memories of terrorizing the halls and the underclass students.

I was looking forward to seeing the old 2:30 Club bathroom where the boy athletes had hung out before practice while taking a dump and sharing stories and rumors from the day. I also wanted to see the spot in the front of the school where I first spotted Jackie, the cafeteria that served the worst food in the world but somehow miraculously passed state inspection, and the boys' locker room where Crazy and Lily cut a heart out of my gym shorts, exposing my jock to all the students attending our first pep rally that year. Other than those places at DuPont, there wasn't too much that held my interest.

Back in the room after saying our good-nights to the group, I literally crashed. I lay down in bed and asked Lucinda to call Oz and tell him I wasn't going on the bus trip, to tell him to tell the others I was coming down with a cold and wanted to rest and be ready for our get-togethers tomorrow afternoon and evening. Lucinda knew it was a lie that I was coming down with a cold. "Are you OK? How come you are blowing off the bus tour? Don't do it for me. I'll be perfectly fine here at the hotel. I'll go to the pool, catch some sun, talk with whoever is down there, and maybe have lunch at the pool. You just go on your bus tour."

"I made my peace with seeing the school today when we went by after our visit to the old home. What with that visit to the old house and school, seeing all my friends after so many years, plus being with Mom at the nursing home this week, well, I'm feeling a little emotionally bankrupt. I need a little quiet time before tomorrow afternoon when everyone will be here. Who knows, maybe even old Star will drag his ass from home and be here."

Lucinda did as I asked and called Oz, broke the news to him and told him to tell the others I would see them tomorrow afternoon. She was such a good woman, after all, even complying with my lie-for-a-purpose.

"Well, Oz wasn't too happy about you not going on the tour. I'm pretty sure he knows you really don't have a cold. He said to tell you that you are a 'puss' for not going with all of them."

I turned on my side and started to fall asleep. I really was emotionally exhausted, and touring the school would have just sent me into a tailspin, requiring me to call a "1-800-psychiatrist" to treat my stressed-out brain. Lucinda got into bed, and that was my last conscious moment. My subconscious started whirling, pulling out some very strange dreams from deep within my mind. I usually can't remember a single dream in the morning, but this night was different. There was one dream I remembered vividly when I woke up.

In the dream, the Mag 6 and I were on my dad's boat on the St. John's River. I was at the wheel of the boat, pulling Oz on skis. Lily, Crazy, and Spiff were having fun throwing empty beer cans at Oz, trying to knock him off the skis. Star was sitting in the chair beside me. The scene was a replay of the day on the river with the Redskins, skiing and throwing beer cans at each other.

Peering forward over the dream-wheel of the dream-boat, I could see a speedboat coming directly toward us. The closer it got, the more entranced I became because it looked so familiar. Within fifty meters, I could see that it was Stacey's bright red, mahogany Chris Craft, and Stacey was at the wheel. Sitting beside her were Jackie and Ginny, and all three were laughing like three witches around a bubbling kettle of witch's brew.

They appeared to be heading directly toward my boat with the intent of ramming it head-on. I jerked the wheel to a hard right to avoid the collision, but the boat wouldn't turn; the steering wheel just turned loosely without the boat responding at all. I yelled at the guys, warning them we were about to collide with another boat, but they wouldn't pay attention; they just kept throwing beer cans at Oz.

I looked to see where the speedboat with the girls was. At twenty-five meters now, I could see their eyes, which appeared to be sightless, cloudy sockets. At ten meters, both boats still traveling fast, I closed my eyes, waiting for the terrible oncoming collision. I waited and waited, and no collision. I opened my eyes and the speedboat was gone, not in front of my boat or to the side or past us—just gone!

I woke with a start, my t-shirt soaked with night sweats and the bedside clock reading 2:43 a.m. I lay in bed for several minutes trying to psychoanalyze the meaning of the three ex-girlfriends in Stacey's boat, trying to collide into mine with all the Mag 6 aboard, but nothing in the dream made any sense to me. Sure, all three of the ex-girlfriends would probably like to "sink my boat," given we ended our relationships on a down note. But why the Mag 6 were dragged in on their quest to put it to me, I could not deduce, except maybe that I cared more for my buddies than I cared for them—which was probably true in high school.

Trying not to wake Lucinda, I got out of bed in the dark, bumped around the room in the direction of where I had put my suitcase, rummaged through it, and found another t-shirt. I put on the t-shirt and got back in bed.

Lucinda woke up and said sleepily, "You OK? What are you doing up?"

"Nothing, go back to sleep. I had to take a whiz."

I hoped she wouldn't notice the change of t-shirts in the middle of the night because then the questions would start: Why? Was I really sick, after all? I didn't want to tell her about the colliding-boats dream, ex-girlfriends and all.

The next day Lucinda and I parked ourselves at the pool. Surprisingly, we were the only ones there. I was very thankful that we had no one to talk with, and I spent the morning getting my brains straightened out and back to some level of normalcy. Quiet is great when you need time and space to recharge your neuron batteries.

Over lunch at the pool's take-out grill, Lucinda and I met a classmate couple who had actually lived twenty miles from us in California for more than thirty years. We went to the same restaurants, shopped at the same stores, rooted for the USC Trojan football team, and thought we might know some of the same people. The couple had moved back east a couple of years previously, but planned to come to California for a visit in the near future. We made a commitment to get together in California. In the end, our intention turned out exactly as I thought it would—zip. Short-term friendships are just that: "short-term," no real future. Oh, well, maybe the next new friendship will extend further than the distance from the pool to the exit gate.

Around 4:00 p.m., Lucinda and I met the group in a hospitality room. Lo and behold, besides Oz, Spiff, Crazy, and Lily and their spouses, there in the room were Star and Freddie the Farter (we had made Freddie an honorary member of the Mag 6) and Freddie's arm-candy wife twenty-plus years his junior. Looking at both Star and Freddie, I initially didn't recognize them. Only when Oz and Crazy spoke to them and thanked them for coming to the reunion did I know who they were.

Based on Star's physical appearance and outward demeanor, I would never have recognized him. He was pleasant, almost outgoing, but when he talked with me, it was clear that he was not the Star I had double-dated with fifty years ago, or ridden out the serious gale storm with, ending up stranded on that godforsaken sandbar behind Pine Island.

Star was cordial and polite to me as if I were one of his plumbing supply customers. At the end of the night, I felt like I should order five hundred feet of twelve-inch PVC pipe for drainage for my front yard. Somewhere in fifty years, Star had forgotten about the Mag 6 and our unbreakable bonds and being a member of the Knights of the Round Table of Camelot. Star hadn't sold out; he'd just found a new life and had forgotten his old ties. I guess Star wasn't sentimental about maintaining our friendship.

Freddie the Farter was an enigma. No one knew what he had done with his life for the past fifty years, but today he holds a top government position, though what he actually does for the government is still fuzzy to me. For years, the rumors were that Freddie was dead or that he was CIA, an undercover agent in some foreign country. I believe some of our classmates prayed for Freddie over the years when no one could find out whether Freddie was living or dead or what he was doing.

Then Freddie magically reappeared to come to our fiftieth class reunion for a few hours. He had a government commitment, he said, but he wanted to stop by and introduce his wife and say hi to his old buddies. Freddie was in supreme condition, probably working out several hours per day. His physique and his arm-candy wife screamed CIA, but that was just a wild hunch based on my limited knowledge of CIA agents—basically zip, except what I've seen on TV. Freddie was probably a CPA instead of CIA, green eye shades and a pocket full of pencils and a calculator, doing forecasts for the Congressional Budget Office. But I decided to believe he was CIA; that was more exciting and romantic. We talked for an hour and then Freddie and his wife left.

After spending some time in the hospitality suite, the entire class gathered near the pool for group photos. Since we had more than one hundred classmates to squeeze into one photo, the outcome was the same as any group photo of that size—lots of body mass and little face recognition. There, in the foreground of the shot, is a huge banner that reads "DuPont High School, Class of 1960, 50th Reunion." The banner was pretty effective at covering most of the body mass, leaving our heads and faces to appear so small that you need a magnifying glass to recognize anyone at all. I had struck up a conversation with a classmate with whom I had never talked in high school and had found her to be quite funny and engaging. We stood together in the group photo, separate and apart from the rest of the Mag 6 in the photo.

After the photo session, the Mag 6 had a group caricature cartoon drawing made of us, a memento I keep on my work desk even today. Looking at the caricature, we quickly decided that none of us looked anything like the artist had pictured us. But besides the real photos of our group, it captured our spirit and love for each other. Star had to push himself to appear in the drawing, but he did try. Spiff, Crazy, Lily, Oz, and I just had to be ourselves. The artist captured our personalities perfectly.

Dinner really became a long program of speeches, including one delivered by one of the former teachers who was now eighty-eight years old but still very sharp and witty. Surprisingly, she remembered many of those in our class who had had her for a teacher. Honestly, I couldn't remember if I was in her class, so her presence at the reunion was less of a treat for me than for those who did have her for a teacher.

Two classmates, both Mormons and brothers, were recognized for having the most children and grandkids combined—over thirty and growing. I wondered if Mormons and Catholics used the same birth control manual. Lucinda and I were recognized as having travelled the farthest to the reunion. The only other California classmate had died a few years earlier. I recognized the name, but I hadn't even known he had lived in California.

Much like the night before, at the end of the dinner, we all retired to our rooms with promises to get together in the morning before we all headed home. In the old drinking days, we would have been up till the wee hours drinking and laughing, reliving great memories, teasing each other, and lying about our conquests. Now, we were like a bunch of old farts headed to bed before midnight, putting on our night caps to keep our balding heads warm, and when turning out the bedside light, dropping our false teeth into the bedside glass of Polident solution. Sad. Sad. Sad.

The next morning, I was very apprehensive about the day. I would say goodbye to my best friends without knowing when, if ever, we would be together again. My mother's condition in the nursing home wasn't improving. Lucinda and I had purchased a custom-manufactured home for my son and his family who were relocating from Washington, D.C., and had already scheduled the home's delivery to a park community in Laguna Beach. Lucinda and I needed to be back in California immediately to finalize the home's move to the park. Oh, and of course, my company was asking when I was coming back to take care of the usual f***ups, and my blood pressure was higher than my weight, both not good.

Star never came back in the morning, so it was pretty simple to say goodbye to him. Oz and Lily had early morning flights, so I barely got in a hug and a promise to keep in touch. Lily was more emotional than Oz, as I felt he really loved our friendship even though we had never said "boo" to each other over the fifty years since we had seen each other last.

I told him, "Lily, if you ever need me for anything, please phone me and I'll come." I really meant it; I would jump on a plane and fly anywhere to help out my old friend. I said to him as we parted, "You were a great co-captain. Couldn't have wished for Coach Luck to pick anyone else." With those words spoken and a tear in his eye, Lily left the lobby for a cab to the airport.

Oz and I looked at each other and said nothing. There was nothing to say. We instinctively knew that the time had come to say goodbye, so I just gave him a big hug, kissed him on the cheek, and said, "Been great seeing you. We were the best, the best Knights of the Round Table of Camelot." Oz just looked at me and nodded in agreement, and with that, he and his wife left the hotel.

Spiff and Crazy came down to the lobby in leisurely fashion, as they were the only ones driving home and weren't in any hurry to leave. I had regained my composure and was busily drinking hot cups of coffee. Rather than jangling my already sensitive nerves, surprisingly enough, I found all the coffee actually had a calming effect on me. My caffeine high was smoothing out my emotional roller-coaster ride. Lucinda was upstairs still packing, and she knew I wanted to have the last few minutes with the Mag 6 by myself. Her intuitions were always bang on, and for this one, I really owed her. I wanted more than the husbands and wives exchanging niceties; I wanted to tell my buddies how much they meant to me.

Spiff and his wife were gracious and told me how great it was to be with Lucinda and me at the reunion. After fifty years, I finally realized why Spiff was a good friend of mine; simple—it was always in front of me and I just never got it: Spiff was "a good friend, period." He had no hidden agenda, no emotional baggage; there was no questioning Spiff's motives or actions. He was solid and predictable and fun to be around, except when he was in his Mr. Chamber of Commerce mode.

I told Spiff I really enjoyed our relationship and missed his very early Saturday morning telephone calls when we were in high school: Spiff munching cereal, asking me what I was doing for the day. Sometimes I wish my cell phone would ring on a Saturday morning and Spiff would be on the other end: "Rollo, what are you doing today?" His were the kind of unexpected, early morning telephone calls I love. All the others I've gotten have seemed to be the bad kind filled with horrible news of one kind or another. Now, Spiff and I had a slight embrace, and then he and his wife were gone and headed home.

That left just Crazy and me to say goodbye. I dreaded this goodbye more than any other because Crazy had always been there for me—on the defensive line with me against the monster Jackson High School football team, bailing my ass out of jail early on a Sunday morning, in the back of Miss Hamilton's English class with #2 pencils stuck up his nose trying to rattle me in front of the class, in the football stands with his bright red sweater waiting for his anonymous admirer. These are the images of Crazy I will cherish forever—because I cherish Crazy.

When we met in the lobby, I became a sobbing idiot; I could barely tell Crazy what he had meant to me and continues to mean to me after all these years. I think Crazy was a little embarrassed for me and my multi-Kleenex, teary goodbye. We hugged for a long time. I simply did not want to let Crazy go, but out of the corner of my eye, I could see his wife, and she didn't want him to get any more emotionally upset than we already were as we were saying adiós to each other.

"Crazy, time to go," I said. "Thanks."

Crazy looked at me with a quizzical expression, "Thanks for what?"

"Just for being you, Crazy."

I think Crazy understood what I was trying to say. He gave me another quick hug, looked to his wife, and the two of them walked out the front door. I laughed to myself—Crazy had on the same Hawaiian shirt from yesterday; must not have packed enough Hawaiian shirts for the weekend. He still reminded me of a tour bus operator at Leisure World Florida sans the lei. I will simply always love the guy.

Lucinda and I packed, checked out of the hotel, loaded the car with our bags, and headed toward the airport. Our forty-minute drive was fairly quiet conversationally. Lucinda knew I was an emotional mess after saying goodbye to my buddies, and I was leaving Jacksonville, my old home and stomping grounds, probably to never come back again.

I don't think I'll be around for the seventy-fifth reunion. I'm sure by then, the number of surviving alumni will just be sufficient to populate the corner booth at an IHOP pancake restaurant.

Was the fiftieth reunion what I anticipated it to be? Did I reconnect with my buddies after all these years? Did I come away with a renewed commitment to stay in touch with them? Would I have changed anything about my reunion with the Mag 6?

The answers to those questions are: Yes . . . Yes . . . Yes . . . Nothing!

Post-Reunion Emails
From Oz to All (May 24, 2010)

Guys,

Terrific weekend. Got a ton of good shots but here's one. Can't wait for the "official" photos. Star said he'd call me with his correct email address. If so, I'll pass it along. Let's don't drop the ball about getting together after we've had a chance to recover from this one!

From Lily to Oz and Rollo, cc All (May 25, 2010)

Great job and a terrific attitude by your wife. What a blessing to have been able to get together. Let's not drop the ball and stay in touch.

From Lily to Rollo (June 2, 2010)

Rollo,

Thanks so much for the DVD . . . DAMN I look old. You win buddy . . . you looked the best. Great to see ya, it has been only fifty years. Seems like last week we talked just before fb practice was to start (you at Tech and me at Millsaps) and we decided the popular song then "Please Mr. Custer I don't want to go", said it all for us.

My best to y'all and I will assume the last sunset segment of the DVD was shot from your veranda.

Captain Lily

From Rollo to Lily, cc All (June 3, 2010)

Dear Co-Captain, sort of like being a pilot and sitting in the second seat of an airplane beside the real captain . . . oh well, what's in a title?

It was great seeing you and all the Mag 6. Too bad we are spread all over the place, especially me in California. Surprisingly, Crazy and Star rarely see each other even though they live in same town. I told Oz that Bill Swift and his wife lived 20 minutes from me for 39 years and we never knew it. I would not have recognized him even if I did bump into him at the mall. His weight is way down from high school and his little goatee makes his face different. I am glad none of the Mag 6 has gone for the old man mustache which really dates you. In my 30's when big hair was the in-thing, I grew a beard, looked like Gabby Hayes, side kick to Roy Rogers, my wife hated it. I looked 70. That lasted 6 months.

Every once in a while, on one of the oldie but goodies radio stations, they play "Please Mr. Custer, I Don't want to Go." I smile and think of sitting in Tech locker room waiting to go to practice and get KILLED and hearing that song over the intercom. I can smell the locker room today when I hear that song. At practice, they had me as a linebacker going against Rufus Guthrie, second team All American guard and Maxie Baughan, All   American center, played pro for several years. I was pure road kill for those two. Custer had a better chance against the Indians than I did against those two gorillas. Somehow, I lived through it.

As for the DVD sunset, it was actually the sunrise form the veranda, maybe at Millsaps they missed teaching the jocks that the sun rises in the east and sets in the west. See we were on the east coast so the sun would not set on the ocean, but rise from the ocean. Guess that is why as captain, I had to fly the plane.

Take care, Captain Lily.

<u>From Lily to Rollo (June 3, 2010)</u>
Co-captain Rollo,

I beg your pardon, but on the DVD the sun is melting into the ocean . . . hence setting and would therefore be on the west coast. I suppose through some photographic screw-up it was recorded and saved in reverse. This all proves why you are indeed the captain . . . . . CAPTAIN OF A KAMIKAZE PLANE.

Spiff said my title was "ceremonial" . . . what a ass clown. Hope to see you before another 50 years.

Captain for life . . . . Lily

Chapter *18*

Shotgun Shell
May 2012

*A*fter getting into the rental car and firing the engine, my next action was to push all the various chrome-covered buttons that would slide open the moon roof and slowly lower the windows into the doors. The gentle wind blowing off the Atlantic Ocean entered from all directions to refresh the stale air and stuffiness that had built up inside during the hours I had walked the beach and remembered times long in the past but fresh in my heart.

Rental cars always seem to have the same unique scent; anyone who has driven many of them will recognize it instantly. It is the combination of left-behind odors from previous drivers and passengers. Apparently, smoking is always allowed in a no-smoking car; wine or beer spills from illegal open containers with startling regularity; fast-food ketchup, mustard, and onions drip from triple-cheeseburgers and greasy french fries drop onto the seats and floor with such frequency that it's hard to believe *all* the spills are accidental.

Sometimes the food smell is mixed with the scent left by a pet along for the ride: shed hair from a cat or dog, or even droppings from a bird cage or grimy water splashed from a fish's bowl. The wretched top note of the scent mixture is that of cheap cologne used to try to cover the olfactory assault left behind before turning in the rental car. Thank goodness the beach air is God's room freshener and well able to mask the undeniable stink of the vehicle.

When I had first picked up the rental, I had spent a few extra minutes programming the GPS system I'd gotten with it for "just" an extra $15 per day. I set as "My Favorite Places" the current addresses of Stacey, Jackie, and Ginny, my planned destinations over the next three days on my way to Key West. I had been a detective on a par with Sherlock Holmes or Dick Tracy as I tracked down the residences of my three ladies through a combination of skill, perseverance, deductive reasoning, and an unmatched level of innate intelligence.

Well, maybe that's stretching the truth a little. The facts are that I tracked their whereabouts down through the same contacts that had put me on the way to my fiftieth reunion. I had been able to get the roster of the Class of '62, Jackie and Ginny's graduation class, with no trouble at all. The same reunion contact had Stacey's address and phone number as well, having invited her to all the previous reunions and even my fiftieth, since she had been at DuPont for all but her senior year, during which she had been sent into exile at a private school by her daffy mother. Stacey was a no-show for all the reunions.

A week before I would be in Florida, I blew into each of their lives like a freak summer storm, meaning that I telephoned each of them. I purposely didn't send them a "storm warning alert" in advance of my telephone call. I could have sent them an email or a note in the mail for the non-computer owners (believe it or not, two of them actually didn't own a computer). But I wanted to personally phone each of them and pose the invitation and see if they would like to meet me simply to renew our old friendships and to compare our lives over all these years. Of course, I never mentioned that my true motive was to see if I could spark some magic and create the chemistry we once had between us.

I made no pretentions that any of my Sleeping Beauties would open her eyes and tell me that she had waited all this time for me, her Prince Charming, to literally walk through her front door, hold and kiss her, and carry her away on a magnificent, white steed. For the Sleeping Beauties, their ride away to the land of enchantment would have to be in my "rental horse," a 280-horsepower, white-on-white, four-door, Ford Taurus, the only mid-level rental available at the airport rental company.

Using the analogy of a tennis match, my rehearsed phone strategy was based on how they would return my opening introduction. "Hello, Stacey [or Jackie, or Ginny], this is Rob Strand; remember me?" For all three, my opening line was the same, trying not to ace my initial serve to them but, rather, to provide a soft lob to their back court, giving them time to react to the impending conversational back-and-forth. I waited patiently near the net to see how each of them would return my serve.

Without exception, all three reacted with a measured, polite, but questioning service return: "Rob . . ." Long pause, as if in each case her brain was computing why I was calling after fifty years, and possibly questioning the authenticity of the voice on the other end of the line. "Wow, I don't know what to say after all these years. I must admit I lost track of you and really haven't thought of you [measured reaction]. How've you been?" I gave a polite response to each, which was followed by a question about my motives: "Why are you calling me?"

Picking up the pace to get a sense of how each match was going to play out, I returned the serve with, "Well, [insert name,] I apologize for not staying in touch somehow. We've lived other lives these years. You and I were each married, had children, so it would have been awkward, if not inappropriate, for us to stay in touch. Plus, living three thousand miles away put a little crimp in my ability to accidentally run into you in the fresh-vegetable section at the local Piggly Wiggly." By design, the reference to the old-time grocery store chain would, hopefully, get them to giggle, putting a nice crack in the ice between the two of us.

"I want to say I'm sorry to hear about the death of your husband. [Insert name of reunion contact] told me of your loss; I'm really sorry."

Now I settled back to wait for the return volley which would be either a blast to my corner or a lob barely over the net. She might say, "Well, Rob, I'm sorry, but I really have no interest in continuing this conversation." If she hung up, well, point, match, game over. But if she stayed on the phone, there was an opening to keep the match going. Or she might say, "Rob, how wonderful to hear your voice after all this time. How are you, still married?" (The "still married" was my opening to either rush the net for a smash and go for the close or continue to lob soft returns to keep the match going and see if her question was merely a polite response or if she was actually curious about my marital status.

Going for a controlled conversational game while steering clear of any confrontational interaction, I would reply softly, "My wife is institutionalized for the rest of her life with Alzheimer's disease. I've lost her, not to death but maybe to a worse fate—the loss of her knowledge and memories of me and the boys." Now, the match would continue, either with sincere condolences or with a response of "I'm sorry to hear that. I wish you well. Goodbye."

If the match was alive and well and I was keeping the ball continually in play, I would go for what is referred to as a "soft close." "[Insert name,] I'll be in Florida in a week on my way to Key West to possibly establish a second home and watch those stunning sunsets over the Gulf of Mexico. I've been watching spectacular sunsets over the Pacific for most of my life. Now I am looking for a new life, a new beginning." The unsaid in the mention of a new beginning was, with whom? "I was hoping I could stop by for a few minutes to say hi as I pass through on my way to Key West." The conversational strategy here would be to minimize the expectation of some grandiose meeting—just two old friends getting together over coffee at Starbucks or wherever. The match would now move toward giving the other a sense of control as to how the remaining serves would be played—fun and open, or competitive, one winner, one loser—while I actually still stayed firmly in control.

"Would you like to meet at some local Starbucks or your favorite place to get something to drink and just talk?" This would take the pressure off; it wouldn't be "a date"—no dressing up, and we'd meet in a public place in case either person had morphed over the years into some sort of weird kook.

The return service was always predictable: "Why not come by my place? I have a coffee machine, or I can maybe even offer you something stronger, like beer or wine? I'd love to show you some pictures of my family. Do you have pictures of your family? We can take a little time and get caught up after so long." The conversational game would end with both sides coming out winners and getting to see each other. The meeting might be strictly out of curiosity for her, but for me, it was definitely to see if the particular "her" I was meeting might just be part of my new beginning.

Each lady invariably gave me her address, not knowing I already had it, and we set a day and time to meet at her home. Stacey lived in the

Jacksonville area. What's more, she was living in her parents' home, which she had inherited through the family trust upon both parents' passing. Jackie was further down the state in the city of Cape Canaveral, home of the Kennedy Space Center. It figured that Jackie would be near something related to space, the vast unknown. Ginny was in Miami Beach, home of the three B's: beach, booze, and babes. But for Ginny, Miami was home to her and her deceased husband's big-time law firm, which she had taken over as Managing Partner upon his death in the crash of the firm's corporate jet.

I would soon discover why each had made her home where she had, and if any of them might desire to sail off with me into the Key West sunset.

My GPS sent me on a short trip back to Jacksonville and then south on Highway 13 to Stacey's house. I had thought at first that I didn't need some high-tech, electro-robotic gizmo to tell me where I was going, but I was wrong. The swampy area going to her parents' home, the old Ponderosa ranch, was now developed housing tracts and strip malls, complete with the required Home Depot and Wal-Mart. I marveled at the change in the area, remembering the night I had come to a dead stop on Highway 13 at the imaginary railroad crossing before coming to my senses that there was no railroad crossing there. That night I swore that would be my last trip to the Ponderosa.

At the turn off the highway onto the dirt road leading to Stacey's house, the site of the old Adams General Store was now a mini shopping center, servicing the owners of the exclusive homes that now occupied what used to be the wooded area that dominated the local geography. The shopping center had the usual selection of establishments, a Starbucks, a few upscale women's clothing stores, a trendy sushi bar restaurant, and a grocery store catering to the vegetarian set. I'm sure Mr. and Mrs. Adams, owners of the old general store, got so rich with the sale of their property that their grandkids are now driving BMWs and going to private colleges.

I never understood exactly where Stacey's parents' property started as I left the highway and drove toward the house. If they owned a chunk of the acreage, then Diane and Bob Purcell made a helluva lot of money with the sale of the land for real estate development. With money in the bank, Bob Purcell could have bought himself a new shotgun to shoot pine cones, like in the woodsy campsite where he hid from his wife each day all those years. He would have had to find a new campsite, of course, as the developers' bulldozers would have leveled his old retreat.

As I turned onto what used to be an ass-bouncing dirt road, I marveled at the landscaped, street-lighted, paved parkway that went toward Stacey's house. At the end of the pavement, my GPS directed me onto a dirt road, and I passed through a big, rusting, wrought-iron gate and under a semi-circular, matching wrought-iron sign that proudly proclaimed "Purcell Ranch." I was happy to see that there was still a piece of the old dirt road and that the road could still jar the kidneys like no other. As I carefully proceeded up the road to the house, I wondered if Stacey had the same type of tire-eating, incessantly barking Weimaraner dogs her mother had so proudly owned. Upon reaching the house, I was thankful not to spot any dogs to scratch the rental car and cause me to pay contract-specified damages to the rental car company.

When I stopped the car and opened the door, the scent of pine trees and fallen needles was very pronounced. Adding the cool breeze off the river made the atmosphere idyllic, almost mesmerizing. I felt like I was on a Shangri-La–like movie set. Standing by the car, I surveyed the house and the surrounding grounds, wracking my brain to think whether the place had changed over the years. My brain server kept coming up: "Same place, no changes."

I was a little dumbfounded that the house and property hadn't been changed structurally in fifty-plus years. Sadly, the house also looked like it hadn't had any upkeep, including fresh paint, since the last time I had stood in this same exact spot. While still grand in its initial impression, the house appeared worn and run down. Maybe Stacey hadn't had anyone to help her keep up the house and property. As I stood there, I found myself thinking, "It's a shame the place is so run down. I wonder if the dock and Chris Craft are still there."

"Welcome to Purcell Ranch!" sounded in my ears and broke the spell. I looked quickly toward the sound of the voice. My mouth almost dropped to the ground. There, standing by one of the monster pine trees that dotted the property, was Stacey . . . only now, she was a dead ringer for her mother Diane Purcell. Stacey was wearing a pair of old riding pants and boots, a plaid shirt knotted at the waist. Her hair was pulled back in a tight bun. From where I stood, Stacey's beautiful, bright white smile illuminated the pathway between us.

Thank God Stacey didn't have a smoldering cigarette dangling from her hand like her mother always had. Stacey hated the smell of smoke and, therefore, never took up the habit. Later, I did learn that, though she wasn't a smoker, she did like her glasses of wine very much. She explained that they were the best medicine to take the edge off the stress of managing the Purcell Ranch. Well, maybe letting wine fill her brain with a pleasant haze was better than filling her lungs with smoke to relax.

"Stacey . . . wow . . . I almost didn't recognize you, but you sure are still as beautiful as always and still shining that million-dollar smile!" I walked to her and stopped within a couple of feet to take her into my mind and do the usual comparison to the girl I had dated in high school. She still had the same striking blonde hair with just a very few detectable strands of gray, the same sea-blue eyes, and that Coppertone tan that now came from working daily around the property instead of sunbathing on the dock.

"Stacey, you look like the clock stopped; you haven't changed a bit, except . . . you do look a little more like your mother the last time I saw her."

"Rob . . ." Stacey paused as if to catch her breath. "I can't tell you what a thrill it is to see you, and ditto, you look like the same guy who used to hide in the pitch dark on the dirt road to take me on a date."

We moved at the same time to close the two feet between us, embraced in a warm hug, and pulled back while still holding each other. Then we kissed with a "great to see you again" kiss, as if by some unspoken mutual agreement. We pulled back again and just looked at each other for several long seconds. Then we both started to giggle, maybe the nervous giggle of not knowing what to say or do next. Our giggles quickly turned to a fun laughter, the type common between two long-lost friends who see each other again, like at an airport or a high school reunion or, like now, on the pine needle–covered grounds of the Ponderosa.

"The place hasn't changed since the last time I was here. Do you still have the boat dock with that beautiful speedboat? Remember on our first date when we took it out?" I knew I was pressing a little on the remembering bit, but time was short and I needed to start to understand where Stacey was with her perception of me.

"Yes, I still have the boat dock. As a matter of fact, it was just refurbished ten years ago before both my parents passed away. I had to replace most of the pilings and deck boards, and I added lights for security. Too many houses are getting broken into from predators coming up from the river. That old speedboat? I sold it to a boat collector before it could sink while still tied to the dock. The boat needed a lot of work, more work and money than I was willing to put into it, and the collector gave me a good price. Come on, I'll show you the dock."

Stacey and I headed toward the dock, passing the very spot where Diane would plop her ass in her Adirondack lawn chair with her pack of Winston cigarettes and hold court over her domain. I stopped on the way to the dock, looking around for the chair; somehow, I had a feeling Stacey might have created a monument for her mother around her favorite spot. "Sorry about your mom and dad passing away. Are they buried at a cemetery in Jacksonville?"

Stacey stopped dead in her tracks, spun around, and looked at me with those beautiful blue eyes, now a little fiery. "My parents died within six months of each other, both from cancer. Mom had lung cancer; Dad had liver cancer." She paused for just a minute to regain her composure. "They're both over there by the big pine." Stacey nodded her head in the direction of a massive pine tree farther down the bluff overlooking the river.

Looking in that direction, I could see a fenced-off area around the huge pine, and right in the middle of the space, the Adirondack lawn chair and what looked like a cement replica of a hunting dog. Wanting to laugh, I looked at Stacey and asked her with as straight a face as I could deliver, "Your parents are buried by that tree with the lawn chair and hunting dog headstone?" I was actually thinking to myself, "My God, tell me it isn't true—Bob and Diane planted on the property within one hundred feet of the house."

Stacey was now more reflective and replied in a sober tone, "Yes, Mom and Dad's last wish was to be cremated and have their ashes distributed on the property. I thought a little memorial was appropriate, so I had their ashes buried by the pine tree overlooking the river. I put Mom's chair over her ashes after having it coated with some preservative that lasts a hundred years. The hunting dog headstone is over Dad's ashes. I found it at a pet cemetery that had put it up for sale since the previous owner had died and quit making payments on Rex's gravesite. Every day, I keep the memorial site clean because that tree drops a lot of needles on the chair and headstone, and little critters get in and eat the flowers I put out."

Now, I really wanted to fall down in gut-wrenching laugher, thinking to myself, "Oh, come on, a memorial park on the property for Bob and Diane with a mummified lawn chair and a recycled headstone from some dog's gravesite? Daily she cleans the site because of critters? Lung and liver cancer, duh—maybe the daily three packs of cigarettes and the daily pint of Kentucky whiskey at the campsite had something to do with their kicking the bucket? Stacey, what's happened to you?"

Thankfully, I was smart enough to keep my thoughts to myself and instead politely said to Stacey, "You must be proud of your memorial to your parents. Not many people could have their deceased parents so close to them. Do you have plans to join them when you leave this world for the next?"

"No, silly, I plan to leave the Purcell Ranch to my daughters. They can bury me with my parents, throw my body in the river, put me through the branch shredder, I really don't care. Once I'm gone, I'm gone. The kids can do what they want, but . . . I guess if it *were* up to me . . . yeah, I would like to join my parents under the pine tree. My whole life has been here on the ranch; I never want to leave it."

Well, that was really all I needed to hear because there was my answer about Stacey going to Key West with me: nope. Only if I dig up Bob and Diane and cart along the mummified Adirondack lawn chair and Rex's headstone and maybe the two-hundred-foot pine tree. But I'm sure I can't quite get all that in the Taurus along with Stacey and her luggage.

"Here, hold my hand as we walk down the hill to the dock. I don't want you to slip and break any bones in that beautiful body," Stacey said as she looked at me and winked.

Taking hold of her hand, I was shocked by how rough it was, callused and hard. Glancing quickly at her hand, I saw that her nails were broken and had not a speck of nail polish on them. My mind went to the movie *Gone with the Wind*, when Scarlett O'Hara, now laboring in the fields of her home, Tara Plantation, and having gone from being a Southern belle to working as a common field hand, pulls up a filthy radish and says, "I ain't going to be hungry no more." Stacey seemed to have that appearance, one of just getting by, working at hard labor to keep the ranch going. I wondered where all the money from the real estate sale had gone.

I said to Stacey, "You don't have to worry about this body. I'm in great shape. A little slip and fall won't kill me."

"Well, while I wouldn't mind having you holed up in the house and me taking care of you, I'm sure you have other plans, especially getting on to Key West. Have you found a house there yet?" Stacey was suddenly hitting me on several buttons, openly hinting that she could take care of me and inquiring about my living plans in Key West. I started wondering if the Taurus's trunk really *could* hold the lawn chair and Rex.

"Well, I am sure you'd be a great nurse. I could use a little loving care . . . I'm pretty sure both of us could use a little loving after the last several years. It's been tough on both of us. But no, I have a small rental to stay in till I have more permanent plans in Key West."

Stacey and I were now on the dock. We slowly strolled out to the end of it, where two fairly new jet skis were moored. I grinned. "I'm impressed— jet skis? You were always a water wonk, swimmer, skier. Now jet skis?"

Stacey laughed. "No, these are my grandkids' jet skis. They come here every summer for weeks on end. They just left last week and will be back next month. I'd be joining Mom and Dad if I tried to take one of these jet skis for a spin on the river."

Looking at Stacey, I found it easy to see that she still had a trim little body, probably from working the ranch, and my impression was that she could probably easily handle a jet ski and probably run circles around the grandkids while doing so. Prompted by the mention of her grandkids, I said, "You'll have to tell me about your family. I don't know a thing about you since DuPont. Let's go to the house and you can bring me up to date."

Stacey held my hand and led me back up the hill. I kept thinking as I felt the callused hand, "Where did the money go?"

While the outside of the house was in desperate need of paint, the inside was clean and well-kept, though aged. The furniture looked to be the same pieces her mother had owned, and nothing looked newer than twenty years old. The inside of the house had the scent of a frequently used fireplace; I supposed there was no central heat. Passing through the living room and den to the kitchen, I noticed Stacey had her dad's gun rack on the wall with the shotguns still in it. I commented while looking at the display, "Ever shoot the guns?"

Stacey stopped, looked at the gun rack and guns, and said matter-of-factly, "Yes, I go out frequently. Still some spots around here with quail and wild turkey. I sometimes see a deer or two, but I can't bring myself to shoot them. Buck fever, I guess."

Stacey opened the top drawer of a nearby antique desk and, from it, took out a spent shotgun shell and handed it to me. "Here, take this shell. Dad would have liked you to have it. The grading contractor found a number of the spent shotgun shells at a campsite, probably where Dad used to go hunting, and the contractor gave them to me. Dad always liked you, thought you were a great athlete. Mom, on the other hand, well, we both know what her thoughts were."

I took the spent shotgun shell and said, "I never knew your dad liked me. I remember the first time I saw him. He was walking on the dirt road back to the house, shotgun breeched, just sort of meandering back home. Thanks for the shotgun shell; I'll definitely keep it as one of my cherished mementoes." I put the shell in my pocket and followed Stacey into the kitchen.

"Would you like a glass of wine, coffee, soft drink?" Stacey asked as she opened the refrigerator, scouting to see what was inside. "How about a glass of chardonnay? Got a cold bottle in the refrig."

Now deciding it was time to step up and press my luck, I responded, "Sure, I'll have a glass of chardonnay. Just don't take advantage of me if I get tipsy." I wanted to see if Stacey was up for a little teasing, see if she still had any sexuality about her.

Laughing her unforgettable, angelic laugh, she replied, "I think it was always the other way around, me worrying about you taking advantage of this poor little country girl." After pouring the wine into two glasses and noting that the bottle was almost empty, Stacey said, "Open the pantry. Inside is a small wine refrigerator. Get us a fresh bottle."

In the pantry, I opened the small refrigerator to find it stocked full of cold chardonnay wine. I also noticed a case of wine on the floor for refilling the little wine unit. In the corner of the pantry were cases of empty wine bottles, probably to be returned for a bottle refund. Judging by a quick count, Stacey had twenty or thirty dollars of bottle return monies due her. All this led to a fairly obvious observation: Stacey likes her wine—and lots of it.

I gave Stacey a new bottle, which she uncorked and placed on the kitchen table, where we sat down. I opened the conversation about her family: "From the photos on the wall in the den, it looks like you have a couple of children and four or five grandkids? Are they living nearby?"

"Two kids, both girls, both live within an hour or so of the house, and both have two children, all boys, no girls. I really hope one of my girls has a little daughter. Don't get me wrong, I love my grand boys, but I'd love to have a little girl to dress, fix her hair, and tell her not to date good-looking track athletes because they'll only break your heart."

Stacey looked at me with a twinkle in her beautiful blue eyes. It was obvious time hadn't diminished her ability to give it back to you in a tête-à-tête. "Well, she couldn't do any worse with a track guy—better than a Speedo-clad swimmer showing off all his goods, if you know what I mean." I laughed at my Speedo line, thinking it was a pretty quick comeback to her dig about me "breaking her heart."

I then asked Stacey some more personal questions. "Stacey, how are you doing out here all by yourself? Seems like a lot of work for a single woman. How come you don't hire some help? Your family must have made out OK with the housing development."

I think I caught her off guard with my questions; she was anticipating more of our fun bantering. Stacey got very serious and outlined her financial situation for me in a nutshell: "Yeah, we hit the mother lode with the sale of the property. Mom and Dad had paid off the mortgage on this place and put the house in a trust for me and any surviving family members, along with a fund to pay the yearly property taxes. Some hotshot investment banker put most of the money in the stock market just as Wall Street collapsed. Well, we went down the financial tubes with this asshole's piss-poor investments of our money. Of course, he collected his commissions, and our family ate the losses. I think it was the loss of the money that killed my dad. He literally drank himself to death. Now I get by on a little money we salvaged from the stock market and my Social Security check. The kids help out as best they can, but they have their own lives and families and expenses."

Stacey became very stoic in her demeanor, and I reached out and took hold of her hands. I decided it was a great time to put the big question to her to see if she was going to be my Sleeping Beauty. "Stacey, I am going to be on this side of the world for a long time. Would you like to come to Key West to see me and maybe be part of my new beginning?"

Slowly raising her eyes to meet mine, a chipped fingernail circling the top of her wine glass, she gave me a very deliberate answer, which I believe came from deep within her heart: "Rob, I couldn't think of anyone I would like to spend my last remaining years with more than you. After my husband and I divorced so many years ago, I have to admit I've thought quite a lot about you. It's been lonely, especially since the girls got married and moved out and on to their own lives. Now it's just me and the critters that invade Mom and Dad's gravesite, and my grandkids on holidays and vacations. It gets pretty lonely out here."

My mind soaked in her words, and I was almost sure she was going to say "yes" to my offer. Looking at her closely, I could see that Stacey had the makings of an even more beautiful woman; all she needed was some TLC, a trip or two to a full-body make-over spa and one of those nail salons that restores a bad set of nails by topping them with little flowers or fake diamond dots. I suddenly visualized Stacey and me on one of Key West's fabled beaches, hand in hand, watching the burning sunset over the Gulf of Mexico.

Then Stacey dropped the hammer on my dream: "Rob, when I have a free weekend, I'll definitely think about coming to see you in the next several months. But I have so much to do here at the ranch; the kids are coming in a month, and I have to get this house painted, yada, yada, yada . . ."

There it was, a polite "Thank you for wanting me to be with you and your new beginning, but I have my life here on the Ponderosa. I want to be buried with Mom and Dad under the big pine tree with Rex the headstone and the mummified lawn chair."

I looked at my watch, which Stacey caught me doing. "Do you have to leave so soon? Can you stay for dinner?" Stacey quickly realized she had shot herself in the foot with her reluctance to be more open about coming to Key West. Now she was trying to regain some footing and keep me at the house to talk more about us, which, I perceived, would be the only outcome of my staying longer: talk, talk, talk.

"Stacey, when I get settled in Key West, I am going to call you and ask you to come see me. I think you and I would be great together—not here at the Purcell Ranch, but in Key West. I want a new beginning, new surprises each day, not rehashing the old. I think if you give my offer some serious consideration, you'll come to Key West. Will you at least say you will consider my offer to be with me for what time we have left?"

Stacey had tears in her eyes. God, it killed me to see her with tears. I did not come to the Ponderosa to make her cry. I felt like a real louse, and I apologized. "Stacey, I'm sorry if I upset you. I never want to hurt you. You mean so much to me."

"Rob, I loved you so long ago. I think I could love you again. Give me some time."

I got up from the table and took Stacey in my arms and kissed her as passionately as I did when we were teenagers. I needed to see if my kiss would open the eyes of Sleeping Beauty and if she would love me once more. I kept my eyes open and looked at Stacey during the kiss; her eyes were closed and didn't open a bit. So much for this particular Sleeping Beauty going with me to Key West.

Stacey and I stood holding each other for several minutes. I turned and started toward the front door. Looking around in the foyer at the old family photos on the walls, I could swear I sensed Diane Purcell's spirit nearby, grinding her teeth knowing that Protestant boy was back. That thought put a smile on my face.

Outside the house, I said goodbye to Stacey, telling her I would call her soon and that we would go from there. We kissed again, this time more of a friendly kiss than one that might lead to a roll in the hay. I reached into my pocket for my car keys and felt the shotgun shell Stacey had given me. Pulling it out, I held it up to Stacey and said, "Good thing your mom didn't have the shotgun years ago; this shell would have had my name on it." We both laughed.

I got into the car and slowly pulled away from the house, watching in the rearview mirror as Stacey waved to me. Looking to the right, in the near distance by the big pine tree I could see the mini cemetery with the Adirondack lawn chair and Rex's headstone. I thought to myself, "I wonder what Stacey's ashes will be marked with when she is buried with Mom and Dad. Probably an empty chardonnay bottle."

At the main highway, my GPS gave me my instructions: "Turn right, stay on Highway 13 for ninety-six miles to your destination, Daytona Beach." I would spend the night in Daytona Beach before going on to Cape Canaveral tomorrow to see Jackie and find out if she was "*the one,*" my true Sleeping Beauty.

Chapter *19*

Pendant

*D*aytona Beach is the home of hundreds of low-end motels and a few two-star hotels that cater to underage high school and college students. These beer-loving students, most from the cold northeastern states, but nonetheless sporting a reasonably passable fake ID, migrate to Daytona to party and hopefully get laid. Daytona Beach also has a speedway race track for a little stock car race called "The Daytona 500, The Great American Race." I've been in Daytona for both events: as a teenager partying, drinking beer, hoping to get laid; and as a spectator for "The 500."

Arriving in Daytona this evening, I found the area of the beach with the lower-end motels, which, of course, are miles away from the upscale hotels. With a $49-per-night rate, the motel I selected could have been the Bates Motel from the terrifying movie *Psycho*. Even the night manager— "Stark" was the name on his badge—looked suspiciously like the nut-job Norman Bates. The bathroom in my room had one of those opaque shower curtains that you could see through, the same type as in the movie when Janet Leigh gets sliced and diced by Norman with the type of butcher knife you could carve up a side of beef.

I went to the motel office to ask Stark for a good place to eat. After I rang the desk bell several times, finally Stark emerged from a dark back room. The single bare light bulb hardly gave off enough illumination for me to see him coming out. I surmised that the room Stark had emerged from was where he slept in case someone showed up in the middle of the night to rent a room. I imagined him sleeping in the dark back room with his mummified mother propped up in a rocking chair, just like in the movie. Stark was that creepy of a person.

Stark recommended Tico Taco, his favorite eating place, which was, conveniently enough, located directly across the street. Tico Taco is a fast-food joint specializing in make-believe Mexican tacos composed mostly of premade taco beef, along with refried beans fresh from a can. Each night, Stark must run across the street, grab a few tacos, and then rush back to the motel and his dead mother. I imagined that Stark's room behind the motel's check-in counter must be littered with Tico Taco carry-out bags and food wrappers. But hey, at least his mother wouldn't eat much.

Being from California, I know my Mexican food, and Daytona Beach is far from the center of gourmet Mexican tacos. Farther down the street was a Burger King, which I selected in honor of Jackie. While at DuPont High School, the night I thought Jackie and I were going to make mad, passionate love for our first time, I had driven to Kings Highway to purchase a new condom from the vending machine in the men's room at the Burger King. Now with both of us in our 60s, if anything sexual did happen between Jackie and me, we definitely would not need a twenty-five-cent Burger King men's room condom.

While downing my Whopper burger and fries, I remembered back to 1959, when a few of my high school buddies and I had come to the Daytona 500 to hang out, drink beer, and chase girls. As luck would have it, our superstar football running back scored infield tickets and pit passes for all of us, which had been donated by a wealthy University of Florida alumnus who was recruiting our buddy for the Gator football team.

With the exception of Crazy and Lily, those of us with an infield pass spent the majority of the 500 race going from one beer- and food-laden tailgate party to another. On his own without the rest of us, Crazy meandered to the racing pits, where he watched the pit crews do their remarkable servicing of the race cars in an almost ballet-like display of split-second timing.

As the 500 came down to the final laps, race car drivers Lee Petty and Johnny Beauchamp went back and forth for first place. They crossed the finish line in what appeared to be a dead heat. Beauchamp was declared the winner and Lee Petty immediately protested. It took a committee three days of studying newsreel footage to finally determine that Petty had indeed won. At the finish line, famed race car driver Fireball Roberts had seen that Lee Petty had won and told the press that. Standing on the finish line along with Fireball was our Mag 6 buddy Crazy; thus, Fireball Roberts and Crazy were the only two people of hundreds of thousands of spectators who truly knew the winner of the 1959 Daytona 500 right away. When looking for others to verify the winner, the committee wouldn't listen to what Crazy had to say; who was going to believe a teenager with the nickname "Crazy"?

Back at the motel, I double-latched the door and even slid a chair under the doorknob to prevent any intruders, especially Norman Bates, a.k.a. "Stark." I had a sleepless night, keeping one eye on the doorknob to see if Stark was going to pop in with a butcher knife and try to kill me. In the morning, as I checked out, Stark handed me a pamphlet for "Motel Owners for Christ." Stark seemed to look different in the daylight with the back room brightly lit by the morning sun. I could see a large crucifix on the wall. When Stark gave me the pamphlet, he said, "Hope you enjoyed your stay. If you're a Christian, the next time you're this way, us motel owners get together on Wednesday nights as a Bible study group. We love for our guests to join us."

Boy, did I feel like a schmuck—a double-schmuck—perceiving Stark as a Norman Bates, and needlessly losing sleep. I thanked Stark for the invitation to his Bible study group, but told him I didn't expect to be back to Daytona Beach for a long time, if ever.

On my GPS, I found Jackie's address in the "My Favorite Places" list and got the initial directions to Interstate 95 South. I headed toward Cape Canaveral, eighty miles away. I planned to be at Jackie's residence by 11:00 a.m. so we would have several hours together. Within those precious hours, I hoped to find out if Jackie would be my future companion in Key West.

Florida during the early summer months is incredibly beautiful, balmy in the true sense of the word, so as I drove, I opened the sun roof and rolled down all the windows. I wanted the fresh sea air laden with just a tinge of salt to take me away to a fresh level of consciousness, hopefully replacing the concerns I had for Stacey and her financial predicament of trying to keep the Purcell Ranch from falling apart at the seams. I wasn't sure about Stacey and me and our future, but it bothered me that she was alone and struggling. Those thoughts were a real downer that I didn't want to impact my meeting with Jackie or Ginny. The sea air is a great energizer, and by the time I arrived in Cape Canaveral, I felt like a new person.

Jackie's residence was an attractive, high-end condo unit just two blocks off the beach. My real estate instincts told me that before the market crash, the condos had been in at least the mid-$600,000 range and most were probably in the high $800,000s. I hoped Jackie wasn't upside down on her unit, as Florida was still suffering from a very depressed housing market. After visiting with Stacey and looking at the sad deterioration of the Ponderosa, I didn't want to hear or see more real estate problems. Fortunately, I soon found out that Jackie was doing quite well financially, so real estate was the least of her problems.

I rang the buzzer to Jackie's unit for entrance to the condo lobby and elevators. The return answer was Jackie on the intercom: "Rob, is that you? Please be you."

"Yes, it's me, whoever the hell *me* is," I said in my satirical manner. Continuing on, I teased Jackie, "No, it's really the smell-good plumber to fix whatever you need fixing, lady."

"Oh, Rob, you haven't changed a bit. Get your ass up here so I can do *whatever* to my smell-good plumber."

I was pumped up that Jackie still had a great sense of humor—and that she had never forgotten our *whatever* date when, in some park overlooking the St. John's River, she fed me some tasteless walnut cakes, chased with an 80-proof vodka juice drink, and danced the dance of witches and dragons. God, what a sultry vision she was, barefooted with her white dress flowing like gossamer, her platinum hair glowing in the moonlight as she twirled around and around in a semi-hypnotic trance. If she had done that dance naked, I would have been committed the next day for the simple fact that I would have lost all my rational-thinking ability due to the erotic power of that mind-blowing dance. Instead of taking the elevator, I found myself feeling twenty years younger, so I ran up the flights of steps to the third floor and her unit.

Jackie answered the door and, already out of breath from the stairs, I thought I would need oxygen when I saw her—she was breath-taking. Her smoky gray eyes had not dulled one iota over the years and, if possible, were even more "smoking." Of course, that may have just been due to her eye shadow. Her platinum hair was still platinum without a single gray hair to be seen. I figured it was probably a $500 tint job and definitely worth every dollar. Jackie was still the Kim Novak look-alike I had initially seen on the first day of my senior year at DuPont High School. I just stood in her front doorway and said nothing. I was actually trying hard to just breathe; I didn't want to pass out and make an utter fool of myself by suddenly falling face down on her white carpet.

"Rob, you look great. My, my, you're still a walking and talking heartthrob. Give me a hug and kiss."

I didn't have to wait to find out if Jackie would be a candidate for my Sleeping Beauty, winner-takes-all, Key West contest. She jumped into the fray before I even got through the front door. We came together and now, just inches from Jackie's eyes and lips, I suddenly felt as if I was being pulled to her by some unexplainable force. I let go and surrendered, and our lips met in a passionate kiss that made me wonder who the Sleeping Beauty was, Jackie or me. She still had that magic touch or, in this case, those magic lips.

"Well, hello," I sputtered as we parted from kissing. I was still catching my breath from running up the stairs, which had been a bit of a workout in itself, followed by the very long, unexpected, and somewhat over-the-top welcome kiss from a girlfriend I hadn't seen in five decades. But I had to admit, Jackie hadn't lost any of her unique sensuality.

"Come on in and make yourself comfortable." Jackie stood to one side and, with a sweeping gesture of her arm, pointed me in the direction I should go. She followed me into her living room, which was decorated entirely in contrasting black and white—carpeting, white; sofas, black; pictures on the wall, black on white or white on black; no other colors. One of the abstract pictures was signed, "Picasso."

"Beautiful living room you have. I love the way you did the decorating, all of it, and I mean *all* of it, in either black or white. Sure saves time trying to figure out color combinations. Sort of like Henry Ford when he said you could have his Model T in any color as long as it was black. Well, you threw in white, but who's complaining?"

For a moment, I just stood looking around the room, trying to take it all in, or maybe more to the point, trying to understand why just black and white. Jackie could sense my mystification over her decorating scheme. At length, she said, "I have moved to a minimalist life-style. Partially because it makes my life simple, especially as I get older—not a lot of choices and decisions I have to make: this color or that color, will it work in this room or that room? Also, I've become a Church of Scientology believer, and their credo is also a minimalist structure. Have you heard about L. Ron Hubbard and the Church of Scientology?"

CRASH! I could only think to myself that the roof had just fallen in on what had been an incredible first ten minutes with Jackie and my conviction that she could be the Sleeping Beauty of my dreams. Immediately, I found myself thinking, "Church of Scientology, wow! Not a religion I expected Miss Witch on a Broomstick to gravitate to. Then again, maybe it's not so unusual, from what I've heard about Ron Hubbard and his church. The whole Scientology religion is sort of *out there*."

Then the lightning bolt of awareness hit me with one million volts: "Shit, I bet Jackie's here in Cape Canaveral because of the space thing going on here. Maybe that's why she is into the Church of Scientology. Don't they believe in aliens or something like that?"

Normally, I stay away from discussing someone's religion and religious beliefs, as I do with politics, as there are no winners in those discussions, only losers and hard feelings, and sometimes even tears. In my teens, I had to deal with Stacey's mother and the Catholic/Protestant issue between us, and that only led to Stacey getting her ass pulled from school and sent elsewhere.

But in the case of Jackie and her religion, I had to ask the big question: "So, why did you join the Church of Scientology? I don't remember that church being in Jacksonville when we were at DuPont."

Jackie took hold of my hand and led me to her sofa, which was, of course, black and white: a black fabric covering and big, white, fluffy pillows. Soon we were both sitting on the sofa, and Jackie was holding both my hands in hers when I noticed her fingernails. They were well-groomed, short, pointed nails decorated with black fingernail polish and a white line running diagonally across each nail.

"Hmmm," I thought to myself, "I wonder if she does her toes the same way." Glancing to the floor as if to admire the white carpeting, I could see that Jackie was barefooted—of course, what else?—and yes, her toenails were painted, but with white. "When she wants to really be kinky, she probably does one foot in white and the other in black," I thought, a little bitterly.

"Like my carpeting?" Jackie asked, breaking my trance of staring at her toes. I quickly remembered that she had that extra mind-reading power thing going on so she knew I was ogling her toes and wondering about her paint job on them.

"No, just a little overwhelmed by how beautiful you are. Time has definitely worked in your favor. And it looks like you aren't worried about making your mortgage payment."

"Well, thank you, Rob. And if I may return the compliment, you look great, even with silver hair instead of brown. It's a distinguished look with an attractive richness to it. And yes, I don't have to worry about money; this place is paid for—no mortgage payments."

Continuing on, Jackie asked me, "Remember Reginald Bradley III, family in the urinal manufacturing business? I dated Reginald after we broke up. Well, Reginald and I were married my second year of college. The Bradley family attorney made me sign a prenup. It said basically that I would be financially taken care of in the event of a divorce, but just no ownership of the urinal business. But for me, life took a big turn when Reginald died in a big-game hunting accident in Kenya during our fifth year of marriage. The life insurance payoff was ten times better than the crummy prenuptial. I've been financially independent since the mid-1960s. Not bad, you agree?"

"Well, I'm sorry about Reginald's death," I said. "What happened in Kenya, killed by a lion? Were you there with him on the hunt when he was killed?"

"No, I was at our home in Jacksonville; I couldn't stand the thought of killing something as beautiful as a lion. Reginald was going to bring home its skin and head and have it as a rug in his office. I told him before he went to Kenya that he could buy a lion rug from an import store without going to Kenya, but he insisted he wanted to bag the lion himself. I think he felt like he had something he had to prove to himself and his parents about being his own man. I didn't get it, but proving himself was the driving force behind his Kenya trip."

Jackie paused with a slightly bitter little smirk before continuing.

"Unfortunately, Reginald was killed by an elephant they were using for the lion hunt. The elephant got spooked by some small rodent that ran out, and it bolted down the pathway where the hunting party was standing getting ready to go on the hunt. Reginald was directly in front of the elephant when it started running, and he was instantly trampled to death. Sad. They shipped what was left of Reginald's body back home in a plastic tub about the size of a small garbage can. I guess the elephant did quite a job on poor old Reginald. Life is sure strange—Reginald's life snuffed out by what began with a tiny mouse."

I just sat there, stunned. I wasn't sure what to say upon hearing of such an uncommon event. "Wow, what an amazing story. Losing your husband to such tragic consequences."

"Oh, well," Jackie went on. "I cashed the insurance check and started to find myself on trips through Europe, India, and the Middle East. In 1985, after experimenting with a number of Far East religions, I was returning home when I walked into an airport gift shop. While I was there, I picked up a copy of L. Ron Hubbard's *Dianetics*, and it changed my life forever. After getting back to Jacksonville, I joined the Church of Scientology, and I have been a devotee since."

Then she suddenly changed conversational directions. "Enough about me. Let's talk about you and why you're sitting here in my living room, especially after all these years and not even a 'boo' from you. Are my prayers and wishes and witchcraft chants coming true?" Jackie winked at me on the mention of witchcraft chants, knowing that I would get a charge out of her reference to her teenage fascination with the Wiccan world.

"My wife Lucinda and I had a beautiful, storybook marriage for forty-five years," I replied. "We have one son, John, and I have a son, Darren, with Elizabeth, my first wife, and we have a couple of fantastic grandsons. Business has been rewarding. God has smiled on my life.

Then, slowly over time, Lucinda started acting strangely, doing things like putting food in the freezer that should go in the cabinets. Ever try to pour frozen Heinz ketchup on your hamburgers? Simple little odd actions led us to a neurologist who last year delivered the terrible news on one bright spring morning: Lucinda has a quickly progressing form of Alzheimer's disease."

Jackie looked at me with compassion in her eyes. "I cannot imagine how you and Lucinda handled the diagnosis. You two must have been devastated."

"Lucinda and I crammed in as much being together as we could before she lost her memory of me and the boys. We went on trips, to movies and plays, and even remodeled the living room to a more contemporary style. Those activities seemed to delay the progression of the Alzheimer's, but at some point, we both knew she would need to move into a care unit that could watch over her 24/7. I simply didn't have the time and strength to take care of her as she needed.

"Six months ago, Lucinda was totally institutionalized, and no amount of visiting and talking with her or showing her photos of the family can open a window into her mind so that we can visit with her. I would sit with her for hours and . . . nothing. Not a 'Hello, lover' or 'What are you cooking for dinner?' I finally realized Lucinda was gone to another world, buried somewhere deep in her mind. I just prayed she was happy in her new place.

"A month or so ago, I said my goodbyes to Lucinda and made my way to the East Coast. I've visited old friends, gone by my old home and high school for my second visit in two years, and now I'm here on my way to Key West."

I paused, and after a moment, Jackie spoke.

"Rob, why are you here? Not here in Cape Canaveral at my condo, but why *me*, why *now*?" Jackie wanted answers to the big "why?" and she didn't want to play "cat and mouse" to get them.

"Simple. I wanted to see if there was anything between us that could be carefully stoked, and I wanted to see if we could have a life together for as long as God permitted." Being cute, I added, "Unless I get my ass trampled by a berserk elephant on the loose from the Cape Canaveral zoo. Think we have any future?"

Jackie leaned to me, took hold of my head, and pulled me to her for a very passionate kiss. I had the feeling that the kiss was leading to a trip to the nearby bedroom, with sex on or under what were probably black sheets and a white duvet. While it was tempting to consummate our relationship, since we had never done so in high school, in my envisioning, I could only get as far as picturing myself as Prince Charming, leaning over and kissing Sleeping Beauty, and her waking and smiling at her prince. But the idea of the prince dropping his tights and making love to her—the two of them having uninhibited sex—blew my romantic image of Prince Charming and Sleeping Beauty.

Breathing heavily, I pulled back from Jackie, who also was pretty turned on. "Jackie, we need to take a walk and talk. How about we talk on the beach?" I asked. Jackie stood, walked into the kitchen, and pulled a small basket from the refrigerator.

"Guess what's in the basket. No, not walnut cakes and vodka," she laughed. "It has a couple of veggie sandwiches, fruit, and a couple apple juice drinks. God, have we gotten old? I'd planned that we'd go to the beach and have a little picnic for our reunion. Let me throw on a pair of shorts."

Jackie disappeared for a few minutes, then reappeared in white shorts, a black halter top, and no shoes. She was carrying a small white blanket, apparently for us to sit on at the beach. We got the basket and headed out into the noonday light. Not ten feet from the sidewalk leading out toward the beach was a sandy area perfect for our little picnic. The sun was warm on our bodies as we sat on the little blanket and talked about anything and everything: friends, high school, and her parents. We laughed about her family's Wiccan practices, revisiting the night I had seen them at their camp dancing around in the middle of the night, chanting, and pretending to be working spells of great power on some poor soul, maybe me. Jackie briefly touched on L. Ron Hubbard and how much the Church of Scientology had made her a better person. She said she had donated sums of money to the Church, which concerned me into thinking, "I hope she doesn't give away her livelihood at this stage of her life."

I stretched out on the sand and put my head in Jackie's lap as we talked. She slowly ran her hand through my hair as if I was a Cheshire cat, and I surely felt like purring. Within minutes, I was in a deep sleep from the warm sun baking my body, my stomach being delightfully full of veggie sandwich, and my lack of sleep at the Bates Motel the night before.

From deep in my subconscious, I recalled the dream of Jackie mounted on the red-scaled, fire-breathing dragon, flying in circles in front of me, and each time as she passed by, whispering, "I love you." The dream sequence kept repeating and repeating until I woke with a start, almost nauseated from the continuous circling of Jackie and the dragon. Jackie leaned down and kissed me on my forehead. "It's OK, I'm here."

Sitting up, I said, "My stomach's a little upset; I think it was something I ate last night, like a cheeseburger and greasy fries. Let's go back to your place. I want to freshen up, and then I have to go. I need to get to Key West to sign the lease on my apartment."

Both statements were true. I wanted to get my emotional equilibrium back on track and a little bathroom time with cold water splashing on my face and the use of the potty would help me feel better. As for signing the lease, that was true, too, but *after* stopping in Miami to spend time with Ginny and complete my trifecta of reconnecting with all three of my princesses.

I completed my refreshment routine in Jackie's bathroom, which was decorated with—no surprise here—a black granite counter and sink with white towels. I looked at the toilet as I put down the seat, and I laughed in spite of myself; the toilet was stamped "Bradley"—a product extension, apparently, of the urinal business. Refreshed and relieved, I was ready to say goodbye to Jackie and head to Miami.

In the living room, Jackie was waiting for me because she knew we were parting, maybe for just a short time, maybe forever. I could tell from her body language that she was on the verge of tears. She was beautiful in her little beach outfit; her tanned and toned body, blinding platinum hair, and those smoky eyes made her stunning to behold. "No matter what happens between us, she will always be my Kim Novak," I thought.

Jackie came to me and held out a clenched hand. "I have something special to give to you. I didn't know if I would ever see you again to give it to you. I may never see you again, so here, for you to always remember me and us." I could see tears in her eyes, and her voice thickened as she choked up.

I opened my hand and Jackie placed something small in it. I thought to myself, "Looks like some foreign coin. Odd, why would she give me a coin to remember her by?" I took the coin in my fingers and brought it closer to see the figure inscribed on it.

My mind exploded when I realized what I was looking at. "It's the dragon pendant! My God, it's the pendant you gave me in high school. You've had it for all this time? Did Reginald know you were keeping my pendant when you were married to him?"

"Reginald didn't know everything about me, especially that I always loved you. This pendant was the only remembrance I had of you. I want you to have it now, to keep you safe like when I first gave it to you in the cafeteria at DuPont. Remember?"

"Oh, yes, of course I remember." Now I found *myself* getting teary. To know that Jackie had always cared for me, loved me, and kept the pendant, maybe even occasionally taking it out of her secret hiding place to hold it and think of me—I was having a very difficult time keeping my emotions in check.

"I'll always carry the pendant wherever I go. I'll always think of you and I'll never forget you." I drew in a deep breath, knowing full well that if I didn't leave right there and then, I couldn't predict nor be responsible for what was about to happen between us. I knew I mustn't stop my mission of seeing Ginny as well, and then deciding who would be the best match for me. Another few minutes in Jackie's living room and my mission would have ended; quite simply, I would have stopped and stayed with her.

"I'll call you next week," I said. "We can decide our future and see if there's a new beginning between us. I do want to say that I love you and you mean so much to me." Jackie and I held each other for what seemed a long time. Finally, I pulled away and kissed her goodbye tenderly. She pulled my head to her and *really* kissed me goodbye, with a kiss that practically shouted that she wanted me to remember her while I was in Key West and in the process of making decisions about who would be my Sleeping Beauty.

In my car, I sat and looked at the pendant, turning it over and over between my fingers. The dragon image reminded me of the DuPont Dragons, our high school mascot. I placed the pendant in my wallet for safekeeping. Memories streamed in, and once again, I started reliving those wonder years at DuPont. "No radio music on my way to Miami and Ginny," I told myself. "Just quiet time and mental replays of great times with the Mag 6 knights and our fair maidens."

I programmed the last of "My Favorite Places" into the GPS: Miami and Ginny. Immediately, the little computer started commanding me like my mother: "Turn left at the corner and proceed . . . your final destination is in 105 miles." The GPS would be my companion for the next several hours. My mission was on its final leg.

Chapter 20

Two Classics

Cruising down Interstate 95 to Miami, I started keeping track of the license plates of the cars which were invariably passing me at close to the speed of sound. I wanted to see if any of the plates were from California, but of the one-hundred-plus cars that zipped by me, most of the out-of-state plates were from Alabama and Georgia. Of course there were a couple from New York and New Jersey and, surprisingly, several from various Canadian provinces. I guessed that the Canadians were snowbirds who would head home in a week or so to escape the onset of Florida's mosquito season. Mosquitoes in Florida grow so large that they should have been elected the state bird. I figured the New York plates were attached to Jewish travelers headed somewhere to find great cheesecake, and the New Jersey plates . . . well, what else? The Sopranos were relocating to Miami.

Sadly, there were no California plates. I guess no one from California drives to Florida, especially since flying is so much faster and cheaper. Come to think of it, I never saw Florida plates in California either. No one drives coast-to-coast anymore to visit the America in between. It must be a sign of the times: Americans don't want to take it slow and easy; everyone wants instant gratification—a real microwave society we live in today.

"My life in Key West will be the former," I thought, "slow and easy, no car, no computer, and no television, almost total isolation from everyone else who's so busy hauling ass around in this crazy world and not really knowing where they're going, not even sure where they've been. My next Sleeping Beauty must be on the same 'slow boat to China' I'm going to be on." In a nutshell, at this point in life, I was in no hurry to hurry; with the few grains of sand left in my hourglass; I just wanted to let them drift slowly to the bottom.

My three-hour travel time from Jackie's place to Miami included the required just-off-the-interstate rest stop to refuel the car and drink a McCafé cup of coffee in an orange plastic booth at the next-door McDonald's. While sipping the coffee, I used my cell phone to search for an inexpensive motel in Ft. Lauderdale. One of the online searches took me to an ad for a $45-per-night motel, which seemed reasonable till I read one of the guest reviews:

Worst Night of My Life
Posted April 12, 2012
The hotel is in a ghetto. I was afraid to open my door to the pizza delivery guy. There is no lobby—all the rooms are outside and creepy weirdos were wandering by vending machines on each floor when I checked in. My room—absolutely miserable. There were ants on the walls. I turned down the beds and would randomly see even more ants crawl across the sheets. Cigarette burns in the sheets. The room stunk like musk and old cigarettes. The toilet was filthy, the shower looked like it hadn't been cleaned in weeks—hairs, grime, FILTH. It was the worst night of my life. I barely slept a wink. The other reviews on here complain about the train noise—yes, it was loud and annoying but it was the LEAST of my worries when staying here. I was more concerned with bugs and street walkers lingering in front at night. I googled the crime demographics of the town and read about homicides that occurred right in front of the hotel. STAY AWAY! THIS PLACE SHOULD BE CONDEMNED. No, I would not recommend this to a friend.

I laughed to myself, "I guess this motel owner's not a member of 'Motel Owners for Christ'—no Bible study group on Wednesday night in this rat hole." Searching again, I found a motel at just a few dollars more, with reviews that didn't mention homicides, street walkers, and weirdoes. It's amazing what a few more dollars can buy you in motel quality. The one I selected and called for a reservation promised free Wi-Fi in every room, a continental breakfast, and the morning newspaper by your door. But chiefly, I picked this motel for the simple reason that I didn't want to wake up dead and, having become a crime statistic, miss my date with Ginny.

So, Ft. Lauderdale was my stopping place for the night. In another quest to revive old memories, I wanted to find the Trade Winds Hotel and Bar where, one long-ago summer night while on a quick weekend trip from Jacksonville, our Mag 6 gang had met Liliani, the bar's Hawaiian dance entertainer. Loaded with the worst fake IDs any door bouncer ever checked, we were all still passed to the bar to be served liquor to our hearts' delight. The $20 we pressed into the bouncer's palm most likely modified his vision and helped him see that our IDs were perfectly valid and that all of us eighteen-year-olds were indeed twenty-eight to thirty-one years of age as the IDs stated in plain, if slightly misspelled, English. Crazy never even bothered to get his fake ID out since the bouncer thought he was the same age as those of us with IDs that stated we were thirty. Crazy was the epitome of "looking old before his time."

My online search for the Trade Winds Hotel and Bar didn't produce a location. I thought maybe they had been bought out and the name had been changed. Who knows, maybe the Trade Winds is now a Hyatt or Hilton, maybe even a luxurious Marriott.

Checking in at the motel, I asked the front-desk manager if he knew the location of what was at one time the Trade Winds Hotel. Not recognizing the name himself, he yelled to a man who was maybe in his early eighties and was doing the octogenarian dozing act in an overstuffed chair in the motel lobby. "Clarence! Hey, Clarence!" Come to find out, Clarence had lived full-time at this motel for the last twenty-some years, his Social Security check covering the rent.

Waking from his snooze, Clarence picked his head up and yelled back, "No need to scream at me! I ain't deaf! What do you want?"

"Ever hear of a Trade Winds Hotel? Guy here says it was around here sometime in the 1960s, had a Hawaiian motif to it."

My heart started throbbing with excitement when Clarence said, "Yeah, I remember the Trade Winds. Spent too much of my paycheck on those fancy *Hee-wye-yun* drinks with little umbrellas in 'em. Had a great dance show, pretty girls all of 'em, even though none of 'em would go out with me. Shame, they missed a real dude with me." Clarence started in with a laugh which was actually more like a repeating snort.

I asked Clarence, "What happened to the hotel? The Hawaiian hotel? Where was it located? Near here?"

"Well, Sonny-boy, the hotel burned to the ground in the late '60s. Seems one of the patrons got real drunk on one of those *Hee-wye-yun* drinks with fire coming out of it, a Volcano Surprise or something like that, and he passed out, fell into the drink, grass tablecloth caught fire, and then it spread pretty quick. There weren't any sprinklers back in those days. I think some of the patrons died in the fire and maybe even a couple of the dancers who were trying to get everyone out. That's a helluva shame, dyin' because some drunk fell into his Volcano Surprise."

Thinking of Liliani, I had to ask, "Did all the dancers die in the fire? Did they rebuild the hotel?"

"Don't know how many people died in the fire. Hell, that was a long time ago. Just guessing. I think they sold the land to a developer and he tried a number of ideas for it. They put a Chevy dealership there, lasted a long time, but they went broke with the economy. Now it's a kids' park with rides and putt-putt golf. Place is just a couple of miles away."

With the sun slowly dimming, I wanted to see the spot where the Mag 6 spent one glorious night with an absolutely beautiful Liliani. I prayed she hadn't perished in the fire. I'd have no way of knowing—couldn't even find out from old records of the fire, as all I knew was her stage name. I decided not to relay this piece of information to the Mag 6. I wanted all of them to remember Liliani as she was, a special person who made six teenagers feel special, too, on one beautiful summer night.

Within fifteen minutes, I was standing in front of "Wally's Wonderful World of Wackiness," which turned out to be probably the tackiest amusement park I have ever seen. At the front entrance, you had to pass under a big, ugly cartoonish sign of Wally, an overly made-up clown character with smoke coming out of his ears, except the smoke machine wasn't working correctly, so smoke was only coming out of Wally's left ear. The whole park looked run down, the parking lot had only a few cars sprinkled around it, and my guess was that those belonged to what few employees were left to run the place.

As I walked up to the front, I saw a young teenage girl with a very bad complexion and a purple streak running through her otherwise jet-black, spiky hair. White earphones were plugged into the sides of her head, which was bobbing madly, I assume to whatever music was being pumped into her brain by her MP3 player. She had a celebrity magazine in her hands, and her jaws were pumping furiously on what I hoped was a large lump of gum.

I had to yell to get her attention. "Is the park open?"

Her only response was to look up at me and take the earphone out of one ear. I said, "I just want to come in and look around. I was here fifty years ago. What would it cost me to come in?"

The teenaged ticket-taker just stared at me and then said, "You just want to look? Why not play putt-putt? You can do that by yourself." She looked around me and saw I was alone. "We get old guys like you in here all the time, no one else with them, kind of sad. You want a putter and ball just to whack it around?"

I held my breath to keep from losing my cool and screaming, "Look, you little shit, I'm not some old guy with nothing to do with my life!" I considered telling her about Sleeping Beauty, and me as possibly the new Prince Charming, but she had probably never even heard of the two. The purple streak of hair told me that the only "Prince" she might have heard of was the one who makes music, though I had serious doubts that anyone with purple spikes would appreciate even his musical genius.

"I was here years ago when this dump was the Trade Winds Hotel. I just wanted to remember what the place looked like."

Ticket Taker looked up. "See that umbrella out in the parking lot with the sign that says 'Security'? Go ask the old lady under the umbrella. She's been here longer than me. Owner's kept her around, I think, because they're related somehow."

I walked to the umbrella with the "Security" sign and peered down at a very old woman busily napping in a lawn chair. I jiggled the chair to wake her up. "Hi. I'm looking for someone who might remember the Trade Winds Hotel."

The old lady, who was only half-asleep and had heard what I was asking, answered me in a voice that was only slightly shaky with age, "Why you want to know about the Trade Winds? It's been gone for years."

"I was a guest in the bar some fifty years ago with a bunch of my buddies. We had a great night in the bar and even met one of the dancers, Liliani; had our picture taken with her. I just found out the place burned down and some people were killed. I hope the dancer was OK."

"Only person who died in the fire was the drunk who started the fire. Everyone got out of the hotel, but the fire consumed the place in minutes. No one wanted a Hawaiian hotel in Ft. Lauderdale anymore, so they put in a Chevy place, and now, it's just this dump of an amusement park. Been sold to the Mormons who are going to level it and build a church on it. I'll be out my security job."

"Wow, the Mormons are going to be on the same spot I was drinking Mai Tais years ago. Funny how times change. Funny you're still working security at your age." I was trying to be polite, but it struck me as funny that this old lady was the security for the park.

"My grandson bought the place from the bankruptcy court handling the Chevy dealership. Put me out under this umbrella to watch the place. I have this cell phone with a direct line to the cops if anyone acts up."

"Well, I'm sure you do a great job of protecting the place. I hope you find something when the Mormons move in. Maybe they'll put you in charge of *their* security." We both laughed.

I was headed to my car to go back to the motel and get a good night's sleep for tomorrow and Ginny when, turning to the old lady, I yelled, "Thanks. My name is Rob."

Walking without looking isn't the safest thing to do at any age, and I tripped on one of the concrete parking barriers and fell into a disabled-parking space. I laughed to myself. "Well, wouldn't that be ironic—break my neck falling into a disabled-parking space."

Getting up and brushing myself off, I got to the car to get in and heard the old lady respond, "Be careful where you're walking. We don't want to get sued. By the way, my name is Liliani. Drive careful."

I did a double-, maybe even a triple-take of the old lady. "Liliani, my God!" I called back to her. Then I thought, "Wait till I tell the rest of the Mag 6 that Liliani's alive and well and working security at Wally's Wonderful World of Wackiness!"

I started laughing, and continued to do so all the way to the motel and into my room. That night in my prayers, I thanked God that Liliani was still alive and still entertaining me fifty years later.

The next morning, I was torn about what to wear to meet Ginny at her law firm with its ritzy Biscayne Boulevard address. I was purposely traveling light as far as clothes went. Having figured that all my stops with the three potential Sleeping Beauties would be casual coffee dates, I had packed nothing fancy; mostly just jeans, my Jacks Surf Shop surfing shirts and Sanuk sandals. With Stacey at the Ponderosa and Jackie on the beach, I might have even been overdressed. Now with Ginny at her high-rent business address . . . well, take me or leave me, it would also be jeans and Jacks.

The chrome and smoked window-glass building screamed $800-per-hour, top-of-the-line law firm with big retainer fees. It also came complete with a killer Cuban receptionist on the tenth floor just outside Ginny's office, who had jet-black hair and eyes, natural 36s that were almost visible through her sheer white dress, and legs that only stopped at a booty you could set a martini glass on.

When I asked for Ginny, the receptionist did the required quick glance at my jeans and Jacks Surf Shop clothes and politely asked, "Would you like to meet with one of the firm's junior lawyers? They may be more in line with your budget?" That told me Ginny was in the $800-per-hour bracket, if not higher.

As I started to put it back on Miss Cuba, the glass door of Ginny's office opened and she walked out. There she was: my bright and beautiful swim-team diver, who had given me the greatest thrill of my high school days with her half-naked swan dive off my family's swimming-pool diving board while dressed in not much more than the illuminating rays of moonlight. Now, the Ginny standing before me was a buff, tanned, "The Devil Wears Choo," in-line-for-a-judgeship, all-American woman whom I barely recognized.

Maybe what threw me was her drop-dead designer outfit—Vera Wang?—with jet-black, $1800 six-inch Jimmy Choo stilettos and a perfect tan—legs, arms, face, all equally, naturally bronzed. Nothing about her said "simple girl down the street from Jacksonville, Florida."

I had the immediate urge to rattle off, "I'm so sorry, I've made a terrible mistake, I'm in the wrong place at the wrong time, thank you for your sixty seconds, what will that cost me, $10? Can I put it on my American Express?"

Ginny looked at me and smiled, then said the words that told me I should stay to see how the day would play out: "Well, if it isn't Mister You Ain't Seen Macho Till You Seen Me in Action." Ginny closed the distance to me and we gave each other a hug. She gave me the Middle Eastern kiss, one on each cheek. I felt like I was being greeted by a sheikh prince from Saudi Arabia.

"Ginny, it's really great to see you, and—" I looked around at all the woodwork, the marble floors, the hot Cuban receptionist— "congratulations on you and your firm's success. It looks like you won a multimillion-dollar case, or maybe seventeen of them."

Without a hiccup or a hesitation, Ginny said, "We won a number of big cases; we win 'em all. That's why we get the big clients with big settlements. We always win."

I thought to myself, "Ginny must have a picture of Oakland Raiders owner Al Davis on her wall. Maybe she bows to it daily and repeats old Al's credo: 'Just win, baby.'"

Ginny said, "Come on into my office so we can visit. I want to hear all about you and what you've been doing for the last half-century."

Again to myself, I thought, "Well, here I am in the visiting stage with Ginny. Her idea of visiting isn't gonna be like the family pastor coming by the house on Sunday after church to 'visit,' and after being invited to stay for Sunday dinner, maybe having a beer and watching some football. Ginny's idea of visiting will be more of a deposition. I wonder if she'll have a stenographer there to take down my every word."

Ginny's office was as spacious as the lobby of the law firm, with floor-to-ceiling windows for a spectacular view of Biscayne Bay and downtown Miami. The office was richly appointed with a huge, glass-topped desk, a monster leather and brass-studded executive chair, and an eight-person dark-mahogany conference table, all offset by a matching white leather sofa and club chairs and a glass coffee table.

We positioned ourselves on opposite ends of the sofa. Ginny opened the questioning—more like an interrogation: "Why do you want to see me after all these years? What we had was a high school romance, nothing more, so I'm surprised you want to see me. We certainly didn't part on such great terms. You were becoming a drunk, and I had other aspirations for myself than to have that albatross hanging around my neck. So, what makes you think I want to see you after all this time?" Finally, Ginny stopped asking questions and making jabs at me, and just looked at me with those beautiful dark eyes.

"Simple. I believe you might still have a little bitty smoldering ember deep inside you that never went out the night we broke up. You had a wonderful marriage to your partner in life and in business, and I'm so sorry for your loss. But even with this wildly successful law firm and all its trappings, even with you on the 'A' list for all the political and celebrity parties in this city, I had to see if that itty bitty ember was still there waiting for me to walk back into your life and blow on it and see if I could make a fire start again between us."

Ginny started laughing and shaking her head slightly from side to side. Generally it's not a good sign when a woman does this. "Rob, I've got to give credit where credit is due. You're a macho guy, balls and all. Coming to Miami after all these years . . . I guess you expect me to fall down upon seeing you and throw away everything my husband and I worked so hard for, to walk away from all that and go with you to some menial life in Key West, which, by the way, is full of losers. Wow, you're incredible."

"Well, yes, I knew it would be Mission Impossible to come here and see if we could have something together again. I certainly can't offer anything compared with what you have here. My life is pretty much a pair of jeans and an array of washed-out shirts from a surf shop. My promise is to close out the remaining years in a loving and caring relationship with no other distractions that would take away from the time I have left to share with someone special. No time lost with mundane, time-eating activities like house chores, laundry, shopping, taking the garbage out; we could hire a housekeeper and spend our time walking and talking on the beach, hand in hand, locked in the world's longest embrace. In my opinion, not an altogether bad way to go out of this world."

"Boy, what have you been smoking? You know, they have laws against recreational marijuana. Why would I want to walk the beaches with you? We've had nothing between us since DuPont High School. Are you delusional?"

I could sense that Ginny was really pissed at me for showing up, *But* she hadn't asked me to leave—yet. I figured that her inquisitive mind was simply processing why I was there and, more importantly, whether she still had any feelings at all for me after all these years. So, I went for the "Hail Mary" to see where we'd go from there.

"Nope, Ginny, I'm not delusional, just passionate. There's a big difference. If I've misjudged you and what we might have, then I wish you and your future here with the mahogany conference table, glass-topped desk, leather sofa and club chairs, and Miss Cuban Hot Body Receptionist and all you partners and ass-kissing junior partners the very best. I'll think of you once in a while when I am standing on that beautiful, sandy Key West beach, watching God carefully direct his sun to a spectacular close of the day over the Gulf."

I stood and reached out to shake Ginny's hand, not wanting to do the Middle Eastern kiss on the cheek goodbye. If she stood and shook my hand, oh well, I'd be in Key West a little early today and my Sleeping Beauties went from three to two—still a rather pleasant choice to make, in my opinion.

Ginny stood and took hold of my hand, but instead of shaking it, she pulled me to her and, with tears filling her eyes, said softly, "Rob, I have thought of you. I won't tell you a lie and say different. I'm honestly still a little overwhelmed with losing my husband Everett so suddenly. It's only been six months. Then taking over as head of the law firm, and all while trying to keep up a good front for our clients. I don't have any children; we didn't know I couldn't conceive till after we were married. Now I've got no one to love. The truth is, you may be the only person in my entire world I can hold and share my feelings, and maybe even my love, with. God, does it come down to my future being spent with the Macho Man?"

I took Ginny in my arms and kissed her with an "I'm here, we can be something together" kiss, not a "Let's lock the door and consummate a love we had years ago on this white leather couch" kiss. As we kissed, the buzzer on Ginny's conference telephone interrupted us.

"Shit, stupid buzzer," I thought to myself. Ginny pulled away, walked to the phone, and picked it up.

"OK, thanks. We'll be leaving in a few minutes." Ginny walked back to me and kissed me somewhat more passionately, then said, "I made arrangements to have lunch on our company boat at the marina just down the street. The crew is ready for lunch and a quick spin around Biscayne Bay. I have to be back by 3:00 for a partner meeting which we had on the calendar before you called to say you'd be in town. We can talk more over lunch."

With that, Ginny guided me out of the office and past Miss Cuba, telling her to call the boat captain and let him know we would be at the boat in fifteen minutes. Less than two minutes after walking out her office door, we had taken her private elevator down to street level, where a limo was waiting to take us to the marina.

I made a mental note: "Maybe Miss Cuba could be our housekeeper; I wonder if she does floors."

Walking down the gangway to the yacht, I said to Ginny, "My dad had a boat when I was in high school, the *Miss Marian*. It could have served as a dinghy for most of the yachts tied up here."

When we got to the end of the gangway, there before me was the company yacht, one of the most fantastic marine engineering creations I had ever seen. It was a sleek sixty-five-foot 2009 Fleming motor yacht, appropriately named *Miss Ginny*. A smartly dressed crew member stood at the boarding gate to help us aboard. I was blown away by the whole scene: Ginny looking like a million dollars in her designer clothes, owner of the Fleming yacht which was probably worth multimillions, the swank marina worth maybe a zillion dollars, and me in my $20 designer outfit from Goodwill. Even the crew was better dressed than me.

Ginny took me on a quick tour of the yacht, and I paused at the stateroom with its granite-decorated private bathroom and its plush queen-sized bed with mirrors on the wall behind the headboard. Laughingly, I said, "Ginny, what do you think about us taking our lunch in this stateroom? We could save a lot of time talking. After all, you lawyers like a quick settlement."

Ginny just grimaced. "Well, I see your mind, The Sex Express, still travels on the same old track. I guess you never expanded your intellectual interests beyond reading the main interview in *Playboy*. Or do you even read the interviews?"

Before I could come back with some smart-ass reply, Ginny said, "Let's go up to the main salon. I have something for you."

The main salon was spectacular with sofa and club chairs upholstered in lime-green and white; a glass-topped dining table with a big, square, chrome base; a wine refrigerator and wet bar; and a fifty-inch flat-screen plasma television. The table was already set with fresh flowers in a cut-crystal vase. The steward helped seat us with Ginny and me across from each other, which was not my preference, but what could I do? Neither did she reach across the table to hold my hand as we talked before lunch was served. As we talked, the *Miss Ginny* pulled away from the dock. I could see us pass by the other yachts, and soon we were in the open waters of Biscayne Bay.

When Ginny started talking, I just listened. She told me about getting out of DuPont and going on scholarship to Tulane University and then on to School of Law, Loyola University, in New Orleans, where she had met and married Everett while still in law school. They had moved to Miami, his hometown, and built a mega law firm, specializing in marine law. The oil spills from tankers and oil-drilling platforms provided big settlements from the oil companies for class-action suits; her firm represented the beach hotels, restaurants, fishing vessels, and such that were financially devastated by the spills. The fires that killed passengers on cruise liners were also a real settlement bonanza for the relatives and the law firm, as was practically any other disaster that occurred and allowed for someone's head to be placed on the legal chopping block.

Ginny revealed her and Everett's disappointment that she couldn't conceive, and how, instead, the two became involved with Miami Children's Hospital, holding fund-raising events and even serving on the Board of Directors until Everett was killed in the plane crash.

Selfishly, I thought to myself, "What a waste of money in high school when I purchased a box of condoms at the local drug store in anticipation of having sex with Ginny the night my parents were out of town; she couldn't have conceived anyway." I wondered if her sexual activity, or lack thereof with me, would have been different if she had been privy to that knowledge back when we were in high school. I quickly surmised that it probably wasn't a good idea to ask her.

As we finished our lunch, the steward cleared the table and served us coffee. Ginny pushed away from the table, went over to a credenza, pulled out a gift-wrapped box, and handed it to me. "Remember the St. Christopher medal and chain I gave you on the last day of school to protect you wherever you were? I'm sure you probably don't have it after all these years."

"I actually did have the medal for years," I assured her, "but someone broke into my locker at my gym and took it and my wallet. I cancelled all the credit cards, but I was heartbroken that the medal was gone. Some petty thief is probably wearing my St. Christopher's even today. Maybe God will have a meteorite fall on his head to see if St. Christopher will protect him from an 'act of nature.'"

"Well, maybe the next locker thief will leave this alone and not find it to their taste." Ginny looked very serious. This gift was obviously not a frivolous joke; it was something she really seemed to want me to have.

For some reason, I just can't help myself; I have to make light of these situations: "Maybe there is a new pair of jeans in here."

Well, that seemed to piss off Ginny since I had now made her special moment, which she had planned so carefully, suddenly seem not so special. I had to rally quickly, so I continued, "I'm sorry. The wrap is beautiful, and from the feel of the package, it must be a couple of thick books of some sort." I wanted to poke more fun but thought better of it, and finally succeeded in holding back from saying "Are these books my life story, *Ripley's Believe It or Not* and *Superman*?"

Tearing away the wrap, I was stunned to find beautifully bound hard-back copies of two perennial classics: *War and Peace* and *A Tale of Two Cities*. I was a bit flabbergasted and for a moment sat staring at Ginny with the confused look that I have become so adept at over the years.

She smiled. "Don't remember, do you?" She paused to see that I had no answer before continuing: "Remember that night in front of my house when we were discussing your need to improve yourself, to read more classics like *War and Peace* and *A Tale of Two Cities*, and you told me you had read a version of the two books combined into one, called 'A Piece of Tail'?" Well, I knew in your entire life you would never read those books. So in Key West, while your butt is parked on the beach and you're looking for something to read, I want you, before you leave this earth, to read these two books, and if for some strange reason, I'm there with you, then I can explain them to you."

I thanked Ginny sincerely, and promised to read every page of each book and even write her a book report if she wanted, just to prove that I had read them. Talking with Ginny about her wonderful, thoughtful gift made my mind flash back to DuPont High and Miss Hamilton's senior English class.

Crazy had *A Tale of Two Cities* for his reading assignment. Figuring he'd take a shortcut to reading the book, Crazy had only thumbed through the Cliff's Notes version. Well, how stupid could you be, considering the fact that every single English teacher in the world has read *A Tale of Two Cities* maybe a thousand times and knows every single word in the book.

Crazy had only started presenting his report and Miss Hamilton automatically knew that he hadn't read a word of the book. She had him by the literary balls and started to squeeze in an instant, asking him to tell her what Chapter 1 was about, how about Chapter 2, how about the last chapter. Crazy got a big "F" for his report. I couldn't do the same with Ginny; I couldn't get an "F" with her that would definitely mean I would have to kiss this Sleeping Beauty goodbye.

Even as I recalled Crazy's screw-up in Miss Hamilton's class, the better and saner part of my brain was trying to process Ginny's comment, "If for some strange reason I'm there with you . . ." So I looked Ginny straight in her deep dark eyes, an experience which had always been and still was erotic for me, and said simply and matter-of-factly, "So the deal is, I read the books, you'll come to Key West with me?"

"Not quite. You read the books and I *may* be inclined to *consider* visiting you in Key West. I'd do the same for anyone who took some intellectual interest in the arts."

I didn't have a quick, cute comeback, so I just looked at Ginny and tried to augur whether this day had brought any real clue as to whether Ginny could be my one and only Sleeping Beauty. Her gift of the two classics was a positive sign that she remembered us as we once were. She could have given me a couple of current best-sellers as a gift, She could have given me *nada*, nothing, for a gift. But this gift held a deep connection to our shared past. Maybe she was reaching out to me in her own way to crack the door open and allow me back into her life.

The *Miss Ginny* had arrived back at the dock and the clock on the wall read 2:20, which meant a quick ride back to the law firm. Then Ginny would be off to her 3:00 partner meeting, and I would be on my way to Key West. As we left the main salon, I thanked Ginny for a wonderful time on the yacht, for lunch, and especially for the two books. In front of the crew, she was very much the business person; no kissing or groping, not that we would be making out on the salon's lime and white striped sofa in any case.

Our fifteen-minute ride back to the law firm in the limo was my best shot to have a few more quality minutes with Ginny and to put the sell on her as to why she should come to Key West. So, taking the bull by the horns, I turned to her and took her hands in mine. She didn't seem resistant at all, and seemed to know instinctively that I wanted to speak from the heart.

"Ginny, I did read a book one time, a sci-fi book about a time traveler—can't remember the title, maybe by Jules Verne, whoever. The point is, if I could have been that time traveler, I would have gone back to when we were dating in high school and I would have changed my beer drinking, my casual attitude to my education, anything and everything to have kept you. I really screwed up, losing you to stupid things like too much beer and too much play."

Ginny had tears in her eyes as I told her how I felt about us. She said very softly, "The night you and your buddy showed up drunk for our get-back-together date, that said it all about you. I don't know who was the bigger bum, you or your friend. But I'm glad it happened because I went on to a wonderful, successful life, a beautiful marriage with Everett, and, if not for wind shear that caused the jet to crash, we wouldn't be in this limo together. I imagine you've changed over the years. I am sure your wife wouldn't have put up with your drinking and immature attitude and irresponsibility. I'm sorry she fell ill with Alzheimer's; what a shame for her, for your boys, and for you."

Well, we were getting close to her building, so I simply asked her, "Do you think you could love me once more?"

"Life is full of compromise. Could I love you? Yes, I believe I could fall in love with you again. Can I walk away from this life I have in Miami, my law firm, the Children's Hospital, my friends? The answer is probably no, but . . . nothing's impossible. It would take me years to unravel the ties that bind me here. Could you wait a year or more for me to be with you?"

"If you told me you loved me and would make your life with me, I'd wait." I leaned toward Ginny, took her in my arms, and kissed her more passionately than I have ever kissed any woman, other than Lucinda—even more passionately than I had kissed Stacey and Jackie. Ginny kissed me back, giving me one of her patented tongue-to-tongue kisses that made me want to declare an immediate winner in the Sleeping Beauty contest.

She put her hand to the side of my face and said, "My Macho Man still has it. You were always a great kisser." Ginny then kissed me again, almost sucking my tongue from my mouth. I could tell she hadn't been passionate with any other man since Everett's death. I was becoming the benefactor of the gap in time since she had been affectionate with anyone.

The limo stopped, and the driver opened Ginny's door. I said to her, "Well, that kiss gives me hope that we'll be together very soon."

"Yes, I'll come see you in Key West in the next month or so, after I've completed our current case against British Petroleum for the Gulf spill." Then, looking at the two books on the seat beside me, Ginny continued, "And in the meantime, promise me you'll read the two classics."

I got out of the limo and stood on the sidewalk with Ginny and any number of pedestrians quickly coming and going. We had no chance to finish our romantic mini-interlude in the limo. Ginny just gave me the Middle Eastern kiss goodbye and, almost yelling over the traffic noise from the street, said, "Call me in a week and maybe you can come up for dinner. You're only three hours away. You're welcome to stay on the *Miss Ginny*."

I yelled back to her, "That's a date! Will call! Thanks for the books; my IQ will probably double, maybe even triple, after reading them!"

Ginny laughed, touched my face with her hand, and for a second, I could tell from the smile on her still gorgeous face that she did still love me. The thought of dinner and sleeping on the *Miss Ginny* had a lot of appeal, especially if there was any possibility that Ginny and I could end up in the stateroom together with all those smoked mirrors on the wall.

Ginny disappeared into the building, and I walked around to the public parking attached to it and grumbled, "Damn, I forgot to get my parking ticket validated. Wonder if Miss Cuba would run down a parking sticker if I called the office." Then, "Naw."

The GPS kicked in when the car got out of the garage, automatically finding the satellites to compute my location. "Turn left on Biscayne Boulevard, proceed to Interstate 195 West, then right on I-95 South. Continue 160 miles to Key West."

With the two classics on the front seat, I said to myself, "I have to get an 'A' from Ginny in reading these mammoth books. I wonder if they're available in an audio version."

Chapter 21

Key West

Leaving Miami for Key West put me on the road for at least a four-hour drive, or longer if you stopped along the way to take in the spectacular views. I really didn't mind the long drive because it gave me plenty of time to think over and more or less analyze my dates with Stacey, Jackie, and Ginny. After the last couple of days, I realized it was high time to start coming to some decisions about which one of the three Sleeping Beauties would be the best companion for me.

As I rewound and replayed in my mind the wonderful times I had had with each of the three, the one comment that kept raising its ugly head was what Ginny had said to me earlier today: "Are you delusional, coming here and expecting me to fall in love with you again?" Delusional? No. I figured I was mainly just very lonely and looking for a simple answer to my problem. I realized that I needed a love mate I could feel comfortable with, someone who knows me and loves me for who I am.

At this stage of my life, I figured it would be an enormous hassle to try to start over with a "newbie," especially a *cougar* (the name alone tells me that she always wants to be on top, no missionary position for her), or some *arm candy* twenty to thirty years my junior (erotic thought, but not my ideal to consummate a relationship on a trapeze over my bed—way too much energy for me), or a *blind date* (love seeing-eye dogs, but usually ends up being a woman who really doesn't give a shit about me, probably along on the date just to be seen or out for a free dinner).

Was I delusional to think that any one of my former high school girlfriends would want me back in her life after these many years?

Something told me that I might have been a little forward to make a run at these long-ago loves. But my "just coffee" dates with Stacey, Jackie, and Ginny quickly evolved into reconnecting with each other and finding and expressing at least a renewed interest, if not outright love for each other. Was I just seeing the situation through rose-colored glasses, or did each of them feel some real excitement at me showing up now in their life and forcing them to admit that they still loved, or at least cared for, me? Did any of them really want to give up their friends and family—a career, in Ginny's case—and fly away to Key West to walk the beaches and watch God's majestic sunset every night, hand in hand with an old flame from fifty years ago?

As I pondered Stacey, Jackie, and Ginny, I found I was also concerned, and maybe even feeling a little guilty, about abandoning Lucinda at the Alzheimer's care unit for which I am paying big bucks. Well, I guess the truth is that the trust fund is paying the big bucks, but still . . . I somehow still feel as if I should be there in case she comes out of her condition, even though I know the chances of that happening are, in reality, less than zero. The doctors have told me time and time again that Lucinda doesn't know me or remember me or our boys.

Despite my dates, my Sleeping Beauties, and my dreams for the future, the thought of me in Key West, and Lucinda in a high-priced care unit on the opposite coast all alone—well, something wasn't clicking. The whole Sleeping Beauty and Key West plan had seemed plausible last month when I started down this path to meet up with my three high school sweethearts. But as the spring sun and the sweet Florida air warmed the car and the miles whispered past, I was beginning to doubt myself and my motives. What about the rest of my loved ones? Was this whole scheme of mine really fair to everyone? Not only Stacey, Jackie, and Ginny, but Lucinda, my boys, myself?

As I travelled the one-hundred-plus miles of bridges and suspended roadways that connect the Florida Keys to the mainland, the ride was becoming increasingly surreal. With water on both sides of me, I began to have the strangest feeling that at some point the road would simply end and I would just drop over the edge and off the earth. Only the fact that

I could see the oncoming traffic in the opposite lane assured me that the road actually did end somewhere on terra firma.

Ferdinand Magellan, aboard his three-mast ship *Victoria*, sailed the oceans to prove that the earth was round, or at least that's what the history books tell us. As I looked at the seemingly endless miles of roadway ahead of me with water to each side and below, I hoped the books were correct. I found I had no desire to drive off the end of this road into the netherworld because the whole Magellan history lesson happened to be a hoax.

The drive was becoming hypnotic: the sound of the tires on the roadway, then bridge, then roadway. The sun was bouncing off the water, and the tranquil influence of the fresh air on my senses began to make me feel almost at one with the earth and sea. I know it sounds corny, but for the first time in a long time, I was beginning to understand my true feelings both for Lucinda and for my Sleeping Beauties. I needed someone to love me, and that left Lucinda out because she couldn't love anyone anymore. One of the three Sleeping Beauties could certainly rekindle her love for me, but which one would that be?

I started to recount the last three days and mentally check off the pros and cons of getting back with each one.

Stacey: really very lonely out there on the Purcell Ranch, my first love, great personality, down-to-earth, no space aliens in her beliefs, no career issues, doesn't want to give up the Ponderosa, struggling financially, obligations to kids and grandkids, personal looks need a minor make-over, parents buried in the front lawn, I *cannot* cope with her mother's ever-present ghost, would be an outdoor, log-chopping, shotgun-hunting, jet-skiing-on-the-river relationship. The sexual aspects would be warm, tender, and, given the visiting kids, grandkids, and being pooped from working the ranch, infrequent. Did I want to become a ranch hand in my late sixties?

Jackie: whimsical, a little *out there* with the religion stuff, financially secure, mobile, no kids, still loves me, always has, not sure if the Scientology Church would allow her to split from the Cape and come to Key West, they would fear the loss of a generous devotee, but she really loves me. Sex would be intense, frequent, and spontaneous. Jackie might move to the top of the list—more pros than cons.

Ginny: serious, rich, intellectually challenging, would provide a stimulating relationship, always on the go, no time to relax, not sure if the relationship would be just business, no kids but charities, board meetings, law partners, a teetotaler, wouldn't let me enjoy my glass of wine, would make me do one thousand sit-ups and pushups each day to stay buff, relationship would be like living with a fitness trainer. Sex would be a ritual, probably scheduled on her Outlook calendar.

Winner: Jackie; first runner-up: Ginny.

Now that I had decided upon my best option, I needed to find out which, if any of the three, would be willing to come be with me. There could be a dark horse in my selection—maybe Stacey sells the ranch and throws the family ties to the wind, digs up the ashes of Mom and Dad and properly buries them in a real cemetery. Ginny could do the same—sell the firm, lock, stock, and barrel, sell the yacht, trade in the $1800 Jimmy Choo stilettos for sandals and jeans . . . hmm, not likely, but maybe she would read a book on making your man *your man*.

Could there be other options? Sure, while waiting on my Sleeping Beauty, I could run into Ms. Right on a Key West beach or in a bar. "Not sure there's much chance of that," I scoffed to myself. Key West is loaded with the fun women, not the loving or marrying kind. Could I find happiness somewhere other than Key West?

After the umpteenth bridge, I thought, "God, this road seems endless. Who the hell built this thing?"

In the hours spent pondering my selection of a future mate, I found myself wondering again, "Have I *really* answered Ginny's accusation that I might be delusional?" I believed I was as sane as anyone, maybe more so; who else would have the balls and ingenuity to travel three thousand miles to find his Sleeping Beauty? In fact, I decided, maybe ol' Ferdinand Magellan and I had a lot in common. Maybe Magellan's countrymen thought he was delusional for sailing off into the sunset, to prove that the earth was round instead of shaped like a big cube or a flat saucer or whatever the hell they thought the flat earth looked like.

I began feeling energized, confident. "I'm *not* delusional," I assured myself, "not crazy, for having a spirit of adventure still ticking in my life."

Ginny was way off base with her comment. She just didn't recognize that her Macho Man was really the new Ferdinand Magellan in her life.

As I crossed the last bridge to Key West, my GPS began directing me to the condo I had rented for the next month till I could find a more permanent residence. The condo was off South and Duval Streets and, to my mind, ideally located just a few blocks from the beach. The closer I came to my destination, the more excited I got, and soon I decided that no matter what, that very evening I was going to watch what is advertised as "God's most spectacular sunset."

In that instant, I was sure I knew how Ferdinand Magellan must have felt standing on the bow of his ship every night for months on end, watching the sun set ahead of him and thinking that he was someday going to achieve his mission. I knew I was right in my mission. My GPS, more sure than Magellan's compass, now commanded me, "In one hundred feet, turn right on Second Street; your destination is ahead on your right."

Located within a few blocks of lots of restaurants and bars, the condo was expensive for a monthly rental. "What the hell?" I thought. "The expensive condo will make a good impression on my new soul mate." I was now guessing that Jackie would be "*the one.*" After registering with the property manager, I quickly unpacked—a process which took a grand total of five minutes, what with only another pair of jeans, some socks and underwear, a few more Jacks Surf shirts, tennis shoes, and toiletries. Then I headed over to Duval Street for something to eat.

I made a quick mental note to take the rental car back in the morning so I could save a day's fee. It would be a little sad to turn the car back in since we had bonded over the last weeks. Like Magellan's ship *Victoria*, it had steadfastly and proudly carried me on my mission to find a new beginning. Maybe I should have named it *Dreamer*—or *Delusional*? I decided to go with *Dreamer*, which seemed more befitting of my mission. Ferdie (I decided Magellan needed a nickname) was now officially my new idol, and I was sure he would also vote for *Dreamer*. I needed to clean out all the fast-food wrappers and soft-drink cans and plastic bottles. I chose to eschew using the recycling bins and just put everything into the trash so some scavenging homeless person could make a buck or two at the recycling center.

I had an hour or so to grab a beer and a sandwich before experiencing my first Key West sunset, so I was in no real rush, which was a good thing because on Duval Street, the choice of bars is endless. My selection for dinner and a drink was Cowboy Bill's Honky Tonk, with its loud, high-energy atmosphere. I wanted to get recharged after the butt-numbing four hours of the thumpety-thump ride down from Miami. Cowboy Bill's was also one of the more widely known local hangouts, and after eating there, I figured I could tell anyone I met, "Yeah, been there, done that," so I would sound more like a local.

Inside, I struck up a conversation with the bartender and told him of my plans to go to the beach and watch the sunset. He looked at me quizzically for just a moment before starting to laugh and poke at the other bartender. "This asshole wants to walk on the beach and watch the sunset. Should I bust his balls and tell the truth?"

The other bartender was soon laughing and sharing my plan with some of the obviously local patrons, who looked at me as if I had just rolled into town on the turnip truck.

"So, what's so f***ing funny?" I was rapidly getting more than a little pissed at being the butt of the joke when I didn't even know what the joke was.

"The sun rises in the east on the beach, and sets in the west on the north end of Duval by the piers. You wanna go watch the sunset, you gonna be there with about a thousand other tourists just like you. If you're standing on any of the beaches at the south end of Duval, you'll be standing alone in the dark."

My brain exploded at this startling geographical and celestial fact. "WHAT?! THE SUN DOESN'T SET ON THE BEACH?!" I exclaimed to myself.

My whole vision of my chosen Sleeping Beauty and me locked in an embrace on the romantic sands at sunset was suddenly replaced with the image of us two lovers squashed into a seething mass of humanity jammed shoulder to shoulder on a crummy pier, trying to get a peek at an awesome sunset around all the heads in front of us. Evidently, Stacey, Jackie, and Ginny had never been to Key West to watch the sunset or they would have corrected me about my notion of our romantic evening.

Shit, what a huge disappointment. I thanked the bartender, finished my conch salad and beer, and walked farther up Duval Street to the pier area, along with the thousand other idiots like myself.

Near the corner of Duval and Smith, across the street from the piers, the crowds were being entertained by a sundry collection of mimes, street dancers, guitar players, and a few just upfront panhandlers; all were, of course, looking for money. At least the true entertainers were performing for the crowd with the hopes that money would end up in their tip baskets or instrument cases. The panhandlers were walking around with dirty Dixie cups containing a smattering of change so they could jangle the cup in front of tourists as if to say, "Your change goes in the cup if you want me to leave and not ogle—and if I think I can get by with it, grope—your teenage daughter." Amazingly, the jangling-change Dixie cups were very effective at getting tourists to throw their loose coins in. The street entertainers were getting pissed off since they were working hard for their money and yet their tips were no better than those of the panhandlers. "Well," I said to myself, "that's show biz for you."

I was standing by myself, minding my own business and watching the goings-on, when a fairly attractive woman about twenty years my junior came near me with a small camcorder in her hand. I guessed she was trying to get to the front of the crowd to get an unobstructed shot of the sunset. She wasn't negotiating the crowd very well because she seemed hindered by the black-handled cane in her other hand. I caught her eye and said, "Can I help you get through the crowd?"

Initially, she looked at me a bit suspiciously. I figured it was because I looked a little like one of the locals with my jeans and surf shirt and sandals; Bermuda shorts and argyle socks would have been an obvious give-away that I was an out-of-town tourist. But I suppose my gray hair and my mannerisms gave her a little confidence that I honestly wanted to be helpful instead of just get into her pants.

"Thank you," she said with just a hint of exasperation. "It would be helpful. I want to get a good shot of the sunset, but with the cane, I'm scared someone might jostle me and I could fall."

Gently, I took hold of her camcorder hand at the wrist and said, "Stay behind me; I'll get you to the front."

With that, I started to push my bulk through the crowd, looking to nudge aside the smaller, and thus easier to intimidate, people as I went. I also shouted, "Please move, emergency, please move, emergency." It's funny how people will move when someone is yelling, "Emergency!" Once we'd made it to the front of the crowd, I turned to the woman and said, "Are you OK? I didn't hurt you pulling you through the crowd, did I?"

She looked at me, smiled, and said, "No, I'm pretty tough, and thank you, I wouldn't want to miss getting the sunset on my little camcorder."

She pulled the camcorder just in front of her face and stood watching in the screen exactly what she had come to shoot, the beginning of the sunset.

I turned quickly as it dawned on me that one of God's most beautiful shows was already in progress. I looked toward the water just as the sun was beginning its dramatic slide into the sea. The clear skies and clean air created the illusion that the ocean was almost bubbling from the sun's bright orange and yellow rays.

This was my first Key West sunset, and I was blown away. I thought of Stacey, Jackie, and Ginny and pined just a bit that none of the three was present to share the moment with me. Instead, I was sharing this most incredible experience with a crippled stranger. But then I thought, "Well, if it wasn't for helping this lady with a cane, I would be stuck way in back and would be seeing only a portion of the sunset over the tops of balding heads and greasy spiked hair. I should thank her for being there for me to help her get to the front." Because of her, I got to see the sunset unrestricted. It was almost postcard-perfect.

Once the sun had disappeared into the ocean, I turned to the lady and said, somewhat jokingly, "Well, did you get your Oscar-winning video of the sunset to show your friends and family? Maybe you can sell tickets to the show!"

She laughed. "It may not be award-winning, but my kids and mom and dad will love it." She then got really quiet and her lovely face broke down in sorrow and she started to cry.

I didn't know what was happening. I didn't believe I had said anything offensive to her, but my heart tugged in my chest as her tears flowed. My assumption, wrong as usual, was that she was in pain from her crippled leg. "Are you OK? Do you want me to call for help? Is your leg hurting you?"

"No, no, my leg is OK. It's my emotions that are a wreck," she responded, regaining her composure a bit.

"This was to be my twenty-fifth-anniversary trip with my husband, and our plans were to watch this sunset together." She drew in a deep breath to further steady herself and continued. "Just after making reservations a year in advance to be here for our twenty-fifth, we were in an auto accident the very next week. My husband died in the wreck, and my leg was crushed. We were hit on the driver's side by some teenager who was so busy texting that he ran the stop sign. He also died in the wreck.

"I swore that if I could crawl or walk or limp or whatever, I was coming here on what would have been our twenty-fifth to take this video. If it wasn't for you, I wouldn't have made my quest to see the sunset for me and my husband. I thank you so much." With that, she again lost her battle to hold back the tears.

I reached out and put my arm around her in the hopes of giving what little comfort a stranger could. I let her lean on me instead of trying to steady herself on her injured leg while the intense emotions wracked her heart and body. "Please, let me steady you; it looks like you have a great deal more going on than just getting a video of the sunset."

The crowd had dispersed, no doubt headed to one of the many bars on Duval Street. I glanced around for a place for her to rest a moment and said, "Look, there's a bench over there. Let me help you get there, and if you want, I'd be glad to sit with you for a few minutes."

She nodded, and I helped her to the bench, where we both sat down. I held her hands, trying to comfort her. Her distress at the loss of her husband and having to face what would have been such a romantic moment without him was evident in her flowing tears and shuddering breaths. I sat and held her and glared as menacingly as I could at the few gawkers who slowed down to stare.

"I'm sorry about your husband. I lost my mom two years ago to a similar accident. Same thing—someone texting and not paying attention t-boned her car. Mom never recovered from her injuries and died three months later. The driver didn't get a scratch. Worse yet, he didn't even get a ticket for running the stop sign. Some days I have thoughts of finding him and seriously hurting him."

I paused for a moment and got control of my own feelings before continuing. "I want him to feel the pain my mom felt. For you, at least the teenage driver died with your husband. For the rest of your life, you won't have to live with the knowledge that the punk teenager who killed your husband and made you a widow and took your kids' dad is out joy-riding with his buddies, laughing about the accident."

Despite my efforts at self-control, I was getting upset at the thought of my mom dying needlessly and the person who killed her not giving a shit about what he had done to her. The woman I was with could sense that I was also getting upset, and it was now her turn to comfort me. With her own tears still wet on her smooth cheeks, she said, "I'm sorry, I've spoiled your evening and your sunset. I can't believe we both lost someone to stupid auto accidents, especially since both were caused by some ignorant asshole texting."

I looked at her, tried to grin, and said, "My name's Rob." I left it at that since the last thing I wanted to do was get into a dissertation on why I was in Key West and waiting on one of my Sleeping Beauties to show up. Hell, I had just met this woman.

"My name's Angelina, but everyone calls me Angel. God, I'm sorry about your mom. Seems like we both know what real loss is. I don't think I'll ever get over losing the love of my life so suddenly."

Angel paused to collect her thoughts, then, for whatever reason, started to unload on me. Bitterness, and quite a bit of pure anger, was in her voice as she spoke: "One moment my husband and I are lovers, parents, successful business owners. Then, within a split second, he's gone and I'm reduced to being the single mother of two children—well, not really *children* since both are in college. And all of a sudden I'm president of our small manufacturing company and all alone with no emotional support, no one to tell how I feel or to cry on their shoulder . . ."

Looking up at me, she continued with just the hint of a bitter grin playing around the edges of her lovely lips. "Here I am on a bench holding hands with a total stranger, crying on his shoulder and telling him all my problems." Angel started to stand, still a little wobbly. "I gotta go. I've imposed on you enough."

"Angel, if I might be so forward," I said, "I'd like to ask you to join me for a drink in one of the sidewalk bars down the street. Someplace a little more quiet and subdued, if you don't mind. I'm not a Sloppy Joe's or Boar's Head kind of guy. Come on, whaddaya say? We both could use a little something to settle our nerves. You can grab a taxi from the place to take you back to where you're staying. It'll be my gift to you for your twenty-fifth."

Angel looked at me for a long time, mulling over the consequences of saying yes to my offer. Clearly, there was a huge conflict going on within her as she stood at this spot on Duval Street where she and her husband had planned to spend a special evening. Now, instead of her partner of twenty-five years with her tonight, she was here in the semi-dark with, as she had put it, a total stranger, and he had just asked her to join him for a drink, something almost like a date. Yes, I was a stranger, but not a *total* stranger since I did help her through the challenge of getting to where she could make the video she had planned for more than a year, and I did help her through an emotional meltdown.

"I have to leave shortly. I told my family I'd call them when I got back to the hotel and tell them all about the video. But maybe we can find time for one drink, as long as you let me buy to repay you for your chivalry."

I stood, swept my arm into a deep bow to play on her "chivalry" comment, and said, "Great, if you insist on buying, then I will bow to your wishes, my Lady Angel. There's a small outside café down the street. Do you feel like walking? Or we can take one of these carriages—I mean, bicycle taxis."

"No, we can walk; I'm not a total cripple. My doctors tell me I should be able to get rid of the cane in another six months, but I'll walk with a limp forever. I tell my family and the employees at our plant that I just won't be running the high hurdles in the next Olympics." Angel started to laugh at her own comment, and I could tell she was back on solid emotional ground.

At the café, we spent an hour or more just talking about our families, our backgrounds, our interests, all the little things that make life worth living. She told me she lived in a small town in Indiana and that her company made parts for the auto industry. I explained that I lived in California (I didn't tell her that I had walked away from my ties there). I think Angel was a little surprised that I was a normal person with a great family. She expressed her condolences about Lucinda being in an Alzheimer's unit. I didn't tell her about my Sleeping Beauty contest; not sure why, but I thought it best to keep that little piece of information tucked away in a corner of my mind. I stretched the truth when I told her I was in Key West just to see the sunset and that I was leaving in a day or two and returning to California.

Angel paid the check and said she needed to go. On a separate piece of paper, she wrote down her email address and phone number and handed it to me. "We should stay in touch." That's all she said: "We should stay in touch."

I hailed a *real* taxi, and as she started to get in, Angel turned to me, put her hand on the side of my face, and gently kissed me on the lips. When she kissed me, her eyes were closed, and once her kiss was over, she opened them and said very softly, "Thank you for this evening, my Prince Charming. You helped me awaken from a year-long emotional coma. Please call me sometime." With that, she got into the taxi and was gone.

As the vehicle pulled away, I found myself standing on Duval Street, stunned—speechless even. Had I just *met* my true Sleeping Beauty, the person I should ride out my remaining years with?

The realization hit me that the previous days with Stacey, Jackie, and Ginny were my futile and foolish attempts to recreate a love that *was*—a love that had, as they say, "gone with the wind." I had been trying to convince the three of them and myself that we still had something between us. Yes, we did have something—but just a memory of teenage love, nothing more.

The last hour with Angel had brought to the forefront of my mind the realization that teenage love is so different than adult love, and seldom does teenage love morph into adult love. Life experiences are not the same. The Texas Drive-In, movies at the Florida Theatre, romps on the beach with my teenage Mag 6 friends simply could never compare to the birth of a child, family trips to New York, funerals of family and friends. I had been chasing the memory of teenage love. Now I needed to reset my life compass and re-find adult love. Maybe Angel would be my best bet for doing that.

Looking down at Angel's phone number on the piece of paper in my hand, I laughed. There I was in a honky-tonk town, waiting for some old high school girlfriend to throw away her life and come be with me, and what I really needed in my life—a true love—had just limped onto the scene. "God, you certainly act in mysterious ways," I muttered as I walked back to my condo, to shower and go to bed.

Before going to sleep, I carefully rewrote Angel's email address and phone number on another piece of paper. I didn't want to lose contact with her, although I guess I could've called every parts manufacturer in Indiana looking for a limping, but very attractive, female business owner who would remember some old guy she met in Key West.

I now needed to decide what to do with my invitations to Stacey, Jackie, and Ginny to come be with me. I could call them and tell them the truth: "All that stuff I told you about how much I still love you and how I want you to be with me in Key West, guess what? All crap! I found what may be my future, a crippled auto parts manufacturer woman. Thank you and have a great life." Well, wouldn't *that* be a gallant way to say "goodbye and good luck." I decided to call each of them the next day and bow out gracefully.

I emptied my jeans pockets and placed some pocket change in an ash tray on top of the dresser. Next to it I put the shotgun shell Stacey had given me. I couldn't decide what to do with either the shotgun shell or Ginny's classic books, which still sat on the coffee table where I had dropped them first thing upon arriving at the condo. I pulled the dragon pendant from my wallet and stood for a moment, studying the engraved serpent. I laughed to myself. "After I tell Jackie about my decision, I hope she doesn't put a hex on me or send her fire-breathing dragon to tear me a new one." I put the pendant next to the shotgun shell with the intention of doing something with them and the books—keep them, throw them out, something.

The next morning, before breakfast, I took the rental car over to a local drop-off office just off Duval Street. The big African American car receiver person scanned the car for dents and scratches, and then asked me if I had filled it with gasoline before turning it in. With a few clicks of his hand-held computer, the car rental was paid; my American Express credit card still worked like a charm. I tore up the receipt and dropped it in a trash receptacle; I hate little pieces of paper cluttering my wallet.

Back at the condo, I steadied myself for what I perceived to be a nightmare task: calling Stacey, Jackie, and Ginny and saying "goodbye." Since Jackie was the one I had thought of as most likely to be my Sleeping Beauty, I decided I would call her last. Getting a fresh cup of coffee, I sat down at the kitchen table, opened my cell phone, and put in Ginny's number.

"Hello, this is Rob Strand calling for Ginny Vaughn." Ginny's receptionist, Ms. Cuba, put me on hold for several minutes. Then, after a fashionably businesslike wait, Ginny picked up the phone. "Hi, Rob. I didn't expect you to call so soon. I told you I need some time to think about us. Have you read the books already?"

Looking at the two classics on the coffee table, not even the first page turned on either of them, I replied, "I wanted to call to say how much yesterday meant to me and to thank you again for the wonderful gift. I promise to start on them today."

"Rob, when I got back to the office, the partner meeting involved the litigation we have with the oil companies about the Gulf spills. Come to find out the government is taking a greater involvement and the whole process is now going to take months, maybe a year, to straighten out. Our firm is in the middle of all the lawsuits, and now, with the government wanting their fair share of the money, I can't see that I will have any time in the foreseeable future for us. I want to be honest with you. Maybe you should go back to California and when this is all over, we can talk to see if there is any reason for us to get together."

I had just been dumped by Sleeping Beauty #1, but even so, I had a big smile creeping across my face because she had just saved me the trouble of making up some bullshit explanation about why we weren't meant for each other after all. "Gee, Ginny, I'm happy for you and your firm's apparent success with the government behind you. I must admit to being just a tad distraught that we aren't going to see each other again for some time, if ever. I do want to say, I am going to read the two classics if it kills me."

Ginny laughed. "Rob, on second thought, why not just give the books to someone who would appreciate them. I can never change my Macho Man, and honestly, I would never want you any other way. You're priceless. Never change; you are one of a kind. Call me in a year and we can go from there. I did love you, and maybe I still do. Take care, Macho Man." With a resounding *click*, Ginny hung up the phone and that portion of my life was now history.

Stacey was scheduled to be next on the chopping block. When I called, her phone rang and rang, and I was about to hang up and call later when an out-of-breath Stacey finally answered: "Hello, hold a sec while I catch my breath, was outside." Pause. "OK, this is Stacey." She must not have had caller ID on her old desk phone, but then again, she was never very tech-minded.

"Hi, Stacey, this is Rob. I'm calling to say what a great time I had seeing you and spending a few hours with you. I also wanted to say that the ranch is exactly as I remembered it. You've done a great job of keeping it going. Congratulations." I really meant it when I congratulated her on keeping the dumpy house from falling down around her. The rest of the property, the dock, and, yes, the family cemetery was all evidence that she had worked herself to the bone to keep it presentable.

"Oh, hi, Rob. Yeah, thanks for calling. I have great news! My kids are moving in with me and have used some of their savings to hire a contractor to refurbish the house—new roof, new kitchen, new floors, new bathrooms, everything new. It's like a miracle come true for me, my own Extreme Home Makeover reality show. Needless to say, I am going to be a little busy for the next year or so, so we are going to have to put our plans on the back burner. Once the house is done, I want you to be the first guest. Promise?"

Wow, I was getting dumped by Sleeping Beauty #2—two in a row, and my smile had become a full-on grin. I found myself wondering if Jackie would make it a trifecta. "Wow, that is great news, Stacey. I know you're thrilled to have your family coming to live with you and the house getting a complete do-over. I definitely promise to be your first guest. I just called to say I'm going back to California for a while to see Lucinda, but I'll stay in touch. Thanks for our great date." Even as I spoke the words, I was already thinking that I should send Stacey a case of chardonnay as a housewarming gift in lieu of coming back in a year.

"Rob, you take care. I still love you, and I want you to come be with me and the family. Promise?"

"Yes, Stacey, I promise. I'll call you in a month to see how the house is coming along. Bye now, and take care."

Two down and one to go. I nearly giggled out loud as I got up to take a break and use the bathroom. I took my time coming back to the table since, deep down, I really didn't want to call Jackie. Of the three, she was the only one who was still truly in love with me and would come with me wherever I went in a heartbeat. I had loved her, and still did, for who she was—a wonderful woman with a great personality, a little wacky and offbeat, but genuine.

Too bad I didn't have Jackie's grandmother's tarot cards so I could see if they would deal the Death card for our chances of getting back together. By now I bet Jackie had already dealt the cards and knew the answer.

Chapter 22

Illusions

As I am about ready to call Jackie, the front doorbell rings. Thinking it must be the property manager, I get up and go over to answer it. As I open the door, the morning sun blasts me in the eyes, making me squint, and I can barely see who's there. The shapes of the people standing in the doorway are two men, but I can't see their faces with the sun directly in my eyes. I manage a weak "Yes, can I help you?"

"Hi, Pop."

My mind's server unit spins to find the voice-recall tape. I know that voice, but not *here*—not in *Key West*.

"Pop, it's Darren and John."

My mind automatically goes on overload. It's Darren—my son. My eyes are adjusting to the morning glare now and my sight is coming back. It doesn't take long for me to fully recognize both my sons standing outside my condo door.

"Darren, John . . ." I glance from one face to the other. "What are you doing here?"

Suddenly, my heart is pounding. I start jumping to conclusions, and my mouth goes dry. My voice cracks as I ask, "Lucinda—is she all right? Did something happen to her at the care unit?"

"No, Pop, she's OK. She wants you to come home. Can we come in?"

With that, Darren moves through the doorway with John right behind him. In the living room, I can now see that both my sons look like they have been travelling—jeans, tennis shoes, casual shirts, clothes you'd see on folks on an airliner.

"What are you doing here then if Mom is OK? I don't think the two of you came all the way to Key West to vacation with your ol' dad. You have families and businesses to take care of. So why are you here?"

"Pop, you walked away from the Shady Groves Care Center last week without a word to anyone. You didn't take your medications with you. Hell, you barely took any clothes. Your doctor called Mom, and in a panic, she called us. Well, it does come in handy once in a while to have a lawyer for a brother. John's resources at the police department were able to track you here by tracing your cell phone calls and credit card usages."

I sit speechless and motionless, just staring openmouthed at my boys, astounded at the line of bullshit I'm hearing: "Through your cell phone calls, they were able to track you here."

"Pop," my son John continues as Darren falls silent, "you need to get back to the care unit and get back on track taking your dementia medications. You can't take off like this. You might hurt yourself or, God forbid, hurt someone else. Mom and the two of us and all the rest of the family love you, and we want to take care of you . . . at Shady Groves. We can't help you three thousand miles away."

My mind is a kaleidoscope of thoughts. I stand up and start walking around the room. I say to my boys, "I'm confused. I don't understand what you're saying. Me with dementia? Bullshit! I'm perfectly mentally healthy. Ginny said I was delusional; *she's* the one who's nuts—not me. Stacey and that stupid house and a cemetery for her folks with a cement headstone of Rex and Diane's lawn chair—who's crazy there? Or what about Jackie and her black and white world and waiting on the aliens to come visit?—yeah, *that's* normal."

I notice a puzzled look pass between the two, and Darren speaks to John loudly enough for me to hear: "Who are Ginny, Stacey, Jackie? Has he ever mentioned them to you?" John shakes his head; he looks sad.

John speaks next: "Pop . . . Pop . . . sit down and relax. Here, doctor said you should start taking these pills first thing when we caught up with you. They help make your thoughts clearer, more rational. They help slow the loss of your memory."

John hands me two oblong, white pills. I hold them in my hand. I vaguely recognize the little letters and markings on the pills. I remember pills like these being passed to me in a little white cup from the hand of a male orderly.

I protest, "I don't like taking pills. I'm as healthy as a horse."

John picks up my coffee cup, checks to see that there is a little coffee still in it, and hands it to me. He makes fun of my "healthy as a horse" comment: "Here, you can wash them down with the coffee, Mr. Ed." Probably thought that joke would get by me, but it didn't.

I swallow the silly white pills, but I give John a disapproving look for forcing me to take them.

I see Darren look at John. Then he takes a breath, turns to me, and says, "We're here to take you home . . . today . . . now. We have airline tickets to leave this afternoon from the local airport, connecting in Miami and then back home. Pop, you're coming with us."

"Boys," I protest as emphatically as I can, "I'm *OK*. Besides, I have a month paid on this condo. Why don't you stay with me a few days? You can buy some clothes, kick back, call the family, tell them you're hanging out with me for a while, and . . . then you two can go home without your pop. I have plans to go to Indiana after I stay here for my month."

Darren writes off my plans without giving them a moment's thought. Not even curious about why I might be heading for Indiana. "Pop, that isn't going to work. We have to take you with us. Mom's worried sick and wants you home. Please, just come with us and we can sort out everything when we get back home."

"Lucinda's OK?" I ask. "She's not in the care unit? Then what the hell am I paying for from the trust?"

Darren seems desperate. "Pop, the trust is paying for *your* stay at Shady Groves. *You* are the one staying there, not Mom. You've been there for the last six months. You've been doing really great. The medications have made you almost normal."

"Normal? You trying to say I'm not normal?? What am I? Nuts??" I am more than a little pissed off all of a sudden, and I'm nearly shouting.

John jumps back in: "You're just fine as long as you take your medication and stay within Shady Groves with professional care. You can't do the treatments here in Key West, in this condo, by yourself. Now, again, you *are* coming with us. Darren can pack your clothes. Come on, you can be with Mom in a few hours. Wouldn't you want to see your Lucinda? Be back with your wife of forty-plus years? She loves you and misses you so much."

John pauses, and the three of us sit for a moment, just looking at each other. They're waiting for me to say something.

"Lucinda is really OK? We can be a family again?" This is all so confusing. It feels like somewhere in my mind the wires have gotten crossed and my thoughts have become a jumbled, tangled mess, like a string of last year's Christmas lights coming out of the storage box. It's all so complicated, I can't make sense of it. I thought *Lucinda* was the one with Alzheimer's, but it was *me*? *I* am the one with the onset of dementia?

I find myself wondering if my times with Ginny and Jackie and Stacey were figments of my imagination. "Did I make them all up?" I ask myself in mounting bewilderment. "Did I really spend time with each of them? Didn't they tell me they still love me? I still need to call Jackie; she'll need to know what has happened to me. Wait, what about Angel? I *know* I met her last night and she kissed me with her eyes closed and then she opened them and she said I was her Prince Charming and I made her my Sleeping Beauty and I'm supposed to be going to Indiana to be with her and I'm suddenly so confused . . ." The thoughts whirl and tumble through my suddenly clouded mind. I begin to cry. "Dear God, help me."

John motions something to Darren, who goes into my bedroom while John stays in the living room. In a few minutes, Darren is back. He's carrying my travel bag. He says, "Let's go. I have everything."

John comes and offers me his hand. I stand up—what else can I do? Darren and John both stay close beside me, nudging me along until we're at the front door. Then John stops, like he just remembered something. I see him glance at the fancily bound books on the coffee table. He asks me, "Are the books yours?"

For a moment I stand looking at the two classics, *War and Peace* and *A Tale of Two Cities*. I reply, "No, they belong to the unit; leave them for the next guest." But I think to myself, "She knew her Macho Man would never read them."

The boys have a bright white Ford rental parked just outside, along the street. I look at it and think of the ambulance-white '39 Ford I owned in high school, the one I picked up the other five members of the Mag 6 in each and every morning. A single lucid thought sneaks out from my ball of brain wires: "God, that was a great car; we had great adventures in it. Boy, I miss those guys."

John helps me into the front passenger side of their rental car while Darren walks over to the property manager's office, I suppose to tell him I have to leave and won't need the unit after all. What reason will he give? Family emergency? I watch Darren and the manager walk into my condo, probably doing a quick look-see. When he comes out, he looks happy; probably figures he can rent it again and collect double for the month.

John gets in the back seat; Darren gets in up front to drive. I hear John say to Darren, "Did you get everything? Clothes, toiletries?"

"Yeah. I found a shotgun shell and some scratch paper with numbers on it. I threw them in the trash. What Pop's doing with a spent shotgun shell is beyond me. He probably picked it up off the ground wherever he's been for the last week. The numbers must be for some church, had 'Angel' as a name. Maybe Pop stopped in some church to pray; he's religious, you know, always asking God for guidance." Darren hands me some coins without apologizing for talking about me like I'm not there. "Here, Pop, I found this change in a glass ash tray on the dresser."

I hear John affirm, "Yeah, Pop always asks God for guidance."

Those words ring true, and I close my eyes and begin to pray to my God: "I need help. I can't go back to that Shady Groves. I do now remember those long lonely nights by myself, no one to talk to. Lucinda isn't with me; she's always leaving when visiting hours are over. I've only got the shitty TV to keep me company. Dear God, I need someone."

"Rollo, we're with you."

I turn toward the back seat, seeking the source of the voice echoing loud and strong in my ears. "Oz? Is that you?"

Oz continues, "We're *all* here, Rollo. We'll be with you wherever you go." Looking at the back seat, I now see the Mag 6, all scrunched together beside John: Oz, Spiff, Lily, Star, and Crazy, all dressed exactly as they were when I picked them up the first day of our senior year, and all stuffed into the back seat of that shitty little Ford rental.

Spiff looks at me with his patented Chamber of Commerce straight-face look. "Don't worry, Rollo, your son can't see us—only you."

I turn back around and laugh to myself. "The Mag 6, my buddies, they'll keep me company in my lonely nights. We'll have a blast." I can plainly hear Oz, Lily, Spiff, Star, and Crazy poking each other and laughing among themselves. I sit back in my seat, my face suddenly spread out in one big smile.

Darren glances over at me, then looks at John in the rearview mirror. "Something's making Pop happy. How many pills did you give him?"

John looks at him. "Just the two. Maybe he's just happy to see us."

I start to put the change Darren handed me into my pocket and feel an odd coin. Looking in my hand, I see among the few pennies and a quarter the dragon pendant from Jackie. Darren hadn't noticed the pendant. I put the coins in my pocket, but I hold the dragon pendant in my hand.

From deep within my mind I hear a voice speaking in a sound like soft spring rain after a long, bitter winter: "I'm here with you, *whatever*. Whenever you need me, just think of me."

"Jackie, can I see you? Can I touch you?" I speak the words inside my head, clutching the pendant in my palm.

"No, I'm only in your mind, but you can call me up anytime, and I'll always be with you. I loved you more than any of the others. Lucinda will love you when she is with you; I will love you when you're alone, when you want a tender voice. And when Lucinda and the boys are gone from your memory, I will still be with you. I am a spirit sent from God to be with you till you are with Him. The Mag 6 are here to amuse you and make you laugh. I am here to make you happy and to be with you in your quiet moments. You will never be lonely again. God has willed it."

Darren pulls into traffic at a sign that reads Flagler Avenue. I swat my ear; something wet is in it. "Wet Willy, Rollo!" sounds from the back seat. I pull down the visor and open the flap for the mirror so I can see into the back of the car without turning around. Crazy and all the others are there, laughing. "A Wet Willy for Rollo!"

I know now that God is with me. Words from an old Bible passage flow into my mind: "The Lord is my Shepherd . . . He makes me to lie down by still waters, he restores my soul . . . yea, though I walk through the Valley of the Shadow of Death, I will fear no evil . . . He is with me . . . goodness and mercy will follow me all the days of my life, and I will dwell in His house forever. Thank you, God."

"Rollo . . ." Crazy leans forward to tell me something.

Looking into the mirror, I speak out loud without thinking how nutty it might seem to my boys: "What, Crazy, what do you want to tell me?"

I catch Darren looking at John and shaking his head. "Need to get him home quickly."

"What, Crazy? . . . What?!" I scream in my mind.

Crazy laughs cheerfully and maybe a little maniacally. "Chee-vee-vee, Rollo . . . Chee-vee-vee!"